The Chronic Prudence Fairweather

PART ONE

The Pirate of Heffen

P.A. Taylor

PublishAmerica
Baltimore

First printing

ISBN: 1-4137-6352-9
PUBLISHED BY PUBLISHAMERICA, LLLP
www.publishamerica.com
Baltimore

Printed in the United States of America

Dedicated to my wife Carol and my daughters Jennifer and Gemma. Also to my son Thomas for whom I wrote the words, "Oh it's you."

$\mathcal{M}$y thanks also to Jessica Dean and Chris Barnes who helped and encouraged me so much. Thanks also to Manfred Mann who got me writing again by giving me the chance to do lots of liner notes and other stuff for him.

Special thanks to all at PublishAmerica who gave Prudence a chance to save the world and have done everything they promised to do and more.

Finally thanks to every swashbuckling, whodunit, ghostly, fantasy love story ever thought of.

The Pirate of Heffen takes place on a world remarkably similar to this one about two hundred years ago. It can only be a matter of time before it happens here on our world. Perhaps it already is!

The Chronicles of Prudence Fairweather

PART ONE

The Pirate of Heffen

P.A. Taylor

*O*n the side of a rocky pass, a pathway twisted along a narrow ledge, climbing higher and higher into a stark and barren landscape. There were, here and there, the petrified remains of a tree or shrub.

About halfway up this dusty narrow road it ran alongside a lake, the water so black, it both looked and felt like ink. A little farther on were the remains of what had once probably been a thriving community. In amongst the eerie desolation of broken-down buildings and crumbling roads stood a wooden hut, a weak yellow light flickering from the single tiny window. Inside in the gloom sat an ancient wooden table.

Four frightened men sat around it, the oil lamp swinging slowly to and fro just above their heads. It was held to a beam above them by a rusty chain that creaked and groaned in protest as it swung slowly backwards and forwards. One of the men sitting at the table looked comfortably rich, one was dressed in rags. Another looked quite wise, although a clever man would surely not choose to be in this dreadful place. The last of the men, more scared than his companions, surveyed the scene through frightened eyes.

There was surrounding them an unnatural silence, broken only by the persistent sound of the swinging lamp. Why the lamp was doing this was difficult to comprehend, as the air was absolutely still. The movement of the light created strange moving shadows that seemingly at random plunged different parts of the room into total darkness.

In the centre of the table was an amulet in something that looked like dull gold, on which was carved the shape of a hideous and tormented face. It was no creature any of the men recognised as being from this world.

At the head of the table, in the shadows that were almost still, there sat a tiny figure cloaked in black. A dark shadow blocked its features, from which shone bright blood red eyes. The tiny form was of an innocent, the presence within it pure malevolence.

This terrible thing we should all fear.

I knew I was dreaming. It was very much the same dream I had had before, I knew in my sleep that I, Thomas Arthur Anders, should most probably be dreaming of that most precious and delicate rose whose hand I desired in marriage. I am deeply ashamed to say that Miss Anna Groves was not, however, the subject of this dream.

I was on a long thin strip of golden sandy beach. It was bordered on one side with dense green tropical foliage and on the other by crystal clear, sky blue water. This changed to a multitude of darker, richer blues, greens and purples, as the water became deeper, farther out from the shore. Two very tall palm trees stood over a small clump of rocks, polished smooth by centuries of tides coming in and going out. High cliff faces curved round to help form this natural inlet.

I was trying to think which book or painting had placed this beautiful scene into my mind. There is no such fairytale paradise near to my father's parish. The English countryside, beautiful in its own way, is the only countryside that I am familiar with. Except, that is, for such scenes as I might have seen or read about in the pages of books or paintings. At the far end of this beach was a large rocky outcrop.

The largest of the rocks had been moulded by centuries of sunshine, wind, rain and saltwater into the shape of a face. It was partly submerged into the water, making it almost grotesque, like the features of a drowning man. It was perhaps more beast than man. This face was like I have never seen before. It was contorted into a silent scream of rage and hunger, as if warning unsuspecting travellers to come no closer, or risk being swallowed up.

For a moment I was sucked in by the cold terror of such terrible hunger, but then I could no longer see the face. Instead, draped gracefully over the rocky outcrop, her long and shapely legs dangling down over the twisted face and into the water, was a vision of loveliness such as I have never seen before. I doubt her unimaginable beauty could ever be successfully captured on canvas or adequately described in the pages of a book, but must surely be confined only to the deepest and most private of dreams.

She turned to look at me through large sparkling brown eyes. There was a hint of a smile playing on her fulsome lips. I saw in her a woman of great strength and intellect, truly independent of the constraints that society imposes upon us all. She slipped gracefully from the rocks into the warm clear water. Her long dark red curls fell onto broad smooth golden brown shoulders.

Then this apparition began to walk slowly and seductively through the shallow waters, along the shoreline, towards me. The tall and shapely girl was shockingly naked but for a large piece of orange silk draped about her hips. This covered her thighs and most of one long leg down to the calf, although the material was almost completely transparent.

I should have felt shocked by such outrageous exhibitionism. I should have averted my eyes, but I could not. All I wanted to do was hold her in my arms and feel her smooth silken skin pressing up to mine.

No woman whom I have ever known made me feel like this girl did.

She was now so close to me. I could see tiny beads of perspiration forming around the tight muscles which were holding in the gentle swell of her flat brown belly. I could smell the salt from the sea on her tangled hair.

I reached out to touch her…but she was not really there.

The dream was once again over. I was lying hot and sweaty on my bed in the ancient rooms where I lived during the week. These rooms were at the private school where I had once myself been a student. Here, I now taught boys from good families to understand the fantastic wonders of this mysterious and wonderful world in which we lived. A world I confess I have only ever experienced within the sombre walls of our school library.

It was I, not the imaginary girl, who was perspiring heavily as a result, no doubt, of the most inappropriate nature of my dream. A dream I was having more and more frequently. I shook off the distinctly uneasy feeling I was always left with.

That day I was about to embark upon the most important and scariest adventure of my life so far. I am not a brave man, but I had summoned up every ounce of courage that I had. It was my firm intention to ask Miss Anna Groves for her hand in marriage.

Almost Everybody Dies

Being an account of some of the important and seemingly unconnected events that took place a little over ten years prior to my adventures on Heffen, these events would one day help to determine the survival or the terrible and total destruction of our world. I have come to learn that our world is one of many similar worlds, many of which have already perished. This, however, is our world and surely we must look after it.

From the outside, 31 Charles Square looked much the same as the other forty townhouses that encircled the Park. The inside, however, was another matter altogether. On entering the grand entrance hall, there were large high ceiling rooms on both sides of an imposing staircase. Beyond this were an impressive kitchen and a huge pantry. Upstairs were five further large rooms and an enormous tiled bathroom built around a spacious landing.

What made 31 Charles Square different from the other 39 properties that made the Park, such a desirable place to live, was that despite the bright and spacious nature of the house, it was cold, austere and very, very tidy. It was almost impossible to believe that two children were amongst the residents of this sombre place. Perhaps even more surprising was that the owner, one Charles Raines, was a good-natured seafaring man.

Raines was a big, jovial chap. When introducing himself to guests, he would be eager to point out that the entire square had been named after him. Of course, this was far from the truth. The name was, in fact, that of the builder's favourite King Charles spaniel. Raines would roar with laughter and confess at once. He was a modest and unassuming man beneath the bluster and slightly crude recounting of his favourite seafaring adventures.

Charles Raines had much love to give and was the type of person who needed only to be loved in return. It was Margaret Raines, the lady of this particular house, who should have returned her husband's devotion. In her defence, Charles Raines would be away for many months at a time. Margaret would be left alone with their two children, a boy and a girl. There was no doubt that she was often very lonely. Even when he was home from one of his long trips, he was probably not the easiest man to live with.

Margaret had grown up in a very strict Presbyterian family. Her father believed passionately that to spare the rod, spoilt the child. He also considered that an outpouring of emotions, other than perhaps to God, was quite unseemly.

So Margaret took out her frustrations on the house, the children and the numerous housekeepers who came and just as quickly went from service at 31 Charles Square. The house was kept so clean and so tidy that to find a speck of dust would be as likely as finding a pot of gold at the end of a rainbow. There was no laughter and no fun.

Their first child, a boy, was born with a mop of bright red hair like his father. Margaret was little more than a child herself. She produced two more sons but tragically both were stillborn. Margaret was heartbroken and convinced that God was punishing her for her sins. Charles also had difficulty understanding why fate had dealt so cruel a blow. He began to spend longer periods away from home. Years passed and the Raines had put aside all thought of further offspring. Indeed, little opportunity ever presented itself to make such an event possible. When

Charles returned from foreign parts, Margaret did, however, continue to carry out what she considered to be her wifely duties. She would lie still with her eyes closed and pray that it would be over quickly.

Unexpectedly following one of her husband's brief visits home, Margaret found herself to be once again with child. This time she gave birth to a healthy bouncing baby girl. Her brother was at once allowed home from boarding school to see the tiny baby. All these years he had been the centre of attention, and now suddenly, he had a baby sister. The child was confused. He was not sure if he loved or hated this tiny little thing. A tiny chubby little hand reached out and clutched at his finger with surprising strength.

The children, Silas and Mary, had to be immaculately dressed at all times, and when Silas was home from school during the holidays, they spent most of their day in study. They would also be expected to give a good part of their time to prayer, asking the Lord for forgiveness for the sins they had little opportunity to commit in the first place.

The decoration at 31 Charles Square was colourless and drab. What few pictures hung on the walls were mostly dark and stern portraits, in oil, of Margaret's forebears. One such picture of Margaret's father, Silas Brand, dominated the stairwell, adding to the overpowering sense of gloom. He had what appeared to be the very rod that would never be spared to spoil the child resting across his hands. He also had the look of a cruel man who would take much pleasure from using it.

The children missed their father during his long trips away. Silas was now a young man with a taste for gambling and dubious business deals. His father had often had to clear his debts for him. Silas's baby sister was schooled at home and hardly ever went out. Her teacher was an unpleasant and humourless woman who fitted well into the drab world of 31 Charles Square.

As they grew older, their father's absences seemed to become longer. His periods visiting his family became less frequent. His manner had changed too. He became less willing to tell stories of his trips to far-off places or of his encounters with vagabonds and pirates. Perhaps he felt Silas too old now for such fanciful tales and that Mary, being a girl, would have little interest. Both Silas and Mary missed his telling of outlandish and fantastic adventures more than he could ever have realised.

He would rather sit smoking one of his many pipes. If Margaret's disapproval of this filthy habit had stopped him taking a pipe, he would just stroke his big red beard with massive leathery hands. Most of the time Raines would be staring out of the window, through the trees, beyond the park, the town, the docks and far away to some distance place he would so much sooner be.

The gloomy atmosphere of this dark place became tense indeed. It was only a matter of time before something had to give.

"Margaret, I leave tomorrow."

Margaret looked up over her glasses at her husband. He seemed thinner and looked very tired. There were hints of grey starting to show in the big red beard and the equally bright red mop of hair. Charles Raines looked sad.

"Leaving so soon, dear?" Margaret put down her sewing and stood up. "You have only just got back, husband. Surely you could stay a little longer."

Raines pulled himself out of the chair and began searching for one of his pipes.

"I do not wish you to smoke those horrid things in here and I do wish you would refrain from drinking." Margaret's voice was emotionless. She paused, removed her spectacles and began to polish them and then snapped out, "Rum, whisky, my family has never approved of such evil. It is the devil's brew." Her eyes were blazing. She sat back down, hands clasped on her lap, glaring at her husband.

"You know nothing of the devil," snapped Raines. He forced himself to control his uncharacteristically bad temper. His face, however, had become almost as red as his beard. Raines looked at his wife sadly. "I have tried so hard to explain to you just some of the evil that threatens all of us, Margaret, and it comes not from a tobacco pouch or a bottle of rum. Your father has filled your head with too many images that prevent you from seeing the truth, and he had no right to be so sanctimonious."

"You blaspheme, Charles, and you attack my father's memory."

"I am tired, Margaret, very tired. I am not needed here; you don't need me, Margaret. Far from needing me, you disapprove of your husband in almost every way." He paused to wipe the perspiration from his unusually sad face.

"The children need you, Charles," insisted Margaret, wringing her bony hands together in an attempt to help her stay calm. "And they need you to set a good example as a father," she added. She did not tell him how much she needed him however.

"Silas is no longer a child, Margaret, and as much as I have endeavoured to set him a good example, he is mixing with the wrong types, becoming a wastrel, as well as a fool. I am always paying off his debts to save his hide. That is all he needs me for. I try to do my best for Mary too, but it is her mother she needs most now." Raines was angry again now. Margaret had not often seen the gentle giant so red in the face and so mad. "You know, Margaret, that I have always provided well for you and for my children, who as you full well know, despite my disappointment in my son, I love with all my heart."

He paused as if lost for words, then becoming a little calmer, once again more sad than angry, he carried on.

"Yes, I do like a pipe and a measure or two of rum, but what sin is there in that? Tell me, woman. I am not getting rolling drunk in front of my children, or using foul and abusive language. I believe I have done my very best to be a good husband and a good father."

Margaret laughed, but it was a humourless laugh. She was a smallish, thin woman who had once been quite pretty, but had grown to look much older than her years. Her hair was now grey and matched perfectly the plain dress she almost always wore.

"You think being a father is to return from your adventures with foolish and frivolous gifts and fill their heads with ridiculous stories, most of which are…."

"Margaret, I am leaving and this time I shall not be returning." Raines had stopped Margaret in full flow. For a moment it looked as if Margaret might faint. "I will continue to send money, of course, and perhaps in time, Silas and Mary might come out for a visit."

"Visit!" Margaret was screaming with anger. "Visit some heathen land, populated with the devil's own children, you cannot be serious."

Charles Raines looked sadly at his wife. "Margaret, I have a new family. I know I have in this way let you down, but this woman loves me in return for my love. She loves me unconditionally and without reservation, something you have never been able to do. I do not blame you, Margaret. It is without any question your husband who is at fault, for I have been unable to give you or our children that which you would desire of me. I have failed you and I have failed my son. It's just that my new family loves everything about me. Every little foible, every little eccentricity. They love the smell of my baccy and they love my ridiculous stories, the more far fetched and the sillier, the better."

"*Get out!*" screamed Margaret, tears streaming down her face. It was the first time Raines had seen any emotion in his wife for many years, and he was sure in his heart it had been much his fault.

"Look, I have not kept you or our children a secret. If anything should happen to me, they will be sure you continue to receive money, anything you need."

"Get out! Get out!" wept Margaret. She began to beat her fists on her husband's chest. Then realising that she had lost control, Margaret composed herself. "You are a sinner and a fornicator, Charles Raines. You have let the devil himself possess your soul. You have cheated on both your devoted wife and your adoring children, now get out, get out!"

As the sad and guilt-ridden Raines tugged open the great parlour door, Mary and Silas ran for the shadows. They had been listening to every word. He turned back to his wife. All traces of emotion had drained from her face and she was once again cold, controlled and dignified.

"You are right about one thing, Margaret. The devil's children are at work out there. That is why I have made absolutely sure that if anything happens, you and the children will be taken care of."

"Get out, Charles, I will not be needing your charity, nor will our children." And Margaret turned her back on Charles Raines forever.

Silas Raines clutched his baby sister to him as they watched from their hiding place as their father took his leave of 31 Charles Square for the very last time. Silas had often hidden there as a child at bath time.

"You are right, Father, you have failed me," said Silas Raines softly. Mary was crying.

Some years passed. Raines kept his word and regularly sent money, but Margaret returned all communications unopened. Instead she raised her children on the small savings from her own inheritance. She also took on small jobs. Even so, money became very tight indeed.

Mary grew into a tall, slender and very beautiful woman. She had her mother's pale complexion and light brown hair, but her father's smile, complemented by the most stunning hourglass figure.

Silas, on the other hand, was shorter like his mother, and as a young man thin as a rake with the same cold eyes. He was quite a handsome young man in a rather sly and devious way. From his father's side, he had inherited a mop of bright red hair and an inclination to put on weight far too easily. Silas did not wish to be or intend to stay poor, so he borrowed his mother's remaining money and over the next few years proceeded to lose it all on ill-considered business ventures.

With almost no money left and considerable debt, young Raines at last had some luck. Whilst visiting a rather insalubrious club in the city, he made the acquaintance of a young man by the name of Maurice Jones. Whist Silas's dire financial circumstances were not apparent in his immaculate dress, Maurice was a young man of good means but indifferent appearance. Silas would not have been interested in the scruffy man at all had Maurice not just inherited a vast fortune from his father. Jones, however, did not have the imagination, or business acumen, to know what to do with his newfound wealth.

Silas Raines, on the other hand, had plenty of ideas on how to spend Jones's money. To begin with, he arranged for Jones to meet his beautiful sister Mary. He then spent much time persuading Mary that the future of the family was now very much in her hands. The courtship was short.

Mary felt no love for Jones, although he was a nice enough and kindly man. For his part, Jones had fallen madly in love with Mary. He was well aware that if it were not for his father's money, he would have had no hope of a union with such a beautiful woman.

"I know that you do not love me, Mary," he said, kneeling before her, holding a pale white hand in his. "Perhaps given time, it is possible for me to have hope that your feelings might change?"

Mary smiled and ran her free hand through his unkempt hair. "Yes," she said softly. "I think I could learn to love you, Maurice. You have become a good and kind friend. Without question, you deserve my love and my gratitude." Mary paused and looked into the untidy man's big blue eyes.

Maurice Jones wore some of the best tailored clothes in England, for which he had attended numerous fittings. Unfortunately, the trousers would still look too short and the jacket a couple of sizes too large. He was incapable of tying a cravat properly and his jackets quickly took on a creased and crumpled look.

"If I was to say yes," Mary said carefully, "you understand that my acceptance of your kind and generous offer is influenced much by the security you will bring to me and to my family."

"Of course I do," conceded Jones, "but I really love you, Mary, and it is my deepest hope that in time you will return that love.

Maurice Jones and Mary Raines were married soon after. The Raines family had little money left and Jones had not yet gained access to the bulk of his father's estate. As a result, it was not a particularly grand affair and it rained all day. Silas made sure that he was Jones's best man. Only a short time after the wedding, Mary found out that she was pregnant.

The pregnancy passed without any significant problems, and she gave birth to a plump and healthy baby girl. They named her Victoria. It was shortly after the birth of Victoria that Mary thought quite seriously of writing to her father. She wanted so much to tell him he had become a grandfather. Years before, she had stolen one of his many letters to her mother, before Margaret had returned it like the rest. In the end, Mary could not bring herself to write. Like her mother, she was still too angry with him.

One fine spring morning, shortly after Victoria was born, Silas arrived at the very large and very modern house where his sister now lived. Maurice Jones had spent much of his late father's fortune having this plain and unimaginative home built for his new family. Silas was becoming increasingly concerned that his irresponsible new brother-in-law might flitter away all of his inheritance before Silas had a chance to spend any of it. Even the room they were in was cluttered with expensive and varied furniture that brought to mind a disorganised and overstocked warehouse.

Mary's choice of decor for their new home, an uninteresting mixture of drab and lifeless colour, owed a great deal to her mother's influence. She had also quite obviously inherited Margaret's passion for dark and foreboding paintings of dead people. Despite this, there was much more light, more atmosphere and a great deal more dust than there had ever been at Charles Square.

"I have a business proposition, brother-in-law." Silas smiled. "I need you to finance a deal. I guarantee you that we will both make an absolute fortune, Maurice, both of us." Silas paused for a response. His small, piercing eyes searched Maurice Jones for a reaction.

"How much of a fortune?" Maurice looked nervously at his brother-in-law.

"It means a sea trip, Maurice," he confessed. "Of course there is absolutely no need for you to come. You can trust me to transact the business there without you present, I'm sure. It should take no more than three months at the most."

Maurice turned his head towards the sound of a screaming baby coming from another room. Little Victoria was hungry, as she always seemed to be, for food and a change.

Her father, Silas thought, *is as close to a chameleon as anyone could be.* He could quite easily go unnoticed in an empty room. As dull as the house he lived in, he was in many ways the most ordinary-looking man imaginable. Except, that is, his arms and legs seemed to be too long for his body. The baby's screams became louder now. Victoria was having another one of her tantrums.

"I think three months away on business has much to recommend it, brother-in-law," pointed out Jones with a lopsided grin. "As I have always been guided by you in matters of business, Silas, it would also seem to be wise for me to join in any such venture, my friend."

Silas smiled. It was a smile that would make you check your pockets, or even count your fingers, if having just shaken hands with him. Maurice Jones, however, had never been good in his judgement of other people. He was far too trusting a man. Jones saw Silas only as family and as a good friend.

"I have a ship and a captain subject to...em...."

"Financial backing?" interrupted Jones

"Exactly that, my brother," enthused Silas, grabbing him by the arm and almost hugging him. "And now that you are with me, we could leave as soon as the day after tomorrow." He grabbed two glasses and the crystal glass wine decanter from a polished oak side table, one of about a dozen of various shapes and sizes. "Let us drink to our ultimate adventure together, brother," he said, pouring out two glasses of rich red wine and handing one to Jones.

"The day after tomorrow?" Jones spoke softly as if to himself. "That soon?" He frowned. "We still have to break the news to Mary, and I am not sure she will be pleased with me travelling. I know she already feels deep resentment towards your father as a result of his travels."

"Our father left us," snarled Silas, his cold piercing eyes drilling into Jones. "We could have all gone to the workhouse for all he cared." For just a moment Silas was so angry his demeanour became frightening, even to the insensitive Jones. His thin and normally pale face became ruby red and his blue-grey eyes became almost white. The glass in his hand shattered, spilling a cocktail of red wine and blood onto the carpet.

"I am so sorry, my brother," he said, taking a deep breath to help calm himself down. "Please forgive my outrageous behaviour. You are quite right, of course; neither my sister nor I will ever forgive that man. You must trust me to carry out our business and stay here with Mary and your child."

"No, Silas, I will accompany you. It would be unfair to expect you to undertake such responsibilities alone." Jones poured his brother-in-law a new glass of wine.

Silas knew exactly where their fortune lay. He had found the letter Mary had stolen from their mother. His father's whereabouts were pretty clear, and it was time for Silas to have the revenge he had dreamed about for so long.

"Then we must shake on it, brother dear," he shouted in delight, his steel grey eyes sparkling with excitement. He offered Jones a bloody hand.

At the other side of the world, in the very waters where Silas Raines planned to take his brother-in-law, the ancient pirate was dying. He had captained the legendary *Black Albatross* for many years now, almost the last of a long line of pirates to do so. In the last few years, he had gained two unusual new crewmembers.

Neither Arthur nor Harry had been born privateers. They had, however, quickly become loyal and hard-working members of the old man's crew. As a result of this, he had bestowed great responsibility onto both of them. He used to say that Harry had become his eyes and Arthur his ears. This he assured people was not because Arthur's ears were large, although not so large as his nose, but because he was a good listener. Harry was good at observing others.

Despite their comparatively short time on board the *Albatross*, both men had become devoted to the old pirate. To the casual onlooker, however, Harry and Arthur seemed always to be greatly at odds with each other. The old man had no son to pass on his ship or his knowledge. He knew the time was rapidly approaching when he must choose his successor. It was naturally expected by all of the crew that one of these two men would take command.

They had both had previous experience of leadership before joining the *Albatross*. In these waters it was vital to keep one's wits. Both men had quick minds, as well as the necessary respect of their shipmates. The *Black Albatross* was only one of many pirate ships preying on the healthy trade from the islands of Heffen. Despite the combined efforts of the British, French and Spanish navies, who had taken time out from blowing each other up to put an end to the curse of piracy, the number of cutthroats and privateers sailing these waters was increasing daily.

The three great powers had formed an uneasy and extremely unlikely alliance to put an end to all this. There were gentlemen privateers and honest villains such as this old man. These men had come from a long tradition of piracy. There were also killers and cutthroats like Blind Mario and Jessie Crooks. These were two of the most evil men sailing the tropical waters of Heffen.

What made it impossible for the navy to navigate a path through to the multitude of tiny tropical islands, wherein the pirates hid themselves and their ill-gotten gains, was Gabrielle's Reef. This was a large expanse of jagged rocks, hidden beneath the surface, in amongst the coral that surrounded the smaller islands. More notorious even than the reef was what had become known as Gabrielle's Fault.

Sailors required what had become known as "The Knowledge" to sail a ship through the reef. This knowledge was held only by pirates and perhaps a handful of native fishermen. If the captain of a pursuing vessel was lucky enough not to sink his ship, he became a sitting duck for the pirate he was chasing. It was the legendary pirate, Francis Gabrielle, one-time captain of the *Black Albatross*, who the ancients claimed had discovered the only safe course through the reef.

The legend goes on to claim that it was this same buccaneer who discovered the strange part of these dangerous waters that had become known as The Fault. Gabrielle's Fault was without question a peculiarly unnatural phenomenon. Best described as a ghostly mist that was always present, it could envelop whole parts of the reef without warning. Ships caught in this terrible fog were most often never seen again, or else found floating miles away and empty.

Gabrielle's own ship had been found many miles from the reef, deserted by its crew. It comes as no surprise to learn that many myths and legends had grown up around this unnatural phenomenon. Hundreds of already tall stories had become exaggerated in the telling and retelling over the passing years. Such fanciful anecdotes may be heard in such widely diverse places as sailors' bars and children's nurseries. These are stories that can fire anybody's imagination.

They tell of alternative worlds, of the gates to hell itself being hidden below the great dead mountain, Niridia. People whisper of monsters long extinct. Wild claims insist there are indeed creatures that have escaped through the silvery mists into our world. Beneath these waters, deep underground, it is said a million different worlds collide.

Many sailors had been lost to those dark places. Indeed, there was an old tradition that a bright light should be kept shining at all times near the point of the Fault to help guide missing loved ones home. Sadly, nobody had ever returned.

In truth, the sea was very deep in those parts, so the ships had most likely sunk without trace, or perhaps the crews had perished trying to abandon ship. Whatever the dull but true explanation of this strange phenomenon, it helped to further discourage even the bravest navy captain from chasing any pirates into those waters.

Back on board the *Albatross*, the old man's possible successors eyed each other. Harry was a tall rakish man with curly ginger hair, now touched with grey. He had leathery tanned skin and a finely trimmed pencil moustache. Despite having recently celebrated his fifty-something birthday, Harry looked at least ten years younger, even with the grey hair and wrinkles. He was undeniably handsome and quite dapper, although prone to putting on weight if living became too comfortable.

Arthur was a tall scrawny skeleton of a man and would always be so, even if he ate an elephant. He had a long, thin face, ears that stuck out quite alarmingly and a very pronounced chin. A colossal, beak-shaped nose finished off this hideous mess. The enormous protuberance seemed quite out of proportion with the rest of him, even the ears. To complete this pretty picture, Arthur had narrow ice blue eyes that were filled with mischief passed and mischief still to be done.

He was a quick-tempered rogue, but an alert and excellent negotiator, as well as a clever thief and conman. Both men were good to have on your side in a fight. Harry would constantly provoke Arthur with good-natured banter that wasn't perhaps always quite as good-natured as it seemed.

The old man watched all this with sadness. He knew they had once been very special friends. He also knew that whomever he chose, the rift between them would almost certainly become irrevocable. He alone knew what it was that had come between their friendship. His presence had kept them together and he needed them to stay together. He also understood too well that time was running out. Lowlifes like Blind Mario had their sights set firmly on the *Albatross*, so his choice had to be the right one. The ancient pirate sighed and called the two men to his bedside.

After many months at sea, which included a few truly terrifying experiences, Maurice and his brother-in-law Silas Raines arrived on the islands of Heffen. Maurice did not like being so far away from home and already dreaded the long return journey. He missed Mary very much, and to his surprise, he also missed the tiny little baby, despite her powerful lungs. There was newness, special warmth and even more, a special smell about his new daughter that he would willingly give up his entire inheritance to be with again. He longed to hold the tiny baby, to protect her from all the bad things, like fathers do.

Nevertheless, Maurice was at first quite taken with their new world. He became quickly convinced that they had accidentally stumbled upon something close enough to paradise for anyone. Not just because of the breathtakingly beautiful surroundings, but also the stunningly sensuous island girls, some of whom had provided comfort for the long and lonely nights so far from home.

Within weeks of arriving on Heffen, Silas Raines had almost trebled the not considerable sum of money Maurice Jones had invested into his scheme, although Maurice had no idea how he had done this.

Raines had established them both in the island's cosmopolitan society, although some of their new friends and business acquaintances frightened Jones. The governor's wife, a cold but handsome woman, would flirt with him shamelessly. He knew her to be a cruel and calculating woman.

The governor himself was rogue of a man. He was not more worthy of such a high office than the many pirates who terrorised honest merchants in the waters of Heffen, and apparently had fled for his life. It was, however, the slaver John Burleigh who he most feared and despised.

A short while later, the problems began. Silas gambled almost all their money away,on a deal that could have been very profitable indeed, had it been a success. Sadly, it was not, and Maurice Jones suddenly found that they were both out of money and out of favour.

It was John Burleigh, who along with Jones's brother-in-law, persuaded him to become involved in things he would have preferred not to be a part of. Jones knew they were meddling in places they did not begin to understand.

His fears proved right. A sense of dark foreboding crept upon the islands of Heffen, worse still, an overpowering sense of evil. The superstitious island folk spoke of devils and demons. Even Silas Raines seemed a little afraid.

Then one dark night, the short thin figure of Silas Raines burst into Jones's shabby room, waving a pistol. For a moment, Maurice Jones was convinced that Raines was going to shoot him. He had seen that look of madness in his brother-in-law's eyes before.

"Maurice." Silas Raines was shaking, his face purple, his eye twitching. "I have arranged for a ship to take you away from here." Raines sounded short of breath. He paused for a moment to recover his composure.

"Please do not argue, but trust me," he went on. "There are people who see you as weak and I'm afraid they want you dead." Raines put his arm around Jones's shoulder.

"How do you know this, brother?" Maurice looked confused and frightened.

"Listen to me, you fool, I was given this loaded pistol and told to shoot you with it!" shouted Raines.

Jones was lost for words. He opened and closed his mouth a few times, but no sound came out.

"My sister would never forgive me if she thought I had harmed you in any way. You must leave these islands tonight and, Maurice, you must promise me, give me your word of honour, that you will never return." Raines reached into his faded and threadbare waistcoat pocket, pulling out a fine golden watch. He looked at the time and then back at Maurice Jones.

"There is a ship leaving port in less than an hour," he said.

Silas Raines guided him down dark and slippery cobblestone back streets lit only by occasional torches. There were many of these steep, narrow and twisting lanes, all inevitably leading back to the harbour.

They were both oblivious to the two figures, hidden in the shadows, who watched their progress with a strange fascination.

"I told you he would be unable to carry out a simple task," hissed the woman, her beautiful pale face lit starkly by the dying light of an almost burnt-out torch.

"It is taken care of," promised her handsome male companion, a slim and elegant man in an immaculate grey suit. He wore expensive white gloves and carried a stick with a diamond-encrusted handle. "Maurice Jones will be dead before daybreak, I assure you of that," he added.

Close now to the docks, Maurice realised that Raines had no intention of leaving Heffen with him.

"Will you not now be in great danger too, Silas?" he whispered to his companion as they reached the quayside. It was a wet night, the torches reflecting in the dark puddles that had formed in the potholed road.

"I must stay to look after your interests, brother dear," explained Raines. "You have invested considerable sums of money into my foolish and ill-considered venture. I must try to recover our investment, brother dear. It is the least I can do."

Raines saw his brother-in-law safely on board the ship, departing on the long voyage home. It was a freighter and the accommodation poor, but all Raines had been able to afford. He looked nervously around for evidence that they were being watched. He sensed that they were, but still failed to see the eyes fixed upon them.

Some months passed before Mary received any news of her husband or her brother. Victoria had started to walk, and Mary was sad that Maurice had not been there to see his daughter's first faltering steps into her beautiful mother's arms. Mary did not love Maurice, but she had grown fond of him. She was sure that he would be a good and kind father. The young mother missed her husband more than she had excepted.

It was almost two years before Maurice returned home. Even then he was alone. He walked into the house unexpectedly one late summer evening, thinner than he had ever been. Mary's husband looked unwell.

She was pleased to see her Maurice again, although she was angry that he had been gone so long. Mary had not enjoyed being alone.

Maurice Jones was reluctant to talk about her brother Silas, or to discuss much of what had happened to them during his time away. He would simply try and reassure her that Silas was most probably in good health and safe. Over time, however, Mary was able to piece together some idea of what had happened to the two men.

There was something in the way Maurice spoke of his adventures that made his wife certain that he was still withholding much of the truth about what had befallen them. Then there was the haunted look in his eyes, where prior to his adventures there had always been a look of childlike innocence. Maurice no longer trusted anybody, and worse, he had become afraid of the dark.

He did, one night after a terrible nightmare, tell her, as she held him close, how near he had come to death on the journey home.

"The ship had not long got underway when a group of cutthroats, the like of which I hope I never see again, boarded. Their leader was a gross-looking man, if you can call him a man. I don't quite know how he managed to move he was so fat. They quite obviously intended to kill me."

"Oh my poor love," Mary held her husband tighter. "But the ship's crew, they repelled these blaggards?"

"No, that's just it. The crew was frozen in fear. It seems the fat man I described to you was the notorious pirate Jessie Crooks. A man, I am told, who very much enjoys his work."

"So how did you effect your escape, husband?" Mary sat up and looked at Jones, her beautiful eyes filled with concern.

"Well, it was very odd," he replied slowly. "Something, I am not sure what, seemed to frighten them and they fled the ship."

"You must know, Maurice?"

"It is preposterous I know, but as they fled, I was sure I caught a glimpse of a strange little man. At a guess he must have been much less than five foot, dressed in black and wearing a bowler hat. Yet this is most peculiar for I promise you, Mary, there was no such person on board; indeed, I was the only passenger."

For a little while Maurice and Mary were almost happy. She still, however, worried about his terrible nightmares. About a year after his sudden return, Mary gave birth to a second child, a little boy they named Rupert. Maurice was incredibly proud of his new son. Rupert reminded Mary very much of her father. A tubby little thing, he had the same mop of red hair.

Maurice worked hard to regain some of his lost wealth, providing adequately for his family. The trouble was that neither he nor Mary could put Silas from their minds. Jones knew that he probably owed Silas his life. Mary wanted badly to know what fate had befallen her brother. Maurice seemed haunted by the very thought of him. So once again bags were packed and Maurice set out on the long sea journey in search of his brother-in-law. Mary remained at home alone again, this time with two young children to look after.

For a very long time Mary and the children heard nothing of Maurice or Silas. When news arrived, it was the news she had most dreaded. Pirates had attacked the ship; her husband had been a passenger. It was said to have been the notorious Jessie Crooks. If this was true, then this time the evil pirate had not failed. Maurice Jones was dead.

The shock of all this was attributed to the rapid decline in Margaret's health.

Mary spent what little money they had left on health bills, but it was to no avail. Margaret died, leaving Mary alone to bring up Victoria and Rupert. As money became tighter, Mary remembered the conversation between her mother and father all those years ago.

"*Look, I have not kept you or our children a secret. If anything should happen to me, they will be sure you continue to receive money, anything you need.*"

There was no word from Silas, who was most likely also dead. So Mary decided to open the letter from her father, the letter they had stolen all those years ago. It was on that day that she noticed it had already been opened. The handwritten note begged Margaret to accept the money enclosed. It went on to ask how Silas and Mary were, ending somewhat predictably with a paragraph of self-recrimination and a plea for forgiveness. Mary guessed that most of her father's letters would have followed a similar pattern.

I am, I confess, very happy with my new family and yet I do miss you, Margaret, and the children. The letter ended with the scrawled signature: *Charles Raines.*

Mary wrote a few times but never received a reply. She preferred to believe that her father was dead, rather than face the harsh reality that he might have finally abandoned her and the grandchildren he had never known.

They moved from the grand house to cramped and dirty rooms in a poor part of the city. The sale of the property barely covered debts and mortgages left by her missing brother and late husband. Mary took many low-paying jobs to earn enough money to put food on the table. In a way it was worse, because both children could still remember the better times. They wished so much that one day they might return.

Often Mary would be forced to go without food so that the children could eat. All this inevitably began to take its toll. The beautiful woman's handsome features were becoming drawn and haggard. She was becoming noticeably weaker and thus more vulnerable to disease every day.

"Why our mother?" sobbed Rupert. "Why her? She is so beautiful, so beautiful."

Victoria took his hand. "We must try to be brave, Rupert. For our mother, we must try to be brave."

It was less than a month later that Mary passed away. She was so tired, but Mary hung onto life for as long as she could, for her children's sake. Now the battle was over. For Rupert and Victoria, however, the battle was about to begin.

Most of the ranches and plantations on Heffen's north island had given the slaves their freedom, offering work at a fair rate of pay. It was one such ranch on the very northern tip, known locally as the Sunshine Ranch, that had led their neighbours into enlightened times. The Sunshine Ranch was one of the first to build villages for their former slaves to live and schools to educate their children.

Although it wasn't all sunshine, the people of the north seemed happy and contented. Inevitably, of course, these modern and liberal ways were spreading to the south. People in positions of power and authority, however, were afraid of the new ways, as people like that so often are. They could see neither the commercial logic nor understand what other possible advantages could be gained as a result of slaves being paid well. Even more confusing was the principle of treating them like fellow human beings, never mind as equals. The terrible evil trapped thereabouts could dine well on such feelings.

The ancient pirate died. His choice had been a difficult one to make. Arthur was born to be a pirate. He showed unquestioned loyalty to his dying leader. When called upon, Arthur could be a calculated and cold-blooded killer. He never showed any sign of remorse, although he obviously preferred to make profit by clever and peaceful means. He was fearless in battle.

Arthur was little concerned with the idea of honour amongst thieves when it came to a fight for survival. Despite having the appearance of a rat, and an ugly one at that, the ugly beanpole of a man exuded immeasurable charm. He could not only remove a man's wallet without him noticing, or win himself a position of importance and responsibility, but also had earned himself tremendous popularity amongst the other scoundrels on board the *Albatross*.

Harry, on the other hand, was not and would never be a natural pirate. Although both had come to serve the old man through unforeseen circumstance, Harry, unlike Arthur, had not been born to become a crook, although certainly an adventurer. Harry was perhaps the better sailor, but only the most astute and observant would have come to realise that he had the ability to make any task seem effortless.

Harry had strong beliefs of right and wrong. He had no problem taking a man's wallet, if the man deserved to lose it, or plundering a slave ship. He would view profit from such an exercise that might also see the liberation of many people quite justifiable. Although a brave man, he took no satisfaction in killing others. Above all else, Harry had a conscience, something not always considered to be a good attribute in a pirate. So Harry was surprised when the old man chose him.

"Why me, sir?" He knelt at his dying leader's side. "Everybody knows Arthur is the man to take your place, and I promise I will stay and serve him, as I have you, despite past differences. If he desires me to do so."

The old man chuckled and began to cough. He swallowed some water and sat back on his pillow. "I am very old and very tired, young man, and I do not take kindly to having my decisions so questioned. I would write my choice in my own blood or yours for that matter, if it were to help you understand." He laughed, which brought on another coughing fit.

"The written word," he went on after he had recovered his breath and taken another drink, "is a skill that for all these many generations my family has never mastered I am afraid. We have always had little call for reading and writing. Even the most famous of my forebears recruited learned men to read treasure maps for him, yet he could sail the Fault blindfolded. You are the learned man I recruited, Harry my boy. It is my view that your brain will be as important to the survival of my ship and crew as your sword arm. Now ask Arthur to join us. I have little time left, and if I don't tell him myself, I don't suppose he will believe me either."

He looked sadly at the handsome man on whom he had bestowed far greater responsibility than just one small pirate ship. He wondered if he understood that yet.

"He will most likely try to kill you, of course, Harry, and take the *Albatross* by force. Many of the crew will be expecting Arthur to be my choice as well, so if you are not man enough for the challenge?"

"I will go get him, sir," said Harry. "If it is your wish, sir, and your true desire, then I would be honoured to take charge of the *Albatross*." Harry went to leave the cabin and fetch back Arthur.

"There is a lesson to be learnt here, Harry," the old man called after him. "Beware the obvious path to salvation, for sometimes more danger lurks there than you might think. Arthur still has a part to play in all of this. It is up to you to convince him."

After he had spoken with the old man, Arthur left, swearing to put together his own pirate crew and take back the *Albatross* by force. More of the crew than Harry had hoped left with him.

"At least he has not tried to kill me yet," Harry said to the old man.

"Arthur is not your enemy, Harry, and with luck, he will come to realise that. Your enemy is much more dangerous. I am trusting you to give your help unconditionally to someone we both love, if we are to beat this terrible evil."

Harry had so many questions, but the old man was staring up at him through lifeless eyes. The new captain of the *Black Albatross* gently closed his leader's eyes.

"Goodnight, sir," he said softly. "I hope I never let you down." One large tear rolled down his face.

Pirates hit the Sunshine Ranch without warning. Some say the evil cutthroat Jessie Crooks was seen to be leading them. They were not looking for gold or treasure. There was no obvious profit in the pirate's actions. They were simply looking to burn, rape and kill. Crooks would have no doubt enjoyed that. They killed the freed slaves, the owners, and their animals, in fact, every living thing on the Sunshine Ranch. Within an hour or so of the attack, a sickly red glow filled the sky over the northern tip of Heffen. Thick acrid smoke filled the once clean fresh air. Even the fish in the river were still. Some tell of the terrible and monstrous wailing of a wild beast trapped somewhere in the burning jungle that struck fear into the very soul of anyone who heard it. It was the sound of no creature known to man.

Superstition says that the sun now never shines on the burnt-out shell of the Sunshine Ranch. Especially not on the monstrous edifice that now stands upon the charred earth where the grand ranch house once so proudly stood. It is also said that little now grows upon land so stained in the blood of the good and the innocent.

Once again mankind had demonstrated its extraordinary ability for cruelty, murder and destruction. It had not been difficult to manipulate these human creatures at all. There was plenty to feed upon in this sad and pointless little world. It would be a few years before it could be free again, but it could wait a little longer now, and what a feast it would have.

The children were taken to the workhouse. A large plump man took a stick to Rupert on the very first day. It seemed certain they would soon be separated, and Victoria knew that Rupert was not coping in this dreadful, dark and dirty place. For now, both the boys' and girls' wings were already crammed so full of broken children that there was no more room until a couple more died of malnutrition. So they had been found temporary accommodation in the stable block.

As they lay together on damp and smelly straw one evening, a short while after arriving in this hellhole, Victoria saw a dark and shadowy figure in the doorway of the old stable which they shared with three ancient and undernourished carthorses. The figure paused for a moment until illuminated for a second in the lights of a passing carriage.

"Rupert, did you see that?" whispered Victoria, her voice filled with fear and wonder.

"I thought I saw Mother." Rupert had gone as white as a sheet and was shaking like a leaf. "A ghost, Victoria, a ghost." The boy's voice was stricken with terror.

"Shush now, Rupert dear," whispered his sister. "If it was a ghost, then it was mother's ghost, and that means she is still watching over us." She hugged her brother to her for both comfort and warmth. "There is nothing to be afraid of now, Rupert. Everything is going to be all right, I promise."

Chapter 1

To the explorer coming to the end of a long journey, the tropical islands of Heffen are, on first sight, like discovering Paradise, or at least that is true of two of the three larger islands. The third, in stark contrast, is reputed to be much closer to hell.

Along the shoreline of most of both the north and south islands, there is mile upon mile of golden sandy beaches. Palm trees and dense tropical jungles cover much of the northern island, the fertile land scattered liberally with many large plantations, growing mostly food and timber and providing work for many hands.

The south island is smaller. At one point, an extremely narrow channel, through which it must be difficult to navigate a larger craft, is all that separates the two landmasses. There is a strong likelihood that once, a very long time ago, Heffen had been one much larger island. The British, French, Spanish and Portuguese have cultivated the south island, which is governed, in theory at least, as part of the British Empire. Here has grown up a thriving harbour and a fine and colourful multinational settlement.

At the far end of the north and south island lies the third and *smallest of the larger islands. In a shocking contrast to the rich and lush green vegetation and golden sands of the two inhabited islands, it is said to be a stark and barren mass of burnt earth and black sand, out of which rises the awesome spectacle of the volcanic rock Niridia. Nothing grows here, although there is evidence that at one time the earth must have been as fertile as its neighbours.*

Beyond the mysterious reef discovered by the pirate Gabrielle are grouped a number of much smaller islands, some very close to the north island shoreline. These are uncharted waters except, that is, by the pirates who have made these smaller islands their hideouts. It is difficult to be more precise as to the number or size of these islands or how many of them are habitable.

The ghostly mists can always be seen around the Fault and it is from here that most of the legend, mythology and superstition of these islands has evolved. Could it really be that the spirit of the devil himself is trapped there?

–Taken from the excellent, informative and highly commended *New Worlds to Explore* by Mr Thomas Anders

*I*his informative volume brings together in a most unique and readable fashion all the fascinating research, diaries and records of some of the most intrepid explorers and adventurers of the last few hundred years, up to the present day. Included are twenty hand-painted colour plates and many fine pencil drawings, as well as a fine new map of the area.

I had not seen Sydney for ages. My oldest school friend, Sydney, was the son of a rich merchant by the name of Cuthbert Francis Greenburgh. So money was not in short supply for my old friend. In contrast, my papa is a clergyman with a small country parish and a very large family. I am the youngest of four boys, all of whom have turned out quite different; although I think Papa is equally proud of us all.

I also have two sisters, whilst Mama persuaded Papa to adopt another boy and girl, as well as three dogs, a goat, chickens, ducks, geese and countless cats. Mama has a soft spot for cats.

"Thomas Anders," Sydney Greenburgh embraced me warmly, "you haven't got any prettier, old man," he went on cheerfully. "Still got your nose stuck in all those stuffy books you love so much, or have you discovered women yet?"

"Sort of," I mumbled, not wishing for one minute to discuss my love life with this man. Sydney had always made me feel awkward on this particular subject. He was a tall, dark and richly handsome man with deep blue eyes that were filled with passion and good humour. He wore his curly jet-black hair quite long.

Sydney would often talk openly about his most recent conquests amongst the fairer sex. Conquests which had more often than not caused him much trouble. One lucky girl, for example, had turned out to be a foreign princess, the daughter of an eastern potentate who held vitally important trade ties with England. When Sydney broke his promise to marry the girl, as he always did, it not only sparked a diplomatic crisis, but also resulted in Sydney's expulsion from college.

I had always been a little shocked by his rather crude and explicit accounts of his latest bedroom adventures. I confess, however, that I was probably also a little jealous. I have had little good fortune in the search for love. For a year or more, I had been courting Miss Anna Groves. She is the daughter of the parish physician. I was at that time madly and hopelessly in love with the elegantly beautiful Miss Groves. She had a delicate, china doll kind of beauty, added to which she had the most adorable laugh. As if that was not enough for any man, she was an accomplished pianist and an artist as well.

"Don't tell me you are betrothed at last, teacher man?" Sydney slapped me hard on the back, and although I am anything but a violent man, I wanted so badly to hit him.

"You know that I am not, Sydney," I replied sourly. "I know you have been speaking with my sister Susan, so I am sure you have aquatinted yourself with all the news of the Anders clan."

"Twenty-seven cats," confirmed Sydney.

"You know more than I do then," I confessed. "I long since lost count of the number of cats Mama has adopted."

"And let me see, little Fred has just married the farmer's daughter," went on Sydney. "That makes you the only one still available, doesn't it, old boy?"

I tried my very best to change the subject. "I heard you are something important in government nowadays, Sydney?" I looked at my old friend. "Diplomatic corps, someone told me. Presumably we badly needed to start a war or something?"

"Very funny, Thomas," Sydney laughed. "No, I am still a tradesman like my father, that's all. Now tell me, Thomas, is it really true that Anna laughed when you proposed?"

"I don't believe you, Sydney."

"I heard tell that even whilst you were on one knee proposing, she was overcome with a fit of the giggles and had to have smelling salts."

"Look, this is painful for me to discuss, Sydney, so can we please change the subject!"

"Never liked the girl myself, old boy," he went on, clearly having no intention of changing the subject. "Having to sit through all those dreadful piano recitals, and that dreadful cackling laugh used to set my teeth on edge. If you ask me, Thomas my friend, you are well out of that one. China dolls are too easily broken, old chum, and let's face it, she was terribly plain."

"Well, I didn't ask you, Sydney, as I recall."

We were in the empty classroom where I had spent the last couple of years trying to persuade small boys to learn something of the wonders of our world. It was a dowdy sort of room, with desks set out in rows and a grand if rather careworn desk on a raised dais, looking down upon them. The tall and muscular Sydney Greenburgh leaned nonchalantly on the blackboard. Then, picking up a pointer, he began to walk around the classroom, pointing at places on the maps that lined the walls and added some colour to its otherwise drab surroundings.

"All right, Thomas my old friend, I will change the subject if you so wish." He pointed at a map at random. It was the Americas. "Been there, have you, old boy?"

"No!"

"What about there then?" He had the pointer somewhere in Africa.

"No," I said again.

"Or here, or here, or perhaps here?"

"Sydney, you know full well that I have never travelled much farther from my father's parish than we are now."

"And yet you teach geography, not to mention writing supposedly authoritative books on the subject. Don't you ever want to explore this exciting world you drone on and on about so much? Would you not love to see these places for yourself and not just as pictures in some silly stuffy book?"

I sighed. "I am sure I would find it interesting, Sydney, but I am a long way from being an adventurer, and as you know I do not travel well, especially by boat."

"How do you know, old man, when in your own words you have hardly ever left the boundaries of Papa's parish?"

"Sydney," I said, walking over and taking the pointer from his hand, "I have not seen you for ages, so please tell me why you are here and why you have such an interest in my travelling habits, not to mention my love life."

"Well, I just thought it might do you good to get away for a while, old boy. You know how it is. So as you can get over the unlovely Miss Anna Groves." Sydney sat down in my chair and picked up an exercise book that was waiting to be marked. "And in truth," he went on a little sheepishly, "if you must know, I need to get away for a while myself. Had this liaison with a very pretty young thing, and I promise you, Thomas old chum, this little filly did not just lie back and think of England. What a body she had too. Her breasts were like big ripe melons."

"Yes, yes, Sydney, I think I get the picture," I blustered, convinced that I was blushing.

For a moment, Sydney continued to dream of this young lady's breasts.

"She also has a very large husband," he said regretfully, at last. "With a record of violence, I might add. Rumour has it he killed the last man who laid a finger on his wife." The wicked grin, never far away, returned to Sydney's face. "And I, my dear old friend, laid more than a finger on the charming thing."

"I think I've gathered that already," I said.

"I have found the perfect job for you, Thomas. Tutor to the children of the governor of some tropical island." He took the pointer back from me and showed me on the map. "I'm pretty sure you wrote one of your dreadfully dull books about that part of the world, didn't you?"

"You want me to go near to Gabrielle's Fault?" I asked, raising an eyebrow in surprise. "Sydney, those are dangerous waters, and one hell of a long way away."

"You're just frightened that if you go there it will prove what a load of baloney that book of yours is," insisted Sydney, rather unfairly. "Come on, Thomas, you are always banging on about mysteries and things. It's time you took a peep at the world out there. I need to be a long way away from the angry husband. You have a broken heart to mend. Thomas, it is ideal. I've even found you work to keep you out of mischief whilst we are there. I can do some trading for Father's company. I am in no mood to travel alone, old chap, what do you say?" He paused only for breath. "Anyway, Thomas, you don't believe in all that mumbo jumbo you've written about Gabrielle's whatever, surely?"

"I know those waters are riddled with pirate ships, Sydney. In any case, as I have already said, I do not travel well. The answer is no, definitely no, Sydney. You once nearly had me expelled from school. On another occasion, thanks to you, Sydney, I recall escaping being thrown into jail by the very skin of my teeth." I glared at the man who was still grinning broadly at me. "Now you wish to see me scuttled by pirates, eaten by sharks, or lost inside Gabrielle's Fault," I said, a note of incredulity in my voice. "I am telling you now, Sydney," I added firmly, after a pause to calm myself down, "I am not going and that is my final decision and I will never be moved from it."

"I cannot believe you have agreed to go with him, my little angel."

My mother is short of stature and perhaps a little on the stout side. With her long dark hair and eyes as brown as mine, she is also a handsomely attractive woman for her age. She has, as well, a most motherly look about her, which is not surprising, considering she has given birth to six healthy children. As the youngest of the boys, the price I pay is that I will always be seen as her baby. Add to this, my rather absentminded way of muddling through a life, in which a trip into the city library is a big adventure, and I'm afraid I will always suffer an excess of fussing from my dear mama.

"I cannot believe it myself, Mama," I agreed. "I suppose the position of tutor to the governor's wards seemed a promising prospect and a welcome relief from that dismal school."

Mama did not look convinced.

"And," I went on before she could interrupt me, "it is true, I have been thinking for a while now that as I love my research and enjoy writing supposedly authoritative books on faraway places, then perhaps I should travel. It would surely make good sense to experience at least a little of what I am trying to tell my readers."

Mama grunted and began to busy herself around the old farmhouse kitchen. This part of the already ancient manse had been where all of us as children had spent most of our time. A couple of hares hung in the back next to two brace of pheasant. My papa's great coat and huge leather boots and stick were draped on the old scullery sink where he and the dogs had left them after his parish visits.

He would constantly threaten to beat the dogs' brains from their bodies if they did not obey him and without question. The dogs took no notice of his rantings, which is not surprising, as not one of us has ever seen him use the stick. Mama always says that like her, the dogs are not fools, but humour the bad-tempered old goat. This, she insists, is always good in long-term relationships.

My papa is a short and rather portly man who has the ability to always look untidy, even when naked, according to mother. He had been sat in front of the log fire supposedly working on next Sunday's sermon. It would be another long one. There would, as always, be a section on shooting rabbit, hare or pheasant. He passionately believed that God had put these poor creatures on earth for him to shoot and then later eat.

"Trouble is, boy, if you are going anywhere near water, you are sure to drown," he mumbled. "It's not your fault, lad. I'm afraid it's just how you are," he added in a futile attempt to try to make me feel better.

My eldest brother Joseph was at this time somewhere in the Amazon rainforests indulging himself in the ridiculous theory that long extinct reptiles and mammals could be found there somewhere. It was Joseph's dream to see a mammoth. He claimed other explorers had reported sightings of very large furry elephants, so my scepticism was unfounded.

"You didn't fuss like this when Joseph went off," I pointed out. I knew before either of them spoke that this argument would hold no sway with either of them.

"Joseph can look after himself, my darling," Mama replied gently. "I'm afraid that all of your brothers and sisters are better equipped for this trip than you are, my dear."

"The dammed goat is better equipped for this trip than him." My father did not even look up from his work.

"I have to go, Papa, to get away from your dreadfully long sermons for a while." I went over to sit in the chair opposite him by the open fire

"I mean no disrespect, sir," I went on, "but I am now well practised in begging the Lord for forgiveness and shooting innocent bunny rabbits."

"He's making fun of my sermons now, wife," complained Papa, glaring back at me through round spectacles repaired with sticking tape.

"It is not your wonderful and inspiring sermons that are driving the lad away," Mama told him. She had been washing dishes in the big sink. She seemed to be always washing dishes in the big sink. Papa would often comment that Mama was only happy with her arms up to her elbows in hot soapy water or having babies.

"So what on God's wonderful earth could posses this young man to leave his books and his students to sail across the world. Stay home and marry yourself a good woman and be blessed with many children from that happy union as I have done."

"That, dear, is the problem, you silly old thing," interrupted Mama. "The young lady has turned down our son's advances. She is, in fact, to marry Simon Fallow."

"Young Simon Fallow? Why he's a blithering fool like his father." Papa sat up, angry at this news.

"But a very handsome fool whose foolish father is foolishly rich," replied Mama as she dried her hands on a bright yellow towel, which she then threw at her husband. "Not that I am saying you are not handsome, my dear," she added to me. "You're handsome to me anyway," she added unhelpfully.

It was all news to me. She had promised me when she had turned down my proposal of marriage that there was no other suitor. My already heavy heart became a good deal heavier.

"The school has promised to keep my position open for when I return," I explained, still trying to deal with this new information.

Mama could tell at once how upset I was and put her arm around me. "I am so sorry, Thomas," she spoke softly now. "We all thought that she would be only to pleased and honoured to be your wife. I am sure she will regret her choice before long."

"Maybe so, Mama, but I will be a long way away when that happens."

"The boy is set on this foolhardy journey, Mother," observed my papa. He removed his glasses to clean them and quickly wiped away a tear we were not supposed to see. "Are my sermons really that bad?" he asked me.

"No, Papa." I tried to laugh to calm the atmosphere in the kitchen. "But a break from them can do me no harm"

The old vicar laughed. "You will get them twice as long when you come home."

"What better incentive to ensure my speedy return, Papa," I lied and we hugged.

"It's just that Sydney Greenburgh I worry about." Mama was lying too, now. She worried about everything. "He has always been a bad influence on you, Thomas. You know he has. If any one of your friends is going to get you killed, it's Sydney. It's not that I dislike the boy. He is a charmer, I grant you, but also a bad lot and it makes me worry even more about my little baby." She was hugging me now and had begun to sob.

"I will be fine, Mama," I assured her, but I wasn't sure how fine. "I will miss you both, all the family, even the goat. I will miss this kitchen, its warmth, and the way I feel so safe when I am here. I will miss your fussing, the smell of freshly baked bread, or meat roasting. I will miss walking the dogs with Papa. I'm afraid I shall even miss his sermons just a little."

Once final goodbyes had been said, Papa and the dogs walked with me down the overgrown cart track to the gates. We embraced again.

"Look after, Mama," I said, my own voice starting to crack.

"You take care, Thomas Anders," ordered Papa. "I didn't spend all these past years getting you educated and into good employment for you to become shark bait for some pirate."

"I will take good care," I promised him.

"Watch yourself with that Sydney Greenburgh as well. Your mother is right to be concerned about him."

"I will," I promised again, kneeling to say my goodbyes to the dogs.

"Don't forget," Papa reminded me, "the sermons will be twice as long, at the very least, when you get back."

He watched me walk over the hill to the road, where I waited in the late afternoon sunshine for old Jake. The old carthorse turned the corner. Throwing my bag into the back, I pulled myself up next to the old man, who as always smelt strongly of sweat and old chewing tobacco.

Papa watched the cart disappear over the horizon. It took sometime, as Jake's horse, even when younger, was not known for its speed. Once he had lost sight of the wagon, he turned back towards the manse, calling the dogs to follow. The sun was setting fast now and the sky on the horizon blood red.

"Twice as long, maybe three times as long, when you come back." He stopped to threaten the puppy with his big stick. It was, however, an even less convincing threat than usual. Tears now streamed down his face. "When you come back. Don't I mean *if* you come back? Listen God, I know that I have never been the perfect servant, I realise that and maybe I do go on a bit, given the chance. But please Lord, if I have offended you, it was never deliberate and I always do try my best to carry on your good works. So please keep our little boy safe. So far you have kept all our children safe, for which I am grateful. You may, however, find young Thomas a little bit more of a challenge."

He turned back to his dogs, took out a huge handkerchief and blew his bulbous nose. "Right, lads, we can't let the good wife see us all in this state, now can we? We have to be strong us fellas, so once round the field whilst I compose myself."

My dog, Mama told me in a letter that found me just before our ship left, had stayed by the gate. A daft-looking black and white collie with enormous ears, he sat watching the hill over which I had disappeared.

"Come on, lad," Papa called him, "and don't you worry yourself. He'll be all right."

More than ten years before we left England, an old man sat in a wooden rocking chair on the porch of his rustic homestead on the north island. He stared in despair at the dark clouds of black smoke rising above the jungle from where until a few hours ago had stood the Sunshine Ranch.

Richard Boscastle ran a small horse ranch that bordered onto the largest plantations on Heffen. Fairweather had taken up most of the land to the north of the Boscastle ranch on which to build the Sunshine Ranch. Boscastle had arrived on Heffen already well into his twilight years. He had been persuaded to move from the inclement conditions of Scotland at the behest of the businessman, John Burleigh, who promised the sunshine would be kinder to his rheumatism than another highland winter.

He brought with him from Scotland his considerable wealth and a most attractive young wife. Patricia Boscastle was often mistaken for his daughter, such was the difference in their ages. It was said by some that the marriage of the aging Boscastle to this pretty young wench had caused much controversy back home in Scotland. It was even suggested that this had been the overriding reason he chose to sell up and make the long sea journey to Heffen.

Old Man Fairweather had been a good friend to the newcomers. His wife, a native girl who was still breathtakingly beautiful despite her advancing years, befriended the young Scottish lass. She introduced her into the north island society, whilst her husband did much to protect their new neighbours. The two islands mixed very little, other than on business. Once a year, however, all the landowners in the north would head south for the governor's ball.

The south island boasted the main commercial harbour, the banks and the library, as well as the governor's brand new and as yet unfinished palace. The south of Heffen had what little industry existed on either island. The north was mostly agricultural land, or where man had been unable to tame the wilderness, tropical rain forests.

It had been the enlightened minds of some of the north islanders who had started to run their plantations, ranches and small holdings in what became known as the new way. Old Man Fairweather had been one of the pioneers of this new way, before he, his lovely wife and family had been slain by the pirates. The Sunshine Ranch had been burnt to the ground. The village for the freed slaves was set alight and many of the workforce brutally massacred. Others were rounded up and sold back into slavery.

Patricia Boscastle had that day been in one of the remotest spots on the island. She was in a place on her husband's land that bordered onto the Sunshine Ranch. Boscastle could not find his beautiful bride. He was out of his mind with worry. A cocktail of fear for his precious wife's safety and a consuming, jealous rage that tore at his very soul.

This drove him on in his desperate search to find her. As he hunted everywhere, he imagined her lying naked with one of the many men with whom she flirted so brazenly. He half expected to come across her at any moment, entwined in the arms of today's lover, their naked bodies sprawled out dead in this tropical hell.

Even in death, she would, he was sure, be beautiful. As victims of the madness that exploded all around them, there would be a certain irony. A harsh lesson to those who cheat on the one who loves them.

Boscastle had fought so hard to stop Patricia being stolen from him.

Down near the hollow by the old fallen tree, Patricia had been looking for wild flowers, or at least that is what she intended telling Boscastle later. The wild flowers that grew here were like nothing the Scottish lass had ever seen before. Flowers as large as small trees with so many different and brilliant colours. Reds, blues and yellows, some stood almost six feet tall. It was then that Patricia first heard and then saw the terrible carnage. There were bodies everywhere. It was difficult to make out anything, but it appeared to be the remains of a small group of workers who had been fleeing from the Sunshine Ranch.

Their corpses were sprawled in a bloody mess, desecrating this normally tranquil place. There was so much blood. Patricia screamed in terror. Now three pirates had seen her and were coming after her. There was, however, a man running towards her that Patricia knew well. It was the young and dashing Henry Jessop. He pulled out a pistol and shot the first pirate in the back at a range where it was impossible to miss. The pirate coughed blood and fell on his face in the dirt.

One pirate was closing in on Patricia. The great fallen tree behind Patricia and slightly to her right began to send splinters of wood all around the clearing. It was at that point that a small dark-skinned boy ran from the undergrowth to her left, heading for the trees at the other side of the clearing.

The boy was naked and his large eyes were filled with contempt for his pursuers. He might have been any one of the many black slave children at work on the islands, or even the child of one of the free workers at the Sunshine Ranch, fleeing for his life. Something inside her told Patricia that he was none of these things. There was something very different about this child.

Even in the fleeting moment that Patricia's eyes made contact with his, she felt something strange and very special. A strange confusion of fear and unconditional love flooded into her mind.

"Never mind her," yelled one pirate. "It's the boy we want."

The boy was incredibly fast, his wiry form zigzagging between the pirates and nearly causing Jessop to fall flat on his face. A moment later he had vanished back into the thickest part of the jungle. Two or three of the thugs gave chase, but they had little hope of catching him now.

Patricia turned to find another man close behind her. He was a tall, very thin man, whose eyes were filled with the enjoyment of a life of wicked mischief. His enormous curved nose seemed to bend over to a sharp point. There was an even sharper knife in his mouth.

Jessop had stumbled, recovered, reloaded and fired. The shot missed the pirate who had thrown himself onto the girl. The bullet had come close to hitting Patricia, who was now sprawled near the gory remains of one of the bodies. Another loud shot came, but this time from the other side of the clearing and the skinny rat-faced man disappeared into the thick green vegetation in much the same direction in which the child had fled. Patricia screamed again and began to sob. Boscastle leapt down from his horse and ran to her.

"What the hell are you doing here, Jessop?" He stared up at the younger man, his plump, red face filled with hatred. Jessop was not only a great deal younger than Boscastle, but so much better looking, in a sly and rather condescending way. He was one of the young studs who had been paying too much attention to Boscastle's pretty young wife. What was worse, Boscastle was sure Patricia was returning the favour.

"Doing your job for you, old man, and protecting your lovely wife." Jessop was brushing dirt from his well-cut and fashionable topcoat, before brushing the side of his black silk top hat with his sleeve. He offered the stricken girl a finely embroidered handkerchief before helping her to her feet. Patricia continued to sob.

"Unhand my wife, Jessop." Boscastle lurched himself at Jessop, waving a stout stick. The younger man easily dodged the clumsy attack, and putting a foot out tripped Boscastle into a pile of mangled bodies.

"You been drinking again, Boscastle?" he sneered at the man on the ground. "Perhaps it would be wise if I saw Patricia home. You are obviously incapable, you drunken old fool." Jessop turned and walked away, his arm around the sobbing girl.

Boscastle fumbled for a moment and then pulled a pistol from his belt. He pointed it shakily at Jessop's back.

"I wouldn't pull the trigger, Richard my old friend," said a silky new voice. Heffen's newly appointed governor sat uncomfortably on the back of a fine grey mare. Although Boscastle had done business with the new man and had once even counted him as a friend, their relationship had become increasingly strained. The governor was accompanied by a platoon of His Majesty's redcoats.

"We would not want to arrest you for murder, would we now, captain?" The little man made up for his short stature by his imposing presence. He turned to the well-starched young officer standing stiffly to attention at his side. Captain Philip Baldock nodded in agreement. The governor slipped rather awkwardly from the saddle and stood over the prostrate figure of Boscastle.

"Let's face it, Richard," he went on. "I told you all along that you're too old for her. Learn to live with it and let Mr Jessop see to her needs for you." He laughed and pulled the old man to his feet. "Perhaps he will let you watch." The governor slapped him on the back. "I regret I have more terrible news, my old friend," he continued in an over-dramatic way.

"Old Man Fairweather has tragically perished in the pirate attack, as has his wife, his children and many others." He paused to study Richard Boscastle's chubby face. "I did try to warn him, Richard, as I have tried to warn you. I'm afraid these new ways of yours are extremely dangerous, socially unacceptable and quite, quite unworkable, my man." For just a moment, Boscastle believed there might be a trace of genuine sadness betrayed in the governor's eyes.

"Perhaps you will heed my well-intentioned warning now," he added brusquely. "What chance do the brave new ways have of working now?" Silas Raines began to laugh hysterically. Or was the new governor crying? Captain Baldock was not sure. They were both so far from home, their minds haunted by so many terrible things they had seen that night. The horrors they had witnessed would drive many better men insane.

I had disliked boats even as a young child. Joseph, Mathew and Frederick loved to take me out on the boating lake, simply to enjoy the obvious terror I was always in on water. That, I suppose, is brotherly love for you. The craft that was to take us on our adventure was called *Sally O.*

It was a smallish schooner with patched sails and a patched hull. Some of the timbers, although now quite old, had at one time been replaced. Going on the evidence of the remaining older timber, I guessed there had probably been a fire in the galley at sometime. Probably it was when the ship's cook had burnt the cakes. Our cabin leaked and it was not even raining. Just moored in the safety of the harbour, it gave me the distinct feeling that it could sink at any time.

The only comfort I could take from this creaking tub on which our lives depended was simple. There could surely be no self-respecting pirate, anywhere in the world, who would want to scuttle it. The docks were full of tall ships loading or unloading their wares before setting sail for another trip on the high seas.

I had received the third letter in the same number of days from Mama. It contained further instructions on how to stay alive. Instructions which included not picking fights with pirates and various ways of avoiding scurvy. There was news of the family too. My sister Emily, a teacher like myself, had been put in charge of the lower school infants.

My brother Mathew had a new bull. They had heard from Joseph in the Amazon, who was alive and well, or at least had been when his letter set out on its torturous way home some three months ago. Sadly, however, despite of all his best endeavours, his search for the great mammoth had so far proved fruitless.

> One good thing that has come out of your departure, Thomas my dear, is that your father's sermons are quite a lot shorter. God moves in mysterious ways. Do take good care. We all love you and miss you greatly. Mama.

Sydney had spent much of his time in dockside inns, brothels and opium dens. He had also added at least two more angry husbands to the long list of people who wanted to kill him. It seemed so unfair that he could just smile and wink at a lady and receive her favours, whilst I was still a hopeless fool and a failure when it comes to such things.

I was becoming increasingly nervous about the voyage, and the days of waiting to embark upon this long journey did nothing to help improve my rapidly deteriorating state of mind. This coupled with a somewhat alarming moment with one of Sydney's angry husbands was making me feel physically sick. As for the crew of the good ship *Sally O*, they could quite easily have been pirates themselves.

A more motley crew of outcasts, cutthroats and vagabonds would be hard to find. Captain Jakes was a very big man, tall and muscular despite advancing years, with enormous leathery hands. Dressed in a heavily stained tunic, grubby white pants and a battered hat, his clothes looked almost as old as their owner. He inspired little more confidence than his raggedy crew. To be fair, his uniform had probably once been very smart, and there was no doubt he had been a handsome man in his youth. Even with the ravages of time, Jakes still betrayed a hint of his boyish good looks.

The day the *Sally O* was due to set sail for Heffen did not come a minute too soon. First there was my growing apprehension at the prospect of the long voyage ahead. My anxiety grew closer to panic with every hour we waited for the tide to change. I can only liken this to a condemned man in his last hours on death row. Worse, however, than my shattered nerves was compelling evidence that some of the more indignant husbands had formed their own private army.

It was clearly their intention to board the *Sally O* and deal with Sydney, and anybody associated with him, in a most unpleasant and permanent way. It would be ironic I thought, if Sydney got me killed before we had even left England. Perhaps in view of the ordeal ahead, it would be a blessing in disguise.

Only my pride and determination to prove my parents' fears unfounded prevented me from returning to shore and the safety of Mama's kitchen. At last, with much running about and shouting of orders, the *Sally O* cast off. Accompanied by much creaking and groaning, not to mention a good deal of rocking from side to side, she turned slowly in the water to point towards open sea and set sail on the long journey to the islands of Heffen.

A little over ten years prior to our departure from England on board the *Sally O*, a very young Captain Baldock was being ushered into the imposing entrance hall of the Boscastle ranch.

"My wife has had a terrible shock, Captain," pointed out Boscatle. "I think it unlikely she saw anything that will help you catch any more of these murderous scum."

Boscastle paused to gauge the captain's reaction. As stiff and starched as ever, Captain Baldock stood respectfully motionless in the centre of Boscastle's grand hall. The house was built entirely of local redwood. The hall formed an impressive entrance to what was in fact a simple home. A high-vaulted ceiling complemented polished wood-panelled walls. These were decorated with interracially carved swirling patterns through which perfectly crafted nymphs and cherubs appeared to dance. Paintings of many of his Scottish ancestors graced the walls.

There were also many paintings and pencil drawings of his pretty wife. In some of these, she wore little to cover her very pleasing curves. Philip Baldock tried hard not to look at these alluring pictures. There were no windows in the hallway and yet it was surprisingly light and airy.

"I am sure you're right, Mr Boscastle sir," agreed the captain, still doing his best to look smart in his torn and blood-stained uniform.

"Any help we can give, you understand," Boscastle assured him. "Old Man Fairweather was kind to us when we arrived here and a very good friend. I owe him a great deal and shudder to think what life will be like without his guidance and his protection." Boscastle showed the young soldier out.

The most unwelcome guest of the day was Henry Jessop. Dressed in a most fashionable and expensive matching topcoat and mid-green velvet breeches, topper in hand, Henry Jessop cut a dashing figure.

"Go to hell, Jessop," Boscastle told the fop.

"Are you sure, Boscastle?" sneered the rake, examining a gloved hand rather than look Boscastle in the eye.

"She had a terrible night and she was greatly fond of Mrs Fairweather," insisted Boscastle. "Now leave, Jessop, before I have you thrown out."

"Is that Henry's voice I hear?" Patricia, dressed in her nightgown and still looking pale and drawn, stood at the top of the grand redwood staircase. "Please send him up, Richard dear."

"I am going out to check the horses," snapped Boscastle, reaching for his coat and hat. "They too must have been scared witless by the terrible events of last night." He strode to the front door and then turned angrily to his pretty young wife. She had not moved from the top of the stairs and was clutching the banister rail for support.

"At least my horses need me," mumbled Boscastle and he left, slamming the door behind him. Jessop and Patricia were alone.

Despite the relatively calm seas, I was sick as a dog for three or four days. The crew of the *Sally O* thought my suffering very funny, and by far the best entertainment the old bathtub had seen since it last sunk.

Although in a terrible mood, having been celibate for a record four days, Sydney nursed me well. He made me drink plenty of water, which already tasted pretty awful. As I began to feel a little better, Sydney began forcing hot broth into me. He was remarkably long suffering as I am, without question, a most awful patient.

On the fifth day, the down-at-heel captain came to visit us in our cabin.

"How is he today?" he asked cheerfully, bending low to fit his tall frame into the low-roofed cabin. "I ain't got to do a burial at sea in a very long time."

Sydney laughed. "I think he is going to live, captain, unless he goes on trying my patience like he has been." Sydney glared at me. "Then, Captain, I promise you will have your funeral at sea."

Sydney took out a bottle of scotch and poured the captain a drink.

"All that trouble to save his hide, Mr Greenburgh, and the pirates will probably get us all," chuckled Jakes, stroking his untidy grey beard.

The old seadog had been sailing these waters since a young lad, some five decades ago. His hair was almost white now, longish and always untidy. His face reminded me of a piece of comfortable old leather.

"Pirates," I groaned weakly. "Where?"

"I have heard much about these pirates, Captain," enthused Sydney Greenburgh, suddenly more interested in what the captain was saying. "These are some very bad men indeed, from what I've heard," he added, encouraging Jakes to continue.

"Bad men?" the old captain was laughing. "That, my friend, is the past. The pirate we most don't want to run into is a very bad woman. She is as beautiful as she is deadly."

"Sounds my type," mused Sydney. "I have been without a woman too long already."

"No pirates, Sydney." I had pulled myself up in the bunk, still pale and gaunt. I grabbed a weak hold on my friend. "Promise me, Sydney, promise me, no pirates."

The captain laughed again, but it was a nervous laugh. His voice was trembling as he spoke again. "You don't ever mess with Prudence Fairweather." He said her name with fear in his voice. "She is the only survivor of the family who owned the Sunshine Ranch. The rest of them were massacred. Terrible thing, it will be more than ten years ago now, although it still seems like it happened only yesterday. Somehow she escaped and now...." his voice trailed away into a tense silence.

"Now what?" I asked hoarsely.

"Yes, good question," agreed Sydney. He had spent much of his time below deck caring for me. Despite this, the wind and what little sun we had seen on the voyage had brought even more colour to his already dark complexion. "And now what exactly?"

There was still fear in the eyes of the ancient mariner. He nervously pulled at the braiding on his faded and work-stained tunic. "Come now," he said. "We don't want to be talking of pirates and things of that sort, now do we?" And before anyone could reply he continued, "In any case, who would want to steal my pension? I mean it is worth nothing to anybody else and with Mr Anders not well."

Sydney pulled himself up into the bunk above mine in the cramped little cabin. "Pension?" he asked, feeling his head gingerly where he had just banged it on the low ceiling. He poured the old captain another very generous helping of best malt whisky into his battered tin cup.

The captain studied his replenished drink carefully. It was almost as if he might be thinking this Prudence Fairweather had slipped aboard and poisoned it. At last he took a long slug of the golden nectar, taking a moment to enjoy the warmth and smoothness of the liquid as he felt it slip down his throat.

"This is my pension now." He gestured around him at the creaking bucket we had all entrusted our lives to.

"Not planning to retire soon then," observed Sydney, dryly. "Just drown. It's a novel approach to retirement I'll grant you that."

"She'll get us there," insisted Captain Jakes. "Never underestimate the *Sally O*."

I could imagine that this old seadog had, like all of us, set out with great expectations of what life had in store. You could see in his eyes that life had knocked most of those expectations out of him. He stood sadly, gazing at the bottom of his empty tin mug. Although Jakes had let his appearance go, probably because he could not afford a new uniform, underneath the threadbare clothes, he had kept his body in pretty good condition for a man of such advancing years.

"It wasn't always like this," he went on, after Sydney had refilled his cup again. "I had a partner on Heffen and we were doing well. We had a shop in the harbour."

"What did you sell?" I croaked.

"Almost anything really, but mostly sail cloth, rope, good marine ply, tar and general supplies of course. My partner was the shopkeeper, him being married, with a boy of his own. I don't have anyone myself, so we got me a woman of my own." He gestured around him again. "The *Sally O* is my woman."

"No offence, old thing, but I prefer the ones made of flesh and blood," observed Sydney.

"It sounded a good idea to me," I said, deliberately ignoring Sydney, whose mind had already drifted to some more recent conquest. By the look in his eyes he was already comparing the *Sally O*, very unfavourably, to the lady in his thoughts.

"No contest," he muttered dreamily to himself.

"Sydney," I said, reproaching him sternly.

"Sorry," he said sheepishly. "Do carry on, Captain."

Captain Jakes was now quite drunk, although he still accepted another top up from the rapidly emptying jug. I found myself hoping that his degenerate shambles of a crew would at least have some idea of how to steer the captain's pension.

"I was saying," I tried again, "it sounds a very good plan. If the research I have carried out is anything like true to life, Heffen is a major trading point in this part of the world, and a growing one, despite the pirates."

"After long journeys, ships need supplies and often repairs to the structure, or at least the sails," agreed Jakes. He was now beginning to slur his words a little. "My partner and I were doing well, until all the troubles started. We had acquired extra land for our own little boatyard in the old dock. He wanted to build me a new ship, but I am loyal to this old girl." He tapped the bunk I was lying on with affection.

"You said troubles, Captain?" I was interested now and wanted the old sailor to carry on.

"There were those who didn't like the new ways," he said quietly. "We had no strong politics, especially me. We both, however, refused to trade in people though. I draw the line at that. It ain't right, or at least, I don't think it is anyway. Well, that went down none too well, added to which my partner had become a rather pious man. He used to find it difficult to forgive them who sinned and especially his own." Jakes looked sadly at us. "The truth is he never realised how much of a sinner his own business partner was. I would never entertain the slaver's mind."

"Slavers," muttered Sydney, for once with no trace of humour in his voice.

"And I don't care what you good gentleman believe, I agreed with him on that point. It just don't seem right to me somehow." He drained the tin cup in one long slug and then carried on. "Many of the landowners in the north and some in the south had in any case been freeing their slaves and paying them fair for the work they did." He held out his tin cup to Sydney, who drained the last of the good malt into it. "Suddenly the pirates were raiding the northern islands, massacring many good people. Most of the people killed were also our best customers. We had a new governor who they reckoned was doing his best to catch those heartless bastards." Jakes looked sadly at his empty cup and the equally empty jug next to it. "Then the pirates got a new leader, the woman I mentioned, Prudence Fairweather, and now nobody is safe in their beds. Mothers use her name to frighten the little ones when they're doing bad things."

"Now there's a new experience for you, Sydney." I smiled up at the top bunk. "With this one, it's normally the ladies who don't sleep so well when he is on the loose."

"You shouldn't joke about Prudence Fairweather. She is a heartless killer." The captain was now swaying more than the *Sally O.* "I better go check what's going on up top," he decided.

"Careful you don't fall off your pension, Captain," warned Sydney.

"Captain," I said, as he tried to get his big, gangly frame out of the doorway of our tiny cabin, "you and your partner, have these troubles put you out of business?"

Jakes turned and tried to focus drunken eyes on me. "No, Mr Anders, Prudence Fairweather put us out of business. She killed my partner and set fire to our boatyard. So much tar and gunpowder, you can imagine how little was left. The boy Daniel probably perished in the flames. Anyway, he's never been seen since." For a moment, Captain Jakes seemed to be a very long way from the *Sally O.* Sydney took it to be the drink, but I was not sure. It seemed to me as if some past memory had stolen him from us. "The old boatyard and warehouse have never been used since. People say it's cursed in someway. I once tried to go back there. They're right, there is a sense of something terrible hanging over the place. Believe me, I didn't hang about for long. Whatever it is, it's bad that's for sure." Jakes was staring blankly out of the porthole, his normally weather-beaten face drained of colour.

"Captain?"

"Sorry, gentlemen, my thoughts were miles away," he said. "I lost something pretty special the night my partner was murdered."

"Didn't you get some compensation for the yard and stuff?" Sydney asked in a characteristically unfeeling way.

"The governor wasn't interested," he said. "Anyway, now you know why I hate the name of Prudence Fairweather."

The captain gave up trying to squeeze himself through the small doorway, staggered back over to examine the empty bottle that had so recently been full of the best malt whisky. Discovering that this was not only empty, but as we were still a very long way from Gabrielle's Fault, unlikely to refill itself, he faltered momentarily and then collapsed in a heap on the floor.

"Now he's going to have one hell of a bad head when he wakes up," observed Sydney.

Over the next few days, I began to get my sea legs, and even began to venture up on deck now and again. Just as I was able to drink Sydney's revolting broth, without the need of threats, though it still tasted like very salty cabbage water, we hit a storm. This wasn't any old storm and there was little doubt the captain's pension was very much in peril.

The sky was a rich deep blue and the sea seemed calm. Already the shambles of a crew was, however, showing signs of panic, if not blind terror. All Sydney could see was a vertical grey line coming down from the sky into the water somewhere around the horizon.

"What's that odd wiggly thing in the sky, old chap?" he asked me, pointing towards the twister.

"Wind," I said weakly, as I felt the panic start to strangle my words.

The huge swirling mass of the tall grey cloud was travelling fast towards us. "Lots of it," I added lamely.

Captain Jakes was unconscious again and the crew seemed now to be frozen in terror. I could not blame them; the whirlwind was now so close you could almost reach out into it.

The Sally O was being thrown violently from side to side. The familiar sounds of creaking and groaning were interspersed with the less familiar sound of splintering wood. She was now turning about in the water like a demented spinning top.

I stood transfixed, staring up into the great column of wind and debris it had already sucked in. The twister now rose almost majestically up to the sky. As I watched, a small clipper, probably slightly larger than the *Sally O* and still fully sailed, spewed out of the grey cloud. It was tossed up into the sky like a child's toy before hurtling back down to smash into tiny pieces on a few small rocks showing out of the water only a few hundred yards away. Was this to be our fate too?

"Thomas, look out." There was panic in Sydney's voice. Then I heard the dreadful sound of splitting wood and canvas. Instinctively looking above me, as if sensing the danger I was in, I saw one of the *Sally O*'s masts hurtling down towards me.

More than ten years or so before we had set out on this foolhardy adventure, the northern island of Heffen was trying to come to terms with the pirate attacks on the Sunshine Ranch and the brutal murders of so many people. Old Man Fairweather and his lovely wife had been well liked, except that is for those opposed to the new ways. It would be a little while yet before the new governor would give much of the old Sunshine Ranch to Sir John Burleigh. This was a man who ironically had made his fortune, and probably his knighthood, trading in human flesh.

The young redcoat Captain Baldock was appointed to investigate the atrocity. Whilst those who appointed him might not have been very concerned in finding out who sent in the pirate Jessie Crooks and his men, the captain took his role very seriously. Beneath the starched exterior, the young man was as shocked as anybody was at the dreadful sights he had seen that night. Baldock had already fought in numerous skirmishes with pirates in his short career. He had seen plenty of pain and death already, but nothing like he had seen that night.

The soldier was eager to interview Mrs Boscastle, who he knew had been gathering flowers when she had been caught up in the pirates' attack. True she had only become involved because of the close proximity of Boscastle's small holding to the much bigger Sunshine

Ranch. So far Richard Boscastle had refused to let the captain interview his wife, because she was so upset. The captain was a little surprised, as he had met Patricia Boscastle at many social events, including the governor's ball.

She had always impressed him as fiery, strong-willed Scottish lass. She flirted shamelessly with all the younger men, including the captain himself. Patricia was without doubt a good-looking girl who loved to wear the most revealing as well as tight-fitting ball gowns. Dresses that clung to her shapely body with low necklines and long slits down the side to show a glimpse of her long and perfectly formed legs.

She seemed most happy in the company of the young fop Henry Jessop, and the officer was sure in his own mind that it was to meet him that she had gone to the great fallen tree the previous evening. He questioned Jessop, of course, who insisted that as a gentleman and a man of honour he could not and would not betray a lady's trust.

The soldier decided that whilst waiting to meet with Mrs Boscastle he would visit other neighbours. Was it possible that the Fairweather family, on the surface so kind and such stalwart members of the community, had enemies he did not know of? The captain knew that it was most likely those who disapproved of the new ways who had directed the killings. That would put the island's governor in the list of possible suspects, and the soldier knew that to investigate him would be to invite a court martial and certain hanging.

Then there was the other matter, but there could surely be no connection with that. This was murder plain and simple, and Baldock was sure he knew who was behind it. Proving it and living to tell the tale was another matter altogether. With all this running through his mind, the captain took a small unit of handpicked men and went visiting. His first call was to the mad professor.

Raymond Kidner lived on the very edge of the north island, a short boat trip from town, where he ran Heffen Library, as well as acting as chemist and physician for many of the island people. Kidner was a tall, untidy but clean-shaven man with longish grey hair. He wore thick bottle-glass spectacles for his deteriorating eyesight. Kidner would hold papers up to his slightly red nose to read what was written upon them.

A very clever man, his eccentricity was simply a manifestation of the millions of thoughts his brain was cluttered with every second of the day.

He was known to be a great supporter of the new way, and a good and kind, if equally forgetful and sometimes distant sort of man.

He could shed no new light on the tragic events of the previous night. So the captain and his small unit went visiting elsewhere. If Kidner's house was similar to a grass hut, if not quite as luxurious, George Mansfield, the famous architect, lived in a grand red brick mansion that would have looked more in keeping with the English countryside than a clearing in a tropical jungle.

He was an architect of some considerable note, who had not only moved himself and his family to Heffen, but also their country home brick by brick. He was responsible for many of the buildings on the two islands, including Boscastle's great wooden ranch house and the still incomplete, but magnificent palace for Heffen's new governor.

It was not clear to folk where Mansfield's sympathies lay, as he was something of a recluse. The captain climbed the grand entrance steps of Westmoreland stone to the huge claret-painted front door. He ordered one of his smartly turned-out men to put down his rifle and ring the bell.

"Go away," a muffled voice came from inside. "Who is it anyway?"

"Captain Baldock of the His Royal Majesty's Heffen Island Guard. I wish to speak with Sir George Mansfield if I may, sir."

"You are speaking to him, make it quick," said the voice behind the big red door.

"It was about the events of last night, sir," ventured the young captain. "If we could come in, just for a moment?"

"What events are you referring to? I know nothing of any event," the muffled voice replied. "The sun could have fallen from the sky for all I know, or moved. It hasn't moved, has it? Always have the sun on the gardens in the afternoon, so the sun mustn't be moved. If the sun moved it would ruin everything."

"No, sir," Captain Baldock sighed. "The sun only moves on its usual path," he reassured the voice behind the still closed door.

"Good, good that's all right then. Now go away please, I am very busy."

The soldiers looked at their young commander enquiringly. Did he want them to smash down the door?

"Let's go, men," he said softly. "We're wasting valuable time here." Baldock marched his troops back down the long driveway.

Patricia Boscastle kissed Henry Jessop one more time. Her dark brown hair was everywhere. She was naked, her perfectly formed body pressed up close to Jessop. The girl had been genuinely upset and a little shocked by the massacre, and few events ever shocked Patricia Boscastle. She had been very fond of all the Fairweathers. Jessop offered some distraction for her from such unpleasantness. She did not like to dwell on such things for long. It was not as if it would change anything.

It had not been Henry Jessop she had planned a secret assignation with by the fallen tree. In fact, she wondered why he had come there looking for her. Like all men he must be jealous of the attentions of others.

"Must you go, my lover?" she whispered in his ear, which she then began to nibble.

Jessop laughed. "Your husband will return soon, my love. We must keep some sense of propriety."

The girl watched Jessop as he dressed. He had, she thought, the most perfectly formed bottom she had ever seen on a man. Not, she reminded herself, that she had seen that many men's bottoms. She fought with him, trying her best to prevent him pulling up his trousers, a fight which ended in a long and passionate kiss. Jessop freed himself from the naked girl's clutches and pulled a frilly lemon shirt over his hairy chest. Patricia was now playing with her firm and plentiful young breasts in an attempt to bring him back to her bed. Jessop was not to be tempted.

"I must go, my lovely," he whispered softly. "I will come back tomorrow."

"And what am I to do until then, my lover?" She moved one slender hand slowly and very deliberately down her body, pausing whilst the very end of her long red fingernails stroked her flat, smooth navel. Then, just as seductively, she moved her hand between her legs. For just a moment it seemed Jessop's resolve was weakening. He laughed and threw an ivory white silk gown over her.

"Dress up nicely for your husband," he suggested, pointing at the gown. It was a beautiful garment ornately embroidered in gold silk.

"You look stunning in that." He leaned forward and kissed her on the forehead. "He deserves a treat," he went on. "Having just lost a good friend like that. Who knows, it might prove too much for the old fool." He was halfway out of the door when Patricia spoke.

"Henry dear," she said, sitting up on the bed, holding the gown in front of her breasts.

"Yes, my love?"

"What were you doing down by the fallen oak last night? You haven't told me yet."

Jessop grinned. "Why meeting you, my love, or at least that is what you will tell the good Captain Baldock."

"Sure you were not meeting someone else, Henry? After all, I do know of your reputation with women."

"Of course not." He came back over to the bed and kissed her again. "I have eyes only for you, you know that."

"Do I? Well, you will have to wait and see what I tell the handsome Captain Baldock," she laughed. "He is rather handsome, isn't he?"

Jessop looked quite angry. For a moment Patricia thought he might hit her. He had always looked capable of that. Instead, he turned on his heels and left her bedroom, slamming the door behind him.

"See you tomorrow, my sweet Henry," said Patricia to herself.

The front door slammed.

"Well, maybe I will," she added.

Patricia had done very much as Jessop had suggested. First she had bathed before sending her two servants home. All Boscastle's liberated workers had their own homes, although they were little more than mud huts. She had dressed in the shapely silk gown, slit down one side from

66

the thigh to the floor, so as to give tantalising glimpses of a long slender leg. A quite stunning diamond necklace, a present from her husband, set off her perfect and fulsome cleavage. The necklace reflected the light from the flickering oil lamps and dozens of candles that were lighting the great hall in a million or more directions.

She was becoming concerned as to Boscastle's whereabouts. It was very dark out, and with the servants gone, she was now alone. Patricia opened a draw in an expensive, handcrafted cherry wood writing desk and took out a single-shot pistol, which was always kept loaded, just in case. A moment later, the front door opened.

"Oh it's you," she said.

Her pretty eyes were drawn to the two pistols being pointed at her. She forgot about the weapon in her own hand.

"Can I ask why?" she asked, surprisingly calmly. Patricia had never been one for hysterics. She was already backing away towards the staircase. She knew already that she was looking at her murderer. She was sure her killer fully intended to empty both the pistols into her. Patricia continued to back away slowly, starting backwards up the staircase. Her mind was still struggling to work out why anyone might want to kill her when the first bullet hit her in the stomach.

Her body jerked forward, but she remained standing. Her eyes widened a little, blood forming at the corner of her mouth. No reason she thought, looking down in resigned disbelief at the red patch on her silk nightgown where the bullet had entered.

"I would have loved you," she lied, staring wide-eyed at the person who had shot her. A second bullet hit her in the chest, this time throwing her back onto the staircase.

There was a strangled scream. Patricia's body slid slowly back down the stairs, spasming for a moment and then lay still, sprawled out at the bottom. Her blank eyes stared out across the hall at the many portraits of her on the walls.

The scream had brought Boscastle's manservant running through the front door. He stared at the girl's lifeless body and then at her assailant.

His face was filled with disbelief. The assailant picked up the single-shot pistol that Patricia had dropped and shot the manservant between the eyes. He was dead before he hit the ground.

A little more than ten years after the murder of Patricia Boscastle and the carnage of the previous day, the *Sally O* faced the eye of the storm. I could pretend that it was some miracle that saved our lives. Maybe Papa's prayers had been answered. I did not even throw myself out of the way of the crashing mast. I was trapped under sailcloth for a short while, until Sydney and a couple of the sturdier crew pulled me out.

The mast itself had missed everybody, although the hull structure had taken some damage. I had read once in a book somewhere that these typhoons often did change course very suddenly. Our twister had done just that.

Nevertheless, the *Sally O* took the most incredible buffeting. So close were we to the eye of the storm that we were showered with the debris it had sucked in and was now spitting back.

Some of the sights were quite bizarre. A horse and cart flew through the air before us. Part of a barn and a wooden church. Considering we were still some distance from land, I wondered if these strange sights could have given birth to at least some of the mythology of Gabrielle's Fault.

Then the rain came and I do not recall ever seeing rain like it. Waterproofs were of no use. Every hand was now on deck, doing what they could to keep the *Sally O* on course.

We were at sea it seemed for an eternity. I swear on the Bible that I will never find one of Papa's sermons anything other than mercifully short by comparison. At last we were able to make out land. The weather was now hot, although the breeze helped cool us down. There were seagulls and much bigger dark brown birds with huge beaks, following close to the *Sally O*.

"I told you she would get us here," her captain told us proudly.

Our progress, now that we were in sight of land at last, seemed even slower. I was longing to set foot on firm ground once again, but it didn't seem to be getting any nearer. At last we could start to make out the shoreline more clearly. Our first sight was of the glorious golden beaches I had read so much about. Captain Jakes began to point out the land before us.

"Those barren rocks that look like mountains coming out of the water mark the start of Gabrielle's Reef," he explained. "Beyond the narrow channel are the small islands."

"Do you know the way through?" I asked.

"I used to," he confessed. "My father taught me, as his father taught him. I've never tried to use that knowledge though, nor told anyone I have it."

"Why? Would it be a problem?"

Jakes scratched at his beard. "I would much sooner it went no further, Mr Anders."

"Your secret is safe with me, Captain Jakes," I assured him. "Why didn't you find a good woman, settle down, start a family?"

Captain Jakes laughed. "I was in love once, Mr Anders, suppose I still am, but it was not to be." For a moment, the old captain looked very sad.

"That is why I have come to Heffen. To mend a broken heart," I told him. "I hope one day that I will love again."

"When you have loved as I have, Mr Anders, you will understand that it is most unlikely you will ever find such love again."

The sky was clear blue now, without a single cloud. The sea was as calm as a duck pond. The storm seemed a long time ago as the *Sally O* put about to approach Heffen Harbour. Out of the corner of my eye I saw the mist hanging low on the jagged rocks. Some rose like razor-sharp teeth from the deep, close to the mountainous black rock. Many more remained invisible to the eye below the surface. I pointed at the strangely surreal cloud that seemed to hover menacingly over the surface of the water.

"What is that, Captain?" I asked, although I was pretty sure that I knew the answer already.

"We will not be going there, Mr Anders," promised Jakes. "That is what they call Gabrielle's Fault."

At long last, a few hours later in burning hot sunshine, the *Sally O* docked at the South Island Harbour. About half an hour after docking and only a few months more than ten years since the terrible, senseless killing, Sydney and I set foot for the first time on the islands of Heffen.

All those years ago, only hours after the massacre on the Sunshine Ranch, two more cold-blooded murders had been committed. The tall man with the piercing eyes and the big pointy nose was leaning over Patricia's body when Captain Baldock entered. The soldier had dismissed the unit that had been accompanying him all day. They had all remained in the tavern at the crossroads, where the captain had found a very drunk Richard Boscastle.

"I've been out back and thrown my guts up twice," he told Baldock.

"I must talk to your wife about yesterday," explained the boyish-looking soldier. "Why don't you come home with me?"

The drunken Boscastle laughed. "My young wife is entertaining," he explained slowly. "You're not a bad-looking young man, Captain Baldock. I would be very careful with my wife, or you might wake up one morning to find she has ruined your life too."

Now, the young captain stood grimly surveying yet another scene of carnage, this time in Boscastle's house.

"Stand where you are." Baldock pointed a pistol at the beak-nosed weasel in the striped shirt. The cornered man's eyes darted about the great hall, looking for some way of escape.

"One sudden move and I will shoot you dead, where you stand," barked the soldier. He wasn't quite sure what to do next. One thing was for sure. Patricia Boscastle would not be ruining many more lives. Then he noted the manservant shot between the eyes.

"Captain, please put down your gun." It was the voice of someone who was little more than a child. The captain dropped his pistol and turned to face a tall and usually pretty girl. Her olive skin, however, was unusually pale. Like her torn and ripped clothing, it was heavily bloodstained. The young girl's eyes were deep brown and very beautiful. They were filled with a confused and deeply disturbing mixture of grief and hatred. She looked as if she had been crying for a long time. Something about this girl grabbed hold of the young officer's heart. But then it always had.

"You," she snapped at the rat-faced man in the striped shirt. "Turn down your offer of a free passage by any chance, did she?"

"I never got chance to ask her," said the man sadly. "And before you ask, I have nothing to do with this and that is the honest truth. I swear on my mother's grave."

"I heard that you didn't have a mother and even if you did, I doubt you have the slightest idea where she's buried. So why are you here?" persisted the girl, who was by no means as confident as she at first appeared to be. One pistol remained steadily trained on him.

"It's a long story," he said sulkily. "I told you, she was a friend."

"I thought you had deserted us," the girl said. Both men could hear the emotion in her voice. She looked at Captain Baldock.

"This has been another bad night, Captain," she said softly.

"Yes, ma'am, it has," agreed Baldock.

"I will not kill you. There has already been too much killing. In return, you will deliver a message from me to our charming new governor. Tell him that one Fairweather is still alive and kicking and that one day soon I will drop by to see him."

"You were little more than a child when I first knew you," said Baldock. His mind drifted back to happier times at the Sunshine Ranch.

"Last night I grew up, Captain Baldock," she said softly, "and trust me, the world is going to regret making me grow up quite so suddenly."

"I am so sorry," whispered the young captain. "If there is anything I can do."

The young girl laughed and moved closer to the soldier. Perhaps she was still a child. Philip Baldock had visited the Sunshine Ranch many times. Over the last year or so, he could not help noticing how her body had changed. Suddenly it seemed to blossom into that of a very beautiful young woman. She came very close and the captain felt her breath on his face. She had always enjoyed teasing the starched young officer.

"There is much you could and should do, but knowing you as I do, I doubt you will, Philip Baldock." Her hand gently stroked his unshaven face. "I know you are sorry though," she added softly. "And I know what you have seen these last two nights has hurt you very much too."

The young captain found himself alone in the great hall of Boscastle's ranch, with only the dead for company. Even the dead could offer Baldock no comfort.

He delivered the young girl's message to the governor, who became both angry, upset and Baldock thought, a little frightened.

For the next year or so, the name was not heard of again. The governor seemed to relax and put her message out of his mind. Then the stories began to filter through of a mysterious girl who was slowly taking control of the pirates. It was said that even Blind Mario had died at her hands. He was one of the most feared and dangerous pirates in those waters.

About eighteen months after the Fairweather massacre, the governor entered his new office, in his unfinished palace, to find a beautiful young woman sitting cross-legged on his grand oak desk.

For some time now, the notorious pirate had enjoyed a large price on her head, dead or alive.

Silas Raines never told anyone what he and the pirate girl talked about. What was certain was that Prudence Fairweather had announced her presence on Heffen. Everyone, especially the island's governor, knew that she was still very angry.

Whatever she did or did not say to the governor, the price on her head was trebled that day.

Chapter 2

*T*o be trapped anywhere for so long can be terrible. However, such awesome power cannot be held captive for very long, and whilst a few hundred of our years might have come and gone, to the creature it was more like a few hundred minutes. It could not begin to understand why these foolish humans would even wish to delay the inevitable for such a short span of time. Not withstanding the uncompromising savagery they had used against it, the creature was still in control. Those filled with greed, cowardice, jealousy or wicked and murderous ways would be attracted to it just like a moth is attracted to a naked flame.

I had left my companion Sydney at the harbour. The position I had taken was as personal tutor to the governor's young wards and included board and keep. Captain Jakes had promised to find Sydney rooms in town. I could only hope that fathers were locking up their daughters, and husbands were taking any measures necessary to protect their wives, now that Sydney had arrived in town. I had been given little detail of my new charges, other than that they were a girl and a boy. At the ages of about twelve years and ten, they were younger than most of the boys I had been used to teaching.

It was a combination of this and the very different world to which we had come that made me feel very nervous. For much of the long, tedious and sometimes terrifying voyage, I had been seasick. Now for the first time, I felt very homesick.

The harbour itself was much like any other. Great stone warehouses surrounded the bustling scene. People of almost every nation on earth mingled together in a cacophony of colour and sound. There were sailors, soldiers, smart in their uniforms and carrying very large rifles. There were Chinese men wearing those huge hats, Asians wearing turbans, and Arabs in baggy trousers carrying huge curved swords stuffed into belts at the waist.

Mingled into this melting pot of people were finely dressed women in large-brimmed fancy hats, carrying parasols to protect them from the burning sun. There were beggars, often with limbs missing, and children in rags, trying to pick the pockets of the unwary. Then there were a myriad of different smells, from burning tar and freshly treated wood to the rich scent of spices from all imaginable parts of the globe.

It hit me then that no amount of reading and researching could replace seeing all this for myself. Someone shouted a warning and I turned to see a fire-breathing monster bearing down on me. Made mostly of wood and iron, the monster had an incredibly tall chimney stack at the front with lots of moving metal parts on top of what looked very much like a large wooden barrel. It was heading right towards me, for no more malevolent reason than the fact that I stood on the metal rails that guided its journey. I was aware of such contraptions of course. Back home in England the principle was even being developed for the carriage of passengers. I had never, however, been so close to the noise, the heat or the smoke.

As I pushed through the crowds, to the point where I was to be met, my senses took in as much as they could of the sights, sounds and smells of this amazing place. There was a small caged animal, a monkey of some kind, but not one I had seen in any books. Its owner, a toothless one-legged seadog, held out his begging bowl to me. There was a look of hopeless desperation in his ancient face. The blue skies, sunshine, golden beaches and palm trees might look like heaven, but Heffen was clearly not everybody's Paradise.

I had been told that the governor's household would send a carriage to pick me up. If I just took a small bag, the rest of my luggage would be collected from the *Sally O* later. The sun was now high in the sky and the heat was intense. I found shelter in one of the harbour offices. It was in this darkly lit sweathouse that I saw her again, the girl from my dreams.

It was a faded picture, already partly torn from the wall. An artist of some considerable skill had drawn it in pencil and crayon. The picture was a portrait of a fine-looking woman. This was a lady who would surely captivate the heart of any red-blooded man. So taken was I with this heavenly apparition that I did not even think to read the faded and torn writing below.

"Mr Anders?"

I turned to see a surprisingly tall pencil-thin man with white hair and aristocratic features standing before me.

"I am Simms, sir," he introduced himself, bowing his head slightly. He wore a dark black tailcoat and pinstriped pants. His somewhat sombre dress also included a tall if slightly battered top hat. The governor's head butler put me more in mind of an undertaker. He took my bag from me.

"The carriage is outside, sir. It is about a 25-minute ride to the palace."

"Well, thank you, Simms," I said, recovering my composure as quickly as I was able to. To see the likeness of the girl from my dreams had been another shock to my already shattered nerves. "Lead the way then. I confess I am looking forward to a few comforts that are absent on board ship."

Simms did not answer, and I followed him from the shelter back out into the burning sun.

"Tell me one thing, Simms?" I asked, just before we left the shelter.

"Sir?"

"Are all your girls here on Heffen as pretty as that one?"

Simms looked slightly thrown by my question. Recovering his composure, he spoke coldly to me. "Mr Anders, it is true that the lady is," he paused and coughed awkwardly, "as you have observed. She is very attractive. She is, however, also a killer. She is a privateer, a pirate, wanted for countless robberies and murders. A most dangerous lady indeed, and not one to be trifled with I fear."

"Oh I see now," I said softly, almost to myself. So it was this notorious pirate, Prudence Fairweather, who I had for some unaccountable reason been dreaming of. I found that very odd indeed.

Our horse and carriage was, it seemed, going far too fast through the narrow and dirty dockside roads. A small almost naked black boy, no more I guessed than ten years of age, was driving the carriage with consummate skill. He managed to dodge laden-down donkeys, overloaded carts and rickshaws carrying important-looking military figures. He even controlled his charges as we passed close to the great mechanical elephant, from which at that point steam was escaping in the most deafening fashion. A little farther on, the wheels hit a huge puddle of oil, mud and excrement, sending a shower of the filthy, stinking liquid over three very well-dressed ladies. They shook their parasols angrily at the disappearing carriage.

"Slow down, boy," snapped Simms. "You covered those poor ladies in mud."

"They should perhaps ply their trade somewhere a little less dirty, Mr Simms sir," suggested the boy cheekily.

"Watch your lip, lad, or the master will have you shipped out with them." Simms pointed at the quayside. It took a moment to see that he was pointing at a large crowd of black people, gathered in front of a large four-mast freighter. It took a moment more to realise that all these people, men, women and children, were manacled together with big heavy chains.

Never in my life have I felt or smelt such a look of stark fear, hopelessness and total despair. These people were being treated no better than the cattle they might well share the hold of a cargo ship with. Many of them would not survive the journey. I had felt sick and indeed had been sick many times on our long voyage. That was nothing compared to the sickness and revulsion I felt now.

You are right, Thomas Anders, I told myself. *This place is most definitely not Paradise.*

For the rest of that day, there were two things I could not rid my mind of, no matter how much I tried. The first was the sight of all those people chained like dogs, and the second, to my great shame, was the faded picture of Prudence Fairweather. The picture I had torn from the dock office wall nestled comfortably in my coat pocket.

The governor's palace stood high above the cliffs, looking down across open and quite barren countryside towards the town and harbour. It was possible from certain parts of the palace ground to also gain views of some parts of the north island, the golden beaches, rain forests and even some of the closer plantations.

The palace grounds, entered through truly magnificent wrought iron gates, were laid out with very fine gardens, designed in a very formal and geometrical fashion. There was the inevitable maze. This was constructed with impeccably manicured hedging, standing more than ten feet high. The gardens themselves were planted out to military perfection.

Row upon row of plants, standing to attention, reminded me of the palace guard in their colourful ceremonial uniforms. Much of the garden was laid to lawn, freshly cut and with perfect stripes. The courtyard before the palace itself was flagged in a complex pattern of red and grey stone and graced by prancing peacocks with their wonderful fantails.

The gardens give the impression that there was neither one weed allowed to grow, nor one blade of grass permitted to be out of place. As our carriage pulled up to the great front door, two young black men were waiting to clean up any dirt our arrival might have brought to the courtyard.

"How do they keep it so clean with all the comings and goings?" I asked.

"Because they are in for a good beating if they don't," chipped in our young driver cheerfully before Simms had a chance to speak.

The palace itself was said to be one of famous architect Sir George Mansfield's greatest works. Constructed mostly of white marble and gold leaf, it was like nothing I had ever seen before. Part of the construction brought to mind ancient Eastern temples and Arabian knights. With its golden domes and carved marble turrets, it also had the look of a fairytale castle.

The palace could be seen for miles in any direction, the gold roofs and window edgings reflecting in the long hours of glorious sunshine.

We climbed the large spiralling marble stairway to the grand entrance. The door itself appeared to be mostly made from gold, although no doubt enforced by stronger metals.

From the doorway, we entered the vast hallway, with its high vaulted ceiling, again mostly finished in real gold. This reminded me of a grand concert hall, although the walls were just plain marble, as was the mighty staircase at the far end. Upon the stairs hung just two dark and gloomy oil paintings in magnificent golden frames. One was of a grey-haired old man in dark clothes, holding a stick that he could well use to strike someone with at any moment. The other was of a handsome but stern and rather sad-looking lady with similar features and hair to the old man.

The man who came out to meet me, although appreciably younger than the subjects of either of the two portraits, was most obviously related. Even so, I guessed Silas Raines, governor of the islands of Heffen, to be in his late forties. He was a short man and good living had filled out his features, resulting in him looking a little less fierce than his forebears had. They had a very lean and hungry look, emphasised by the way the artist had applied the paint to achieve the dark and menacing nature of the finished work.

Even so, my new employer did not look the kind of man it would be wise to pick an argument with. He wore a simple off-white jacket and trousers to complement a fantastic golden waistcoat. His sharp eyes were fixed intently on me, as if trying to read what kind of man had journeyed all this way to teach his wards.

"My grandfather and my mother," he explained as if answering the question before I had time to ask it. "I take it I have the pleasure of addressing Mr Thomas Anders?"

"I am at your service, sir," I replied lamely. I had no doubt that this was my new employer, although he had not yet introduced himself.

"I am the Governor of Heffen," he told me proudly, with the slightest of bows. "Appointed by His Royal Highness to oversee these islands on behalf of our great empire and greatly honoured to do so."

"They are most breathtakingly beautiful, sir," I said.

"Really, Mr Anders, I am pleased you think so. I too appreciate beautiful things. Many say this palace and the gardens will become one of the great wonders of our world, that is if the dammed place is ever finished." Raines waved his hand at his unquestionably breathtaking surroundings. "Still such beauty cannot be rushed, can it? The basic design is that of the famous architect Sir George Mansfield. You will have heard of him no doubt, Mr Anders?" It was a rhetorical question. "Much of the finer detail, however, is to my own design. I am one of very few people Sir George has ever agreed to deal with on a personal basis you see."

"It is truly magical, sir," I said.

"Of course the islands are much more than some kind of paradise, Mr Anders. Most of the islands in this part of the world have palm trees, golden beaches and clear waters in which to swim. Heffen, however, is the centre of all commerce in this part of the world." The governor took a timepiece from his bright yellow waistcoat pocket and flipped it open "And trade has become extremely buoyant indeed since I took over the reins, Mr Anders, if you will forgive my little play on words. Never has Heffen enjoyed quite such prosperity." He paused as if looking me over to check my suitability for the position. "Still," he blustered on, "you must forgive me, I talk too much. You have had a very long journey, although I trust a good one." He smiled warmly. "Mrs Moffat, my housekeeper, will show you to your room, Mr Anders. I am sure you need to freshen up after such a long time at sea. Then, when you are refreshed, she will introduce you to your new charges."

"Thank you," I said.

"Well, if there is nothing else, Mr Anders, I am a very busy man and

I really must be getting on." A finger played against his narrow lips and his eyes sparkled.

"I think we have covered everything. If there is anything you need, just ask Mrs Moffat or Simms." He turned back to the room from which he had come, then stopped suddenly, as if he had remembered something of great importance he had forgotten to tell me.

"One more thing, Mr Anders," he said, holding one hand to his forehead, as if thinking out exactly how to explain something so complicated to me. Silas Raines had a prominent forehead, his receding hair well greased back. He fixed me through those cold sparkling eyes. "As you can imagine, a great many important people visit me here." He spoke slowly now, choosing each word with the utmost care in an effort to explain something very important to someone of significantly less intelligence. "A great deal of very important business is conducted under this very roof, Mr Anders. The global implications of that business I sometimes dare not think about myself." He walked back over and placed one hand, decorated in fine gold rings, on my shoulder. "You see, Mr Anders, I cannot afford any disturbances," he explained softly in my ear. "The children," he went on almost in a whisper, as if telling me a closely guarded secret, "they were my late sister's and they are here as a kindness to her memory. I do not myself have, nor wish to have, any dealings with them. I would be most grateful, indeed I must insist, that you keep them under control and away from this part of the palace."

He turned back towards his capacious office and then pausing looked back at me. "We do understand each other, don't we, Mr Anders?" He smiled warmly again and the door slammed shut behind him.

Mrs Moffat was a brusque and, it seemed at first, unfriendly woman. She wore a simple grey dress over which was fastened a well-starched black apron. She was, I guessed, somewhere in her middle fifties, of short build, with a matronly figure. Her hair was dark grey and fastened into a severe bun, which did very little to soften her appearance. She spoke with a strong Irish lilt.

"This is your room, Mr Anders," she said sternly, eyeing me dubiously up and down. "The children's rooms are farther down the corridor. The classroom library and your office are at the far end of the corridor." She paused, obviously trying to think what else she should tell me. "The bathroom is directly opposite. There are plenty of towels and there is plenty of hot water." She looked around the room to make sure everything was in order for me. It was very basic. A wash basin in the corner, a wardrobe and a small table and chair were about the only furniture, other than the large bed. The latter filled much of the remaining space. It was quite firm, but in truth anything would have been a vast improvement on the good ship *Sally O*'s sleeping arrangements.

"If you are hungry, Mr Anders, you can pop down to the kitchen and I will make you a sandwich or something," said the Irish woman, her voice softening slightly. "The children always have their dinner at five." She added sternly again, "Oh and another thing, always use the back stairs, especially if you have the children with you." She brushed her hands down her apron. "I'll leave you to freshen up then. You will find the children in the classroom, that is if you wish to meet them today. I am sure tomorrow would do just as well."

"Thank you, Mrs Moffat. You have been very kind. I will, of course, introduce myself to the children before I do anything else. Then when I have bathed, if it is still all right, I might try one of those sandwiches. I find myself quite famished now I am back on terra firma."

"I might even find you a piece of my famous Madeira cake," replied Mrs Moffat. For a moment, I thought I saw a flicker of a smile on her tired face. I found myself wondering what dreadful blow fate had delivered her. There was no doubt that a dark shadow had fallen over Mrs Moffat's life at some time. "You seem a nice enough young man, Mr Anders, and I consider myself a pretty good judge of character. I hope you are happy here and that the same fate does not befall you as did the last one." Before I could ask Mrs Moffat what that fate might have been, she was gone.

The children were sat at desks painting pictures. The eldest, Victoria, a pretty child, had painted a forest with animals including dogs, cats, a snake and a hairy elephant with big tusks. The boy Rupert, a redheaded lad with a face full of freckles, had painted a ship full of pirates. Somebody was walking the plank!

They had stopped the moment I entered the room. They stood up by their desks, almost not daring to breathe. There was an overpowering sense of fear. Rupert threw his picture into the waste bin next to him.

"Why did you do that?" I asked him. The boy stood still silent and to attention. "Why did he do that?" I turned to Victoria in despair for an answer.

"Mr Skeet would beat him with his stick if he painted pictures of pirates, sir," explained the girl flatly. "He didn't like my animals much either, sir," she added.

"Sit down, children, please," I said. They immediately sat down. "Now look, I have no intention of hitting either of you with a sick. I have come here not just to help you learn, but also to learn from you."

"With respect, sir, if I have permission to speak." Victoria paused to await my approval for her to continue.

"Carry on, child," I said, not meaning to sound exasperated.

"I don't see how a learned man such as you, sir, could possibly learn anything from us."

"Well, let me see." I carried a small three-legged stool over to where the children sat. "I am Thomas Anders. I was, until recently, a teacher in England. As well as that gainful employment, I also researched and wrote educational books and papers on geography and history."

"You see what I mean, sir," said Victoria quite bravely.

I took off my topcoat and flung it over a small table. Leaning forward, I was unaware that a paper had fallen from my coat pocket. "I do see what you mean," I said. "But what you do not understand is that up until about a month ago, I had never strayed far from the village where I was born. Never travelled to any of the foreign places I had written so much about. I have already begun to understand, children, that you can learn more from one day of travel and adventure than in a life of studying books."

I stood up from the stool, which was far too small for me and was creaking in a way that reminded me too much of the *Sally O*. I began to pace the small and uninteresting classroom.

"I can learn about lots of things from you, children," I went on. "Animals from you, Victoria. I had no idea that there were elephants on Heffen for example."

"There aren't any real elephants," Victoria corrected me. "Some come in on a ship for the annual ball, according to Mr Simms. Anyway, that isn't supposed to be an elephant. It's a mammoth, sir."

"Thank you, Victoria," I said. "Of course it is, and I can learn all about the pirates from you, Rupert."

"He's scared of pirates, Rupert is," explained Victoria.

"I'm not scared!" yelled Rupert, speaking for himself for the first time.

"Is that why you draw pictures of them?" I asked.

"He has always drawn pictures of pirates. He's scared of them, 'cause there is this pirate that's going to kill him."

"That's nonsense I'm sure," I said. "Why would a pirate want to kill you, Rupert?"

"Because," went on Victoria, "he saw a murder."

"A murder?" My first meeting with the children was proving to be more eventful than I had expected. "Whom did he see this pirate murder?" I asked. "Do you know, Victoria?" I had given up trying to ask Rupert anything.

"Of course I do, sir. I thought you would know too."

"Why would I know?" I pressed, feeling increasingly confused.

"Because it was your predecessor Mr Skeet," said Victoria in a matter-of-fact tone. "In cold blood," she added with relish in an equally matter-of-fact way. "Not that he probably didn't deserve it."

For a long minute, the classroom was deadly silent. So that was what Mrs Moffat had been talking about. Rupert broke the silence. He was staring at a picture in his hand. He seemed to be trembling with fear.

"She's so beautiful, just like our mother," he whispered, dropped the picture back on the floor and running from the room. Victoria picked up the paper Rupert had dropped and opened it

"Oh I see," she said coldly. "This is why he ran out in a fright, sir. It's a picture of the pirate. The one who is going to kill him."

Victoria held up the picture of Prudence Fairweather.

I had no chance to question the children further. Mrs Moffat came to tell me that the children's dinner would be ready soon and that they should be getting washed. She was obviously intrigued as to why Rupert had just charged past her in the hall. She gave me a questioning look.

"It's a long story, Mrs Moffat," I told her.

"Perhaps you would like a glass of warm milk by the kitchen fire before you retire," suggested Mrs Moffat.

"Around the kitchen fire is one of the best places for long stories," I agreed. "Even Papa's sermons sound much better when he practices on us sat around the dying embers of an open fire."

"I got one of my girls to prepare your bath." Mrs Moffat smiled softly and the transformation to her harsh features was incredible. "When you have bathed, there will be food in the kitchen, and I think, Mr Anders, an early night would be of benefit to you."

"You're very kind, Mrs Moffat," I said. "I was feeling rather homesick before and your kindness has helped me no end."

"You remind me a little of someone special I knew a long time ago," she said and before I could ask who, she continued, "I will see your charges are fed and put to bed, so you relax for a while, Mr Anders."

Less than ten minutes later I stretched my weary bones into the enormous bathtub filled so full of steaming hot soapy water that the contents spilt out over the bathroom floor. A shorter man could swim in a tub this size. It was also, I thought, probably far more watertight than the *Sally O*.

Mrs Moffat had been very kind, and there was no doubt I needed to relax. That, however, was not going to be easy, now I knew the true fate of my predecessor. Suddenly, I realised I was exhausted.

I dressed and went down to the kitchens. A massive kitchen served the main part of the palace. Behind the big kitchens was a very much smaller more manageable area, accessible from the back stairs. It reminded me a little of our kitchen back home. For a moment I had an almost unbearable need to be back home with my family. I missed them so much.

I ate a light supper, washed down with a couple of glasses of very palatable local wine and then retired for the night. It was hot in my room even with a window open. I threw off my clothes and crawled naked between the sheets. Perhaps it was because I wasn't used to a proper bed; perhaps it was the slaves on the quayside, or the fate of my predecessor Mr Skeet that made sleep so evasive. Or maybe it was the heat that made me toss and turn, kicking the bedcovers to the floor.

At last I drifted into a disturbed sleep. The little black boy was driving our carriage so fast that we were flung out into the mud and excrement. The brightly clothed ladies began to beat me with their parasols whilst my young driver was dragged away in chains to join the others on the quayside.

I sat up with a start, dripping in sweat. The silhouette of a figure sat cross-legged on the end of the bed.

"Bad dream, Mr Anders?" There was a note of amusement in the voice.

I reached out shakily to turn up the lamp by my bedside. I knew, almost before the flickering light confirmed it for me, who it was.

Only now did I realise what little justice the artist, or indeed my dreams, had actually done this woman.

Perhaps it was just impossible for any artist to captivate such breathtaking natural beauty. There was laughter in those deep brown eyes. A tangled mass of auburn curls cascaded onto strong but shapely olive-skinned shoulders. She wore a low white gypsy top, loosely laced at the front, so as to give tantalising glimpses of perfectly formed breasts. She had allowed her dark cloak to fall onto the bed. Fulsome, ruby red lips smiled mockingly at me. Lips any full-blooded man would die to kiss just once.

For about a minute I was so captivated by this woman that I forgot my fear. For even less time than that it seemed quite normal to dream about a woman I had not only never met, but indeed had never even heard of. Until, that was, I had torn her wanted poster from the customs house wall, just a few hours earlier.

"My, my, Mr Anders." She spoke in the same slightly mocking tone. Quizzical eyes looked up and down my body in a most exaggerated manner. Her eyes widened momentarily, and with one eyebrow slightly raised, she fixed me with her stare. "You are a big boy for your mummy."

I remembered only then that I was stark naked!

"Madam, have you no decency?" I protested, although hardly a sound came from my lips. I reached out for the sheets I had kicked off earlier. Instead, Prudence threw her cloak over my embarrassment.

I could feel my face had gone a crimson red.

"I am a pirate, Mr Anders." Prudence Fairweather was laughing. "I have absolutely no decency whatsoever. You were, after all, admiring my body. Is it so wrong of me to return such a fine compliment? You have a nice body by the way, Mr Anders, in more ways than one. Although I fear you may have enjoyed a little too much comfortable living. Most of my crew are men and I see them naked far too often, so you can take what I say as a compliment, if you wish." She crawled very slowly down the bed towards me, like a big cat stalking its prey before the final kill. Then her face was close to mine. I could smell her own sweet aroma and feel her warm breath upon my lips.

"Are you here to kill me?" I whispered, my whole body trembling with a cocktail of fear and something else quite different.

"No, Mr Anders," she purred, "I am here to kiss you." Those voluptuous lips touched mine, the lightest touch to begin. Then her tongue pushed open my mouth and pressed against my own. The kiss was a long one.

"Why do you expect me to kill you, Mr Anders?" the pirate girl whispered as she continued to gently kiss my face and chest.

"Heard that you killed my predecessor in cold blood," I blurted out without thinking. This information just might have been better kept to myself! It certainly caused a reaction from the beautiful pirate. She leapt off the bed and began to pace up and down. I could see now that she was a tall woman, as well as a shapely one.

"So you know about that already," she said, running a hand through her tangled hair. "My goodness, how news travels, Mr Anders."

"Do you deny it?" I asked nervously, the fear starting to overpower the passion again. The girl's thoughts seemed to be somewhere else.

"Sorry," she said. "What did you say?"

"I said, do you deny it, killing Mr Skeet I mean?"

"No, of course not, Mr Anders," she replied irritably. The pirate came back over to the bed and kneeled down by me. "Are you a spy, Mr Anders, a government agent? Do you seek out something here on Heffen?"

"A spy, me? No, Miss Fairweather, I am a scholar and a teacher. I have come here to teach the governor's wards."

"A trained killer then?"

"Trained to kill what?"

"Don't you mean whom, Mr Anders? Please be honest with me, or I might have to kill you after all." For the first time, the pirate girl sounded like she might not be joking.

"Why do you think I am a government agent?" I sat up in the bed more, careful to keep her cloak over my manhood. "Do I take it that this agent is after you?"

Prudence Fairweather laughed. "Mr Anders, the entire Heffen guard is after me. I believe your government has sent someone to hunt something far more dangerous than me." The tall girl smiled disarmingly. I wondered just what could possibly be more dangerous than this lovely creature?

"I have information from a very reliable source that a British government agent has been sent to Heffen," she went on. "The informant was not certain, however. It was believed that this agent might have been travelling on the *Sally O*. Guess what, Mr Anders? You were the only passenger on the *Sally O*, according to the ship's manifest. So it struck me, simple pirate girl that I am, that there was the teeniest, weeniest possibility that you could be our spy."

"But I wasn't..." I was about to say the only passenger. At last, however, my brain was working again, if not particularly well.

"You wasn't what?" asked the girl.

"A spy, " I said quickly. "I am an academic, a teacher, a bookworm; I have never travelled in my life before. I have come here to fill the position of tutor to the governor's wards and to continue my studies into this part of the world. Up until now, my work has been confined to dusty old books and records." I paused and swallowed hard. My heart had stopped trying to leap out of my chest but was still beating quite fast. "Anyway, what do you want of this spy?"

Prudence Fairweather frowned and her nose wrinkled up in a most appealing manner. "To stop him before he does untold damage to me and many others."

"You mean kill him?"

"If I have to, if that's the only way to stop him."

Although I was not feeling brave at all now, I leaned forward, so that my face was close to hers, our noses almost touching.

"Is that why you killed Mr Skeet? Was he a spy? Did he threaten your idyllic pirate life perhaps?"

"Believe me, this is just a little more important than my so-called idyllic life you speak of, Mr Anders."

There was clear evidence that this woman had an unpredictable and fiery disposition. The anger faded from her big brown eyes.

"Why, Mr Anders, you are shaking like a leaf." She looked at me wide-eyed and innocent. "Do I make you nervous?"

"A little over a month ago," I said, "the most exciting thing I ever did in my life was to help a friend steal back some love letters. I fell off a drainpipe and broke my ankle." I could feel her sweet breath on my face again. "I am desperately homesick and yes, Miss Fairweather, you make me very…" She kissed me again. Another long and extraordinarily passionate kiss that left me quite breathless. "Nervous," I gasped.

The girl laughed. "I hope I don't have to kill you, Mr Anders. As a matter of fact, I think you're quite cute." She stood up and tried to fix her clothes and hair. "I have to be going now," she said. "I would be very grateful if you could give me five minutes before you raise the alarm, although there is really no need, if you are very angry that I disturbed your beauty sleep. Oh, and I would wash your face before you sound the alarm. It has red from my lips all over it." She checked her hair again in the wall mirror

"And what if I didn't wish to raise the alarm at all? What if I would rather like you to call again?" I was blushing again and shaking once more for quite different reasons.

"You really are not what I expected, Mr Anders, government agent or not. But I would really quite like you to raise the alarm. It's a bit childish of me, I know, but I would rather like the governor to know I dropped in." She took her cloak back and did a mock examination of my manhood before I had any chance to make myself decent.

"I may even give that a try sometime," she laughed. "No promises though." The pirate leaned forward and kissed me on the forehead, then on the lips one more time. "Goodnight, Mr Anders," she said softly, and slipped out of my window and was gone.

I waited exactly five minutes before raising the alarm.

The good ship *Wild Swan* had docked not long after the *Sally O*. Oddly, nobody disembarked until the sun began to set and another very dark night on Heffen had begun. At the harbour tavern there was much noise and merriment. A girl was dancing on a table, clothed only in her underwear. Many of the sailors were grouped around the table, ogling the almost naked girl.

Most were singing bawdy sea shanties and spilling more ale from their tankards than they ever got to drink. Others were sat in dark corners with well-dressed or undressed ladies. These ladies could manage a good many men in one night. A sailor who had been at sea for a month or more took very little managing.

In a very dark corner sat a lone figure, toying with a glass of rum. Captain Jakes enjoyed the drink and the camaraderie, even the foul smell of sweat, stale beer and old tobacco. As the first evening back on shore passed, his mind drifted to the woman he still loved and his mood became quite morose.

"If I was you I'd get some fresh air, Captain," the barman suggested. He had known Jakes for a long time and knew what he was like.

The old captain did not argue. He was relieved to be out of the tavern in the quiet night air. Heffen Harbour never slept, but there were far fewer people around at this late hour. The captain swayed along the path, back to his beloved *Sally O*.

He was drunk, but still alert. It was even more important to have your wits about you in the harbour at night. There was the noise of men talking softly on the *Wild Swan*, a smart, modern and well-turned-out schooner. Jakes had always thought that the *Swan* lacked character. The old sailor froze to listen to the voices. A moment later, a slightly built man came down the gangplank.

He was carrying a small bag and paused briefly by one of the quayside lamps. In that brief moment Jakes got a clear view of the stranger. He was dressed in a dark-tailed jacket and pinstriped pants. A bowler hat was perched on his head. Jakes saw the little man check his pocket watch. Seconds later, a small black-covered carriage pulled up. With a last look around, as if to check he had not been noticed, he climbed aboard, and the carriage moved swiftly away into the misty night.

Sydney Greenburgh had also settled into his rooms, which were situated in a narrow cobbled street close to the old harbour. Despite the fresh coat of paint they had recently enjoyed, the well-kept and ancient stone built properties gave the impression that they might crumble to the earth at any moment. This impression was no doubt emphasised by the way they all seemed to lean precariously, both forwards and to the sides.

Sydney's father was quite well known in these parts, although in recent times his visits had become more and more infrequent. Miss Badger, the dumpy but jolly landlady, reminded Sydney that his father had stayed here many times whilst negotiating new trade deals for King and country. Heffen was a major meeting place for dealers and traders from all parts of the globe.

"And now you are following in your father's footsteps," fussed the little woman.

"More like following in his shadow," corrected Sydney gloomily. He had hoped he had at last found one remote outpost where is father's reputation did not proceed him.

The rooms were adequate but fell far short of the levels of comfort the wealthy young man had grown accustomed to. There was a table, four chairs and a bed in the first room. Washing facilities were next door in a small annex barely larger than a good-sized cupboard. The small high window, draped with faded floral curtains, overlooked other narrow back streets leading down to the harbour. Consequently, it got very noisy at certain hours.

Sydney, once bathed, dressed and full of Mrs Badger's shepherd's pie, headed for the officers club. It offered the best opportunity to purchase a fine brandy or two, enjoy a quality cigar and some good company. Sydney sought the way from a passing merchant, a corpulent man accompanied by three very pretty girls.

Strolling in the humid night air, his thoughts drifted to his companion. He wondered how I was getting on. Sydney was very conscious that this was my first journey so far away from home. We had arranged to meet in what Jakes had promised us both was a better class of inn, quite close to the governor's palace, but not for a week.

Sydney was by no means convinced that I would survive that long. He knew Papa and Mama would never forgive him if something were to befall their precious baby. He blamed all this firmly on Anderson, whose idea it had been to ask me along.

The officers club was close to the centre of town. The exterior was unimposing. An old town house, it was much in need of renovation. Paint hung from the walls, and the window frames were rotten. Inside, however, was a different matter. The impression on a first visit was that you were entering the captain's cabin on a very large ship.

He recognised at once a tall handsome man who was standing at the bar.

"My god, Philip, is it really you?" Sydney embraced the tall soldier, spilling his drink in the excitement.

"I'm sorry." For a moment, Philip Baldock was confused. "Hang on a minute," he went on, recognition slowly coming to him. "Sydney Greenburgh, what on earth are you doing out here in hell?"

Baldock was drunk. Last Sydney had heard, his old school friend had been doing well. What was more, he had been one of Sydney's more temperate friends.

"I heard you loved it here on Heffen, old boy." Sydney looked surprised. He shouted an order to the barman. "Didn't you even marry a local lass and sire a load of kiddies!"

"All true, my old chum," slurred Major Baldock. "Guilty as charged. They let me pretty well run the regiment." He accepted the drink his old school friend had bought him.

"You still with the government then, are you, Sydney?"

"Department of Trade, you know the sort of thing, Philip." Sydney Greenburgh leaned forward. "Just a puffed-up salesman, that's all I am, when all's said and done. Although I confess that civil servant impresses the ladies a great deal more." He looked at the major's smart tunic. "Not as much as that I wager," he went on, with obvious envy. "I tell you what, old boy. You should lend me your uniform sometime. Ladies love a man in uniform."

The major stood up. "You will forgive me, Sydney. It is wonderful to see you after so long, but I really must go. Mia and the children will be expecting me." He picked up his hat and started for the door.

It was something in Baldock's deep blue eyes that alarmed Sydney so much. The elegant young beau swung round and shouted after the major. "Philip," he called out, "perhaps you should tell me what it is that has caused this terrible fear in you?"

A portly naval officer dropped his monocle in his brandy. An officer of the Scots Guards choked on excellent malt. To call a man a coward is, after all, to call a challenge. Major Philip Baldock turned to face the mercifully quiet club. There was only one other customer in the place. A very old admiral had been sleeping in a dark corner since the middle of the day. He snored loudly. The old man could be found there asleep almost any day. One day he would die there and it would probably be ages before anybody noticed.

"It's started to happen you see," said Baldock, despair in his voice. "Nothing anyone can do now, too late I'm afraid. It's terrible, Sydney, and you don't know how terrible. This time it will bring about the end of the world. Nobody, I mean nobody, can stop it, especially not me." He looked around the small group of astonished onlookers. "And yes," he was almost screaming, "I am frightened too right. I'm bloody well frightened and if any of you blind, stupid fools have any sense whatsoever, you will be frightened too!" Baldock kicked open the door and left.

"It's the drink talking, that's all." The fat naval man was shoving his monocle back into the folds of flesh around his piggy eyes. "He's a brave young man, the major. They say his wife is one of the most beautiful girls on Heffen. No nothing could truly frighten the young major. He's made of stronger stuff than that."

Sydney Greenburgh did not agree.

Chapter 3

*T*he creature knew that the hunt had begun, and although it did not feel pleasure as a human might, it was pleased that the final game could start. These were such primitive animals, so it viewed recent developments with only passing interest. Yet unlike its hideous protector, the creature was unable to lodge its restless spirit in one of those pathetic human vessels, unless that is, the host was willing or of very tender years. So perhaps it should be worried. Twice it had been slightly inconvenienced by one of those wretched inferiors, and the creature knew that it did fear at least one. If any of these pathetic things could prevent the reunion, or even discover how to kill the creature, then it was the female it feared. Perhaps because of this it still liked the darkest places, still preferred to lurk in shadows, even though it had absolutely no reason to do so.

The consequences of Prudence Fairweather's uninvited visit to the palace were more far reaching than I had expected. Within a few minutes of my raising of the alarm, there were soldiers everywhere inside the palace. The grounds were also overrun with the military, bayonets fixed ready. Big army boots unceremoniously trampled over the beautiful flowerbeds in the frantic search to apprehend the girl.

It was incredible how much fuss my unannounced visitor had caused. I was beginning to understand why she had been so keen for me to sound the alarm. More than half the island garrison had been put to work searching inside and out. They looked in every conceivable nook and cranny. Every dark place in the palace and its grounds was searched and then searched again. Prudence Fairweather, however, had gone. I was sure that even had I not given the pirate the five minutes she had asked for, they would still have found no trace of her.

Rupert was shaking with terror. According to his sister, the boy was convinced that the pirate had broken into the governor's palace for one purpose only. That reason was to kill Rupert. No amount of reasoning would persuade him otherwise. The little redhead sat on his bed chewing at a fingernail, his night light turned up as bright as it would go.

Even reminding the terrified child that the palace was crawling with heavily armed soldiers seemed to offer no comfort. The boy, it seemed, believed none of this would stop the pirate returning whenever she desired. Privately, I could not disagree with him.

Mrs Moffat also seemed upset and withdrawn. Simms told anybody who wanted to listen that, had the lady climbed in through his bedroom window, he would have dispatched her with ease.

"After all," he said, in the condescending manner that every butler seems to speak in, "she is no more than a slip of a lass."

The simple fact that this slip of a lass had evaded two hundred or more of Heffen's finest soldiers seemed to have passed by Simms unnoticed.

The most startling effect of Prudence Fairweather's decision to drop by the palace was the effect it had on the governor, Silas Raines.

The little man stormed from room to room, ranting obscenities at anybody and everybody. Any pretence of pleasantness had, for now at least, disappeared. Uncle Silas was, to say the least, frightening when such a foul mood as this took him. His normally greyish face became ruby red. His eyes became white slits. He also developed a nervous twitch to his left eye and around the corner of his mouth, causing him to dribble like a baby. I had managed to keep well out of his way until his disposition had improved a little.

"Mr Anders, how long was it before you managed to summon help would you say?"

"About five minutes, Governor," I replied. "I had time only to slip into this old dressing gown, sir."

"Why so long to put on a dressing gown?" demanded my employer.

"I was rigid with fear, sir."

The governor laughed. "You are afraid of a mere woman, Anders, surely not?"

"To be honest with you, sir, I was afraid," I confessed, although not, I thought, as afraid as the governor so obviously had been. "I have had a most sheltered and protected upbringing you see, sir," I explained. "My father is a man of the cloth and although he holds liberal views on most matters and has always strived to raise his children accordingly, I have never met the like of this woman before."

The little man sat down stiffly in an armchair and rang for Simms. "You have had quite a fright on your first night, Mr Anders. Perhaps a nightcap would help you sleep."

"You're very kind, sir," I said. "My state of mind has been made no better by the discovery that my predecessor was brutally murdered."

"It is not something one would be inclined to make much mention of in the situations vacant column, Mr Anders." There was a hint of mockery in the softly spoken words. I noticed for the first time just what an unpleasant smile the governor sometimes had. "Let me reassure you, however, Mr Anders," the sugary sweet voice went on, "Mr Skeet very foolishly wandered alone outside the palace grounds. It is an invitation to be killed. She, or any of her cutthroats for that matter, would not dare to harm anyone inside the palace grounds."

I doubted that was true. Prudence Fairweather had left me with the strong impression that she would do whatever she wanted, wherever she wanted. It did, however, seem prudent not to argue the point with my employer. Beneath the exaggerated concern for my health and well-being, there was an indefatigable feeling of menace mixed with an even stronger sense of blind fear.

"If you will forgive me, Governor," I said, rising from my chair, "I will retire for the night. The nightcap you so kindly offered me has made me feel sleepy and tomorrow is going to be a busy day." I passed back through the cavernous main kitchen where, despite the lateness of the hour, many unpaid servants were polishing brass and silver cooking utensils. Others were already preparing breakfast. It was, I realised, only three hours before they would be serving the governor his freshly baked bread, bacon and goose eggs. The smell of the bread cooking slowly in one of the enormous ovens made me once again long to be home in Mama's kitchen.

Mrs Moffat was still very upset. She sat by the fire in her small back kitchen. Simms was making her sip a glass of sherry. There was little light in the room other than the glowing embers from the fireplace.

"Is Mrs Moffat all right?"

"She will be fine, won't you, Mrs Moffat?" Simms assured me in his condescending way.

"You must think I'm a fool, Mr Anders, getting all of a doo-dah over some strip of a lass."

"Not at all, Mrs Moffat," I disagreed. "Prudence Fairweather is a scary lady."

"She's evil that woman, evil." There was so much hatred in the words the housekeeper spat out. "Look at me blubbering on again for goodness sake," she said, wiping her eyes with Simms' serviette.

"I was just going back to bed," I explained. "Unless there is anything I can do?"

"You go ahead, sir," whispered Simms. "Mrs Moffat believes the pirate girl and her cutthroat friends responsible for a most tragic and distressing experience. Don't worry, I'll stay and look after her. She will be fine in the morning."

Hung on to one end of Sir John Burleigh's dark and monstrous home was the conservatory. Solid plates of glass were held together with an ugly dark wrought iron framework that fitted well with the gothic splendour of the main house. This ironwork seemed to creep and slither around the walls and ceiling space of the conservatory as if it were growing there and always had been. It was not surprisingly also very hot.

Sir John was having a fencing class. He was an elegant man who when fencing had the poise and deportment of a ballerina. He was exquisite to watch as he pirouetted gracefully and athletically around his bemused opponent. Poetry in motion, thought his doomed competitor. Sir John was not only skilled with the sword, but also skilled at playing mind games with his opponent. This would always create plenty of frustration and confusion in the enemy before going in for the final kill. It was this skill, rather than his undeniable artistry with a sword, that made him such a formidable adversary.

Sir John was without question considered to be one of the finest swordsmen in the world. He needed to be able to defend himself well. This man had taken hundreds upon thousands of innocent people from their homes and sold them into servitude. He killed anyone who got in the way of his plans or threatened the profit of his evil trade. He, however, mostly killed for enjoyment.

His grand house was another of the architect Mansfield's works. It was built from black stone and rose gloomily towards the sky in all its medieval splendour. Burleigh had insisted that this monstrosity stood on the very hill where once had stood the Sunshine Ranch. This had been a very different building.

Burleigh was a single man. And being wealthy and good looking, never short of willing female companionship. He had been married more than once, but had never yet paid a penny of his vast wealth in alimony. Indeed, nothing had been heard of his ex-wives since their divorces. He assured any acquaintance foolishly tempted to ask that the separations had always been on a most agreeable basis. He did once, however, tell one business associate (Burleigh had no friends) that he had never once got a good price for any of them!

Now he had the pick of the latest merchandise to satisfy his desires. He also had an interest in the black arts, which he shared with, amongst others, the island governor. He enjoyed hunting, especially if the quarry was a young black slave. Girl or boy, he had no particular preference. A few on the islands had tried to stand up to this man and not one of those had lived.

To Sir John, killing was a sport. When murder was required for business reasons, or perhaps as a favour to a good customer, Burleigh much preferred to use a professional. In his view, it was money well spent. There was far less risk of complication, no personal danger and the security that, as he only used the best, the job always got done. In any case, he had never believed in mixing business with pleasure. He had been let down once, just recently, and blamed no one but himself for not checking the man's credentials and his methods more carefully. Above all, although as a swordsman there could be few anywhere better, he was a terrible coward, as most terrible bullies are.

Take away all his riches, remove the trappings of success, such as his knighthood obtained with the help of the many people in government who owed him favours, and you were left with nothing more than a typical playground bully. His swordsmanship had, however, suffered recently for different and far more sinister reasons.

Burleigh had become careless at times. Even the man he was now sparring with, who had little if any discernible skill, had managed to sink the point of his blade an inch or so into Burleigh's arm. The problem had much to do with the fact that Burleigh was, it seemed, no longer able to die. He was becoming bored with his sparring partner. The man was irritating him and the cut in his arm was hurting, even though it had already begun to heal.

The knight was as always immaculate in tight-fitting, light grey breaches and a frilled shirt. The debonair look was finished off with big cuffs and a plain grey tailored waistcoat. After playing with him for a little while longer, he ran his opponent through. It did not come as a great surprise to the dying man to find himself impaled upon Burleigh's sword. Sir John's reputation for such brutality was no secret.

It was his contacts in government who had sent him Peckham, or at least that was the name he had been given. The little man in the bowler hat, dark frock coat, pinstriped trousers and spats was not at all what he had been expecting. His face had a child-like quality that matched his size. His large eyes had very dark pupils that glistened disturbingly as he spoke.

"It is not usual to meet like this," he told Burleigh coldly, speaking with a pronounced speech impediment that made him difficult to understand. This was more noticeable as the tiny man also stuttered. "I was briefed in London, I know what I have to do and it will be done."

"The last one they sent messed up," explained Burleigh. "I just wanted to be sure that you will not. I would do this myself but I never like to mix business with pleasure."

"Had I been given this rather simple task sooner it would have been done by now," hissed Peckham "It is not something I do, however, when I do dabble in simple kills, I have a one hundred percent success rate." He turned his little black case still clutched in his gloved hand. "Oh and, Sir John," the stutter if not the lisp had suddenly gone. "On the odd time a government or a customer of any kind has tried to swindle me in anyway, the consequences for them have been unspeakably dire."

His strange eyes fixed Burleigh's cold grey eyes in a terrible stare then took in the other swordsman who was on his knees choking and gurgling.

Burleigh moved very quickly, pinning the little man to the dark rough stone wall, knocking his hat to the floor. His foil was at Peckham's throat. "No little creep will come into my house and threaten me, Mr Peckham."

Peckham blinked unnaturally at Sir John, but never for a moment broke eye contact. "Should I flick a switch on my little bag, Sir John," he whispered into Burleigh's ear, "a six-inch blade will bury itself in your guts. "Worse still, should I let go of the trigger on the handle of the case…bang, Sir John." He started to chuckle, making odd snorting noises as he did, like a wild pig. "And guess what, Sir John," he went on in the same croaky voice, still giggling to himself. "We are both spread all over the walls, like strawberry jam, only not so tasty, eh? Although we suppose that depends on whom you are talking to," the odd little man added with a stifled giggle, after a moment of exaggerated thought.

"You are good then." Burleigh did not move. The darker part of him was wondering if he could even survive being spread over the walls. He was sure he could. "Yes, you're good, Mr Peckham. You will do me very well."

"Then could I trouble you for my hat back please?" hissed the little man, still keeping eye contact with Burleigh. He pushed him away and smoothed out his odd-fitting frock coat.

"I realise, of course, that it is not why we are paying so much gold to secure your special services, Mr Peckham, but the boy is the most immediate task," said Burleigh. "As to the other matter, it is not time yet, but I want the little brat Master Rupert Jones dead as soon as possible. The child could ruin all my plans."

The children looked tired when I joined them in the small classroom.

"Today, Mr Skeet would have made us read poetry, sir," Victoria told me. She handed me a large and battered book entitled *The Anthology of Great British Poets*.

"Yes," said Rupert shakily, "let's read poetry."

The two children sat very still, looking expectantly at me. Victoria was a pretty child. Ringlets of dark brown hair had been brushed back and tied with a pretty pink ribbon. She wore a white blouse under a sober grey pinafore and sensible shoes. Rupert also wore predominantly grey. His ginger hair was in a mess and his heavily freckled face was still filled with fear from the night before.

"You like poetry?" The question was meant for Rupert; however, as usual, Victoria chose to answer.

"Mr Skeet liked poetry, sir," she explained carefully. "And Latin," she added. "He liked them so much, he forgot his stick most of the time." Victoria shuddered visibly.

"He didn't forget his stick when we were doing sums," interrupted

Rupert. They looked at each other for a moment. Two children sharing a terrible secret.

"Right," I said. "It may not have come to your notice yet, but I don't have a stick. So we can all relax." I looked imploringly at my new charges. "Now I want you to tell me what happened to your previous tutor and why, Rupert, you believe that the pirate lady Prudence Fairweather wants to hurt you?"

"Not hurt me, sir," the redhead corrected me shyly. "Kill me, sir. Prudence Fairweather is going to kill me."

"That will hurt, Rupert," pointed out Victoria unhelpfully. As she spoke, she deliberately snapped her pencil. "Ouch!" she added and laughed.

"You're scared of her too!" Rupert sent an exercise book flying at his sister.

"I am not!" she yelled, expertly ducking the projectile and hurling the broken pencil back at the boy.

"Is this by any chance why my predecessor had a stick?" I hit the desk loudly with my hand and they stopped bickering at once. "Children, I would like our time together to be both educational and fun, but I will not tolerate such behaviour." The children looked as if they might burst into tears at any moment. "I think you should start by telling me a little about yourselves, how you came to be on Heffen with your Uncle Silas."

Once again, Victoria elected herself as spokesman. "Our mother died," she explained sadly.

"She tried so hard to look after us," interrupted Rupert.

"We were sent to the workhouse," Victoria continued, glaring at her brother for his interruption. "We had no money left when mother died."

"It was horrid," chipped in the boy again.

"I'm telling the story, Rupert, so shut up and stop interrupting."

"Shut up, yourself."

"Children, do I really need to go out and buy myself a stick?"

"Sorry, sir," they mumbled in unison.

"Please carry on then," I urged impatiently. I was not at all used to having such young children in my care.

"We were not at the workhouse long," Victoria went on. "Although it felt like it was forever," she added with a shudder. "Somebody from the mayor's office found out that our uncle was still alive. He sent for us at once. That is how we came to be here, sir."

"Do you get on well with your uncle?"

"He scares me," said Rupert.

"Everybody scares you. Even Mr Anders scares you."

"No he doesn't."

"You're just a big scaredy cat."

"Children! Not again please."

The children lapsed into silence.

"Tell me what happened to Mr Skeet then."

This is my understanding of the events, from the story they told me. Skeet was very tall and very thin, with short black hair. He wore clothes that looked about a size too small for him and detested bright colours on him or the children. Skeet had a very slight limp, no doubt the other reason he always carried a large walking stick. This was most often used to hit the children with.

He had what looked to the children like a permanently bad smell under his small pointy nose. The teacher was quite humourless and difficult to listen to in class without falling asleep. The most likely reason he had obtained the position was through the governor. He would often meet with their Uncle Silas and another extremely unpleasant man the children feared even more called Sir John Burleigh.

Another occasional visitor to the palace was the old man Richard Boscastle. He was a far nicer man who often produced candy for Victoria and Rupert from his waistcoat pocket. These men would sometimes lock themselves away for hours in Uncle Silas's offices. Sometimes they would overhear the men engaged in what sounded like heated arguments.

Someone else who visited Skeet was the nearly blind man. He was almost as tall and almost as thin as Skeet, only his hair was very long and slate grey. He wore thick bottle glasses, carried a big magnifying glass in his coat pocket and sometimes when he remembered a white stick.

In contrast to Skeet his clothes were at the very least two sizes too big. If called upon to read a document, the academic would take out the reading glass. Sometimes he would simply have his bright red nose pressed to the page. The children were nervous of this man at first. It transpired that his name was Kidner and he was in charge of the archives and library on the south island. In fact, he was always very pleasant to the children and often, like the old gentleman, would slip them candy when nobody was looking.

The children noticed that Skeet had been going out alone. They had watched him walk down towards the Sailor's Rest, a rough and unruly drinking house close to the beach. A notorious place which was frequented by all the lowlife, pirates and scum of the earth.

"Victoria likes pirates," put in Rupert. "It was her idea to follow Mr Skeet, 'cause she hoped to meet a real-life pirate."

"That's just not true," argued his sister, her face going crimson.

"We think our granddad was a pirate," insisted Rupert. "We never knew him, because he was probably hung before we was born. Mother used to tell us some of his stories though. I don't remember them much, 'cause I was only little."

"They were tall stories Mother always said," explained Victoria.

"Fantastic stories of sea monsters, strange worlds, men with horns, and incredible storms." Victoria's eyes sparkled as she remembered. "First, Mother would always describe Grandpa to us. I think he was quite fat, with red hair like Rupert and a big beard. I wished I had known him." Victoria's voice trailed off.

"See, I told you she liked pirates, sir," interrupted Rupert smugly. "When we got here, Victoria would pretend she was the famous pirate queen, Prudence Fairweather. That was before she wanted to kill me. Only Victoria would most probably give me up, if it was to help get her to be a pirate."

"No, I wouldn't," snapped Victoria angrily.

I decided not press them further for now on what had happened when they followed Skeet. I was, of course, extremely keen to know, in case a similar fate awaited me. To be forewarned is to be forearmed. That is, if I was to have any hope at all of surviving on this so-called Paradise Island.

Harry looked out towards the black mass which was Niridia. The volcanic rock that towered above the *Black Albatross* had been inactive for ten years now. Nothing lived anywhere on its great mass. No trees, no animals, no people, nothing lived there, except it seemed the rock itself.

A great deal had happened to Harry in that ten years. He was sure that many questions would be answered soon now. He found himself wondering if he would survive this time. If he did, what fantastic new stories might he add to his collection? Harry, however, felt a strange sense of foreboding.

It had been little more than ten years ago that the old man had passed away. In his dying breaths, he had given the *Albatross* to Harry. Harry had the sea in his blood. Too long on dry land made him moody and restless. He had started out an honest tar, rising to a position of considerable importance. He had enjoyed an interesting and privileged life, until driven into piracy by circumstances beyond his control. He was perhaps a little too soft with the men, but his compassion had earned him the loyalty of all around him.

On the other hand, Arthur, his weasel-faced rival in the matter of succession to the captain's quarters, was a cutthroat and had always been a cutthroat beneath a cloak of respectability. The good thief and superb con man had the ability to show great loyalty. He would have died for the old man. Indeed, he had on more than one occasion nearly done so. It was only natural that Arthur would expect more for such unquestioned loyalty. He had never in his life been loyal to anyone before other than himself. It was not in his nature to make friends. It had always led to pain and disappointment. So he was angry. Anger without reason, for he and Harry, although from different backgrounds, had once been good friends.

Despite the dying captain imploring him to stay and help as Harry's first mate, Arthur flew into an uncontrollable rage. He swore that he would return to the *Black Albatross* with enough men to take the ship for himself. In his last moments, the old man begged Harry not to ever forget his friendship with Arthur.

Almost all of the crew stayed loyal to Harry. For a short while they got on with what pirates do best: sailing the high seas, plundering other people's treasure. These were, however, strange times. Rumour, mythology and most of all superstition were rife amongst the crew. As a much younger man, before his ginger hair had became mostly a silvery grey, Harry had seen some very strange sights in these waters himself.

Not long after Harry had taken command of the *Black Albatross*, Blind Mario had decided to attack and capture his precious ship. It came as almost welcome relief to Harry. He had started imagining strange and unexplainable things in these waters again. Nothing you could put a finger on, more a glimpse of something just below the surface, or a sense of evil lurking in the shadows. Like before, these were things he did not begin to understand.

On the other hand, Blind Mario and his ship full of cutthroats were something Harry understood all too well. The battle was fierce and bloody. Harry's men proved their worth, as did the old man's choice of successor. Although heavily outnumbered, they fought bravely from the biggest oaf to young Monkey, the ship's boy. The skinny lad swung through the rigging, sometimes making seemingly impossible leaps from mast to mast. He would perch high up, naked but for a loincloth and a long knife, his keen eyes watching for a shipmate in trouble.

Swinging down into the thick of battle, he would take many of Mario's men by surprise. All went well for Monkey until one ugly, toothless, one-eyed blaggard shot him. The young lad looked surprised at the blood spilling from his side and fell to the deck. Harry and his crew fought on, hacking back at their attackers with grim determination.

The crew of the *Albatross* suffered very heavy casualties. Many good sailors died protecting their beloved captain and their beloved ship. The screams of the dying fading away into the darkness, as the light faded on that bloody day. Their spirits would haunt these waters forever.

Despite such uneven odds, the passion, love and dogged

determination of this motley bunch prevailed. Blind Mario's men were beaten back into the blood red sea. At last, Harry and Blind Mario came face to face. The goliath of a man had only one eye that worked. The one eye, however, was good enough, as the giant lurched at Harry, sabre poised for the kill.

It was Blind Mario's bulk, not his eyesight, that was to be his undoing. Although weak from his wounds, Harry was able to side step the attack. His sword plunged into his enemy's gut. The momentum of Mario's attack took him to the very edge of the captain's deck. He turned, Harry's sword through his belly, and glared back one-eyed at the victor.

Then Blind Mario fell backwards into the bloody water below, another feast for the waiting sharks. His dying screams were so terrible; they could haunt a man forever.

"That is what will happen to anyone who tries to take my ship," said Harry through gritted teeth. He staggered over to the point where his enemy had fallen and looked down into the darkness below. "Do you hear me, Mario?" The warm dark night was suddenly very quiet.

The *Black Albatross* lay moored a short way out from one of the most inaccessible beaches around Gabrielle's Reef. The ship's crew was much reduced in numbers as a result of the terrible battle. Many were still recovering from their wounds, some much worse than others. A watch was being kept at all times. The evil pirate, Jessie Crooks, would no doubt have heard of the high price the crew had been forced to pay to repel Blind Mario and his men. The *Black Albatross* would never be more vulnerable to attack.

What Harry did not know was that a Spanish war ship had engaged the dreaded pirate Crooks on the other side of the north island. Things were not, however, going well for the Spanish ship. Jessie Crooks was not only a foul and sadistic man who took great pleasure in inflicting pain on his victims, but also, unfortunately for the Spanish crew, a brilliant tactician. Just when it seemed to the Spanish captain that things could get no worse, a second smaller vessel entered the narrow straits. The lookout on the Spanish vessel had reported another pirate ship coming to help Crooks; not that he was in need of help. There was nowhere to run, so the ship's captain, an honourable and God-fearing Spaniard, was forced to consider surrender. If Crooks's reputation was true, a fight to the death was preferable to any such alternative. Then, to the surprise of everyone on board, the small ship began to fire on Crooks. The balance was back in the Spaniards favour. After a long, bloody and bitter battle, good prevailed. The odious pirate Jessie Crooks was taken alive.

Within the hour, Captain Baldock had taken charge of this, the vilest of men. He was secured in a cell at the Garrison building and heavily guarded by a detachment of hand-picked men. Baldock's superior officer, Major James Scott, personally supervised construction of the gallows. In contrast to the young captain, Major Scott was an untidy man who seemed incapable of fitting into his clothes. They seemed always to be either far too big or far too small for his oddly shaped frame.

The capture and hanging of such a notorious pirate as Crooks, Scott hoped would help to regain the respect of his men and the local island community after the recent massacre at the Sunshine Ranch. This was despite Scott having absolutely nothing to do with the villain's apprehension whatsoever. The crew of the Spanish warship remained silent on the matter of the strange little vessel that had come to their aid. All the captain knew was that he owed the beautiful young girl his life.

When news filtered back to Harry that Crooks was in jail and soon to be hung, there was great celebration amongst his battle-weary crew. This was the opportunity Arthur had been waiting for. Late one night, so dark not even the moon was shining, the *Black Albatross* rested, still moored someway from shore in safe waters.

Monkey, who had been close to death, had been nursed day and night by his captain. It had been touch and go if the child would pull through. The boy had been found a month or so ago by some of Harry's crew, lying washed up on the rocks, close in to the mists. They had thought him dead, presumably drowned.

On closer inspection, they had found the boy to still be alive. He was naked and had no means of identification. The boy himself had no recollection of who he was, or how he had got there. For a while he was known just as boy. He was, however, both a mischievous and agile lad, good at swinging through the rigging. This earned him the nickname Monkey and the name had stuck.

Despite the calm waters and the stillness of the night, the lookout heard nothing. Arthur's men climbed silently up the sides of the *Albatross*. The attack came without warning. With many of his crew still injured, Harry had little hope of saving his ship this time. He decided that rather than let Arthur take it from him, he would scuttle his beloved *Albatross*.

"You are not taking her, Arthur!" he bellowed. "Before that happens, I will take her down, I promise you that, you ugly oaf." He moved towards Arthur, sword drawn ready. "And you and I, my horrible old friend, will go down to our watery grave with her," he added.

Harry had already heard plenty of stories of the notorious pirate Prudence Fairweather. As at last the moon came slowly out from behind dark clouds, the tall and shapely young pirate girl stood before him, illuminated only by the ghostly silver light.

"It is I who want your ship, Captain." Prudence Fairweather bowed gracefully to Harry. "Your men are exhausted," she went on cheerfully, "and I should point out, heavily outnumbered. So I am asking you ever so nicely to surrender, Captain."

Harry looked at the girl in disbelief. "Let me ask you, Mistress Prudence, how exactly would your father feel about his precious little princess turned into a thief and a cutthroat?" he asked scornfully. "She not even in her twentieth year yet." Harry stared at the beautiful girl. Could this really be the child he had once bounced on his knee? The same long auburn curls. The same captivating brown eyes. It seemed she had blossomed almost without warning into a fully mature woman. How could it ever have come to this?

"He would blame you, Uncle Harry, despite your friendship," said Prudence sweetly. "Remember I could never do no wrong." She laughed and tossed her hair away from her face. "Well, what is your answer, old friend?"

"Surrender to a strip of a girl like you? That is one story I will never tell." He charged at the girl. Their swords clashed together. Each of Harry's attacks was skillfully executed but effortlessly parried. Twice she sent him hurtling to the ground. The girl fought with such a relaxed style. It was reminiscent of the cat playing with the mouse before the kill. This made Harry angry, and anger is not good for swordplay.

"Was it really you who taught me to fence, old man?" she asked in wide-eyed innocence as Harry stumbled again. "I recall you being so much better with a sword than this, Uncle Harry."

"I should have listened to your father. He did not wish his little princess to play with swords, in case the little bitch was to cut herself." Harry lunged again, but the girl had stepped aside even before he had begun his charge.

"I assure you, Uncle Harry, he would be most grateful to you now, had he lived, for your lessons have saved his precious little princess's life a few times already."

"You still lean to the left too much," observed Harry "I have always told you it is all about balance."

"No, I don't," replied the pirate girl sulkily, but she paused to check her stance.

Harry made one last desperate charge at the girl. With a final flurry she send his sword spinning from his grasp, her own sword plunging towards him. The ship's boy Monkey, still weakened by his wounds, as indeed was his captain, saw his captain's dilemma. Mustering what little strength he had, the boy flung himself between the pirates. Prudence's sword stopped, pressed against the boy's bandaged torso.

"Get out of the way, child." Prudence glared at the lad angrily.

"No, ma'am," stammered Monkey. He was trembling with fear, sweat running down his bare chest. "My captain has stayed by my side when I had the fever. If you wish to harm my captain, then you must kill me first."

"Monkey, get out of the way," snapped Harry. "And that is an order, boy. I am sure Prudence Fairweather will give me her word that she will not harm you, other than perhaps a flogging for insubordination. Perhaps you need a ship's boy?" he added to Prudence.

"I will not move," said Monkey, who now held his long knife in front of him in a rather pointless gesture.

"What stone did you find this under, Uncle Harry?"

"You can excuse the lad a little, Prudence. We found him close to the Fault."

"He seems to be a useful waif to have around." Prudence laughed and sheathed her sword. "Although," she added, glaring again at Monkey, "a good flogging would certainly do you no harm."

"I have not surrendered, Prudence," pointed out Harry.

"Don't be silly, Uncle dear, I could always wrap you round my little finger, just like Daddy." She smiled sweetly at him.

"That was when you were a little girl," pointed out Harry weakly, offering her his sword reluctantly. His crew had easily been overpowered. This time, thankfully, with few further injuries.

"But I am still only a little girl, Uncle Harry." Prudence fluttered her sparkling brown eyes at him. She looked down at the sword he was offering her. "I don't need your sword," she said softly. "It is your sword arm I need."

"Well, you have seen how good that is nowadays." He laughed.

"Good enough for Blind Mario, I heard." Prudence smiled. "Anyway, in truth, it is your wisdom I need. I have plenty of good fighting men."

A skinny shorthaired black girl, no older than Monkey, was standing close by the lady pirate scowling. "And what about me?" she demanded sulkily.

"I have plenty of good fighting men and my little Meg," Prudence sighed.

Arthur walked nervously towards them. Prudence continued.

"It was the old man's wish, was it not, gentlemen, that you two should be friends. If he were now to get that wish, I would have the wisest council any girl has the right to wish for. What a team we would make."

Arthur walked forward and offered Harry a large and hairy hand. He grinned, his eyes still filled with years of mischief.

"The old man did right in picking you," he said softly. "Much better than an ugly thief."

"You were special to him too, Arthur," Harry said, gripping Arthur's hand. "Although God only knows why," he added with a smile.

All that seemed a long time ago now. Older and perhaps a little wiser, Harry watched the wisp of acrid black smoke drift from the peak of the mountainous rock.

"Are you all right?" A tall young man, dressed in striped trousers and a leather vest, had climbed up on deck to enjoy the late afternoon sun. He was a handsome lad, his face blackened by constant exposure to the sun. His short spiky hair was bleached blonde. His bronzed body rippled with muscles.

"I have never made you stay with me, lad." Harry was passed his sixtieth year now, but fit for his age still. "Me, I've had an interesting time. Accused of treason, disowned by family and friends and condemned to be a privateer. Always on the run and living on my wits. You can get away. You're a bright lad and very presentable. I have taught you good manners and how to behave in polite society."

Monkey laughed. "I have been privileged to have served you. You have more loyal friends than anyone alive and you have become a father not just to me, but to Meg and even dare I say Prudence. What we would do without you when our leader has one of her moods, God only knows. You have seen sights few men could even begin to imagine, and you have done a little good in a world where not enough good is ever done. Is it any wonder that I choose to stay?"

"Monkey speaks the truth, old man." Prudence Fairweather was sitting, her knees hunched up to her chest, on the cabin roof. The pirate girl had not been there a minute before, but looked as if she had been there all day. She wore a short baggy white top and had a piece of animal skin fastened around her slim waist, her tangled hair blowing in the gentle breeze.

"What moods would you be referring to exactly, Monkey?"

"Did you find your government agent then, your demon hunter?" asked Harry, quickly changing the subject.

"I am not sure," she answered, jumping down to join the others. "Are you absolutely sure that this Anders was the only passenger on the

Sally O's manifest, Monkey?" She looked questioningly at the young man. "If it is Mr Thomas Anders," she went on, "then he is quite the most unlikely candidate I have ever met."

"I don't suppose they would advertise their business," pointed out Harry. "In any case, how many government agents of any kind have you known?"

"I will check again," promised Monkey.

"Oh, and check the *Wild Swan* as well, Monkey," said Prudence. "I know it's a cargo ship, but it was the only other vessel to dock last evening, so it's worth a try." Prudence stretched and yawned. "I need something to eat, or at least my stomach is telling me I do." She gently rubbed her smooth olive-skinned navel. "I worked up a bit of an appetite upsetting our esteemed governor," she explained. "If I end up fat, I shall have another score to settle with that man."

A muffled explosion came from just behind them. In the reddening sky of dusk, the volcanic rock looked even more intimidating. The black smoke had become thicker and blacker, and fire was licking around the edge of the mouth.

"It's beginning," said Harry softly.

"No, Harry, it began a long time ago," replied Prudence. "We have to end it."

I had been on Heffen for a week. I had learnt no more of Skeet's final fate, or the part the children had played in it. Despite my eagerness to learn more, I felt I would risk upsetting my charges, before I had gained their confidence, if I pressed them more. They still did not seem to have had time to mourn their mother's untimely death. I had ascertained that she was only a young woman when she had passed away.

From what I could make out, the poor lady had died from exhaustion trying to look out for her two children. They had also suffered the cruelty and ignominy of the workhouse. Mercifully, after being so well protected from the harsh realities of our world by their mother, their time in this most dreadful of places, whilst bitter, was also short.

This was entirely due to what struck me as the most uncharacteristic kindness of their Uncle Silas, who had them brought out to Heffen to live with him. I could only presume that his actions centred on the overwhelming guilt he must have felt, knowing that his sister had died in poverty, whilst he had become rich beyond his wildest dreams.

Rupert remained frightened. Every dark corner, every shadow, could be Prudence Fairweather waiting to leap out and kill him. Any noise, any creak in the floorboards, was also the pirate coming to get him. Victoria was putting on a brave face, but I had no doubt that beneath that she, too, was both frightened and disorientated by this strange new world so far from home.

Then there was this feeling that something else wasn't quite right. I mentioned this to Sydney when we met, as promised, at the local inn. The inn turned out to be a good-humoured establishment, housed in a pretty, white-washed stone building with a roof made mostly from palm leaves.

It was crowded inside. Most of the custom attracted by this jolly place could be directly attributed to the close proximity of the governor's unfinished palace. Although there was still that hill to climb to reach the place. There were paid servants, tradesmen, clerks and craftsmen from the estate, all mixing happily together. The room they were in was probably big enough for half the number that actually was squeezed into it. A great fire in one corner, over which a whole wild pig was roasting, made the room very hot indeed, although few seemed to notice.

Sydney and I took our drinks outside into the gardens at the back. Although it could become quite cool at night on Heffen, this was a mild evening. The views from here across the cliff edge were breathtaking. The rich deep blue waters formed a small channel between the cliffs of the south, to the golden beaches and tropical forest of the north.

"I have to explore that, Sydney," I said in total awe of the scene laid out in front of me. "Pictures in a book can never capture any of that."

"I don't know, I take you away from home for the first time. It was old Anderson's idea to ask you, you know."

"Anderson?" I raised an eyebrow. "I thought you said you were just a tradesman, Sydney?"

"I am, old lad, trust me on that one." He paused and pulled a face at the beer we were drinking. "What is this dreadful concoction?" he said. "It's horrible. Anyway, I said I would never talk you in to it, as you need your mama too much. He seemed confident I would. Of course, I didn't know about her then."

I suddenly remembered that this journey was to help me recover from a broken heart, and it was already working. I hadn't thought of Anna Groves once since we had arrived. Love is a strange thing, if it ever had been love.

"Now home-loving boring old Thomas wants to go wandering about rain forests," finished Sydney, who I had not been listening to.

"I have begun to realise, Sydney," I replied, "that whilst books will always have their place, there is nothing like seeing things for yourself."

One of those splendid birds that looked too heavy to fly had landed, surprisingly gracefully, near us as if to emphasise the truth of this discovery.

"Books can never explain how things smell. You cannot feel the grains of warm sand trickling through your fingers." I looked at my friend. "Now that you have bought me here, Sydney, you need to show me around." I was still looking at my dashing companion, but my expression must have changed.

"What?" I was making Sydney feel uneasy.

"Just something I meant to ask you earlier," I said casually.

"Well?"

"Well, I was just wondering why your name wasn't on the ship's manifest?" I had hoped to catch my companion unawares and succeeded. Sydney spat a mouthful of beer on the floor. For a moment, he looked a little flustered by my question. I would normally have considered this to be quite an achievement. Sydney is never easily flustered.

"Pretty obvious if you don't mind me saying so, old chap," he said at last, wiping his face with a well-starched hankie. "What with so many angry people looking for me, I thought that to advertise my presence might be just the teeniest bit unwise, don't you think?"

"I thought that would be the reason." I smiled.

"Gives me plenty of extra scope with the ladies." Sydney laughed. "Mind you, there is somebody who knows I have arrived. Do you remember Philip Baldock?"

"Yes, of course I do." Sydney had already reminded me that our old school friend was stationed at the garrison here. "You told me he was out this way somewhere. Don't tell me you have run into him already."

"He was drunk, which is unlike the Philip I remember," said Sydney. "He took a boat over to the north island," he added, "although someone else was rowing."

The landlord brought us out another foaming jug of their best ale. We were both beginning to think that maybe the local beer was an acquired taste. Each mug seemed to taste better than the last.

"You followed him?"

"Well," pointed out Sydney, "if somebody tells you the world is coming to an end, what would you do?"

I agreed. "So who was rowing the boat then?"

"I have absolutely no idea, Thomas. He was a skinny-looking chap with long grey hair and funny glasses."

"I have heard that description before from the children," I confirmed. Sydney was very excited by this news and urged me to tell him more. So I told him everything that had happened to me since our arrival. I might even have exaggerated Prudence Fairweather's visit to my room just a little bit.

In my defence, all those years of hearing Sydney boasting about his amorous adventures had taken their toll. Watching the expression on his normally unruffled countenance change from incredibility to shock and, best of all, to pure jealousy was more than any man could hope to resist. The more his expression changed, the more I exaggerated my encounter with the pirate. So much did I embellish my night of passion that by the end of this boastful tale I was blushing at my own words.

I would never sully the name of a lady, but surely a pirate, by very definition, cannot also be a lady. I decided it better, however, not to mention how much I wished she would call again.

"That's not fair," he moaned. "It was probably me she was looking for anyway."

"I would be careful if I were you, Sydney," I suggested. "I think she might be!"

I was determined to win the confidence of my new charges. Their story had without doubt affected me. When they did not look afraid, instead they looked sad. I worked hard in the classroom, trying to get them to enjoy their lessons. I remembered some of my own teachers had managed to make the most interesting subjects quite dull.

As well as struggling with the children, I was also struggling with my own head. For some unaccountable reason, I could not stop thinking about the pirate, Prudence Fairweather. No woman had ever moved me like this. To be fair, I have never dreamed about a woman prior to meeting her before, especially such a life-like and disturbing dream.

I didn't want to stroll in the park holding hands with Prudence Fairweather, or sit in the parlour sipping afternoon tea. I most certainly did not wish to hear a recital on the pianoforte. I wanted to make love, then lie naked side by side talking about anything and everything. Discover what each of us cared about most. I was not desperate to marry Prudence Fairweather. I felt, however, that I would happily spend the rest of my life with her.

I realised also that what I had told Sydney was not just revenge for the years of listening to his conquests, but my innermost dreams of what I hoped might happen, if she were ever to call again.

Late one evening I slipped quietly down to the big kitchen for some supper. Mrs Moffat had already caught me, on more than one occasion, stealing from her pantry. Tonight she was sitting in the dark once again, illuminated only by the dying embers of the fire.

"Mrs Moffat, are you all right?" I asked her. "I am afraid I was trying to raid your larder again," I added ruefully, like a naughty schoolboy who had just been caught scrumping.

"I'll make you something. "Mrs Moffat started to get up. "It's almost ten years since your pirate woman killed my old man." She obviously thought I needed some explanation.

"I'm sorry," I said. "I didn't know. Do you want to talk about it?"

"What's there to talk about? We hadn't been getting on too well him and me like. He was a good man to be sure, but also a pious man. His principles were his downfall in a funny sort of way. I suppose that I knew it was going to end bad and I was right." She looked at me, sat holding her hand in a comforting way. "Learn from me, Mr Anders. Let your heart rule your destiny and don't you be worrying about the affect it has on others. I made a terrible mistake and the Lord has made me pay for it. The sacrifices we make, they are just not worth it."

Captain Jakes had searched out Sydney in the officers club. It was even quieter than it had been a few days earlier.

"Captain Jakes, how nice to see you," Sydney greeted him. "Can I get you something to drink?"

"A nice malt whisky would be just what the doctor ordered, Mr Greenburgh." Jakes sat himself down at the bar.

"Is this just a social visit, Jakes, or do you have something to tell me?"

"Well, sir," replied the ancient captain of the *Sally O*, "you know how you asked me to keep a look out down at the harbour for any strange comings and goings."

"Yes, Jakes, I do remember," confirmed Sydney. "Please go on."

"Well, sir, I was on my way home the night you and Mr Anders arrived, and I saw a strange man disembark from the *Wild Swan*. It was very late and I'm afraid very dark."

Sydney jumped to his feet. "Why didn't you tell me this sooner, Captain?"

"I didn't think it was of that much importance to be honest, Mr Greenburgh," confessed Jakes. "In any case, I've been seriously indisposed," he complained. "Confined to my hammock as they say, I was." In truth, Captain Jakes always went out for a little light refreshment the first night back on shore. The result of this over indulgence was that Jakes couldn't even climb into a hammock, never mind be confined to one. Sidney had no reason to know this and had hoped for better warning of any new arrivals on Heffen. He glanced around the almost empty officers club.

"You can't see him in here, Jakes?" he whispered.

"Why are we whispering?" whispered the still inebriated sailor.

"Walls have ears," explained Sydney, tapping his nose with his finger.

"Oh I see," said Jakes, who did not see at all.

Rupert was in his bedroom. Clothed in his pyjamas and a thick red-and-yellow-striped dressing gown, he sat, looking into the mirror. This was stood on a chipped and stained dressing table under the small window opposite his bed. The small boy walked over to the dresser and pulled open the bottom drawer. From it he took out a small wooden box. It had once contained half a dozen good quality cigars and still smelt strongly of tobacco.

Inside there were two things. The first was wrapped in a small piece of navy blue felt. He wasn't sure what the small, oddly shaped chunk of gold was. The important thing was that it was his. The other item in the box was a crumpled picture of Prudence Fairweather. The same pencil sketch declaring a high price for her capture, dead or alive, that had been posted all over the islands.

"Beautiful," said the boy staring at the picture, a shaky finger, gently stroking her face. "She is so very beautiful, just like our mother."

Chapter 4

*H*effen Library was in its own way as self-indulgent as the governor's
palace. Unlike the palace, designed in a modern style with large
windows and the bold use of marble and gold leaf, the library was of
much more traditional construction. Inspired by the temples of Rome
and Athens and built of stone, it was situated in the centre of the
municipal park.

The centre feature of the park was a large boating lake, set in
amongst orange groves, which nestled into the side of Uqua, the great
mountain of the south island. Here the cosmopolitan population of
Heffen would laze away the long hot summer days, punting, or
picnicking, with wives, families, or mistresses. In this place the French,
the Spanish and the English, amongst many other nationalities,
seemed to forget old grievances and live in total harmony.

The design, like most things on Heffen, was by the notable architect
Sir George Mansfield. The effect upon the visitor was to step out of this
alien world, back into an English country park. I had decided that I
would take the children there to see the great collection of books,
records and archives about the island that was now their home. After

we had spent some time in useful study, I thought, despite my aversion to being on water, that they might like to try out one of the paddleboats on the lake.

The interior of the main library was breathtaking. The entrance was through a grand hall. Scattered about the hall was a collection of classical Greek statues. Carvings of anatomically perfect, nude figures, of both sexes, had been honed out of lumps of solid white rock. Their blank eyes followed visitors as they entered the library through the grand doors into the vast circular central chamber. The floor was laid in the most intricate mosaic, using a multitude of pastel colour to remarkable effect.

Tables were set geometrically down the centre of the floor. Here students of the sciences and the arts sat pouring over books, oblivious to their wonderful surroundings. Shelves filled to overflowing with books rose majestically towards the high-domed ceiling, far above our heads. A grand stone staircase led to a series of wooden walkways, of which I could count more than a dozen levels, spiralling towards the complex floral designs on the great copper roof.

There must be more than a million books in Heffen Library, and it occurred to me that a student in certain subjects would need to keep very fit. Unlike me, a good head for heights would also be essential. The thought of being on those walkways gave me that horrible sensation of panic and dizziness. I had, of course, read of this famous library in books. It claimed to be the largest in the world. My cynicism at such a dubious boast was very quickly evaporating.

Young almost naked slave children were in fact used to run up and down the precarious walkways to collect books for their readers. In charge of all this activity, which took place in an unnatural silence, was a tall thin man with long straight grey hair and bottle glasses.

I recognised at once who this man was. There was little doubt that this was the man that Sydney and the children had both described to me. The same man who had met our old school chum, the frightened Philip Baldock.

The librarian's name I knew was Kidner. A large part of my research into this mysterious part of the world was from Kidner's many books and papers on the subject. A noted and well-respected scholar and explorer, he had settled on Heffen many years ago. I did not like to guess his age, but he was credited with building this incredible collection of books and archives into one of the modern wonders of the world. Quite how he had managed to assemble such a remarkable collection of rare books and manuscripts was difficult to understand.

There was also something else unusual about this cavernous place that I came to notice. The temperature inside never seemed to vary by so much as a single degree. Perfect conditions in this otherwise hot and humid land for the storage of all these valuable books.

Kidner was a quiet and unassuming man. It was said that he preferred to live a reclusive existence, happier dealing with books and ancient scrolls than with people. I was excited to meet him.

Kidner looked surprised by our arrival. Before I could speak a word, he put a finger to his thin lips and beckoned us through a doorway almost totally camouflaged by the books surrounding it. The room led to a much smaller gallery, off which there were a number of anterooms.

"Forgive me," he spoke in almost a whisper; the hint of a smile flickered on his face. His eyes looked out of proportion to his thin gaunt features. This was due to the magnifying effect of the thick bottle-glass spectacles he was wearing. "The library is a place of quiet," he explained. "I am always delighted when children visit. After all, Mr Anders, they are the future of our world, if it is to have one."

"You know me, sir?" I asked, unable to disguise my surprise.

Kidner laughed. "I know of you, Mr Anders." He turned and knelt to the children's height. "And although we haven't been formally introduced," he said to them, "you are our governor's niece and nephew, if I am correct."

"You are, sir," said Victoria very properly. "We have seen you at the palace from time to time. I am Victoria and this is my younger brother, Rupert."

"A pleasure to make your acquaintance." Kidner shook the children's hands.

"I am not one for meeting people, Mr Anders, but I confess, I did enjoy your excellent papers on the isles of Heffen. I encourage the students here to read them as part of their core study of our islands' geographical and social history."

"I used much of the writings of one Professor Kidner in my research for the meagre effort you speak of." I smiled. "He must, I am sure, take much of the credit, if there is any due."

Kidner bowed. "The trouble is, he does not have your easy, good-humoured and most readable writing style," he said. "It is such a style that encourages the student to read on," the professor insisted. "Although I concede that I am delighted you have at last chosen to travel. There is much you cannot get from books."

"I am quickly coming to understand that, Professor," I assured him.

The long gallery walls were lined with paintings. Some were dramatic paintings of the islands. Others were portraits, one of which the current governor dominated. The children stood in awe by the giant oil painting.

Uncle Silas, looking much taller than he really was and much grander, stood proudly by his desk. He wore the royal purple ermine lined cloak of office. He was holding the governor's grand mace in his left hand and the Bible in his right hand, on which he wore an irregular-shaped golden ring. A great chain of gold hung around his neck. In fact, this precious metal was everywhere in the portrait. Even the fine detailed carvings of the grand desk were highlighted in gold leaf. The children gazed up at the man as if they had never seen him before.

My own interest drifted to the other portraits. There were many fine paintings of previous governors and people who had contributed to the island's history, for good or for evil. It was interesting to see Prudence Fairweather's bewhiskered father, a giant of a man beaming down proudly from the wall. Stood around him were two boys and a little girl, cuddled up to the big man's substantial girth. Next to him stood a woman who looked familiar to me.

She was tall with dark long curls, sparkling brown eyes and the most disarming smile. The artist could surely not have done her beauty any more justice than he had. She was holding a baby in her arms. Farther down the hall there was a small and gloomy portrait of a man by the name of Boscatle, with a very pretty younger woman draped around him.

"It is generally believed that he killed her," explained Kidner. "He was so consumed with jealousy when he found she was sleeping with another, some say others." The professor sighed sadly and continued, "Do you know, it is exactly ten years since the murder? The family in the portrait next to them had been brutally murdered by pirates and cutthroats only the night before. It was a terrible time, terrible."

There were many more portraits. One was of the obscenely rich slaver, Sir John Burleigh, who now owned and ran huge plantations in the north, as well as owning a large fleet of ships. He was a darkly handsome man with cruel iron-grey eyes. One of the pictures of the islands' previous governors, in fact the previous incumbent of that exalted position, was missing from the wall.

A fine portrait of a handsome lady hung next to the lighter patch on the wall where the missing picture should have hung. She was, according to Kidner, the missing portrait's wife and a wicked woman. Anyone looking at the picture of Lady Catherine, who trusted in the artist who had painted the portrait, would have had no doubt Kidner was right. Something more than the undeniable beauty of this woman had been captured on the canvas, something quite evil.

As well as portraits, there were some fine paintings, drawings and etchings portraying different parts of the area. One painting in particular caught my eye, perhaps because of the richness of colour, or the tranquil beauty of the scene portrayed.

"This one is lovely," I said. "Where on the islands is it?"

"Funny you should ask about that one." The professor frowned. He put his nose close to the painting and squinted. "I have spent many hours trying to determine the location. I know every inch of these islands, Mr Anders. I am one of the few to have explored some of the pirate islands beyond the reef. I have even explored the Fault, although perhaps mercifully, the skies were clear and the sun shining bright that day." He paused and touched the texture of the paint with a gnarled and shaky hand. "I do not, however, know the location of this picture, except that I am sure that it must be somewhere on Heffen. All the others are."

The children had found paintings of some of the cutthroats, privates and explorers who had sailed the seas in these parts. Some I had heard of, some I had not. A very small sketch dominated this group of pictures. It was in a simple frame and portrayed a most ordinary-looking sailor in his advancing years. I felt strangely drawn to the picture.

"That is believed to be Francis Gabrielle himself," Kidner answered my question, before I had chance to ask it. "Like all good legends, he was nothing special," went on the professor. "A very ordinary man by all account. I have some of his original notes in my study. The parchment is now yellow with age, but still easily legible. It tells a little of the reef, although all the charts are missing. I am still studying the rest, but it seems to shed little new life on the Fault, except that Gabrielle it seems desperately wants the reader to destroy it."

"Destroy it?" I interrupted. "How can you destroy something that is not even remotely understood?"

"Come to my office if you like," suggested Kidner. "Perhaps you could give me your view on the authenticity of the scrolls."

As we spoke, two slave boys ran noisily down the corridor. They were carrying a stack of old manuscripts. The smaller child went flying on the slippery floor, sliding towards me.

"Be careful boys, please," complained Kidner. "Those scrolls are extremely ancient and certainly not used to being sat upon."

"Good afternoon, Mr Anders, sir." The boy sat up on the floor, grinning at me.

"My driver," I said, recognising him at once from the day of my arrival. "I thought you worked for the governor?"

"Don't you mean owned by the governor, Mr Anders sir?" asked the boy cheekily. "I am, but the prof. lets me come here sometimes."

He picked himself from the floor, muttering an apology to the tall librarian. Kidner had become oblivious to his surroundings. He was examining his precious scrolls with great concern. The boy winked at the children and ran off down the gallery.

"How many more times, boys!" the professor shouted irritably after them. "Walk, don't run!" Kidner sighed. Seeing the slightly perplexed look on my face, he smiled weakly, deciding I needed some kind of explanation. "As I said, Mr Anders, I love to see children visit. The children you see here are here because they want to be. I don't own a cat or dog myself, never mind a human being."

"Why is there another painting missing?" Victoria pointed at a much larger light patch on the wall, next to a particularly ugly and unpleasant-looking man called Blind Mario.

"That was a portrait of the pirate Prudence Fairweather," he explained. "The governor made me take it down as well as the portrait of his predecessor. He has forbidden any pictures of her in the gallery." Kidner began to chuckle to himself as we followed him down to his office. "It's not often the governor doesn't get his own way, and I mean no disrespect to your uncle, children."

I couldn't quite understand what Kidner was trying to say. He smiled, realising my confusion. "The baby in the picture," he pointed, "the baby in the picture is Prudence Fairweather." He laughed again and disappeared down an annex to his office. The children had to run to keep up.

"Walk, don't run," reminded the professor firmly.

His office was a jumble of papers, scrolls, books and parchments. They covered the floor, the rickety desk, the chairs and the large fireplace. There was clutter everywhere. Dominating the wall over the untidy fireplace was the banned painting of Prudence Fairweather. Like the picture of her mother, it captured her natural beauty almost to perfection. She stood in cavalier pose, in tight leather breaches, worn low on her hips, around which was buckled an ornate belt. The sword was drawn in her right hand. One booted foot rested on a fallen redcoat. On her top half she wore a matching leather bodice. This was laced up at the front, managing to almost contain her lovely breasts. A long dark cloak fell from her shoulders. She had a three-cornered hat placed jauntily on her head and that familiar mocking smile on her face.

"The governor also wanted to know who the artist was. Unfortunately, the paint was a little wet still."

Rupert stepped behind his sister, as if expecting Prudence to leap down from the picture and get him. I stared open mouthed. For some unaccountable reason, I could feel my heart beating faster in my chest.

"I thought you said the governor had banned her painting from hanging here?" I said. It was easy to see one reason why he would. The painting was greatly more imposing than his own portrait. "My understanding is he would far sooner hang the pirate than her picture."

"He did ban the painting from the gallery," confirmed Kidner with a rueful smile, "but he said nothing of my office. Anyway, he never comes in here," he added.

"It is a particularly fine painting I agree, Professor Kidner." I was managing to recover my composure. If I reacted like this to an oil painting, how in God's name would I cope if I ever came face to face with this pirate again? I was somehow certain that I would. "She is a pirate and a bad one at that, I am led to belief?"

"Mr Anders," said the professor softly, feeling the texture of the paint with the end of a nobly finger, "my eyesight may be poor, very poor." He chuckled. "But I can still recognise a pretty girl when I see one." He took his hand away from the picture. "Prudence Fairweather is a very pretty girl. "Don't you agree, Mr Anders?"

"She is beautiful like my mother was," said Rupert softly. He was staring up at the painting, still hiding behind his sister. "Only my mother's dead." Tears welled up in the small boy's eyes. "She should be dead, not our mother," he sobbed.

Once we had calmed the boy down, I spent much time examining some of the treasures in Kidner's office. The professor, who by and large seemed to lead a lonely and closeted life, was however a man of surprises. Somehow he found drinks and big iced cakes for the children.

This was instrumental in putting a rare smile back on the youngsters' faces. He even found ale for us that tasted much closer to that which I was used to at home. I decided not to mention Major Baldock for now. In any case, I was quite enthralled by some of the ancient scrolls and parchments heaped about his room. Some were directly linked to Heffen and the surrounding area. Others shed new light on other parts of the world. I marvelled at how they could have found their way to Heffen and could not wait to study them in great depth.

"We could learn much about our world from what you have here," I told the professor, unable to conceal my excitement. It was apparent the professor not only realised this himself, but believed he might have found someone today who could help him in his research.

"There is too much here for one man to plough through," he conceded.

"I would be honoured to help in my free time," I ventured cautiously, dreading the possibility that he might decline my offer.

He did not. Clapping me across the back, he became visibly excited. "Excellent," he replied. "I was so hoping you would say that."

The children had been very well behaved. They had enjoyed looking at some of the less valuable old books and scrolls. Victoria spent so much time pouring over an ancient pirate's chart that Kidner suggested she could borrow it. Nevertheless, they were both now starting to get restless. I had foolishly promised them a paddleboat trip on the lake, so we said our goodbyes to the professor and I promised to return at the earliest opportunity.

The paddleboat did not feel remotely safe. We were low in the water, and as nobody seemed able to paddle in unison, we spent a great deal of time going round in circles! More out of good luck than skill, we managed to make it to a small island in the centre of the large boating lake. The island boasted no more than two wind-damaged palm trees and a rocky outcrop.

We could have gone much farther, but it occurred to me that it might not be advisable to drown the governor's children. As we splashed around in fairly shallow waters, the children were laughing loudly. Rupert splashed Victoria. She splashed him back and then they both soaked me. There was immediate silence as they nervously waited my reaction. I regret that to my absolute shame I retaliated by splashing them back and the laughter began again. I had never heard Rupert or Victoria laugh together like this, and it was good. Sadly, it was not to last.

We had landed on the tiny island. I suggested to the children that they build a cairn on top of the rocky outcrop, a custom I explained of explorers when they reach the summit of a mountain.

"But it's not a mountain," said Rupert.

"Yes it is, it's our mountain," argued Victoria indignantly. She ran up the short summit to the top. "Rupert, look at me!"

"I think it's a mountain," I said.

Rupert ran after his sister yelling, "I saw it first!"

I decided to follow. It was not high but I imagined it would afford a good view of the lake and mountains beyond. It should also be possible to see the harbour. I wondered if the *Sally O* was still in port, or if Jakes had set course back to England.

"I saw it first!" shouted Victoria. "I'm the king of the castle, you're the dirty rascal."

"No, you didn't, I did and you're the dirty rascal." Rupert had caught up with his sister

"Actually," purred a new voice that brought the two children to a sudden halt, "I think you'll find this is my castle!"

Prudence Fairweather was standing on the top of the hillock, the gentle breeze rippling her loose white top. She wore skin-tight breaches, like in the picture, and knee-length boots. She smiled sardonically at the children, almost as another child might do.

There was a good-looking young pirate, clothed only in striped pants and a gold chain which was fastened around his large bronzed neck. There was another girl, her skin a rich and very beautiful chocolate brown. She was thin and not very tall, with short frizzy jet-black hair. Her dress consisted of a black-and-white-striped top and dark red leggings. A massive black man, who could easily have been as tall as our mountain, stood looking down on us. His big lips were shaped into an even bigger grin, showing off a mouthful of brilliant white teeth.

All I can imagine is that Rupert must have thought his sister to be in mortal danger. She had stopped about two paces ahead of him. Whatever his motivation, Rupert launched himself with surprising velocity at the pirate, sending her flying off the edge into the rather muddy water below.

"Run, Victoria!" he shouted back at the girl, and the clearly terrified little boy turned to face the rest of the pirates.

The black mountain of a man was blocking our retreat now. I am ashamed to say I had become a little breathless just running up the hill. I was trying to catch my breath and decide what best way I could protect the children. The three remaining pirates were, however, helpless with laughter. The black man, I heard one of the others call him Joshua, had an infectious laugh. The girl with black hair, whilst trying to help her leader out of the muddy water, dropped her back in at least twice; she was laughing so much. The deeply bronzed muscular young man had scooped up Rupert with one hand. Victoria was pummelling him with her fists, with no effect whatsoever.

Prudence Fairweather sat down on the rock from which she had fallen. Her auburn hair, matted with mud, was stuck to her face, which was also splattered with muck. Her beautiful brown eyes were very angry. Wiping something unspeakable from the end of her nose and brushing hair away from her face, she glared sulkily at her crewmates. She pulled off one of her long boots and, slowly up turning it, watched with exaggerated fascination the dirty water pour slowly out onto the rocks.

"Prudence," the other girl was pointing, "redcoats." Where she was pointing, one of the lake patrols was heading towards the little island in something that owed its origins to an oversized gondolier. A dozen or so very smartly turned-out men stood to attention like toy soldiers on the strange craft.

"We really should be going, Prudence," pointed out the girl.

"We could take them." Joshua laughed. "Me and Monkey could sort them easy, whilst you dry the boss." Prudence glared at him.

"Meg is right. Sensible on this occasion to disappear, I think," said Monkey, dropping the boy to the ground.

Prudence got up and limped in one squelching boot to Rupert. Her wet shirt clung to her body, showing off much more of Prudence than a gentleman should really see. She picked the terrified child up by the scruff, and holding him at arm's length, she turned to Victoria.

"Can your darling little brother swim?" she demanded.

"Not very well." Poor Victoria had almost lost her voice.

"Well, he should learn then, shouldn't he?" Prudence said sulkily and she dropped him over the edge. It was not a long drop, and the boy didn't even have time to scream. He hit the water with a big splash.

I had no choice but to leap in after my charge. It was probably a most foolhardy action. I am, at best, a very weak swimmer. I think in the end that Rupert and Victoria probably rescued me, rather than the way it should have been. By the time we dragged ourselves out of the dirty water, the pirates had vanished. In all the confusion I did not see where they had gone. I did, however, have a strong feeling we were still being watched. We all sat on the bank of the little island shivering until the patrol picked us up and took us back to shore.

It must have been a bizarre sight in the red-tinged light of the balmy evening. A gondolier filled with us and ten stiffly starched soldiers, two more peddling our little boat frantically behind.

I had told Rupert how brave he had been to defend his sister like that. When it was time for bed, he said goodnight to Mrs Moffat, then he hugged me.

"I've never seen him do that before," remarked the plump housekeeper. "I hope you're not planning to go home soon. I don't think anyone has done so much for those children and in such a short time as well."

I called in to check on Rupert on my way to bed. It was still quite early. I was, however, very tired. Victoria was sitting on Rupert's bed.

"He is sure the pirate lady will come back for him in the dark," she said.

"What, after the way you stood up to her today, Rupert?" I laughed. "I shouldn't have thought she would dare." I leaned forward to tuck him in. "Anyway," I pointed out, "she didn't harm you today, did she? If you think about it, the pirate only did to you what you did to her."

I am not sure that Rupert believed me, but he did look a little happier. I stayed awhile and read them both a story. Rupert quickly fell asleep, and Victoria and I crept out. On the landing, she flung her arms around me.

"I have had the most wonderful day ever, Mr Anders, thank you." She was sobbing.

"What, even the pirates?" I said.

"Especially the pirates," she replied.

I smiled and walked to the door of my own room.

"Mr Anders," said the girl.

"Yes?" I said.

"You won't leave us, will you? Not for a little while anyway."

"No," I said. "I won't."

In the morning at breakfast, the talk was again about pirates. Victoria was full of questions. She had borrowed a book from Professor Kidner. This told the story of many of the pirates who had sailed these waters during the previous two centuries.

"Did you know the pirate Clarence Collingwood?" she asked Mrs Moffat.

"Good lord, child, how old do you think I am now?" She was taking the dirty dishes from the back kitchen table and Victoria was helping. "Let me see now," she went on. "Collingwood had his neck stretched, must be nigh on fifty years ago now. And if you want to know my opinion, that's what they should do to all pirates."

"The only trouble, Mrs Moffat," I interjected, "is that I think Victoria is considering a career as a pirate."

"Well, it would be a very short career, you silly girl," scolded the housekeeper. "I wouldn't let any child of mine be a pirate," she added.

"But you haven't got any children, Mrs Moffat, have you?" asked Rupert. He was still shovelling porridge down his throat as well as his shirtfront.

Mrs Moffat looked at him strangely and took his porridge bowl before he could say he had not finished. "None of your business what I have and what I don't have now, is it, Master Rupert?" she snapped.

I thought this might be a good moment to find out what had happened to Skeet. I walked over to the fireplace. "You were going to tell me what happened to my predecessor," I said. The account that follows is very much as Victoria told it.

"We followed him twice to the Lighthouse Inn on the cliffs about two miles from here. He went twice and we saw him meet with some of Prudence Fairweather's cutthroats."

"They shouldn't go anywhere near that place," interrupted Mrs Moffat. "There are pirates afraid to go in there, to be sure there are." She saw me glaring at her and went quiet.

"We couldn't tell what he was doing. So we decided the next time, one of us had to get into the inn to hear what was being said. We decided that as Rupert was smaller, he would be less likely to be seen. So I stayed on watch outside and Rupert went in. On that occasion, we had not followed Mr Skeet, but walked with him. He seemed to be expecting to meet somebody, only we never did. Rupert sneaked into the inn without being seen."

Mrs Moffat let out a gasp of horror, but catching my eye remained silent.

"Can I tell the rest?" asked Rupert.

"Well, I suppose you were there not me," agreed the girl reluctantly.

"It was horrid inside. The floor had wet straw over it, and it was very hot and very smelly, and it stank. The smell was awful, worse than the workhouse. There were lots of fat men and lots of ugly men too. It was scary; I didn't want to be in there. There was lots of smoke from the big fire and from all the pipes and cigars being smoked.

"There was a group of really ugly pirates surrounding Mr Skeet. I think it was the ones he had talked to before. That black man we saw yesterday was one of them too. Then I saw Prudence Fairweather. I think she was arguing with Mr Skeet." Rupert's voice trailed off and tears welled up in his eyes. He sniffed loudly, cleared his throat and continued. "She stabbed him with her dagger," he finished. "I saw him die."

"You poor little mite," fussed Mrs Moffat.

"And she saw you?" I asked.

Rupert nodded. "She was looking me straight in the eyes whilst Mr Skeet was still dying." Rupert wiped a big tear from his nose. "I heard her tell one of her men to catch me, so I ran."

"We ran," added Victoria. "As fast as we could. I thought Rupert had made it all up, only Major Baldock came in the morning to see Uncle Silas." She stood up from the table and walked over to join me at the fireplace. "So you see, Mr Anders, Rupert saw her kill Mr Skeet in cold blood. We didn't like Mr Skeet, but it was a terrible way to die."

Rupert was upset now. I asked Victoria to take him for some fresh air in the walled garden.

"See, I told you she killed my Bert and probably my son too."

"Your son, Mrs Moffat?" I asked, dropping a log into the stove. "I didn't know you had a son die too. I am so sorry."

"They never found the child's body." The housekeeper looked ready to burst into tears. "I pray every night he may come back to me." She wiped at her face with her apron. "If there is a God, that is," she added. "Now," her tone became brusque, "I have lots of chores, so I hope you aren't going to be under my feet all day, so be off with you."

"Me under your feet?" I said in a voice that lacked confidence. "I am going on a jungle safari."

Chapter 5

Sydney had dressed in style for our adventure. He was clothed from head to heel in an expensive white safari outfit, tailored in the very latest fashionable style. He had on a white safari helmet that seemed to me to be at least a size too large for his head. The coat too looked baggy; the trousers, I felt sure, were meant to be. These were tucked into large white leather riding boots.

Sydney had about his person at least two pistols, a large knife, not to mention a larger, lethal-looking machete. All these items were stuffed casually into his trouser belt. He also had a brace of fine-looking and well-kept rifles over his shoulder.

I had done the best I could from a rather more limited wardrobe. A wide-brimmed hat to protect me from the burning sun. Lightweight khaki jacket and sensible walking shoes completed the picture. I had an ancient pistol that had most probably not been fired in years. The rifle was even older.

In place of a machete, I carried a short blunt sword that Simms had loaned me. The rifle would be of little use, for although I had been shooting many times with Papa, I had never once managed to hit anything. Even worse, the mechanics of the pistol were a mystery to me. The sword would serve only to cut back the undergrowth that impeded our progress.

Our guide was a sombre man who was very thin and had the familiar olive skin, suggesting that he was probably native to the islands. He glared at us through intense eyes that darted nervously from one person to the next. Two strong black men were carrying enough supplies for one night away from home.

"Why are we doing this?" I asked my companion, eyeing the two small rowing boats that were to carry us the mercifully short distance between the two islands.

"Research for your next book, old boy," came the cheerful reply. There was no doubt Sydney, at least, was enjoying himself.

I looked at the two men who were laden down with tents, cooking utensils, food and other necessities. "We are paying these men well for this, aren't we, Sydney?"

Sydney took off his helmet and wiped his already sticky forehead with a large white handkerchief.

"It is bad to become involved in local politics, Mr Anders, sir," said a familiar voice from nearer the floor. Standing between us was my young chauffeur boy, a large grin on his face. "Mr Simms quite likes you, so he says, 'Odi, you look after Mr Anders and his friend.'" As always, the child wore only a loincloth. As thin as a rake, there was not an ounce of fat on him. He did look to be a strong lad.

"You don't need to come with us, lad," said Sydney. "What did you say your name was?"

"I am Odi, sir." The boy offered his hand and we both shook it.

"As I said, Mr Simms likes you Mr Anders, sir, and I like you, so I want to look out for you, sir." He looked at Sydney. "I'm not sure if I like him though." He looked sternly at Sydney. "I think his eyes are probably too close together, which means he definitely shouldn't be trusted."

"You would get on well with my mama," I said.

"I would love to meet your mama one day, Mr Anders, sir," went on the boy. Behind the ever present mischievous grin, I thought I could see great loneliness in the small boy. "I think she must be very special your mother. I don't remember ever having a mother." He ran off quickly, down to the boats, to pull one out of the water for us.

"Are you a demon hunter, Mr Greenburgh?" Odi posed the question cheekily, in a poorly disguised effort, not only to change the subject, but also hide the fact that he had nearly cried. "I wonder what big game you hunt for in the jungle, Mr Greenburgh?" Odi looked questioningly at Sydney.

"Why?" snapped Sydney. "Is someone looking for me?"

"See what I mean, Mr Anders, sir," Odi said to me. "Can't be trusted."

The boats were laden down with far more supplies than we could possibly need. The crossing was mercifully short. This was just as well. Our boat was taking on water so fast that, had we needed to travel another ten yards, I am certain that we would have sunk without trace.

This end of the north island was sparsely populated and covered in thick jungle. At the far end of the island, the two landmasses almost touched. A short ferry connected to a rough road which passed through most of the populated areas on the other side of the mountain range. This side of the north island was, however, untamed. Relieved to be back on dry land, I was nevertheless apprehensive as to what the next couple of days held in store for us. For the first time since we had arrived on Heffen, I was standing on one of its famous golden beaches. Summer was almost over, but it was still very hot, although the nights could now be quite cold.

"It's too hot," I complained bitterly, looking at Sydney. He was melting under the weight of his ridiculous helmet.

"This isn't hot, Mr Anders, sir." Odi grinned. "It is almost winter time. We will soon be in the rainy season. It gets very wet then."

"Not in the next two days, Odi. I hope."

Our guide and Odi were deep in conversation. The guide glanced furtively around him, as if expecting trouble. We were sheltering from the blazing sun beneath a small copse of coconut trees. One of the fruit had put a dent in Sydney's helmet, which fortunately he had not been wearing at the time.

"The guide wants to know what you would like to see, Mr Anders, sir," explained Odi.

"Anything in particular you want to see, Sydney?" I said, passing on the question.

"Well," said Sydney, slowly and thoughtfully, "I want to know if there is any truth in the legends."

"You have to be careful in the forests, Mr Anders, sir," pointed out Odi in a half whisper. "Smugglers and pirates sometimes hide here you know. Then there are terrible wild animals," he added as an afterthought.

I looked over at our bearers, sitting some distance away in full sunlight. "What is wrong with them, Odi?" I enquired.

"It is simple, Mr Anders, sir," replied the boy. "Some people let you take away their freedom and some never will." He grinned and ran off to talk to the guide.

Sydney and I brought each other up to date on developments since our last meeting.

"So why didn't you ask Kidner about young Baldock? From what you say, he seems a decent enough old chap."

"I am sure you're right, Sydney," I agreed. "He seems to be a good man. Maybe there is something going on here that we should stay out of."

"Trouble is, old chum, I find it really difficult to stay out of things." Sydney smiled broadly. "Especially a good mystery. I am sure Baldock is terrified about something and your professor chappy probably knows what."

"Any news on the man seen leaving the *Wild Swan?*" I took a long swig of warm water from the pouch. I was desperately hoping we would wait until it cooled down to move into the jungle. Sydney killed another bug.

"I am pretty sure he could be your pirate's government agent," he confirmed, "which is a bloody relief, old man. Thought at first that one of the angry husbands had caught the next boat out."

138

He swatted another bug on the side of his face, took the water from me and continued.

"I saw Jakes yesterday. He's got a load of fruit on and the *Sally O* leaves for England today, on the late tide. He has picked up talk round the harbour of this government spy, this so-called demon hunter too."

"Odd this chap followed on the next ship out to us, Sydney." We smacked our arms in unison, followed by the back of our necks and four more mosquitoes died.

"I see what you mean," agreed Sydney.

"How was Jakes by the way?"

"Still the same. Do these dammed flies ever give up?" Sydney killed two more. "Like you, Thomas my old friend, Captain Cornelius Jakes will no doubt spend the rest of his days suffering from unrequited love I'm afraid." Sydney thought for a minute. "The other thing I noticed was that our good captain was quite jittery himself. I tell you, Thomas, something bad is going down here. Something sort of evil, can't you feel it!"

"Perhaps we should have gotten on the *Sally O* ourselves," I said.

"I would not joke about that, Thomas." Sydney was now waving his helmet at the bugs, some of which had squashed on his nice white safari coat.

"I wasn't joking Sydney," I said grimly. "I am not convinced you have picked the best time to bring us out to these islands, are you?"

We set out into the dense jungle about an hour later. Our guide led us along a narrow overgrown path through thick vegetation. It was not long before we saw examples of our first wildlife. Two or three varieties of monkeys were seen swinging high up between the trees. The noise could at times be deafening. It was relatively easy going for the first half-mile or so until we came upon a building that was very little more than a grass hut.

"Our friend lives here," said Odi to me. "The professor," he added in the way of further explanation.

"Shall we see if he is in!" suggested Sydney. "I could kill for a tankard of ale just now. Even that dreadful local brew would taste like nectar," he added dreamily.

"If you want to see anything before dark, we need to keep moving, Mr Anders, sir," Odi pointed out.

As we got deeper and deeper into the jungle, we were forced to use machetes and swords to slice our way through the vegetation. It was extremely hard going, and I felt myself starting to tire quite quickly.

We were all hot and sticky, and I noticed that both our guide and our bearers were becoming very agitated.

Not much farther on there were brightly coloured birds perched in the trees. Parrots of some kind, they glared down at the intrusion with obvious disapproval, muttering to each other in a complaining tone.

"Fantastic, what?" muttered Sydney, now bright red in the face.

At the foot of an ancient tree, with a great gnarled trunk and many broken branches, were large groups of enormous flowers. The flowers were over five foot tall and in a variety of bright colours. The bearers looked nervously on as we examined them.

"I have never seen the likes of these before," exclaimed Sydney.

"No," I replied quite softy. "Nor me."

We rested for a little while in the clearing, close to these remarkable plants. With Odi's help, I managed to get some samples, taking care not to damage the plants themselves.

"Our guide is eager to continue, Mr Anders, sir," Odi said in a low voice "He wishes to make camp before dark."

So, although tired and hot, we continued into the gloom. Hacking away at thick vines that choked our path made progress so very slow. As the evening drew on, the air became a little cooler. The mosquitoes became less troublesome and the monkeys it seemed had retired for the night as the persistent chattering had stopped.

This made the forest very still and uneasily quiet. We made the only noise to be heard as we cut a path slowly towards the place where we would pitch camp. The roar of an unseen beast, which shattered the eerie silence, sent a cold chill shuddering down my spine. It was the sound of pain, anger and desperation, all mixed up together. It tore through the still evening without any warning, making everyone in the party jump out of their skin.

"What in God's name was that?" whispered Sydney, clutching hold of me. Despite a very healthy tan, he had gone as white as a sheet. His face now at least matched his clothes. His expensively tailored outfit had become badly stained with dirt, sweat, dead mosquitoes and rotting foliage.

"This is not good." Odi could not hide the fear in his normally happy young face. Our guide and our bearers turned on their heels and fled. "The beast has our scent."

Only seconds later, the beast plunged through the undergrowth to face us. It was monkey-like in shape, but about the height of a two-story building. The creature's gigantic body was covered in matted grey hair. The stench from this monstrosity was foul. Its face had a disturbingly human quality. As well as being fierce and angry at our presence, there was also an aura of great sadness about the monkey creature.

It stood with its long arms stretched out, roaring at us. The large mouth was filled with jagged yellow fangs that would easily rip a man apart. The sound from the angry beast was deafening and made it difficult to think. I was coming rapidly to the opinion that our guide and bearers had made the right choice in running.

Sydney wanted to shoot the thing. I pointed out that a bullet was unlikely to penetrate its thick hide. It began to advance slowly towards us, scratching at the ground with a huge hairy foot and salivating from the mouth. It was then the pirates came. Some dropped from out of the trees, others from under bushes or rocks.

"Just when you think it can't get any worse," moaned Sydney, shouting over the cries of the beast.

Prudence Fairweather walked out into the path in front of us and stood hands on her hips facing the creature.

"Mable my love, I am sick of telling you, your babies are not here." The creature stopped advancing, and the noise it was omitting came now more out of despair than anger. "And you can stop feeling sorry for yourself as well, Mable." Prudence was shouting over the wailing of the giant ape. "Now go back to your bog and be good."

Mable had gone quiet now, other than the occasional whimper. Slowly the huge animal turned and lolloped back towards the trees. It paused and sniffed at a terrified Odi and a huge hairy hand touched his face. The creature lowered her face to the small boy, cocking it to one side. For a moment, Mable gazed upon Odi in reverent fascination. It was as if the child was in some way special to the creature.

"It's all right, keep still," ordered Prudence. "She wouldn't harm a child. She likes children."

The pirate went over and pushed the giant away from Odi. Even Prudence Fairweather looked tiny next to Mable.

"Go home now," she ordered the creature. "And for God's sake, Mable, take a bath!" she yelled after her.

Prudence turned to look at her new captives. After Mable, even Prudence Fairweather did not seem quite as frightening a proposition. Despite this, Odi was behind my back, whilst Sydney's face was a picture of both fear and the possibility of another conquest.

"Good evening, Mr Anders." She gave me her sweetest smile. "Are you going to introduce me to your friend whose name was most conveniently missing from your ship's manifest?"

"This is Sydney Greenburgh," I said nervously. "Sydney, may I introduce Prudence Fairweather."

"Miss Fairweather, I am honoured to make your acquaintance," purred Sydney, although he was noticeably lacking his usual confidence. "Thomas is correct. You are a vision of loveliness indeed. By the way, what was that horrid thing?" He gestured in the general direction the giant monkey had gone.

"Mable? Oh, she's not horrid. She's the stuff legends are made of. She's the swamp creature, just part of our rich and varied wildlife here on Heffen. Only poor Mable has lost her babies. They are dead I am afraid. Didn't make it through the Fault, but I can't make her understand, so she spends most of her time looking for them."

"How sad," I said.

"Yes, it is," agreed the pirate, her mood becoming sombre for a moment. "Escort Mr Greenburgh to the ship," she ordered, recovering her composure. She spoke curtly to one of her crew. "And who is the young man hiding behind your back, Mr Anders? I don't believe I have had the pleasure before."

"I am just a worthless slave, madam," stammered Odi. "Of no

consequence to anyone, I assure you. Most people don't even notice me."

"Mable did," said Prudence softly.

I looked the tall and shapely lady directly in the eyes. "Odi is a very good friend of mine, and despite being only a small boy, I would be most grateful if you didn't try to drown him this time." I may have sounded brave but my legs, which were shaking like mad, felt like they would give up at any moment.

Prudence Fairweather laughed. "Mr Anders, it was almost impossible to drown in that depth of water. Although come to think of it, you rather than the children seemed to give it a very good try." She nodded to another of her crew, who took a firm hold of my arm and led me onto a downhill path the same way Sydney had been taken.

"Now, young man," Prudence said to Odi, "I wonder if you would be so kind as to escort me back to my ship."

The *Black Albatross* was anchored some distance from the shore in a surprisingly large natural harbour. This was a place that would be almost impossible to find, unless you already knew it to be there.

The beach itself was narrow and mostly shale. The channel then widened out into a large semicircle, before narrowing again at the mouth. The secret harbour was surrounded on all sides by high cliff faces, covered in many shades of rich green vegetation. The water was deep and varied in colour, from light to dark blue, with patches that were more a turquoise in shade.

Small boats took us out to the *Albatross*, which stood proudly in the centre of this peaceful place. It was hard to believe that anything or anyone in our world could be wrong when surrounded by such a picturesque and tranquil scene as this. It became impossible to grasp the reason why anyone would wish to inflict pain and suffering on others. On the other hand, it was easier to understand how some very lucky people, like my father, had been able to come so close to God.

The big black man Joshua rowed the boat containing me and a few other rough-looking crewmen out to the ship. Our rowing boat felt so small and its passengers, so insignificant, in this grand setting. I stared up at the great cliffs, feeling overwhelmed by their size and unspoilt beauty. This was a place man could never hope to tame.

"Looking up there can make a man go dizzy." Joshua grinned. His skin was very black. He had classic Negroid features, such as the large flat nose and pronounced mouth that was always, at the least, close to a smile. He was without doubt a good-looking man. His eyes were filled with a love of life and the challenges it had to offer him. It occurred to me, with considerable discomfort, that in all my years of writing about different lands and different cultures, I had met no races other than my own. At that moment I felt an overwhelming sense of inadequacy.

The *Black Albatross* was everything the poor old *Sally O* was not. Although much older and much larger than Jakes's beloved craft, the *Albatross* was in tiptop condition. There was an overpowering smell of freshly treated wood and new paint, mixed in with the more familiar smells of a ship. The hull had been painted by a craftsman, as had the detail work on the cabins.

"You like our ship?" The man speaking was in his sixties with silvery grey hair worn in a ponytail at the back. "I am Harry." The man smiled and offered me his hand. "By rights this ship is mine, but this ugly thief here called Arthur, who claims to be my blood brother, helped the infamous Prudence Fairweather steal it from me."

A tall, thin weaselled-looking man, the devil in his eyes and a large hooked nose, bowed in exaggerated fashion to me.

"Have you ever heard anybody go on so much? He speaks the truth, of course. He did lose his ship to a slip of a girl, but it must be heavy work, carrying so large a chip on one's shoulder." He gave me a sly grin. "I tell you he has been bellyaching on about it for more than ten years now. Would you not have thought it time he gave it a rest?"

Joshua was chuckling. "You can stand here and listen to these two bicker, Mr Anders, or I can take you below to join your friends," he said.

"Tell me, Mr Anders." The smile had gone from the rat-featured Arthur. His sharp eyes seemed capable of seeing right through me. "Is this friend of yours the government spy, the demon hunter, our pretty leader seeks?"

"I think it most unlikely my friend Sydney is a government spy, and I doubt he knows anything of demons, sir," I said. "He is a fool, a fop and a womaniser. I can't see our government back home entrusting Sydney with anything of national importance myself." My legs still felt weak and unsteady, and from time to time I felt the start of another panic attack. I was, however, much calmer than before.

Joshua took me below to a small cabin, where I found my very dishevelled companion pacing up and down.

"Don't let Arthur intimidate you, friend," said Joshua. "Or old Harry, for that matter. They've been arguing between themselves since I joined the crew." He laughed and his whole being seemed to laugh.

"Prudence gets really mad with them," he went on. "She doesn't have much control of that temper of hers. It doesn't do any good though. Nothing stops them bickering with each other, yet two times, I have seen one save the other's life." Joshua looked around the cabin. "I'll get someone to bring drinks down." The big man left, closing and locking the door behind him.

Sydney was looking very worried. The usually unflappable man's feathers had been seriously ruffled. The dark side of Thomas Anders was, I confess, quite enjoying this, and the realisation was slowly unfolding that much of what had always caused Sydney to make me feel inferior was no more than bravado. Beneath this poor disguise he was as unsure of himself as I was. Even those darkly handsome features that had won over the hearts of so many ladies were looking at the best quite comical.

Joshua returned with some refreshments for me and to announce that Prudence had requested the presence of Sydney in her cabin.

Sydney looked at me. His bedraggled appearance painted a picture of total despair. Then with visible effort, the young Romeo pulled himself together. He rinsed his face in a basin of cold water, ran his hands through his oily black hair, straightened his travel-stained coat and spent a full minute admiring the results in a tarnished mirror which hung lopsided from the wall.

"Not bad," he told himself, studying his own reflection in the cockeyed mirror. "Not bad at all." Sydney was clearly planning to rely on what he knew he was good at and seduce his way out of trouble.

When he reached the door, he turned to look at me. There was much of the old Sydney bravado about him and a brief smile flickered on his lips.

"Don't you worry, old chap," he said, less than convincingly. "Everything is going to be all right."

At the palace, the governor was sat in his long office at the large curved desk. Behind the small man, a grand window looked out over the perfectly manicured gardens. To each side of the window hung the flags of Heffen. On the left, the British flag, and on the right Heffen's colours were displayed. The Heffen flag was blue with a large yellow circle in the centre, over which stood a mythical fire-breathing beast.

A long polished oak table was set up down the length of the room, stretching out from Silas's desk. The centre section was covered in dark green leather, held to the surface with large gold studs in a similar fashion to the desk and chairs. Sir John Burleigh had already taken his seat at the table.

He was a tall man, who had kept himself in good physical condition. He had a handsome but cruel face, yellow hair heavily tinged with grey. This simply helped to give him a look of great authority. His clothes were always dark greys and immaculately tailored. Burleigh always wore white gloves and carried a black cane with a diamond-encrusted handle. The diamonds, worth many thousands of pounds, had been paid for with the lives of the many hundreds upon thousands of people whose freedom he had stolen. This man had been known to order the slaughter of a hundred or more people because they were substandard merchandise, or simply because he could not get the price he wanted from them.

Richard Boscastle also had sticks. Two to be precise, but for far more functional reasons. Bent over with age, he leaned heavily on both sticks for the long, slow and unsteady journey from the door to his chair by the table.

"Is it coming today?" His eyes showed him to be a man who lived in constant terror.

"Gentlemen, I fear we are playing with things that we don't understand," said the governor. "I fear our little scheme might have gone too far."

Burleigh looked down a small but somehow prominent grey nose at the other men. "I have agreed to cooperate over the years, gentlemen, in return for some favours," he told Boscastle and Raines. "We were all very quick to accept the favours offered, gentlemen. I have been able to continue trading in certain extremely profitable commodities that liberal-minded do-gooders in so-called civilised parts of the world are having banned. We cannot show weakness now." Burleigh stood up and walked over to the window. "As for you, Richard, my old and pathetic friend. Major Baldock is still very angry that the governor would not let him hang you for the cold-blooded murder of your lovely young wife. He knew you had murder in you."

"That is true," pointed out Raines. "Why only the day before, you would have shot Henry Jessop in the back had I not personally intervened." Silas took a very large cigar from a solid gold case in front of him.

"If we all play our part and you stop bumbling like an idiot, Richard, then the world is not going to end," Burleigh reassured him.

The governor, however, did not sound so confident. Boscastle had noticed that one of Raines's eyes twitched when he was worried about something. It had been twitching a great deal just recently. The two younger men watched Boscastle hobble slowly from the room without offering any help or assistance.

"He is becoming a liability, Governor," said Burleigh unpleasantly. "Richard Boscastle is surely of little further use." Silas gave Burleigh a nervous smile. It was starting again, and he was afraid that nothing could stop it this time. "I will arrange that for you then, Silas," he promised.

The governor sighed. "I become tired of the killing. Surely Richard Boscastle has not many months left."

"It is necessary, Governor, that is all. After all these years, perhaps we should let the loyal Major Baldock catch and hang his man."

Burleigh pondered his suggestion and then continued as if talking mostly to himself. "No, I think not," he decided. "The young major is already more involved in our affairs than I would have liked. As I said, I will arrange it, perhaps at the annual ball. That is, of course, if God doesn't save us the trouble."

Silas shakily filled two large crystal glasses with port. The patterns cut deeply into the glass reflected a myriad of colours from the rich purple liquid. The two men raised their glasses.

"Your very good health then," said Silas.

"And I drink to our partner Sir Richard Boscastle," said Burleigh with a nasty smile.

In Kidner's office, the professor was pinned up against the fireplace. His thick bottle-glass spectacles lay smashed on the floor and his almost blind eyes were filled with terror.

Standing before him was the apparition of something hideous, but also no more than a child. It was covered completely in a black hooded cloak. Only blood red eyes were visible from the dark shadows of the face, and the voice that spoke was both terrible and pure evil.

"You will not let us down, Professor, you will do what is expected of you," hissed the creature. Its voice was coming from every part of the untidy office, rather than from the hooded child. "What you promised you would do, Professor. If not, you burn in flames for an eternity, screaming in never-ending agony." For a moment, Kidner glimpsed the unspeakable horror of the creature as it clawed at its face. "There is not much time left," it went on. "I have much to settle in your world."

He reached beyond the terrified professor's head. Although seemingly impossible to reach so high, something resembling a hand or perhaps a claw reached out and touched the painting of Prudence Fairweather. The cold empty voice spoke again.

"And you, a mere woman, you will not stop me either, child, only think that you can."

The picture began to burn, and the hooded figure collapsed. The malevolence had left the child. The slave boy's naked remains lay lifeless on the floor. Kidner recognised the child at once. One of his book boys he had been teaching him to read and write.

The *Sally O* was clearing the headland before turning into the wind and setting course for home. It looked even more battered since the storm. Its proud but sad captain stood aft, gazing out over the wake of his leaky tub, back towards the islands. The hastily repaired mast creaked ominously in the strong breeze. For a few more precious minutes, it would feel as if he could reach out and touch the hot golden sand. Tears rolled down his tired and weather-beaten face. He never wanted to leave Heffen. He was always afraid that this time might be the last time he set eyes on this beautiful place. The woman he loved lived here, although he could never tell her that. He had not even been able to bring himself to call this trip.

His mind drifted back to the day of his partner's murder. The day of the fire at the boatyard. It was always easier to tell people it had happened whilst he and the *Sally O* were far away. If he had been far away then he could have done nothing to help his partner. He had been a good man, worth ten of Jakes, probably more. He would have laid down his life for old Jakesey without a moment's thought.

The keener-eyed might have noticed the old and faded marks on the bow of the *Sally O*. They were unmistakably scorch marks. Not obvious was the fact that the scorch marks were a result of the *Sally O* being in dock at their boatyard on the night of the fire. It had been lucky to escape the fate of almost everything else in the yard that night. The crew was a fine bunch of seadogs at that time. Nothing like the motley bunch of reprobates that Jakes could just about afford to pay almost ten years later.

They acted quickly to move the ship away from the blazing dockside. Jakes went looking for his partner. Heffen was in the grip of a tropical storm. The wind was becoming stronger and heavy rain drove across the boatyard. His friend had been shot, although it was difficult to tell how badly. He was sprawled against the shell of a new ship, the first all-new construction job the yard had ever taken on. He was conscious and was calling Jakes to help him. It was clear his wounds were at least bad enough to prevent him from moving.

Jakes at once ran across the open yard towards his prostrate partner. There were fires burning all around him, seemingly unaffected by the torrential rain that impeded the captain's progress. Billowing clouds of suffocating black smoke rose high into the night sky, as orange flames licked up the side of buildings and spread rapidly across the oil-soaked earth.

The first of a number of large explosions shook the ground from under Jakes, and he fell, smacking his head on the hard damp floor. The captain of the *Sally O* struggled back to his feet with some difficulty. Blood pouring from an ugly gash on his forehead, Jakes struggled against the intense heat towards his stricken friend. It was hard going, walking directly into the wind, whilst trying to wipe a combination of blood and rain from his eyes. The look on his friend's face would haunt him forever.

The heat from the flames had become unbearable. Jakes could feel the skin on his face start to melt. Thick acrid smoke was now choking his lungs. A better man Jakes knew would have got through and dragged their friend to safety. The pain and the smoke overcame him and for a moment he lost consciousness. He opened his eyes to see a beautiful girl, her own face blackened by the smoke and heat.

The girl dragged him away from his friend. He could hear him screaming after them. More deafening explosions sent columns of orange flames high up into the sky. The fires burnt for more than two weeks, spreading to the forests behind the boatyard.

It was days later that Jakes realised that the girl had not been an hallucination, but the pirate who had shot his friend and set fire to the yard. The combination of his own terrible cowardice and her interference had prevented him from saving his partner's life. In public he loudly blamed the pirate, Prudence Fairweather, but in his heart he always knew that most of the blame lay with him.

Jakes found it difficult to believe that all that had happened almost ten years ago. The overpowering feeling that something very bad was coming, coupled with the guilt he had always felt, had brought him close to breaking point. That was unfortunately only too obvious to his crew.

A short dumpy man with a fat face and a wooden leg limped across the deck to stand next to Jakes.

"I am afraid we've decided to take control of the ship, sir." He was pointing a pistol at the captain. "Now I could shoot you now, but I would really prefer to wait until we are a little farther out to sea. Mr Burleigh wants us to go back and pick up a more profitable load." The fat man smiled at the captain. "And looking on the bright side, it gives you a little more time to be miserable."

Captain Jakes knew there was nothing he could do now. He knew he was going to die soon. The *Sally O* was not much of a ship, and he knew that too. Most of all, though, he knew that whilst there was a breath left in his body, nobody was going to use the *Sally O* to carry men, women and children into slavery.

Chapter 6

Sydney was gone for what felt like ages. I was left below, on my own, locked in the tiny cabin. The *Albatross* was still anchored in the quiet haven where we had boarded. Despite having stayed in the same place, just bobbing gently up and down in the calm waters of this natural harbour that concealed the ship so well, I was feeling queasy again.

I must also have problems coping in a confined space. Inside the claustrophobic cabin, it was beginning to feel more and more as if the walls were closing in on me. At that moment, Mama's homey kitchen had never seemed so far away. I longed for the warmth and safety of that place.

I was beginning to think that Sydney's charm had won him the day, yet again. I had been convinced that in Prudence Fairweather, he would have met his match. She did not strike me as a woman who would easily succumb to my amorous friend's advances. Feeling terrible now, I was just beginning to wonder how I could have been so wrong when Sydney entered the cabin. I heard the door lock again behind him. The turning of the key in the door was the last straw. It served only to remind me of my confinement in this dingy place.

"I can't stand it in here any longer!" I screamed at the door. "Do you hear me! I need to get out of here!" I began to kick the door and hammer on it.

"I say, old chap, steady on." Sydney got hold of me and sat me down on the bunk.

"Sorry," I said, trying to catch my breath. "Lost my mind for a moment then." Sydney offered me his big handkerchief, with which I gave my nose an almighty blow. "I feel much better now," I said, offering him his handkerchief back.

Sydney pulled a face. "No, old boy, you keep it," he said, eyeing the hanky with distaste. He fetched me a drink of water, and once he was satisfied that I had calmed down, told me how he had got on with Prudence Fairweather.

"Mostly she wanted to know if I was this British government agent, thinks I might be hunting demons or some such nonsense. I asked her why she was so worried about this spy person. She said that our government was meddling in things they did not understand, whatever that means. She said the results of this meddling could be very dangerous, although she did not enlarge on that either." Although I was listening intently to Sydney's account, I couldn't help noticing how strained he was looking.

"I told her that I wasn't her killer spy and, of course, that you weren't either," he continued. "Then I told her about the chap who Jakes saw. If he were an angry husband, he would have surely found me by now, so he has got to be our government agent, hasn't he? I suppose it's possible that he could have no connection whatsoever with this affair."

"So she believed you, Sydney? That you are not a trained killing machine or any kind of a spy for that matter," I asked, half jokingly.

"No, I don't think she did, come to think of it," admitted Sydney. "To be honest, Thomas old bean, she's a scary lady, if as you may have mentioned just a couple of times, a bloody good-looking one. I take my hat off to you, old fella. It would take a far braver man than I to lay that filly." Sydney was speaking from the heart. "I played a lot on you and me being good chums, of course," he went on awkwardly. I gave Sydney a worried look.

"Well, we are," he continued. "I mean there's nothing wrong with that, is there? A lady like Prudence Fairweather would not let a chap bed her unless she at least had a soft spot for him. She didn't disagree with me either. Then we just got talking about what a great time you and her had the other night. You know, what you were telling me the other day."

"What!" I said. I felt all the blood draining from my face. If I had felt bad before, I was beginning to feel terrible now. "Please tell me you didn't tell her everything I told you, Sydney?"

"Well, yes, I did actually, old boy. It was all I could think to talk about."

"Mama was right. You are going to be the death of me." I clutched hold of Sydney's jacket lapels. "You stupid, blithering idiot," I said, followed by perhaps a few more things that a gentleman should not say. "Some things you tell a friend are meant to be in confidence, or has nobody ever bothered to explain that to you!" I knew I was shouting, but I no longer cared. "I wouldn't go blabbering to anyone about all your romantic adventures, Sydney. Oh, but I forgot, I respect your privacy."

"Probably take too long as well," replied Sydney, attempting in vain to be funny. "Anyway, I wouldn't mind at all, old man, long as you weren't talking to her old man that is." Sydney, who was not always exactly good at diplomacy, could see he was getting nowhere. "Look, Thomas, you can't blame me. I was frightened, and in any case, she was sort of encouraging me."

"Sydney, I exaggerated!" I was shouting at him.

"What!" said Sydney, now looking genuinely confused. "What do you mean exaggerated?"

"Do I have to spell it out for you? I mean, I made a lot of it up. Well, most of it actually."

"Why would you do that?" asked Sydney, incredulously.

"Because I am so bloody fed up with hearing about your conquests." I was angry now, quite oblivious to the fact that the cabin door had opened.

To be fair to Sydney, whom I was closer to killing than ever before, he did everything he could to try and warn me. Unfortunately, the sickness, claustrophobia, anger and embarrassment made me quite oblivious to anything he tried.

"You heard me! I made it up because I'm fed up with you, Sydney, having yet another conquest. For the first time that night, I really, really wanted to do all those things. That woman fires up passions in me I never knew I had. You are right, Sydney, she is a scary woman and she's bloody good looking, and for some inexplicable reason, I was dreaming about her stark naked—three months before I even knew she existed. So what do you make of that then!"

"Good evening, Mr Anders."

I turned to see Prudence Fairweather leaning against the cabin door.

"Am I interrupting anything?"

I looked at her, my mouth open, lost for words. Then I looked at Sydney.

"Don't look at me like that, old chap. I did try to warn you."

"I think I am going to be sick," I said.

Prudence was laughing now. "It's a pity you are feeling ill disposed, Mr Anders." She giggled, clutching at her stomach in an effort to stifle her laughter. She looked at me, tears streaming down her pretty face. "I was just going to ask if you would like to take supper with me," she explained, trying hard to stop herself from giggling.

Sydney was laughing now too. Prudence Fairweather had slid down to the floor helpless. Every time she tried to stop laughing, it just made her worse. Both of them just kept on laughing. I stepped over the pirate's helpless body and climbed angrily up on to the deck. Then I was sick.

In contrast to our temporary quarters, Prudence Fairweather's cabin was larger than anything that I had come to expect in my mercifully limited experience of ships. True, this consisted of little more than the *Sally O*, a sort of gondolier and a peddello. Not that I should ever forget my brother's small and anything but watertight rowing boat. The pirate girl's room was, however, impressive.

It had the usual low ceiling from which swung oil lamps. These just at the right height so that I constantly banged my head on them. There were the usual dark polished oak walls and fittings and shiny brass rings round the portholes.

The cabin was L shaped. As well as the usual table, covered in charts and the implements to plot and measure the ship's course, there was a small dining table set for two, a single candle burning in the centre. There were high-backed chairs around the tables and a couple of well-loved easy chairs placed at random on the slightly sloping floor. Large and colourful cushions were scattered everywhere.

In the other half was the bed, which filled most of that part of the room. The drapes were made of fabrics from all over the world, but mostly I guessed the Far East. A variety of pastel colours were used to portray flowers, birds and even a ferocious golden dragon. As a rough-looking pirate called Clarence showed me in, a voice commanded me sternly to wipe my feet. My nerves were already shattered into a million pieces, so I automatically obeyed.

Prudence was standing round the table with four men and a woman. They all looked up to watch me wipe my feet. They quite obviously found this amusing.

"Bad boy," said the parrot from his cage by the door. Joshua burst out laughing and the rest joined in.

"You have a parrot?" I said.

"Well," replied Prudence with a wry smile, "it's sort of expected of you when you're a pirate. Personally, I'd wring the little bugger's neck if it were up to me. He was the old man's bird, and Harry here protects him with his life."

"It's a little clichéd, isn't it?" Arthur laughed. "It don't know how to swear either, pathetic creature," he added.

"It was only a young bird when the old man died and had never spoken a word until it moved in with Prudence," Harry explained. "Parrots can live to a hundred you know."

"Not if I can help it," said Arthur. "Mr Anders is right, the scraggy thing does nothing for your image, Prudence."

"He's not on my shoulder, he's in a cage," pointed out the girl. "He has a habit of crapping on my shoulder and digging his claws in.

Anyway, do I look like a cliché, Mr Anders?" She cocked her head to one side and gave me a mocking look of wide-eyed innocence.

"No, you don't," I said. "Although I confess I am not certain what a cliché actually looks like."

"Our guest has a sense of humour," observed Arthur approvingly.

I looked around at the others in the room. Sydney had been alone with her. Most probably as a result of my embarrassing outburst, coupled to Sydney's babbling, she had decided on safety in numbers. As for supper, she had probably decided that as I had spent some considerable time throwing my guts up over the side of her fine ship, I probably wasn't hungry.

Harry, the elderly but handsome buccaneer, stood by her side. Arthur, on the other hand, was almost anything but handsome. He stood next to the man he loved to bicker with, his ungainly frame dressed in a striped top and spotted headscarf. Ironically, it was Arthur who would have looked just right with a parrot on his shoulder. Joshua wore his leather waistcoat open and had to crouch beneath the low ceiling even more than Arthur. The muscle-bound young man they called Monkey had at least put a shirt on. Meg was dressed much like Arthur, but looked even tinier than she was, next to the tall men. She sat on the edge of the table, swinging her legs. Prudence had on a high-necked plain grey vest and short leggings. She wore a small black leather waistcoat over her vest.

"We were just wondering, Mr Anders," Prudence said, after Meg had stopped giggling. "We were just wondering why the *Sally O* should turn around so soon out of harbour?"

I was wondering if Meg was giggling at my unquestioning obedience to a bird, or worse, my earlier indiscretion. As long as they were still laughing at us, there was less chance Sydney and I were going to get our throats cut.

"I really have no idea," I said. "Perhaps Captain Jakes forgot something."

"Such as a boatload of slaves?" suggested Joshua. There was anger in the question.

"Heavens no," I replied, walking reasonably confidently over to the desk. "The last thing Captain Jakes would ever allow on the *Sally O* are slavers. I am quite sure of that. Jakes is a sad man, but I believe mostly a good one." I wondered if being good was much of a recommendation to pirates.

"We thought the same," observed Harry.

"Don't you mean I thought the same?" interrupted Arthur.

"Right, listen." Prudence Fairweather stood up as straight as she could in the low cabin. "Monkey, take as many people as you think you might need and bring me back the *Sally O* and its captain. She's fast in the water and could be of use to us. Meg and Arthur will go with you. You might have need of a good burglar and a good murderer." She paused and looked at the charts on the desk.

"Harry, you take charge of the watch, will you?" She turned and looked softly at Joshua, who had been unusually sullen and quiet.

"I know you want to go help some of your brothers and sisters, Joshua, but you get too emotional and then you get careless. You're too important to me to lose." She touched his face gently with a strong slender hand. "Instead, Joshua," she went on brusquely, "I want you to take over watching the boy Rupert." She looked at me and smiled ruefully. "Try not to let him see you, Josh," she added. "Mr Anders here wouldn't want us to scare his precious little charge more than we already have."

They all obeyed her commands with good humour and without question. Even Joshua, although clearly unhappy not to be going with Monkey, seemed to trust in her judgement. Without considering the risk I might be taking, I caught hold of Monkey's arm.

"You won't harm Captain Jakes, will you?" I said with less authority in my voice than I would have liked. "Only he is a friend of mine," I added lamely, as if trying to explain my suddenly rash behaviour.

"Their instructions are to bring Captain Jakes back here, Mr Anders. If it is possible, that is what they will do." Prudence called Harry back. "Sorry, Harry, could you tell cook that assuming Mr Anders here has stopped being sick now, he can serve supper."

Harry smiled. "Of course I will." He looked at me and bowed slightly. "Good luck to you, Mr Anders, she has a hot temper that one. Believe me, I know her too well." Harry dodged the object thrown at him and left.

For only the second time since I had first heard the name of Prudence Fairweather, we were alone together. My legs had once more turned to gelatine, and my heart was beating so loud I was sure she could hear it too. Nobody in my life had ever had this effect on me.

Prudence poured me a small silver goblet of red wine, which I took with a shaky hand.

"Look, Miss Fairweather," I started awkwardly, "please forgive my outburst of earlier. I assure you it was out of character, as well as being most ungentlemanly of me."

The pirate moved catlike towards me, her big brown eyes teasing every nerve in my body, her lips once more so close to my lips, I could taste her sweet fragrance. She pushed me down onto one of the comfy chairs and sat on my knee. It was abundantly clear that she wore no undergarment beneath the tight grey vest.

Her warm body pressed hard up against mine. Her eyes looked sensually into my eyes, her ruby red lips just slightly apart. I felt her warm sweet sensuous breath tickling my skin.

"I'm rather afraid I seem to bring out the worst in you, Thomas Anders," she whispered into my ear. I kissed her. A kiss that was long and filled with crude animal passion, a kiss that took our breath away. My whole being was consumed with desire for this woman.

"Thomas Anders, you forget yourself," she said, freeing herself from my embrace. Her eyes sparkled playfully with what a man would hope to be mock indignation. "I may be a brigand and a pirate, but I am not a harlot, sir."

"I am so sorry, please forgive me. As you say, madam, I do not as a rule behave in this way." My face was going as red has her lips. "You do indeed seem to bring out the very worst in me."

"I take it, sir, that you excuse your forward behaviour by blaming this fiery passion, of which you speak so eloquently about, on some ancient dreams." The tight grey vest had ridden up Prudence's lithe body to reveal the gentle swell of her tummy. She pulled the vest down and gave me an aggrieved look. Once more the pirate leaned close to me again and whispered.

"In any case, Mr Anders, you were spilling a perfectly good wine that

I went to a great deal of trouble to borrow from a very unpleasant Spanish merchantman." There was a loud knock on the cabin door.

Prudence did not avert her deeply sensuous eyes from mine. It was as if she was trying to read my mind. Perhaps understand exactly who it was she was sat upon. At last she stood up, leaving me still shaking a little just from being so close to her.

"Come in," she said, still not averting her gaze.

"I've brought your supper as requested," said the cook glumly.

"Wipe your feet," said the parrot.

"One day, when we are far out at sea with no food left, I'll get to cook you, you scrawny little bastard." The cook looked almost as wide as he was high.

"Bad boy," said the parrot, glaring at the man in disdain.

Prudence was still staring into my eyes. "Put it on the table, Neville, and stop being rude to my parrot."

"But you hate the bloody thing, Prudence," argued the fat chef.

The cook waddled over to the table with the tray of food, mumbling to himself. "It ain't right, is it? A pirate's bird should be screaming obscenities," he complained. "I ran away to sea to get away from my mother always telling me to wipe my feet, and I have to put up with an undernourished bird nagging at me all the time."

"He's annoying my cook, don't you think?" Prudence, her eyes still on mine, ran a long slender finger through my hair. "I could have him strung up from the main brace."

"Is he a good cook?" I asked, searching her eyes back with mine.

"The very best," she said.

"And have you other cooks on board?" I enquired as my hand gently stroked the side of her face.

"None," confessed the pirate. A smile flickered on her lips.

"Then surely hanging him would be misguided and not a little foolish no matter how irritating the man is," I decided. "In fact, I would go so far as to suggest that if he is a very good cook, you should humour him. Better hang the blasted parrot."

Prudence was giggling again, her eyes filled with laughter. "You give good counsel, Mr Anders," she said, breaking away from me at last and going over to the table.

The cook, Neville, waddled out in a hurry, pausing only long enough to scowl at the parrot. "Hanging would be too good for that bird, if you want my opinion," he grumbled. He slammed the door, and the bird made a tutting noise.

"So tell me," Prudence poured herself more wine, sat down and began to help herself to food, "how do you find your young charges?"

I remained standing in the centre of the cabin. My heart rate had slowed down a little; however, I was still very hot.

"As a matter of fact, they are very nice children," I said. "I am afraid no one has given them the chance to mourn their mother's passing, and you give the boy nightmares."

"I give him nightmares, why?"

"Because you terrify him."

"Do I give you nightmares, Mr Anders?" Prudence asked me innocently. She was laughing at my serious face. "Or perhaps the dreams you mentioned before are of a different kind?" I was blushing, beetroot red again. "Are you not joining me at the table?" asked the pirate, that familiar look of mischief back on her face. "I promise I won't bite."

I sat down opposite her and helped myself to some food.

"Rupert is scared of you," I insisted. "You don't really mean to do away with the child, do you?"

Prudence's expression changed to something like that of a sulky child. "No, of course I don't," she said. "I don't mean him to be scared of me either," she assured me. "I like the governor's wards."

"And dropping the poor lad off a cliff was a good way of showing that I suppose?"

"It wasn't a very high cliff," pointed out the girl. "And anyway the little monster had got me all muddy."

"Why did you send Joshua to watch him tonight?" I asked, taking a mouthful of strongly spiced meat. I had not realised how hungry I was until now.

"Because someone else really is trying to kill him," explained Prudence flatly.

"Who?"

"Steady on, teacher man, I heard these kids were getting under your skin." Prudence was serious now. "There has already been one attempt on the boy's life."

"Who would want to kill a small boy?" I asked in disbelief. "I never believed that you did."

"There is a great and terrible evil at work in these parts," she said quietly in a very matter-of-fact way. "If I were you, Mr Anders, I would take your silly friend and go home to your mother. You chose a bad place to have your first adventure, and a very bad time to come to Heffen."

"I promised Victoria I would not go away," I said in reply. "I may be beginning to regret my foolishness in making such a promise, but I will not break it."

"You are a braver man than you look, Mr Anders."

"No, I am not," I answered truthfully. "Who is trying to kill the lad then?" I asked. "He does think it's you."

"Well, on the last occasion, it was your predecessor Mr Skeet," explained Prudence. "He hired some lowlife to help him, only we got wind and sort of swapped Mr Skeet's lowlife with one of our own. One piece of lowlife looks much like another, don't you find. I am not short of lowlife here, as you have no doubt noticed." Prudence smiled and refreshed my drink. The wine was smooth and easy on the palate, if perhaps a little stronger than I was used to.

"Unfortunately," she went on, "just when I thought he was going to tell me which scumbag had hired him, or why, he managed to impale himself on my dagger." Prudence sighed.

"So you didn't kill him?"

"To a frightened child it would have looked very much that way. I was holding the knife." Prudence looked at me, and there was fire in her eyes. She was toying with the knife she had just used to carve off a large hunk of meat. She stared absentmindedly at the cruel-looking blade. "Anyway, let's face it, I would have killed him eventually." Her words sent a cold shiver down my spine.

"Does that shock you, Thomas Anders?" Her eyes bored into mine. "I would have got from him what I needed to know and then killed him.

Can you feel pity for a man who kills children for money?"

"No, I couldn't," I said quietly, not wishing to debate the rights and wrongs of cold-blooded murder with a pirate. "Have you no idea who hired this man?"

"I have been reliably informed that Sir John Burleigh wants Rupert dead," she replied. "I am not sure how reliable the informant really is, or why he would want a little boy dead, however."

"Burleigh is the slaver, isn't he?" I asked.

"He's a monster Sir John. He is a bully, a killer and a coward. He kills for enjoyment, for sport, usually slaves. He is someone I very much look forward to meeting again soon." Prudence paused, as if to compose herself. "Although I cannot for the life of me think why this evil bastard would buy a highly paid assassin to kill the governor's orphaned nephew."

"This danger people feel," I said, "this sense of doom, is it connected?"

Prudence Fairweather stood up from the table and walked over to a deeply cushioned seat by one of the portholes. I wanted so much to kiss her again.

"You are a strange man, Thomas Anders." A warm smile lit up her lovely face. It was as if the sun had come out from behind a cloud. "You are not like any man I have ever met and that is for sure."

"You don't think I would make a good pirate then?" The wine had begun to make me feel very much more relaxed. I could even pick up the goblet without spilling most of the contents, and my legs too had stopped shaking. My heartbeat was also almost returned to normal.

"You would need to find your sea legs I think, Mr Anders." She laughed. "Did you really come all this way to get over a woman?" Prudence bit into a peach, its juices spilling around her lips.

"Sydney talks far too much," I said in a tone of voice that might belong to a man contemplating murder. "The truth is, my eldest brother is an explorer, something that never appealed to me, but even he has a woman at home waiting on his return. All my other brothers and sisters are married or at the very least betrothed. So the question on everybody's lips is, when is Thomas going to marry, or what's wrong with Thomas? Knowing what was being said behind my back made me feel under pressure to marry someone, anyone. I don't think I came to Heffen to mend a broken heart, so much as to get away from the pressure of the parish mafia." I poured more of the rich red wine into my goblet.

"You must have a boyfriend?" I asked apprehensively.

"Suppose we have something in common," admitted Prudence. "I did a lot of studying when I was younger. My personal tutor, Mr Quigs, is now also our personal physician and a very clever one. He made me study and that was what my parents wanted. Anyway, putting aside false modesty, something I confess I am not well known for, that makes me both clever and a fair swordswoman." She walked, swinging her hips in an intentionally seductive way, back to the table and sat down close to me again.

"And many men find me quite attractive, I think," she added innocently, just the trace of a smile flickering on her lips. I was sure I had started to perspire heavily.

"I do not see what you think we have in common," I confessed.

"Men find me intimidating, Mr Anders. Women find you the same." She shrugged her shoulders.

"They do?"

"You scare women off because you're shopping for a wife. I scare men off because, well, because I just do."

I wanted to kiss Prudence again so much. The palpitations were returning as I tried to pluck up the courage. As I went to kiss her, she stood up again.

"It's late, Mr Anders, and I am on early watch. I trust also that Monkey will bring me back a nice little schooner to play with."

I stood up.

"So if you will excuse me, Mr Anders, I think I would like to retire."

"Of course," I said. "Forgive me, I should not have stayed so late. I also need a little word with Sydney before he tells anybody else all my secrets." I walked to the door, where the parrot glared at me, as I imagine a very superior race might do. I did not want to leave. I did not want this evening to end.

164

"Thomas Anders." Prudence stood looking at me as I opened the door. "It is customary to give a lady a goodnight kiss in these parts."

I went back over to her at once, longing to taste her lips once more that night. She offered me her hand to kiss. There was laughter in her eyes.

"Goodnight, Mr Anders," she said.

"Thank you for my supper and for your company." I kissed her hand, bowed slightly and left.

"Bad boy," said the parrot with conviction.

Sydney was asleep, snoring very loudly, having drunk far too much grog of some kind. There was little doubt he would have a bad head in the morning. Odi also gave the impression of being asleep. He was lying on the floor by our bunks.

"Mr Anders, sir, you ok?" he asked me.

"Go to sleep, Odi," I whispered. "I am absolutely fine."

I was not really fine. My head was reeling. I wanted to get back to the palace to protect the children, although I knew Joshua was already watching over them. Then there was the pirate Prudence Fairweather. From the day I had first seen her face on the torn and faded wanted poster at the harbour, something new had been awakened inside me. I longed to be with her still and wondered if I had any hope at all that my feelings for her might be returned.

Sydney was in very bad shape when he woke in the morning. Odi had never had the chance to sleep so long. I went up on deck for some relief from the confinement of the cabin.

"Good morning, Mr Anders," Harry greeted me. "It is one of those mornings when it seems impossible to believe that there can be anything wrong in the world." It was a beautiful spot where the *Albatross* was anchored, the cliffs soaring high up above us towards a clear blue sky.

"Any news of the *Sally O*?" I enquired.

"No word yet." Harry's deeply lined but handsome face broke into a smile. "Arthur will not have allowed Monkey and Meg to do anything rash," he assured me. "They will bide their time and go in when the moment's right." He paused to beckon over a burly sailor. "Mr Anders is wanted on the beach, Moby," he said. "If you would be so kind."

The big man rowed me to the beach without speaking a word. Much of the beach was shale, but one part was sand. There was a low table protected from the already powerful sun by a large striped parasol. On the table was fruit and drink. There was no sign of Prudence, or anybody else for that matter. The sand was already very hot beneath my feet. Down on the shore where the cliff jutted out over the water, I could see somebody in the water. I decided to walk down and investigate.

"Good morning," said Prudence.

"Good morning," I replied.

"Did you change your mind and decide to go home, Mr Anders?" she shouted. There was a small waterfall cascading off the rocks into the natural harbour. Prudence was silhouetted against it.

"I told you I can't," I shouted back.

"It may get very dangerous," Prudence said. She was wading towards me. Her clothing consisted of a brief loincloth, fastened about her waist. Other than that she was naked. I tried my best to avert my gaze and hide my embarrassment, but I was enchanted.

"And I do mean dangerous, Mr Anders." She paused and looked at me curiously. "Does my appearance offend you in some way?" she asked.

"No, not at all," I said. "On the contrary, you look very beautiful. It's just that I'm not quite used to the liberal ways of Heffen yet."

"I do mean dangerous," she persisted, ignoring what I had said completely. "For example, you can't even swim from what I saw."

"I swim a little," my reply was defensive.

"Let me see you then." Prudence Fairweather stood tall, hands on hips, in the shallows. I could see small fish swimming around her. The waterfall surrounded by luscious vegetation formed the perfect backdrop to the beautiful olive-skinned girl.

"If you insist on staying on Heffen, Mr Anders, I suppose I will have to try to keep you alive." She sighed and plunged back into the crystal clear water. "I think a swimming lesson might be a good place to start, don't you?"

"I am hardly dressed to swim," I protested.

Prudence Fairweather laughed wickedly. She pushed at a few strands of her long and normally curly, auburn hair that were stuck to her lips. When wet, her hair fell straight and shiny onto her broad shoulders.

"It is better when swimming here, Mr Anders, to be undressed." She waded to the shore and slowly but deliberately removed my shirt.

"Come, Thomas Anders." She was smiling at me. Prudence shook her wet hair, splashing me with cool salt water. Little drops of water ran down her face and down her chest onto perfectly formed and deeply tanned breasts.

"There are none of your prospective wives here," she teased me. "Miss Anna Groves might well need smelling salts at the slightest glimpse of a naked man. I have grown up with pirates and have seen far uglier sights than you without clothes."

"Is there anything about me my loyal and much trusted friend Sydney didn't tell you?" I asked sarcastically.

"Nothing he knows I wouldn't have thought," replied the girl. She was laughing and started pulling me towards the water. Reluctantly, I removed my trousers and plunged in after her. The water was warm and very calming. For a while we just played like two children might play, splashing each other or diving through the little waterfall, which was much, much colder than the sea and took your breath away.

Prudence had me trying to catch the fish that swam with us. I never did, but then neither did she. The pirate girl may not have caught any fish; she could, however, swim like one. As she took me out deeper, she would disappear for ages under the surface. Then she would reappear unexpectedly some distance away. Sometimes she would come up beneath me, grabbing my legs, or leaping onto my back and pulling me down underwater.

"If you wish to swim more effectively," she said, as I had just swallowed about a gallon of water and she was laughing at me, "you must be prepared to get your hair wet, Thomas." She began to teach me with surprising patience. Seeing how uneasy I was out of my depth, she would urge me to relax.

"If I was going to let you drown, Mr Anders," she pointed out quite sternly, "why would I go to the trouble of teaching you to swim better? Trust me and trust the water. If you relax and lie still, your body will float."

We spent ages in the water. My swimming improved as my confidence grew. I was made to dive from rocks. These were not high rocks, but high enough for me. It dawned on me quite quickly that I had probably never had this much fun before breakfast, or indeed at any time of the day.

I had also never enjoyed the company of a person, or laughed as much as we had. I had lost most of my inhibitions with regard to our nakedness. It should have been impossible for me to completely accept such an extreme change in acceptable behaviour. Here, however, in this beautiful place, it seemed so normal. The naked pirate looked so natural in these surroundings, like she was a part of them.

I did not at any time try to take advantage of her. In truth, this was more through fear of rejection than out of any sense of moral decency on my part. Then there was also an innocence, that went somewhere beyond just sexuality, in two naked people playing in paradise. I felt privileged to be with Prudence. Which is not to say that every part of me did not ache for her.

The *Sally O* had not taken long to load her evil cargo. In any case, she did not have very much room. The bulk of the merchandise had been taken from Heffen's south island harbour by a freighter some hours earlier. A grim and ugly three-mast ship, her hold so full that many of the slaves had been crushed to death before the ship had even left the harbour.

Burleigh always built a casualty rate into the shipping costs, but to lose so many before the ship had embarked was not good business. He was also faced with a small, but potentially costly, group left over from the freighter. To keep them until another of his fleet came into harbour would be unacceptably expensive.

A cull would save any further losses, but Major Baldock would not approve and even the governor might find it difficult to openly support such an action. In any case, he had already suffered too many losses. Then he noticed the *Sally O* and knew she was the answer to his problems. The *Sally O* was a little small. The slaves would have to be packed into the hold like sardines. Many more would perish on the voyage, but it was still, by far, the most profitable solution to his problem. The fat waddling man with the sly grin and shifty eyes acted as spokesman for the lowlifes who crewed the *Sally O* nowadays.

Major Baldock stood by Burleigh, watching the *Sally O* leave down the narrow channel between the two islands. It was sat dangerously low in the water with its heavy cargo. Torches lit the dockside, spreading flickering orange light into the inky darkness.

Sir John Burleigh disliked Major Baldock and planned one day to kill him for the pleasure of it. Major Baldock offered no threat to Sir John. The major disliked Burleigh with equal vigour, but most of all he feared him.

"No offence, Sir John, but I am very surprised Jakes is carrying slaves."

"Every man has his price, Major," Burleigh said in an oily and condescending manner. "Except you, my dear Major Baldock. You strike me as a man who is absolutely incorruptible." The slaver's voice was filled with sarcasm.

The two men were remarkably similar in appearance. Both tall, slim men, they were of approximately the same height and build. They were similarly strong, muscular men, who kept themselves in the peak of physical condition. Philip Baldock was immaculate in full dress uniform. Polished brasses glinted in the fire from the torches. He had once been the most eligible bachelor on Heffen. The years had been kind to the major, adding just an air of maturity to his naturally rugged good looks.

John Burleigh, like the major, had kept his body in very good condition over the years. He too had handsome features, although he had an indefinable coldness. He was most elegantly dressed, a long-tailed coat and a tall hat placed jauntily on his head. He carried a swordstick in an impeccably manicured, gloved hand.

Even as people, there were similarities between the two men. Baldock enjoyed life with his family on Heffen. Such an important trading centre and such a long way from home, there was, as a general rule, little call on the military's time. Philip Baldock also enjoyed a standard of living a good deal better than a major's salary might normally be expected to pay for.

He had married Mia, a very beautiful local girl, whose skin was a beautiful golden brown. Baldock feared a transfer home, as he knew his wife and children would find the climate change so very difficult to adjust to. Then there would be the inevitable prejudices to cope with. Many people in this bad world liked to judge a person on the colour of their skin.

Some of the wretched slaves who had just been loaded onto the *Sally O* looked so much like his own children. So Baldock knew as well as Burleigh did that he was not incorruptible. He had turned a blind eye to all of Burleigh's less conventional business practices. Most of these activities he strongly disapproved of, many appalled him.

Both men were never alone it seemed. A small platoon of infantrymen was on patrol with the major. They stood in line on the dockside, bayonets fixed. Burleigh's men skulked in the shadows, eyes unwaveringly on their leader for any imperceptible signal to act.

"As the governor always is at pains to point out, you do your job well, Major Baldock," observed Burleigh, doffing his hat to a passing lady. "Incidentally, next time you need a break from your wife, Major, that one is both a fine lady and quite inexpensive." He watched the girl all the way down the dockside, relishing the sight of her swaying posterior. "And I am led to believe that she is willing to oblige even the most unusual requests."

"I am fortunate I know, sir, but I am happy to be faithful. I have never wished to stray and never will."

"Really? I cannot imagined one lady satisfying all my needs, Major." He laughed, a cold humourless laugh that made Baldock shudder. "Please do not misunderstand me, I believe very strongly in the institute of marriage. Why, am I not always telling the governor he should find himself a respectable woman and marry her? A wife from good stock and good family adds to the status of a man, don't you think, Major?" Burleigh went on, in his smooth and unruffled way, "Her main function is, of course, to bare her man's children. He can have his fun elsewhere. You should try one of the youngsters from the next consignment, no charge, and I wouldn't even want the bitch back."

Baldock's eyes narrowed. He could feel the hairs rising on the back of his neck. "There is a certain evil in these parts," he spoke with a deliberate calmness. "I am not the only one who feels it coming again. I know that it is evil in its purist form, Sir John, and I believe that in the end, it will take us all. To continue to meddle in such things would be suicide."

"Superstitious poppycock, Major." There was just the slightest trace of uneasiness in the outwardly confident rebuke. "You are starting to sound like our honourable governor." Burleigh's face was now almost touching Baldock's face. "Are you so frightened of your own shadow, little man?" He snorted. "Go home to your little woman. Not such a wise career move, Major, marrying a native whore, was it?" Burleigh was mocking the soldier in front of his men. "And one made to such a specific order, as I recall." He looked upon the hapless major with total disdain. "And all she has given you is girls I hear. Still keep impregnating her and you may one day be blessed with a son, if only a coffee-coloured one."

The young officer could contain his anger no longer. Baldock grabbed at Burleigh, and the two men tumbled into the dust and filth. Baldock wanted to kill him, to tear his head from off his shoulders. The men in the shadows came from everywhere, pistols pointing at the brawling men. Burleigh was on his knees now. Baldock, scrambling upwards, smashed his fist into the side of Sir John's head. Burleigh's henchmen could do nothing, for fear of shooting their master. The small platoon of soldiers remained motionless, waiting for a command to action.

The men rolled about in the dust, kicking and lashing out. At last, Burleigh managed to free himself of Baldock's grip and push him away. Scrambling to his feet, he drew his sword. Baldock drew his weapon, and the two men began to circle each other. Their clothes were ripped and both were covered in a thick lair of white dust from head to toe.

"This evil I talk of, this dreadful evil," gasped Baldock, wiping blood from the corner of his mouth, "it has already devoured you, Sir John. You must know that." Both men were breathing heavily from the exertion. Although late, it was a hot and humid night.

"Me thinks, perhaps it eats at you as well, good Major?"

For a few moments more, the two men circled, eyes fixed on each other, swords ready. Baldock knew he was no match for Burleigh, although he was considered a passable swordsman himself. Burleigh attacked first, his slim blade hacking relentlessly at Baldock's heavier weapon, a sword that was more used to being drawn on ceremonial occasions.

Baldock managed to parry Sir John's first flurry of strokes, but he was being forced back towards the edge of the dock. Baldock tried to bring all his skill as a swordsman to play, but Sir John was little more than playing with him. It was then that the prostitute came back along the quayside. This time, she was in the company of two other scantily clad women and a couple of slightly drunken naval officers. For a moment, Burleigh lost interest in the major, his cold grey eyes drawn to the plumpest of the three women.

Still consumed with anger and hatred, Baldock saw his chance and lunged at Sir John. The sharp point of his sword penetrated Burleigh's heart with little resistance. Sir John's eyes widened in disbelief. Baldock too felt panic welling up inside him. He had not meant to kill the evil businessman. Sir John was for a moment disorientated. He stepped back, watching the sword slide slowly out of his chest. He was already looking little more than inconvenienced by what had happened.

"Once again this terrible evil you speak of, Major, has been of considerable assistance to you," he sneered, brushing at the small red stain spoiling his waistcoat. "The governor would not be too impressed if you were to go around killing innocent civilians such as me, for example, now would he?"

Philip Baldock stood rooted to the spot, mouth wide open, staring at Sir John Burleigh in total disbelief. His sword had gone through the foul man's heart. He was sure of that. So why was Burleigh smiling at him now? What unspeakable evil could do this? It was at that moment that Baldock first fully realised the magnitude of the malevolence that was eating away at his world.

With a simple flick of his blade, Burleigh sent Baldock's sword spinning into the water.

"I think," he said, stabbing his blade into Baldock's shoulder, "I think I will kill you another day, Major Baldock. Perhaps I will kill your wife first, then your pretty little girls, unless I can get a good price for them that is." He smiled coldly at the major. "Yes, maybe I would get a good price for the children."

Baldock's shoulder was screaming with pain. "I will kill you," he whispered through clenched teeth.

"Then you will need to fetch your sword, Major." Sir John smiled. Baldock was sent flying backward into the water below. His corporal reached for a pistol and one of Burleigh's men shot him. The man clutched at his chest and fell. With both commanding officers downed, the remaining soldiers remained still.

Burleigh walked slowly back to where his hat lay squashed and dirty on the ground. He picked it up and tried to straighten it. It was clearly beyond repair. He turned to the frightened soldiers and their dying corporal, holding up the remains of his hat.

"Somebody will pay for this," he hissed. "Such a fine hat costs a great deal of money."

Chapter 7

Just before daylight, the pirates attacked the *Sally O*. The ship's crew was mostly very drunk, having discovered Jakes's hidden store of rum and brandy. The progress of the old tub had been very slow. So low was she sat that she was taking on water at an alarming rate. The damaged mast creaked in the strong breeze as the schooner moved down the narrow channel between the two islands. The air was filled with the moaning and wailing of the captive cargo, crammed into the hold in such an inhuman way. An eerie red glow from the volcanic mass of Niridia mingled with the orange swirl of the dawn skies.

The pirates made no noise. They slipped from the water onto ropes and climbed the side of the *Sally O* with ease and grace. Most wore little clothing and were armed with sword or sabre. Dropping silently onto deck, the men waited for Monkey's signal. Arthur, clothed in short striped breaches, headscarf and earrings, stood motionless, eyes glistening with anticipation, in the shadowy dawn. Although he may have discovered it rather late in life, he was sure this was what he had been born to do. He loved the feeling of adrenaline racing through his veins as he waited for the word to attack.

It was strange how, out of such terrible adversity, he could find some contentment. He never remembered being happy, even as a child. Only once before had he cared for anyone special, and the pain of that still returned from time to time.

Monkey crouched in position by the forward hatch. The blonde and muscular young man wore only a loincloth, as he had done as a child. He pushed his shaggy blonde mane back from his face and gave the signal. The mutineers never quite knew what hit them. Arthur stuck his two long daggers into a couple of the bigger oafs with grim satisfaction. They hardly made a sound as they died. Only a few of the men gave enough resistance to provide some sport for their attackers. Meg, armed with two pistols, slipped down below.

She found Captain Jakes bound and weighted, ready to be dropped overboard. She loosened the gag from his mouth. The poor captain cowered against the hull of his ship.

"Get it over with then," he barked irritably. Although very frightened, Jakes spoke proudly, determined not to lose his self-respect. Meg admired this. "Although you really have no need to drown me, as you are certain to drown us all before this voyage is done."

Meg shrugged, cutting free the sacks full of fruit that had been intended to help him sink. She pulled him to his feet.

"Prudence Fairweather would like to meet you, Captain Jakes," she explained casually, stuffing a pistol back into the belt of her colourful vest. "Shall we go up on deck? Sadly, I think you will find that most of your mutinous crew has slipped and fallen onto my comrades' swords."

On deck, the pirates were cleaning up after the skirmish. A few of the drunken crew had given up without a fight. Arthur had captured the fat man with the sly face.

Late the previous evening, Arthur and Monkey had slipped into Heffen Harbour to drop off Joshua and find out what course the *Sally O* had taken. It had been Joshua's suggestion to check on the vessel's course.

"Save you a good deal of time looking for her, if you know where she's going," he pointed out.

"Quite bright for a babysitter," observed Arthur sarcastically.

The ugly pirate had always enjoyed the cosmopolitan atmosphere of the docks. It was essential to keep your wits about you in Heffen Harbour, to be on your guard at all times. Otherwise you could find yourself conned, robbed, or murdered. The unwary could even end up an unwilling able seaman, having fallen foul to one of the local press gangs.

Monkey had oddly never had reason to be on Heffen Harbour before.

"There is a smashing little inn by the harbour," whispered Arthur to his companion. "As I remember, Eva, a well-proportioned lass and most pleasant on the eye, also serves particularly fine ale. Who knows, we may get in on a game." Monkey could see that his ungainly friend was in his element. "It would be unusual for me to earn some honest loot for a change."

"You call one of your card games an honest way to make money?" Monkey laughed.

"It would also afford an excellent view of the *Sally O*," pointed out Arthur, trying to look hurt at Monkey's insinuation. "Without drawing any attention to us," he added.

So they had slipped onto the main dock road, avoiding the busy stream of horse and cart and fine carriages that moved up and down this busy place with alarming speed. More than once, Arthur had to drag Monkey out of the path of some snorting beast, a fully laden wagon bouncing in the potholes behind.

Monkey was enchanted by the myriad of colours, sounds and smells that assaulted his senses. He had difficulty taking it all in. There were hundreds of makeshift stalls selling everything from the finest silks and carpets from the east. Exotic fruits and expensive sweat meats shared space with fish stalls and butchers. Whole animals hung from big hooks, the smell of which was often already ripe in the warm air.

"We will slip round by the old docks," said Arthur softly, observing the busy scene in front of them. Arthur was good at knowing his way into places without being noticed. He was also, fortunately, skilled at slipping away again. As a thief and a con man as well as a businessman, this had often proved a useful attribute.

The old dock contrasted starkly with what Monkey had seen before. A great stone warehouse stood proud, but derelict, overlooking a yard in which were scattered the derelict remains of a few old boats. All were in various stages of construction and in a wide variety of different shapes and sizes.

Arthur always moved quickly. He knew that it was not advisable to linger for too long in the one place in his line of work. Monkey had no problem keeping up with the rakishly thin man, so Arthur was surprised to find the big musclebound youngster was no longer at his side.

Turning back, Harry scanned the rapidly fading light with sharp eyes. Through the gloom, his keen eyesight picked out the solid shape of his friend. Monkey was sitting on the upturned hulk of an ancient dinghy.

"What's up, lad?" He made the ground back to Monkey's side with surprising speed. "We should be getting a move on you know," he went on. "You don't want the *Sally O* to slip out of port without us knowing which way she is heading."

"I know this place," said the young giant. "I've never been here before, Arthur, and yet I swear I know it." The thin-faced man stroked the end of his large proboscis, as he often did when baffled by something.

"If you ain't been here before, my friend," Arthur decided, after a moment's careful consideration, "then you can't know this place. It'll be reminding you of some other place we have been. One dock looks much like another dock."

"No, you old weasel, I'm telling you, I know this place." Monkey slipped down from the rotting boat and walked into the centre of the old dock, where a large rusting crane stood its ground amongst the weeds and dereliction. "I know this place, Arthur, only there is something missing."

"It hasn't been used in years," Arthur said, his eyes darting about the dark corners of the yard. His keen senses told him that some kind of danger lurked here, preying on the unwary. "There have been some fancy tales about the old warehouse here," Arthur spoke softly. "Ghost stories and other such superstitious nonsense."

"There is no truth in these stories?" Monkey was unable to hide the fear in his question. He was afraid of nothing tangible, but how do you fight a ghost?

"No, of course not, idiot," laughed Arthur unconvincingly.

"I saw a light in there before," said Monkey, pointing at the stark shell of the old warehouse.

"Rubbish lad, I am telling you, nobody has been in that place for years. It's probably dangerous."

"The *Sally O* will not leave for a while yet. I am guessing they'll wait for first light, with that crew. It has to wait for the tide, whatever direction it plans to take." Monkey had the familiar glint of both fear and excitement in his eyes. "Come on, old friend, where is your sense of adventure? Humour me a little, Arthur. I need to know of this place."

Arthur had borrowed a torch from near the road. He had been happy up until now to manage without light. He had found too often how much unwelcome attention a torch or lantern could bring. The warehouse, however, was a very dark place. A large sturdy door, which had at sometime been badly scorched, barred their way. Monkey tried to use his bulk to force it open, but the door held firm.

"For goodness sake," muttered Arthur, pulling odd bits of metal and wire from a pouch at his waist. A few minutes later, the well-oiled lock clicked loudly and the door was open.

"You are good," admitted the blonde man in admiration. "That lock must have been pretty rusty."

"On the contrary, I think I'm losing my touch," grumbled Arthur. "The lock was well maintained if you must know."

"But I thought you said that nobody had been in here for years?" Monkey set of into the darkness, keen to explore.

Arthur held the torch over the lock. A bonnie finger touched the surface, wiping away a fresh coat of oil. He looked at the finger and frowned. "Yes, I did say that, didn't I?"

The inside was a long low room that stretched a long way into the blackness. The torch struggled to light up much of this gloomy place. Instead, the smoke and flame served mostly to create large patches of dark shadow that danced about the walls and ceiling in a most unnerving manner. Through a doorway they found a narrow stone staircase leading up to the next floor. Like the vast area below, every sound they made reverberated back from the dirty whitewashed walls, echoing across the complex of empty rooms. On this floor the rooms were smaller, although the area vast. Each room led through a small door into the next. Both men were forced to stoop down under the low ceiling. Some of the rooms had open loading bays looking down onto the disused dock below.

"What the hell are we doing here?" whispered Arthur. Whatever danger he had sensed below, he was sure was closer now.

"Shush," hissed Monkey. "Did you hear that?"

"Hear what?" complained Arthur.

Dark shadows passed across Monkey's face, the light from the torch exaggerating his already prominent cheek bones.

"There is something in here with us," whispered Monkey.

"I have been certain of that for a while." Arthur swallowed. "I have a bad feeling about this place, lad. I think we should leave, now."

Something moved in the shadows through one of the small open doorways that led from one room to the next. Then the shadow spoke.

"Hungry," it said. It was like the voice of a lost child. Both men knew it wasn't.

"Hungry," it said again.

Just for a moment, their dying torch lit up the creature. It crouched in the darkest corner, in amongst a pile of bones. It was only small and shrouded in a dark hooded cloak that helped to melt it into the shadows. It appeared to be gnawing on a bone.

"Always hungry," it complained, ripping meat with razor-sharp teeth. Then the creature hissed, opening bright red eyes. Both men backed slowly away. The creature let out a chilling cry and scurried into the darkness. A human head rolled towards the men.

"When I say run," said Arthur calmly. "Run!"

They might have imagined the creature, but not the severed head. Both men had put some distance between them and the warehouse before collapsing in a heap, gasping for breath.

"Do you dismiss such nonsense now, Arthur my friend?"

"Not a word of this, Monkey," snapped his rodent-like companion. "Harry would think it Christmas if he was to hear of our antics tonight."

Despite the warm night, both men were shivering with cold.

Fortunately for them, the beast had already dined well that night.

"Monkey!" shouted Meg.

Monkey looked at her, then across to Arthur. Neither man could rid their minds of the apparition in the warehouse earlier.

"Monkey, this is Captain Jakes. We picked him up in one piece."

"Prudence will be pleased," observed Monkey. He looked up at Captain Jakes, and the smile faded from his face. For a moment, he stared at the captain. Jakes looked completely exhausted by recent events. His face was drawn and the look in his eyes betrayed a man who had at last given up. After so many years of fighting to survive in an unkind and difficult world, there was no fight left in him. Jakes was still quite unsteady on his feet. Meg, dwarfed by the tall sailor, was having difficulty keeping him upright.

Jakes glared at the fat crewman now cowering against the bulwark.

"You have always been a coward as well as a lazy man," Jakes observed bluntly. "Now your actions have destroyed us all." He spoke hoarsely with ill-concealed emotion. "If there is any honour amongst you cutthroats and pirates, which frankly I doubt, you will surely grant me a final wish." He looked sadly at the fat man, whose sly expression had been replaced by one of abject terror. "I am not a violent man, but before I face my own fate, I wish to see this man hanged."

Monkey was still staring at Jakes.

"Are you all right?" Meg asked. She looked at Arthur, who was carefully cleaning his beloved knives. "He ain't been right since you took him to the harbour. What happened, Arthur?"

"We saw a rat or something in the old warehouse, only Harry must have read the boy too many fairy tales when he was little."

"Meg," Monkey interrupted, "take the good Captain Jakes below and find him something to eat and someplace he can get some rest and tidy up his appearance." Monkey turned and smiled at the desolate captain. "Forgive my rudeness, Captain, but I cannot possibly present you to Prudence Fairweather looking like that."

Meg struggled back down the stairs with the weakened Jakes. Arthur observed the difficulty she was having with obvious amusement.

"Arthur," there was an urgency in Monkey's voice, "that man Jakes, have we had dealings with him before?"

Arthur held one of his long knives up to the light from a swaying lamp. "Prudence always said to leave him alone," he answered thoughtfully. "Mind you, I don't think poor old Jakes has much worth the trouble of robbing." The thin-faced scoundrel looked about him. "I mean, take this old tub, let's face it, the decent thing to do would be to scupper her."

"I knew his face, Arthur," said Monkey.

"Well, he is well known around these parts," pointed out Arthur. "He has been coming and going as long as I can remember, and before you remind me, I know that is a very long time."

"No, Arthur," insisted Monkey. "There is a connection between me and this man. I can feel it."

Down below, Meg had found the old captain something to eat. Jakes had been determined to refuse the pirate's food. He was, however, much hungrier than he had thought. In any case, he told himself it was his food in the first place and he was, after all, liberating the food from the pirate scum.

Meg watched him eat through big brown eyes. She sat opposite him, leaning on the table, her chin resting on her hands.

"So what happens next?" asked Jakes through a mouthful of food.

"Frankly, I was thinking of throwing you overboard," confessed Meg with a sweet smile. Jakes almost choked on his food.

"To be honest, Captain Jakes, you smell really bad. You need a bath."

For the first time in ages, Jakes managed a smile. "I suppose I do stink a bit," he conceded.

"A bit." Meg laughed. "I would hate to be near you when you smell a lot, Captain."

They lapsed into silence. Meg had explained they would be dropping the cargo somewhere safe before heading for the pirate islands.

"Will they grant me my request?" he asked after awhile. "Not that it matters much," he added. "There is one thing bothering me though."

"You have your ship captured by mutineers and then get captured from them by cutthroats and only one thing bothers you, Captain?" Meg was grinning at him.

"The young man with yellow hair," he said. "What do you call him?"

"He is known as Monkey," replied Meg. "He's gorgeous, ain't he! Although he never notices little Meg." She laughed. "I took over from him as ship's boy and that's how he still thinks of me unfortunately." Meg frowned. "Why do you ask?"

"No reason," said the captain. "Just for a moment, I thought he knew me. I, however, have never mixed with vagabonds."

"Until now." Meg laughed. "Now please, can I chuck you in the sea, Captain?"

We had returned in a small boat to a point where we could easily get back to our own even smaller craft. From here, it was only a short journey back to the south island. Before we left the pretty natural harbour and the *Albatross*, Prudence Fairweather had come out to see us. The tall silver-haired pirate, Harry, was by her side.

Prudence looked down at us in the small dinghy from the deck of the *Black Albatross*. She was dressed in black, her dark curls blowing about her face in the gentle breeze.

"My people have taken the *Sally O*, gentlemen," she called down to us. "We lost nobody. Captain Jakes is well, although sadly many of his small but mutinous crew perished." She smiled and turned to go. "My advice to you both is still to go home. I might even arrange for Captain

Jakes to take you. I am sure Miss Groves must deeply regret her decision, Mr Anders. If not, then she must be a truly stupid woman."

She turned and came back to the edge of the deck. "If you are to find yourself a wife, Mr Anders, maybe in the future you should fight for your love and not run off on some foolhardy adventure such as this. I am quite certain Miss Groves would have admired you for that." She smiled and looked at Sydney. "Oh and the good and respectable womenfolk of Heffen would sleep better in their beds in the knowledge that Sydney had gone home, or at least their husbands would."

"If I could beg one favour of you, madam," I shouted up, "can the lad here not stay with you and enjoy his freedom?"

Harry stepped forward. "If I may, Prudence." He looked questioningly at her.

"Of course, Harry," answered the girl dismissively.

"I did offer young Odi the opportunity you speak of, Mr Anders," Harry assured me.

"He is a man though," interrupted Prudence, leaning over the side and glaring at the nervous child.

"He wanted to stay with you," added Harry in the way of explanation.

"He obviously believes, as I do, that you have a slightly better hope of continuing to breathe with a small child to look after you," concluded Prudence.

Our small vessel was now pulling away from the *Albatross*.

"Try not to be sick this time, Thomas Anders!" she shouted after us.

I was already feeling queasy.

Professor Kidner sat behind the desk in his untidy office. The unfortunate piece of furniture was, as always, piled high with parchments and papers. Behind him, the somewhat scorched portrait of the pirate Prudence Fairweather still hung proud, if slightly askew, above the fireplace. The gold leaf frame had been badly charred in places, but there was little damage to the painting itself. The flames had fortunately been unable to diminish the beauty of its subject.

Kidner looked truly awful, like a man who had not slept for days, who had reached out and touched Beelzebub himself. He sat shivering in the musty heat of the book-lined office, still filled with the overwhelming smell of smoke and the vile stench of something much worse. Only the flickering light of a single candle that sat on the desk in front of him illuminated the room. Now and again, terrified eyes would search the shadows in case the thing had returned, or worse, remained hidden in the darkness, watching his every move.

His poor eyesight made it even easier to see all manners of shapes moving in the shadows that pranced around the bookshelves.

"Yes, it likes the darkness," moaned Kidner to the empty room. "Always hides in the dark."

At last he went over to a small cupboard beneath the books. With a long tarnished brass key, he unlocked the door and opened it. From inside he took out a worn leather case and, returning to the light on his desk, shakily removed the contents. Pushing his broken glasses onto his face, Kidner held the candle so close to the ancient parchment that hot wax dripped onto the fragile paper. The parchment had yellowed with age, and like the painting of Prudence Fairweather, there were scorch marks around the edges, as if someone had tried to burn it before.

The writing was still surprisingly clear. Each page contained a depth of information relating to Gabrielle's Fault and how it could be destroyed. There were drawings and detailed charts. There were pages of meticulously detailed instruction, such as where exactly to lay the charges. A full account of the colossal quantity of explosives required was also included. It was also clear that without this vital information, any attempt to destroy the Fault would most likely be extremely counterproductive. It was, however, the final page that froze Kidner's soul.

If these rough scribblings of mine have been found, then it can be for only one reason. That I, Francis Gabrielle, have failed in my duty to destroy the

Apprentice, no doubt outwitted like the rest by his dangerous and devious guardian angel. I beg the reader to believe my rantings. No man can see what I have seen these past days and still remain completely sane.

What I still know for sure, whatever state of madness might have overcome me, is that the future of our world now depends upon you, dear reader. The Fault must be destroyed. Only I ever knew how to do that. I pass this knowledge to you. Even now perhaps, many years after my time on this earth, I can still help defeat this creature and save our world. Perhaps in the end the guardian was not as clever as it thought.

I pray my notes are in safe hands.

Signed,
Francis Gabrielle, adventurer and privateer

"If I burn you," sobbed Kidner, "I fear that it is not just an old piece of parchment I burn. The consequences of my stupidity are too terrible to think of." He began to shiver violently again. "Is it so bad that I am afraid?" he argued angrily with himself and with his God. "Everybody knows the prophecies are nonsense, superstitious poppycock. Why should I suffer so much pain for some foolish, some pathetically childish superstition?"

He began to sob again, so that now tears mixed with the candle wax, dripping onto the ancient scrolls.

"Why me!" he screamed. "What did I do that was so terrible? Tell me, God, wherever you're hiding. I mean, you always hide just when you're needed, don't you? Why should I be the one who destroys the world?"

The tall thin man wiped his face and shakily rubbed his broken spectacles with a filthy handkerchief.

"No, Francis Gabrielle, I'm afraid Efulric's guardian angel was every bit as clever as you thought it was."

Professor Kidner pushed the parchment awkwardly into the candle's flame and watched it begin to burn.

Philip Baldock, his uniform in tatters, his shoulder roughly bandaged, sat at the bar of one of Heffen's seediest establishments. An old woman with a pot-marked and rather purple face, dressed in the refinery of a woman half her age, had been offering the major her services most of the night. Baldock was so drunk he had almost excepted.

"You never know what you'd catch off that one," said a man at the next table. "Come to think of it, actually I do, 'cause I caught it. 'Twas nearly the death of me."

Baldock tried to ignore the intrusion. He had come to this hovel because he wanted to be alone. He would never have expected to meet with anyone of his acquaintance in this hellhole. Yet the man who spoke had a familiar look about him.

"Can I join you, Major?" asked the intruder.

Baldock eyed the man coldly. This was a man who had the ability to look good even when anyone else in his situation would look very bad. He wore expensively tailored clothes; however, they were old, faded and a little travel stained. His hair was still dark and worn in a ponytail, but with the unwelcome addition of quite a few grey hairs. It was also clearly receding and had been combed in a peculiar manner in an attempt to disguise this fact. The deception had not worked. If anything, it had the opposite effect.

"Go away, I am busy," lied Baldock firmly.

"You don't look busy, friend," insisted the man. "You don't remember me, do you?"

"Forgive my candour, sir," replied Baldock drunkenly, wincing at the pain in his shoulder, "but no, I don't."

"Then let me reacquaint myself, my good Captain Baldock. The name is Jessop, Henry Jessop."

Richard Boscastle lived alone, as a recluse, in what had once been amongst the grandest of the many ranch houses on the northern island. Over the years it had been allowed to fall into little more than a ruin. Despite his enormous wealth, Boscastle had few servants and none that lived in.

The truth was, he no longer trusted anyone. The old man's obsession with security was borne out of an equal passion for owning beautiful things. His consuming fear was that somebody might steal them from him. Most nights he would wake in a cold sweat, convinced that thieves had taken everything. He would not be able to sleep until he had checked that nothing had been touched.

The land on which his home stood was liberally covered in traps. Many of these lethal surprises he had learnt from different parts of the world during his years of travelling. If a visitor should wander away from the main approach road to the Boscastle ranch, then they could spring a variety of different traps, all with similarly fatal result. It could be a spear in the chest, a barrage of poison-coated arrows in the back. Or perhaps the victim could just be left dangling by a rope to starve, or as food for the wild and sometimes rather unusual animals that inhabited this part of the jungle.

Most locals believed that Patricia Boscastle was planning to leave her husband before she was murdered. They also believed that Boscatle himself had killed her, rather than let her go. The then young Captain Baldock had collected together certain proof that this was what had happened. Baldock had been shocked at his discovery. Boscastle had never struck him as a bad man. True, he was a little overzealous in the protection of his land and his possessions. He was, however, a good employer, known for his kindness and generosity to his workers.

Nevertheless, Baldock knew Boscastle must be arrested, tried and when found guilty, as there was no doubt he would be, hung for his terrible crime. It was only after Baldock had arrested Boscastle that the new governor Silas Raines had intervened. Somehow, he had managed to persuade the honourable young captain that it would serve no good purpose to have this popular man tried and hung.

He argued that, in fact, such an action could prove to be greatly damaging to the colony of Heffen. There were a number of important trade agreements under negotiation at that time and a scandal on the island could damage these irrevocably. It was just as easy to blame the pirates. Baldock had done much worse. So why not turn a blind eye to Boscastle's terrible crime? He even began to believe the killer could have been the rat-faced cutthroat he had found by the body. That was what he wanted to believe. In his heart, Baldock knew this was not true.

So it became increasingly difficult to forget that his promotion and generally improved circumstances were as a result of his cooperation. To make his feeling of guilt and remorse even worse, it also transpired that one of the major trade deals under negotiation was with the infamous Sir John Burleigh.

The death of his young wife seemed more than Boscastle could bare. Always a private man, he now rarely left the ranch except to make occasional visits to the palace. Boscastle always attended the annual ball, at the governor's insistence. As he became older and more infirm, even his visits to the palace became fewer, although it was understood he would always put in an appearance at the biggest event in the Heffen calendar.

Boscastle sat in the window of his living room, staring out into the wilderness and the jungle beyond. He sat in a bath chair with a pistol resting on his lap. He sat always in a room, so filled with lamps and candles that it became so dazzlingly bright, it was painful to the eyes. The walls had all been whitewashed and anything not essential that could create a shadow had been removed from the room. Torches burnt everywhere in the clearing outside. Richard Boscastle had better reason than most to be afraid of the dark.

Victoria noticed Joshua first. Naturally, this claim was the subject of some heated argument with her brother later. Rupert insisted that he had seen the giant before his sister. In truth, on a fine clear morning, the massive pirate was not difficult to spot. Mrs Moffat had let them accompany her into town. In the absence of Odi, Mr Simms had opted to drive them himself.

The road was dusty and the ground dry. It had not rained on Heffen for some weeks, as was normal at this time of the year. When the rains eventually hit the islands, much of the highway closer to the town would become impassable.

"We are being followed," Victoria informed everyone calmly.

"Nonsense, dear," scolded Mrs Moffat. She tried to brush the dust from her best frock, which she wore only for trips into town. "With Mr Anders away exploring, they don't know what to do with themselves, Mr Simms."

"The young gentleman does seem to have made quite an impact on the children, Mrs Moffat," conceded Mr Simms. He was impeccably dressed in grey and black as always.

"We are being followed," insisted the girl. "And it's one of Prudence Fairweather's pirates," she added. Rupert's face had drained of all colour.

"Will you stop frightening the boy, you wicked little madam," admonished Mrs Moffat, glaring sternly at them both. "I do hope Mr Anders and his friend will be all right, Mr Simms. I mean, they are not used to jungles and such like, and the guides can be so unreliable."

Mr Simms smiled. "That is why I spared Odi from his duties, Mrs Moffat, to look after them." He paused to negotiate the carriage round a tight bend that dropped steeply down towards the old town. Here the children were afforded a panoramic view of Heffen Harbour, the old town and the newer settlements scattered around the harbour. "And," he added, as the carriage bounced over a particularly large pothole, "some other friends of mine have promised to keep an eye on them too."

"It's the giant," persisted Victoria stubbornly. "The black man with very big teeth."

"Perhaps he is going to eat us," said Rupert nervously.

"You would need cooking slowly, for a very long time, if the meat was to turn out anything like tender enough," pointed out Mrs Moffat unsympathetically. Apparently this was an attempt to reassure the small boy.

"A stew perhaps," suggested Mr Simms, laughing, "with plenty of carrots and dumplings."

"I think his name is Joshua," said Victoria. "And actually, he has very sharp teeth."

Rupert swallowed hard.

Dusty and dirty from our journey, Sydney and I entered Mrs Moffat's kitchen through the gardens. The governor was lovingly tending to his roses. The little man was, as always, smartly dressed. Well-tailored grey pants set off a royal blue velvet waistcoat, from which, on seeing our approach, he pulled out a large gold fob watch, an action as always borne more out of habit than from a need to know the time. He glared at us through his monocled eye.

"You are a little late, Mr Anders." He glared at Sydney. "And who is our unexpected guest here?" he asked with a pretence of sincerity and a humourless smile. Silas Raines was not an ugly man. In his own way, he might once have even been considered handsome. He was certainly an imposing man, despite being short in stature. His blue-grey hair was cut quite short and heavily oiled back onto his square head. There was still a distinct trace of red left in it. The little man's problem was that the more he tried to look sincere, the more insincere he actually looked.

I have noticed that, for some peculiar reason, people like this often seem to become politicians. What confounds logic even more is that they also seem to do well, despite an extraordinary inability to tell or even recognise the truth.

"This is my friend and companion Sydney Greenburgh, sir," I said. "He has accompanied me from England and came with me to have a look at the rain forests."

"I heard you had been exploring, Mr Anders," said the governor carefully, letting his monocle drop. "Of course, the jungles at this end contain nothing like the dangers farther into the island." He shoved his fob watch back into his waistcoat pocket. "You are a writer, are you not, Mr Anders?"

"I have written a number of simple works to aid the study of our planet's history and geography, sir. As there is little money in that, I mostly teach."

"And I am hearing good account of your work with my wards, sir. I am most gratified at the effect your teaching is already having on the children," he beamed, although I was not sure he meant a single word of what he had just said. "Now you have seen one of our rain forests for yourselves, it might be best not to stray too far from civilisation. Heffen may look like paradise to you, but it can be a very dangerous place, gentlemen."

The governor picked a single deep yellow rose and put it to his nose.

"Beautiful, is it not?" He looked at us with a fire burning in his eyes. "I love my roses, you know. Although, as a matter of fact, I think I prefer gold to be honest. Gold continues to glitter forever, you see. Doesn't wither and die on you like a rose does." He crushed the rose in his hand, at least one thorn penetrating his skin, blood welling up through his long fingers. "The prettiest things can sometimes be very dangerous," he added, holding out a handful of blood-stained petals. "Be particularly careful you are not seduced by such danger, Mr Anders, or your friend here."

He turned to walk down the pathway that led to his study. Sydney and I watched him go.

"Creepy or what?" whispered Sydney.

"Gold may not die," I mumbled under my breath, "but it can easily lose its shine and become dull and unattractive."

"Oh, Mr Anders, I forgot." The governor stopped and walked just a yard or so back towards us. I wasn't sure if he had overheard my remark or not. I hoped he hadn't.

"The palace has an annual grand ball, the most prestigious event in our social calendar," he said. "Your friend and companion is most welcome to an invitation."

"You're very kind, sir," said Sydney.

The governor bowed with surprising grace. "It was a pleasure meeting you, Mr Greenburgh," he said. He bowed slightly to me. "Keep up the good work, Mr Anders." With that, the governor disappeared into his office.

The children were without doubt pleased to see me. They also took an immediate liking to Sydney, although Victoria later told me in a very grown-up way that I should be careful. She thought Mr Greenburgh was very nice but could get me into trouble.

Sydney enjoyed the children too. He has never grown up, and if it means taking responsibility for his own actions, probably never will. To be fair to Sydney, I probably haven't grown up either. I work in the same environment as I did when a schoolboy, and have always enjoyed reading and writing more than most other activities.

The children told me about Joshua. I could have tried to explain that Joshua was there as a friend and not as a potential assassin. This would have become very complicated. I would have had to explain that whilst Joseph was no threat, there was somebody who did want to kill Rupert. It seemed much worse to have an unseen enemy who could strike at any time. I was not sure that telling the children about Prudence Fairweather was a good idea either.

I had gained their confidence and, in view of the present circumstance, did not wish to lose that hard-won trust. Sydney agreed, although I felt very uncomfortable. In a strange sort of way it felt like I was betraying the trust I had worked so hard to gain.

I watched the two of them leap on Sydney, who had been dressed up as a pirate, complete with a patch over one eye. He was giving a good account of himself with a few shouts of, "Belay there, you land lubbers," or there would be a cry of, "Shiver me yard arm." In the end, the pirate and his eye patch succumbed to the supremacy of the good guys, as he disappeared under the victorious children. The whole battle took place with a good deal of laughter and merriment.

"It's good to hear the kiddies laughing, Mr Anders." Mrs Moffat was polishing the silver.

"Yes, it is," I agreed. "I thought the governor liked gold," I said. I picked up a fine silver fruit bowl to examine.

"Gold would be his favourite, Mr Anders," she agreed, "but he likes anything that cost him lots of money."

Sydney staggered in, his clothes all dishevelled and grass stained, his hair a mess. The eye patch was still firmly in place.

"Don't you think the old eye patch adds a certain sense of mystery, Mrs Moffat?" He was standing admiring himself in the mirror. I looked at Mrs Moffat and she looked at me, and we burst into laughter.

"You are right, Mr Anders, so you are, that man is incorrigible," chuckled the housekeeper.

"Perhaps not then," said Sydney to the mirror rather than us. He sounded quite offended.

"Oh come now, Mr Greenburgh," scolded Mrs Moffat. "Please don't take on. I haven't laughed like this in years." She wiped the tears from her face and added, "And it does you good to laugh a bit, doesn't it?"

Baldock had sobered up a little.

"You vanished, Jessop, without trace," he pointed out gloomily.

Henry Jessop smiled. "I thought the old fool would come after me next. So I took the next ship out of Heffen," he explained.

"You were probably the last person, apart from the killer, to see Patricia Boscastle alive," pointed out the major, concentrating hard on not slurring his words.

Jessop called over the dirty and disreputable barman. He was a revoltingly grubby man in a filthy apron. The garment was stained with beer, food, general grime and what looked like dried blood, amongst other things. The man was well suited to his gloomy smoke-filled surroundings.

"Another drink for me and my old friend the captain," called Jessop.

"Actually, I am a major now," Baldock corrected him.

"You can have one more, then you get your soldier friend out of here," said the barman, slamming two tankards of foul foaming ale onto the table. "He's bad for business."

"Haven't you done well for yourself, Major Baldock." He passed him his drink and raised his own tankard. "Cheers," he said. "How's Mia by the way?"

"Mia?" Baldock looked confused. "But you don't even know my wife, Jessop, so why would you care?"

"I heard she was very beautiful, that's all, and the spitting image of your long-lost love. Is that true?"

"Mia and I are very happy. I love her very much. We have three girls you know. Anyway, you ran away, Jessop."

"Yes, I suppose I did run away, but I couldn't claim diplomatic immunity from that madman, now could I, Baldock?" Jessop was looking at his own drink as if trying to work out how anything could taste so awful. "Any idea what's floating in this?" He looked up at Baldock, who shrugged his broad shoulders in reply. "Being in the diplomatic corps," Jessop continued, "means I have travelled a good deal. I could not very well refuse when they decided to send me back to Heffen. In any case, it's a chance to look up old friends."

Baldock's tired and bruised face was mostly in shadow. The few lamps still intact after the most recent brawl were not anywhere near sufficient to light up the hovel.

"As I recall, you had no friends, Jessop," he said dryly. "Anyway, when did you arrive?"

"On the *Wild Swan*."

Baldock looked surprised. "That docked ages ago."

Jessop leaned forward in his chair. "I wanted to check things out before I announced I was back," he explained. "Actually, Baldock, I would prefer it if you didn't mention you had seen me just yet."

Baldock sat back in his chair. "You're not this new government agent hunter I hear talk about, Jessop?"

Jessop laughed so loudly that the few other customers in the filthy place looked at them. The painted old lady, Boscastle noticed, had picked up a very young, but not so able seaman.

"As if I would tell you if I was a spy or an assassin, Baldock," Jessop pointed out, laughing

"I really must be going home." The major rose unsteadily from the table. "Mia does not know where I am and she will be worried."

"Does she really look the same?"

"Frankly, if you must know, Jessop, I had forgotten."

"Sure, you can find your way, Captain, whoops sorry, I mean, Major." Henry Jessop smiled. "I would offer to see you safely home, only I heard the governor bought you a nice new house." He raised one eyebrow, looking quizzically at the soldier. The two men stood staring at each other, Baldock swaying slightly, side to side. Jessop was slightly shorter than the soldier was, or it might have been that he had let himself go a bit over the years. He stood slightly stooped with rounded shoulders and an expanding girth. His face was still slim and handsome.

"I also heard it was a very big house," he went on. "So you shouldn't have too much difficulty finding it."

Baldock leaned forward towards Jessop. He spoke in a loud whisper that could be heard by anybody in the tavern who wished to listen. "Do you understand this evil that is possessing our island, Jessop?" he demanded.

"Should I?" said Jessop. "I can feel it all right, Baldock, like you can. Don't know that I understand though. It's just like it was ten years ago."

Baldock's eyes narrowed and his lips pursed. The entire colour had drained from his face. "I should have ended it then." Baldock was talking more to himself than Jessop. "And you are wrong, Jessop, this is nothing like ten years ago. This time, it is infinitely more powerful than before."

Jessop emptied his tankard onto the muddy floor. "Baldock," he said, "it's a shame you didn't, if indeed you could have. I doubt you could have stopped it then and I'm absolutely certain nobody can stop it now."

Chapter 8

I had received another letter from Mama. It had clearly been written before my reply to their last letter had reached home. It contained the usual details on how to survive. These included many warnings about Sydney's unreliability. There was a section on insect bites, running into a section on the importance of eating plenty of greens and a reminder to always boil water before drinking it.

There was a long section on family news. Father had his old problem back. She did not say which one, but I suspected gout. I was, I am ashamed to admit, delighted at the news that Simon Fallow had been caught by Mistress Anna in an extremely compromising situation with the choirmaster's younger daughter. Charlotte Chambers, as Mama pointed out, was well known to be free with her favours.

All my brothers and sisters were doing well, including Joseph, who according to his last letter home had found a giant footprint not far from the campsite. A footprint which could well have been made by a hairy mammoth. Mama ended by pointing out that if Joseph could get letters all the way from an African jungle, the least I could do was to write home once in awhile!

Captain Jakes was not quite sure how he felt. The *Sally O* had navigated the reef. The young man with spiky yellow hair knew the waters very well. The *Sally O* raced along in the strong breeze, frequently changing course to avoid the razor-sharp rocks. These were mostly hidden well, just below the surface.

The great mountain of rock, Niridia, dominated the scene at the entrance to the reef. The volcano seemed to have gone quiet again for now. A wisp of telltale grey smoke drifting from the top was, however, a salutary reminder that the huge volcano was only resting.

Gabrielle's Reef started very close to the rock, but extended a long way beyond. The clear blue water was very deceptive. Many a ship had come to grief there. The water, so deep at that point, had no trouble in devouring ships whole. Many wrecks lay far below the surface on the seabed. The mortal remains of many sailors also found their last resting place in the murky depths.

The secret of navigating the reef was known to very few. One of those few who had been privileged to have the knowledge passed to them was Jakes himself. However, he was sure he could never remember enough to safely navigate the reef.

Beyond the rock, despite the warm hot day, the strange mist hung above the Fault. Now and again the mist would swell, begin to spread and envelop the whole channel, including the tip of the northern island. That day, only the slightest trace of the deadly sea mist was visible.

A small group of tiny islands, protected from the outside world by the reef, formed the pirate's home. Ships that Jakes had thought long sunk were moored outside the large natural harbour formed between three of the larger islands. All the islands had beautiful golden beaches and were rich in lush green vegetation. The *Sally O* stayed on course to another cluster of little islands, where the freed slaves were unloaded into waiting boats.

"Some will find their way home," Meg told Jessop. "Others will decide to settle here. The important thing is it's their choice, right?"

"There looks to be quite a community," observed the old captain.

"We are unable to do much," said Meg sadly. She rested her chin on the bulwark rails. "The compounds are too well guarded, and once out at sea, the big freighters are bloody difficulty to take."

"Unlike my old bucket," Jakes smiled sadly.

Once unloading was complete, Monkey put the *Sally O* about and brought her into the main harbour. She was overshadowed by many of the other craft birthed here. The *Queen Anne* was a fine three-mast brig. There was a fine fully armed warship, cannons polished and ready. By no means the largest vessel, but easily the most infamous, was the venerable *Black Albatross*. The old ship was maintained and painted to the highest standards by local craftsmen. Beautiful though she was, this was the ship any honest sailor dreaded sighting in these waters.

Jakes was taken ashore in a cream rowing boat, along with the sly fat man. He spent the short journey to shore trying to explain to Jakes that Burleigh had forced him to lead the mutiny. Jakes grimly ignored the whining little man. Some of the pretty local girls watched the party land on the golden sand. The old captain had always understood how easily men from the west fell for these heavenly creatures. Perhaps he would have done so, too, had he not already lost his heart.

The buildings that made up the settlement were set a short way back from the beach. Built in a variety of styles and materials, there were quite a few substantial-looking buildings. On closer inspection, some were little more than grass huts. Wood was also a popular source of material, whilst a few of the structures were built entirely of stone. All the construction had been cleverly designed to blend in with the hillside on which it had been built. It was, Jakes thought, the closest he had come to a real paradise. Even the fat waddling mutineer seemed bewildered by his surroundings.

Most of the buildings, whatever they had been constructed from, were of similar size. High up in the centre, however, was a larger building. This reminded Jakes of a small castle keep. The central part was of stone, but much of the rest was built of traditional local materials. A sizeable part of it seemed to have been carved out of the reddish-brown rock face behind.

The pathway to the entrance was paved in red and lined with tall palms. The captain of the *Sally O* followed the others into the central part of the building. The hallway was very plain and surprisingly cool.

Jakes was left in a simple and sparsely furnished room with whitewashed walls. There was just a simple wooden table and two chairs. The fat mutineer had been taken away, protesting loudly to deaf ears. A little while later, Meg brought Jakes some refreshment.

"Prudence won't be too long," she said.

"I wonder if perhaps you would spare me some paper, a pen and some ink. I feel I should put my affairs in order. I have nothing left, now you have taken my ship you understand, but there are things unsaid that need saying."

Meg nodded and returned quickly with the required items. Once he was alone again, Jakes began to scratch away on the paper. He was not sure quite what he wanted to say. He would soon be facing the pirate who many years ago had murdered his partner. There was a large scar on his arm to remind him just how hot the fire had been.

If I could just see you one more time, he wrote. *Hold you in my arms like I used to do.*

Once again, as it had done so many times before, his mind drifted back to that dreadful night. The same question Jakes had been asking himself for little short of ten years was nagging at his brain again. Was it just the heat from the fire that had held him back?

Could he truly blame a slip of a girl? Even if that girl was Prudence Fairweather? She was little more than a child back then, a child who had witnessed the brutal massacre of her family. Had she really stopped Jakes, or had it been because he wanted Benjamin to die so much?

It was the blond lad Monkey who came to get him.

"You sailed my ship well," said Jakes, studying the boy carefully.

"She handles much better than she looks," acknowledged Monkey. He was looking at the old captain in a strange way. "And she has a familiar feel to me. I felt I had sailed her many times before. She could do with a little love."

"Couldn't we all," said Jakes.

"Forgive me," Monkey said at last, "have we met before?"

"I confess I wondered that myself," acknowledged Jakes.

"I came to tell you that Prudence Fairweather would like to see you now."

Heffen Library was bathed in the hot evening sunshine. The closeness of the heat was oppressive, a strong indication that the storms that herald the start of the rainy season were on their way. For now there were just a couple of white cotton-wool clouds floating in a perfect blue sky.

Inside the great circular hall, the naked slave boys ran up and down the precarious walkways, fetching papers and heavy leather-bound volumes for the students to examine. As always, the tall thin figure of Professor Kidner, still tiny in relation to the cathedral-like surroundings of the great hall, was directing operations. He did, however, seem a little vague with his instructions and was uncharacteristically short-tempered with the young lads, who came to the library for a small taste of freedom.

The students sat, heads down, studying the books and manuscripts they had sent for. From time to time, they would call over Kidner or one of the boys and hand a slip of paper on which the name of the next required work was scribed. Kidner had been greatly criticised by some for teaching slave children to read and write. Sir John Burleigh, for example, described it as a foolhardy and dangerous practice promoted by misguided modernists.

The students who came to Heffen Library were from widely different backgrounds. There was an Oriental gentleman clothed in the most beautiful hand-embroidered silk robe. Near to where he sat were a group of monks in shabby brown habits who, by the size of their ample girths, were not at present fasting. There was a man in a turban who looked very important and appeared to have a small posse of bodyguards to protect him.

From the western world, there was an ageing French military man and a middle-aged, grey-haired lady with harsh features and wire-framed spectacles. I recognised the young student types from my own years of study. Most of these had made the journey to Heffen, not to fall in love with the beautiful island, or the beautiful Heffen women, but to spend their days in this vast library. Here they devoured as much knowledge as they could in the time that they had available.

One of these people caught my eye in particular. In more normal surroundings, I am sure I would have not been aware of the existence of this bizarre little man. Clothed in grey pinstriped breaches and a black tailcoat, he sat at one of the tables reading a slim volume. A bowler hat sat on the table next to him.

Professor Kidner welcomed us nervously. It was hard to see the look in his eyes behind bottle-glass spectacles, but I was sure I would find fear there. Odi sensed it too.

"What is the matter with the professor, Mr Anders, sir?" he asked me. "It is like he is scared about something."

I was about to agree when Kidner walked into his office. He had sent us there to wait for him. Rupert was caught red-handed rummaging through some of the papers on the librarian's desk.

"Stop that, boy," snapped Kidner angrily, quite out of character for the normally gentle and kind-natured man. He looked at me and immediately began to mumble apologies for his sudden outburst.

"Please forgive me," he said. "I fear I have been working far too late this last few days." He pulled off his spectacles and polished them with a grubby handkerchief in which he had tied a number of knots. "Please forgive my rudeness, children. It is merely the ranting of a silly old professor and you should take no notice of him."

Victoria curtsied politely. Kidner looked at Odi. "And where have you been, young man? I have greatly missed your assistance here."

"I've had to look after my friends, Professor," explained the boy. "They have pirates trying to kill them."

"Is that true?" asked Kidner, sounding surprised.

"Very close to the truth," I agreed.

We told the professor of our encounter with the pirates on the lake. Rupert and Victoria then went on to tell an exaggerated version of being followed into town by a pirate, as well as describing the defeat in battle of the infamous privateer Sydney Greenburgh. Odi was about to say something about our stay on the *Black Albatross*, so I kicked him hard on the shin.

"Ouch, Mr Anders, sir," he complained. "I thought you didn't believe in beating your slaves."

"You are not my slave, Odi," I pointed out with a warning smile.

"So that makes it all right?" demanded the boy, hopping around the office on one leg in an effort to exaggerate the pain.

"Well, what can I do for you today, my friends?" pressed Kidner. He was oblivious to the boy's acrobatic performance. He had interrupted tales of pirates with the occasional "oh dear" or "how terrible." In truth, he was not really listening.

"Odi is going to keep an eye on the children whist I do a bit of research," I said, "as we agreed the other day. I recall you being quite keen for me to assist in this way."

Kidner stared at me for a moment, his exaggerated eyes blinking in what seemed to be some inner confusion.

"Yes, of course," he said at last. "Odi can find anything you might need. Frankly, he knows where things are better than I do now in this place.

"There was just one thing we might need you to find, Professor." My words stopped him as he scurried towards the door. "You said you had some original manuscripts by the pirate Gabrielle," I reminded him. "I think we can learn much about Heffen from them."

"Original manuscripts you say," said the professor vacantly. "Work in the pirate's own hand is very rare indeed. In fact, I only know of the one." Before Kidner could say any more, Rupert interrupted him.

"Somebody's tried to burn Prudence Fairweather." His voice was trembling as a small hand reached out to touch the charred frame.

I am not quite sure how I had failed to notice the damage to the painting. The fine portrait of Prudence itself had largely escaped any harm; however, there was some damage. The picture was burnt at the edges and part of the frame more badly damaged.

"It was an accident with an oil lamp," explained Kidner hurriedly, answering the question on everybody's lips. "Extremely careless of me," he babbled on. "It serves as a warning, children, as to just how dangerous and unforgiving fire can be."

I was not, of course, aware at that point what had really caused the damage. It was possible I supposed that an oil lamp or candle placed on the mantle shelf of the grand fire surround could have caused such a fire. I doubted in my mind that this was the true cause. I was convinced that Professor Kidner was in some kind of serious trouble. He turned to leave the room again. "Gabrielle's writings," I reminded him.

"You will find some, I mean most of them in one of the piles on the table, or on the floor near the fireplace," he answered. "Or are they in this pile?" He began to search through a mountain of papers almost as tall as himself, discarding unwanted parchments in all directions in his frantic search.

"Was there any part you wished to examine in particular, Mr Anders?" he enquired. He pulled off his glasses and shoved another paper close to his nose in an effort to identify the contents. Satisfied it was of no interest, he flung it to one side and scooped up a few more.

"Although I do have much of a scientific brain, Professor," I admitted. "I was most intrigued with the details of the Fault and Gabrielle's theory about its destruction."

Professor Kidner stared at me again. For a moment, he visibly shook. With tremendous inward effort, Kidner brought himself back under control.

"That's a strange thing, Mr Anders," he said, wiping sweat from his face with the same dirty linen handkerchief. "I have already looked everywhere for that and I am afraid it's gone. It is a tragedy, of course," continued Kidner. "I lost some papers in the fire and I regret to say the ones you speak of were definitely amongst them. Unfortunately, there is no doubt about that."

Before I could question him further on the matter, the professor had gone.

"I do not believe this," I said more to myself than the three children. "If one paper had ignited then this whole room would have been a ball of flames within seconds." I was looking at the piles of tinder-dry parchment around me as I spoke.

"Do you think this could be something?" Victoria held out an old plate on which there was a pile of ashes. "I found it on the desk."

"Yes," I said grimly, poking at the ashes of what I guessed to be three or maybe four rolled parchments. "I am afraid the professor was at least half right. It looks to me as if the parchment I most wanted to examine has been deliberately destroyed." I paused for a moment. Even the children seemed to sense that from this simple act could come something unthinkably dreadful.

"If it is true," I said, as I continued to examine the ashes in the vain hope something had survived, "then judging by his extremely odd behaviour, it is only logical to conclude that Professor Kidner must know who did this."

The tall pirate wore tight black leather pants hung low on her hips. On the top half she had an equally figure-hugging plain leather bodice. A broad belt studded in silver hung low around her bare navel, from which she carried a sword and a long slightly curved dagger. Her shiny auburn hair fell in a tangle of curls onto her smooth olive-skinned shoulders. High boots in soft animal hide completed the awe-inspiring sight that Captain Jakes was met with on entering the council room. In contrast, despite all Meg's efforts to clean the big sailor up, his old uniform was even more travel stained and thread bare than before.

Prudence was perched on a high desk at the far end of the room that contained little more than a long roughly hewn wooden table and a dozen or so high-backed chairs. Apart from a small window, the only relief to the room was a painting of a big, jolly man beaming out of the canvas through a set of thick bushy whiskers.

"My dear father," explained Prudence, noticing the nervous seaman's interest in the picture. "He was murdered," she added softly. "My father, my mother and my brothers, as a matter of fact," the pirate added bluntly. She slipped down from the desk. "Still, that was just over ten years ago now, and anyway, I am sure you don't wish to discuss my problems, Captain Jakes," she observed.

Jakes had heard many stories about how Prudence Fairweather's beauty could take a man's breath away. Now entering his twilight years, Jakes was young enough still to appreciate the truth of those stories. Prudence Fairweather radiated an elegant beauty he had rarely ever seen in all his long years of travel.

"I have given up my last possession to you, madam," he spoke uneasily. "That is having foolishly lost it to them treacherous mutinous dogs." Jakes swallowed hard. "Would it be too much to ask for you to spare my life, madam," he continued, all too conscious of the pirate's sparkling brown eyes fixed on him. "I am no threat to you and I have nothing else for you to steal." Or bargain with, he thought to himself.

"Captain Jakes," said Prudence, perching herself on the table, "I have absolutely no reason, or indeed intention, to cause you harm." Jakes looked surprised at this.

"If you wish you can take your *Sally O* and leave now," went on the pirate, "I can probably even supply you with a crew. One a good deal better than the one you had before." She gave Jakes her sweetest sardonic smile. "I am afraid the fat waddling man will sadly not be able to join you though." Prudence walked to the one small window that looked back towards the beach. "So leave if you wish," she said again. "Of course, you understand, this is not a course of action I would recommend, Captain Jakes. I am prepared to wager a cask of good rum that your mast would not have got you home, even assuming the old tub didn't sink without trace, and that is a big assumption. In short, Captain, your ship needs time for repairs."

Jakes looked at the woman. He was not sure if he fully understood what she was saying. He had not expected this.

"You look surprised, old man." Prudence's face creased into a frown. "It seems that everybody thinks I want to kill them at the moment and they're all wrong." She paused, examining her fingernails carefully. "Well, except for the fat waddling man. I suppose he wasn't wrong, but hey, nobody's perfect." She smiled at Jakes. "Not even me, Captain," she added with a flutter of her eyes.

"You killed my partner," pointed out Jakes. Almost at once he regretted he had said that. "Although I don't suppose you remember, what with all the killing you do. Anyway, it was a long time ago." Jakes looked uncomfortable. "We had a boatyard at Heffen, the old dock," he added, as if trying to help her remember.

"All the killing I do when?" demanded Prudence crossly. "Believe me, there are one or two men on Heffen I would like to kill, Captain Jakes. Only for some annoying and inexplicable reason, when I try, they won't die. Your partner, however, was not one of them."

"You do remember then?" put in Jakes awkwardly.

"Of course I remember. I saved your life that night. Not that I have ever had any thanks for it. Got my hair and eyebrows singed, and I still have a scar on my arm to prove it. And you, Captain, don't even write."

"Saved my life?" muttered Jakes in disbelief, tears welling up in his eyes.

"You were going to commit suicide if I hadn't stopped you," insisted Prudence. "To be fair," she conceded grudgingly, "you were trying to get to your friend, but you had no chance, not a hope in hell. The whole place was about to go up. A couple of seconds later and we would both have been ash."

"All these years I thought…." The big and ungainly old sea captain had sat down on one of the chairs and was sobbing.

"That I had killed him?" Prudence finished his sentence for him. Her voice was filled with disbelief. "I confess, I never liked your partner. I found him a pious and self-opinionated man. Never fully understood how you came to be partners either. Why on earth did you think I would want to kill him?"

"I didn't really. He was not only a very religious man but also a cruel one. If you want the honest truth, I hated him. I could have saved him that night, only I didn't. I let him die. You didn't kill my partner, I did."

Then Prudence Fairweather saw the guilt the good Captain Jakes had been carrying all these years. She came and sat in the chair next to him.

"You silly, silly man," Prudence took hold of one of Jakes's huge weatherbeaten hands. "Why would you have ever thought such a thing?" She pulled a sweet-smelling lace handkerchief from her belt and wiped the captain's eyes. Captain Jakes had not had anyone treat him like this for many years.

"He was, as you say, a pious man. Some might call him a Bible basher. He thought of himself as a missionary bringing the word of God to the natives. Nothing wrong with that you might say. However, he began to believe that those who would not join his own particularly unforgiving brand of Christianity should be punished. He wasn't always like that you understand. Something awful happened to him. I have no idea what that was. For a while after he turned to the bottle and then to God."

"I knew some of that already," Prudence spoke softly. "It doesn't explain why you would blame yourself for his death, Captain."

"We had fallen out over a number of things," confessed Jakes. "I don't think I have ever told anyone this before. Also, he had something I wanted."

"What was that?"

"It doesn't matter what," Jakes replied hurriedly. "When I saw him lying there I was thinking to myself, 'You fry, partner, and all my problems are over.'"

"Instead I had to pull you out of the middle of a wall of fire seconds before about a dozen barrels of gunpowder went up." Prudence shivered at the thought of the picture her words had just painted. "And I wouldn't mind," she added, having composed herself. "You fought to get away from me. You are a big man, Captain. I don't think you know your own strength and it was becoming very hot. It is a miracle you didn't break free."

Jakes was looking at the pirate. "You dragged me to safety," he said softly.

"Luckily for you I have big shoulders too." Prudence smiled.

"So why am I here then?" asked the captain.

"You would be surprised how many friends you have," explained Prudence gently. "People who have joined me over the years always speak well of old Jakes and the *Sally O*. Although, if you will forgive my bluntness, Captain, your ship needs a good carpenter and you could do to spend a good deal more time with a paint brush. Continually patching her up just won't do anymore."

"And that's it?" he asked. "Not that I ain't grateful you understand."

"I think, Captain," smiled Prudence Fairweather, "I have just saved your life for the second time. So you probably owe me, wouldn't you say?"

"I can't argue with that," agreed Jakes. "What do you want of me?"

"For now I want you to start getting the *Sally O* back into seaworthy condition, Captain. I may need you and your ship to do something very important for me."

I had found a number of books in the library to be of interest. In particular, I was trying to find out more about the infamous Fault. It quickly became obvious that most serious historians had paid scant regard to Francis Gabrielle's discovery.

Any volume containing a serious study of the Heffen islands made, at best, only passing reference to the Fault. Those that did cover the particular phenomenon described it as a light mist, probably caused by a mixture of unspecified gasses, emanating from the seabed below. Most, however, did not even mention the Fault's existence.

I found only one serious history that actually referred to some of the strange manifestations that had over the years been attributed to Gabrielle's Reef. Even then the writer in fact poked fun at a select few of the better-known myths. He went on to point out that the people of Heffen and the other surrounding islands were a rather primitive race of people and, as a result of this, very superstitious.

He seemed to view the natives from a position of unquestioned superiority. I found this attitude outrageous, although sadly typical of merchants and politicians. This was, after all, a community that had lived in peace and harmony for thousands of years. Since being discovered by our so-called superior and civilised race, peace and harmony had been replaced by repression and violence.

Most of the more serious and detailed references to Gabrielle's Fault were in books like *Myths and Legends of Heffen*, *Ghosts Stories of the Heffen Isles* and *Demons of the Fault*. These books I found to be crammed with stories. Some of these tales I recalled from books I had read in my studies, before we embarked upon this adventure. Others were new to me. Some of these inevitably contradicted other accounts or explanations, as can often be the case when dealing in superstition and folklore.

One common thread in my research into the myths of Heffen was the devil. Much had been written about Satan himself coming through the Fault. There were pictures to support these extraordinary stories. These included some beautifully painted colour plates which mostly depicted the devil in traditional form, with horns and a forked tale. There was one painting I found particularly disturbing.

The devil in this illustration was depicted in a black cloak. The horns were less prominent under a hooded cloak. Large red eyes shone from the twisted face. I could almost sense the pure evil depicted therein. A similar picture in the same book showed a giant version of this devil, whose giant hand loomed over a small flotilla of tiny ships. The creature was looming out of the mist over Gabrielle's Reef.

In one book I found a colour plate depicting the very creature Prudence Fairweather had rescued us from in the forests. Almost every monster possible was credited as having visited Heffen, according to the many authors whose work I studied. It seemed that over two centuries the stories had become more and more fanciful. It was as if each author had set a challenge for the next. Great prehistoric reptiles, dinosaurs, were talked about and illustrated. I found some fascinating pictures. In one large and ancient tome, there was a description of a great sea monster which sounded much like an octopus, only at least twenty times bigger.

Whilst I was studying each of these and many more books, the titles of which I do not recall, Odi kept an eye on the children, as well as fetching and returning material as required.

I must have fallen asleep just for a moment. In my defence, I had just been reading about reports of strange foliage and the writer's extremely complex hypothesis as to why this was normal and not plant life from another dimension. There were many proponents of the other dimension theories.

"You all right, old boy?" Sydney's bouncy tone woke me at once.

"I must have nodded off for a minute," I mumbled, rubbing my eyes.

"Who started the fire!" asked Sydney, studying the picture of Prudence. "You know, you're right, chum. She is a most attractive woman, Mistress Prudence. Pretty darned scary though!"

"So scary you volunteered all my most innermost secrets to her, as I recall." My mouth tasted dry and unpleasant as a result of my short sleep.

"Oh dear." Sydney managed to look a little shocked and very offended all at the same time. "You're not still upset about a few minor indiscretions, old boy, when after all, I just saved your life?" he asked innocently.

"When exactly did you save my life, Sydney?" He could be so very annoying. "Only very remiss of me I know, but for some unfathomable reason, I don't remember that part of our recent adventures. Inexcusable I know, but all I remember is the bit about you telling Prudence almost everything I never wanted her to know. I'm a laughing stock now, Sydney. Any hope I had of being taken seriously by the beautiful pirate dashed to smithereens. I'm angry with you, Sydney, very angry."

"And ungrateful." My tall, smoothly handsome companion looked deeply hurt by my sudden outburst. It wasn't difficult to see how eligible young women fell for Sydney. He had an irresistible boyish charm which I imagined would easily woo the ladies. "We got home in one piece, did we not?" he said sulkily. I suppose he did have a point. Sydney was poking at the fire-damaged frame. I was looking at the painting as I often did.

"This was done quite recently I reckon," he said.

"Well, it was undamaged when the children and I first met the professor here."

Sydney was paying exaggerated attention to me as I spoke. "Not a bad painting I suppose," he said grudgingly.

I fell straight into the trap my companion had set for me. "What to you mean not bad? She's beautiful, Sydney," I protested. "I do not recall ever seeing such beauty and yet such independence, such free spirit."

"Oh no, Thomas, please no." Sydney grabbed hold of me. "I thought it was just another of your silly infantile infatuations, old boy. You can't fall in love with the pirate Prudence Fairweather. I forbid it. You'll get us both killed for sure and Mama will blame me."

"I haven't," I lied. "Sydney, that is a farfetched and ridiculous notion. My dream is of marriage and a pleasant house in Papa's parish. Of church on a Sunday without all the old maiden aunts telling each other loudly that there is something amiss with the minister's youngest."

"That's just it, Thomas. You never really wanted any of the Anna Groves of this world. If you had, well, they wouldn't have all got away, would they? I mean, even you aren't quite that useless. For pity's sake, man, you are not that bad a catch. A nice young lady could do a great deal worse than Thomas Anders." Sydney looked genuinely concerned. "Come to think about it, maybe you are that bad."

"Is it so farfetched to believe that there is some lady in this world who would find such a union favourable? My feelings for Mistress Anna were perfectly honourable."

"Maybe that's your problem," observed my friend. "Anyway, thank goodness you do not have ideas of going to church with the pirate Prudence Fairweather on your arm." Sydney put on a tone of mock relief.

"Prudence Fairweather," I repeated the name dreamily. "I just want to be with her, talk with her, swim naked with her. I want her to be my best friend, no offence, Sydney. I want to have no secrets from her or her from me. I want to share all her problems and she to share mine. I want to lie for hours, holding her in my arms, Sydney. I want to make love and I don't give a damn what all the maiden aunts in the world say about me behind my back."

"My God, Thomas." Sydney swallowed audibly. "You have got it bad, old son. I don't believe you, Thomas. The first time you truly fall for a lady, you choose an infamous, murderous outlaw with a price on her head. That is just great." Sydney started pacing up and down in Kidner's cluttered office, kicking mounds of jumbled parchments and muttering. "It's ironic, Thomas, is it not, that everybody warns you about me," he went on angrily. "If I get my hands on Anderson, I'll ring the bloody idiot's neck, even if it does cost me my job." He did a poor impersonation of his superior. "*If you feel you need a companion, why not take your old school friend, Thomas Anders?*

"Thomas Anders, I say, to the portly old fool, but he never goes anywhere. I like him of course. Jolly good friend and all that, even helped me out of the odd pickle, but in truth he's a little boring, I say. *Well,* Anderson says, stroking his big girth in that irritating way he does, and chuckling like a convulsed mongoose."

"I thought it sounded more like a very smug attack of hiccups."

"Good one, yes. Anyway, where was I?"

"What Anderson said."

"Oh yes, that's right. Anderson says, *You need someone to keep you out of trouble. Who better than the studious and rather dull Mr Anders?*"

"I am not dull, Sydney, or at least I try not to be. You should be pleased. I may have at long last found the woman of my dreams." This was truer than I dare say at this point. "Anyway, I don't understand why you are taking on so, Sydney," I added.

"You don't understand." Sydney had gone red in the face. "If the pirates don't slit our throats for the fun of it, the very unpleasant governor of Heffen will probably hang us with her."

"Who is going to hang us?" Victoria stood in the doorway of Kidner's office. As always, she looked very grown up for a child little more than ten years old.

"Nobody, Victoria, nobody." I put my hands on her shoulders to reassure her and looked into her pretty eyes. "Nobody is going to harm any of us, I promise you. Are they, Sydney?" I glared at him.

"What? No, of course not," he agreed.

"I can't find Rupert anywhere," Victoria said in a matter-of-fact way.

"What!" said Sydney in ill-concealed alarm.

"Something is wrong," said Victoria, fear showing on her pretty face.

"Is he not with Odi?" I asked, not meaning to sound abrupt. I could feel panic welling up inside me. I had been so busy staring at books; I had not paid enough attention to the children.

"Odi is looking for him." Victoria looked like she might burst into tears at any moment. "The pirate lady has got him," she went on, fighting back tears. "I only took my eyes off him for a couple of minutes, Mr Anders, honestly."

"It's not your fault, Victoria my love. We will find him." I ran out into the corridor, shouting back to Sydney not to let Victoria out of his sight. My feet slipping on the polished floor, I hurtled back towards the main hall. I was sure the people in the dark portraits on the wall were following me with their eyes. Skidding through the small doorway into the gargantuan room, I found the great circular library to be almost deserted. With the light outside fading fast, just a few lamps threw out a flickering yellow light across the mosaic floor.

Rupert screamed. It was a terrible cry from a terrified child that echoed round the copper-domed ceiling, ripping through the normally mandatory silence. The sound came from high up on one of the walkways. I ran up the stone stairway without thinking and out onto the thin wooden decking high above the intricately patterned stone floor below. Grabbing an oil lamp, I began to edge myself along the walkway.

Earlier that day, I had marvelled at the agility of the slave boys running up and down the complex network of wooden paths that zigzagged and circled the towering wall of books like some unfathomable mathematical puzzle. Unlike the children, however, I have no head for heights. The walkway creaked and swayed up and down as well as rocking to the sides under my weight. The drop to the ground was a very long way down already. All there was to hold to was a single rope stretched, but not taut, on either side of the long trestle bridges. I was already frozen with fear as I tried my best not to look down into the main hall below.

In the flickering light from the lamp I held up in front of me, I thought I could see Rupert on the swaying deck a few yards ahead of me. Hardly had I stepped out onto the groaning trestles when there was a loud crack and the whole walkway collapsed beneath me, plunging downwards towards the mosaic floor a long way below. I clung to the ropes in sheer terror.

Panic was welling up inside me. My heart was beating out of my chest and I was unable to move, frozen to the spot with fear. It seemed certain that the collapsing platform would plunge into the ornamental floor that was rapidly coming up to meet us. Instead, the broken section lurched against one of the towering bookcases. Had I not been holding on so tight that my hands were bleeding, the sudden end to our descent would have toppled me over the edge. There was the terrible sound of splintering wood. For a moment we continued the slide downwards until the thing became wedged between two very large and dusty old volumes on something connected to mathematical formulas and probabilities.

I wondered, as the walkway tipped precariously to one side, if somewhere in the many pages was a formula to working out the probability of my salvation. I doubted the odds would be particularly good in my favour.

Rupert's terrified scream broke the silence again, but not from in front where I had seen him before. The sound was from far down below. He must have fallen when the walkway collapsed. Then there was a movement caught out of the corner of my eye and the silhouette of a child was by my side.

"Mr Anders, sir, you ok?"

"No," I gasped. "I have no head for heights at the best of times, Odi, and for some reason, I have never got round to learning how to fly. Look, don't worry about me, Rupert's in trouble and you will get there much quicker than I, even if I can persuade my limbs to stop shaking and start working again."

"Mr Anders!" Rupert's voice echoed up to us from the floor of the library below. The wooden supports jammed into the bookshelf began to break up and the walkway moved slightly in a downward direction.

"Help me, Odi," I said desperately.

"You just trust me, Mr Anders, sir," said the boy "I will get you down ok, sir, I promise." Odi swung the section of walkway he was standing on towards me. He stood on the edge of one of the long support beams, oblivious to the sheer drop below.

"You need to step across, Mr Anders, sir," he said.

"What!" My broken support moved again.

"Please, Mr Anders, the books will not hold it much longer."

"Odi, I can't move," I said.

One of the books stopping the whole structure from crashing down fell. Foolishly I watched the ancient volume fall slowly to the floor. The heavy tome hit the ground with a deafening crash. The sound resonated round the normally silent hall like a gunshot. I knew it was now or never.

The little slave boy grabbed me as I leapt from my walkway onto his. The former crashed slowly to the earth whilst I was still in mid-leap. As I landed next to Odi, the whole thing tipped sharply backwards and there is no doubt I should have fallen. The small child grabbed hold of me and, displaying incredible balance and remarkable strength for one so small, pulled me back.

He guided me back along the walkway to the stone staircase. It seemed to take an eternity to get there, my body still shaking and my legs weak. Nevertheless, I rushed down the twisting staircase, stumbling into the grand hall. I was struggling to catch my breath. Rupert was stood in the centre of this cavernous place.

He looked a tiny pathetic figure in the vast elegance of this temple of books. Next to him was a very small man in pinstriped breaches and frock coat. A bowler hat was perched on top of an oval face, which was mostly in shadow. He clutched a small case in one hand.

"Is this boy your responsibility, sir?" he asked in strange voice.

"Yes," I said, still gasping for breath.

"The boy was alarmed," the man spoke in a smooth and unhurried manner despite his speech impediment. "I think he saw a lady pirate coming after him." He laughed and the hairs on the back of my neck stood up. Sydney and Harry came running over, and Professor Kidner, too, had reappeared from the shadows at the far end of the hall.

"I would take much better care of him, Mr...?"

"Anders," I answered automatically.

"Much better care, Mr Anders, or the boy might come to serious harm." He raised his hat to us. "You don't like heights, of course. Foolish of you to go up there really." The little man gave me a toothless grin as he laughed at me through saucer-shaped eyes. Then he walked passed me, out of the great hall. He left us all motionless, in complete silence amongst a million books. I knew then that he had played some fantastic trick upon me. I didn't know how and I had even less idea why.

"What made you go up the walkway, Rupert?" I asked, still trying to get my breath back.

"I didn't," he answered sulkily.

"What frightened you to make you scream like that, old chap?" asked Sydney, who was looking very pale and shaken.

"I didn't scream," said Rupert. Seeing that we doubted the truth of his reply, he added, "I was too scared to scream, Mr Anders." He ran into my arms.

Prudence Fairweather was lying in a large tub of hot soapy water. There were candles placed all around the room and, in particular, round the bath. The floor was littered with rugs and fleeces. Books and papers were scattered everywhere. Over the fireplace hung a watercolour painting of an English country landscape. There was no fire; instead, a large vase of attractively arranged dried flowers and greenery decorated the hearth. A large four-poster bed almost filled one half of the untidy room, unmade since the last time she had slept on shore.

There was a bookcase down one wall filled to overflowing with a diverse collection of reading matter. There were children's books, plenty of boys' adventure stories, a surprising number of romances, mostly with terribly sad endings and plenty of reference material. The latter included many of her old school books. A large chest in the corner, which should have contained doubloons, pieces of eight and other pirate treasure, was also crammed full of books. So much so that the battered lid had no hope of staying shut.

Meg entered the room and got an immediate order from the parrot to wipe her feet.

"You will be like a wrinkled prune if you stay in there much longer," she scolded.

"It's wonderful in here," moaned Prudence, for a moment disappearing under the steaming water. "You know how I look forward to a long bath," she added sulkily, trying to blink the soap from her eyes. "A girl should be able to pamper herself from time to time."

"You asked Harry to come and see you, and he will be here soon," Meg told her sternly. "Or do you wish to converse with him from the bathtub?" she added sarcastically.

Prudence smiled and looked at the diminutive black girl. Meg had very dark brown skin and was very pretty. She had large eyes, a flatish nose and full lips. Short Afro-styled black hair complemented her appearance. She was less than five feet in height and very slim. The impish girl was difficult to age. Prudence guessed she had been about twelve when the pirates had rescued her, perhaps younger. That was about eight years or more ago, and in that short time she had become indispensable to Prudence, as both a good pirate and a very good friend.

"Harry has seen me without clothes before," she told her.

"When you were about two," Meg pointed out.

Prudence sat up in the bath, splashing water over the floor and Meg. The soap suds still clung to her smooth brown skin. "If I was to get out of here, would you brush my hair for me?"

Meg was only clothed in tight short breeches and a small vest, which her leader had managed to soak. "Why should I?" she demanded.

"Well, obviously not because I am your loved, revered and deeply respected leader, I suppose." Prudence stepped out of the bath. "You couldn't at least pass my towel?" she added.

Meg handed her a large claret-coloured towel, which Prudence wrapped round her shapely curves.

"You've put a bit of weight on, girl?" asked Meg, deliberately to provoke.

"No, I haven't," Prudence answered indignantly. "We can't all be as skinny as you, Meg."

"Do you think that's why Monkey never notices me?" asked Meg. "Because I am so thin?"

Prudence walked over to one of the large cushions flung around the floor at random, collapsed into it and began to vigorously rub her hair with a second towel.

"You have to make a man notice you," she explained, unintentionally letting the top of the claret towel fall from her breasts.

"Yeah, well, I haven't got as much to notice as you, have I?" complained Meg.

"Meg, you are lovely," Prudence scolded her. "And anyway, it's not what you've got, it's what you do with it that counts. Now please, will you comb my hair?"

"You always moan and swear and move your head when I'm trying to get all the lugs out," moaned the elf-like girl. "So why should I?"

"As a friend, and anyway, I always scrub your back for you, don't I?"

Some ten minutes later Harry knocked and entered the room. The tall, handsome, silver-haired pirate threatened the parrot with a very unpleasant end before the bird had the chance to admonish him for not cleaning his long black boots.

"Leave my parrot alone, you big bully," said Prudence. She was sat in front of a large gold-framed mirror, watching Meg comb her hair out. "Ouch, you stupid girl, that hurt," she moaned, as Meg fought bravely to de-knot her long dark auburn curls. "Ouch, ouch, are you deliberately trying to rip my hair from my scalp, woman?"

"Shut up and keep still," said Meg, gritting her teeth.

"Tell her, old man, she shouldn't speak to her leader like that."

Harry laughed. "Perhaps if our leader combed her hair more often, she would not be presently in so much pain," he ventured, with little thought to his own personal safety. "However, as I cannot bear to see you in such pain, perhaps I should return later when you are dressed."

"You don't need to go, Harry," she said. "I promise to be good." Prudence smiled her sweetest smile. Although she had stolen his ship from him nearly ten years ago now, nobody could be more loyal to Prudence Fairweather than the *Albatross*'s former captain. He had become very much a father figure to Prudence, and as such, she put great importance in his council. Her impetuousness and impatience meant she did not always, unfortunately, listen carefully enough. Harry loved her as he had loved the daughter he had once had in another life a long time ago.

"Is Captain Jakes all right?" she asked Harry. "Ouch, Meg!" she yelled. "Comb it, not rip it out of my skull!"

"He is fine, Prudence. I think you lifted a heavy cloud from him today."

"I know," Prudence agreed. "If only I had known, I would have had a word sooner."

Meg had got almost all the knots and tangles out and was now gently running the comb through Prudence's richly dark red hair. Her normally curly locks fell long and straight down her back.

"Harry, I have been thinking," she said, after a moment of silence.

"That was the funny grating noise then," said Meg. Prudence made a point of ignoring her.

"We might know what ultimately we have to face, but I would be much happier if I better understood how some people fit in to all this."

"True," agreed Harry. "It might help a little."

"Exactly my point, old man." Prudence became quite animated. "We can use every little bit of help we can get."

"Keep still if you want your hair combed," interrupted Meg.

"I suppose I'm fed up sitting around, waiting for an unseen enemy to attack."

"What are you suggesting, Prudence?" Harry asked her.

"I thought I might drop in on a few people," she said softly. "The weak but interesting Philip Baldock perhaps. We haven't talked for years now. Or how about old man Boscastle, he definitely has a part to play. I am quite sure of that, I am just not sure what his part is. He is certainly a frightened man."

"There are those who hope and pray that you will be tempted to step back on Heffen," Harry said quietly. "Your foolhardy trip to the palace was totally against my council."

Prudence laughed. "It was great fun though, Harry." She gestured to Meg that her hair had been combed enough and leaned forward to Harry. This time she ensured that her towel did not fall. "I plan to pay at least those two gentlemen a visit very soon. Perhaps you and Arthur might join me." She smiled at Harry in a way that almost always got her her own way. "You can keep a fatherly eye on me that way. Perhaps make sure I do nothing too silly." Harry knew it was pointless to argue.

"I want to come too," said Meg. "And if you say no 'cause it's too dangerous, I'll stick this comb in your ear."

"I rescued her from the hold of a slaver, saved her life and nursed her back to health." Harry knew all Prudence was telling him already, of course, as he had also helped rescue Meg. "Then," went on Prudence dramatically, "we give her back her freedom and what do I get for it?"

"The best friend you could ever have asked for," suggested Harry.

"Yes," agreed Prudence, grudgingly. "But apart from that, what do I get for it?"

Rupert did not know what had happened to him. It even seemed that the sinister little man might have been right. The little boy was absolutely convinced he had seen Prudence lurking in the shadows, dagger drawn, ready to pounce. The trouble was we knew that Prudence was nowhere near Heffen Library.

We had waited until we were safely back in Mrs Moffat's back kitchen before we asked him any questions. We all sat huddled together around the fire. The evening had become quite chilly. There was also something reassuring about the glowing embers, perhaps it was a little bit of home. The big copper kettle hung over the red-hot coals singing quietly. Mrs Moffat had put a great big pan of soup on the stove, which was also simmering nicely.

I found Mrs Moffat's kitchen a comfort whenever I began to feel a little homesick. Rupert seemed to be very quiet after his experience. In truth, however, the rest of us were more shaken than he was. Victoria felt she had let her little brother down. I felt the same. Had I spent more time keeping an eye on my charges and less engrossed in nonsensical books, Rupert might not have been put in danger.

It was difficult to know exactly what danger he had been in. My own terrifying experience was still haunting me. I looked at Odi, who was deep in conversation with the butler.

"He vanished, Mr Simms, sir," he protested. "One moment he was there. I turned around just for a minute, that's all, to get a book or something, and when I turned back he was gone."

The little black lad had proved to be unbelievably strong, almost impossibly so. He had without question saved my life. Odi noticed that I was staring at him and gave me an odd look in return.

"Where did you get to, old lad?" Sydney was asking Rupert.

"Dunno," said Rupert quietly. His freckled face looked pale and tired. "I remember being in the library with the scary-looking man in the black coat and then you ran in."

"Listen, don't worry yourself about it all, lad," fussed Mrs Moffat. "You can have a bowl of nice hot soup and then off to bed. You too, Victoria. And will you lot stop fussing around the poor boy and leave him alone," she scolded the rest of us.

Simms sent Odi on a couple of errands and then the immaculate butler excused himself. Mrs Moffat found Sydney and I a very large brandy each, borrowed from the governor's personal supply. Then she said she would see the children to bed and would retire herself.

"That horrid little man can't get into my bedroom tonight?" Rupert asked.

"No, of course not," Mrs Moffat scolded him.

"Prudence Fairweather can," he said bluntly.

"Why don't you sleep in my room tonight?" suggested Victoria. This was unusually helpful for the boy's big sister. She was obviously becoming just as concerned for her brother as the rest of us.

Once we were alone, I was able to voice my fears to Sydney.

"That was strange today," I said. "Sydney, why doesn't Rupert remember what happened?"

My tall and annoyingly good-looking companion looked more physically drained than I recalled ever seeing him. He had a day's growth of beard and his normally well-groomed appearance had become ruffled.

"I swear I saw Rupert on the walkway before it collapsed and I heard him scream twice, Sydney."

"You've had a big fright, old boy. The way that walkway collapsed on you, well, it was bloody scary from where I was standing."

"Not as bloody scary as from where I was standing, Sydney," I suggested. "It was very odd that the one small section of a complex network of platforms, the very one that I went on, collapsed like that," I went on, shuddering as the unpleasant sensation of falling from such a great height came back to haunt me.

"Perhaps you were a bit on the heavy side, old lad," ventured Sydney, unhelpfully.

"It was if the scary little man was after me, not Rupert. Somehow he made me think Rupert was on the walkway, made me hear him scream even. There was something very odd about him, couldn't you feel it?"

"The little chap? I haven't seen him round before. Suppose he was a bit of an odd sort, now you come to mention it." Sydney spoke slowly as if trying to understand what I had said. "To do what you suggest, well, that's pretty weird, Thomas old chum, you have to admit. In any case, why should he want to harm you? He doesn't even know you."

"You're right, Sydney. I think it's this feeling of impending doom. It's getting to me."

My friend yawned and stretched. "Do you think Mrs Moffat would mind if I slept on the sofa tonight?"

"I am sure she would have no objection, Sydney," I said.

"To be honest," Sydney smiled ruefully, "I don't much fancy the journey back to my digs. Not with pirates, monsters, funny little men and that bad feeling you talk about."

"Not to mention demons, devils and dinosaurs." I forced a laugh. "Heffen is a good place for monsters," I added.

"What monsters?" Sydney now had the look of a man who was starting to wish even more that he had stayed in England to face the angry husbands and outraged fathers. A savage beating from an angry husband was something my companion found easier to relate to than any of this.

"There are some wonderfully painted colour plates of a giant sea creature. The pictures I found varied in detail, but the better ones were in the style of a giant octopus." I flicked through the pages of an ancient volume I had brought back from the library.

"Does Professor Kidner know you are pinching his books?" asked

Sydney, pulling his face at the strong musty smell of the old book.

"Well, it is a library," I pointed out. "Anyway, he has plenty more where this came from."

I found the painting I was looking for. It was a fanciful depiction of three long boats filled with natives and settlers fighting the huge multi-legged monster with spears. The boats were riding the waves and one unfortunate sailor had been caught in the creature's tentacles. Like many of the colour plates in this book and others I had found, this was in the style of a picture you might expect to find in a children's fairy story. Use of clear bright colours helped to bring these pictures to life. The people, particularly the almost naked natives who were either rowing over huge waves or hurtling spears at their attacker, were anatomically perfect.

The monster looked like some kind of octopus, except for its size and razor-sharp fangs. I showed the picture to Sydney.

"Somebody has a colourful imagination," he said.

"I hope so," I agreed. "I would not like to meet that thing and that is for sure."

"What the hell is this one supposed to be?" Sydney had found another plate further into the book. This depicted what I guessed to be the volcanic rock Niridia. Although Niridia is large enough to be considered a mountain, a horned creature with glowing red eyes was towering above it. The creature was sucking in everything around it. This was leading to a similar effect to that of the whirlwind I had experienced. There were indeed, amongst other things, people, a horse and cart, a small ship and a black and white Friesian cow being devoured by the demon. The title of this imaginative work was "Efulric the Apprentice Feasts."

"Efulric is one of the most commonly referred to devil-like creatures that the mythology of these islands is so keen to promote," I explained. "Like all the other weird things in the various different works I have had a chance to examine, all these apparitions are blamed firmly upon Gabrielle's Fault. In the case of Efulric, a battle was fought with the infamous pirate Francis Gabrielle, who it is said separated the monster's soul from his body."

"Efulric is a little large," observed Sydney nervously, which was, to say the least, an understatement.

"It is not the size of this creature that frightens me, Sydney," I interrupted. "Although I am sure it would if I was to meet this thing in the flesh," I added quickly. "It is the eyes I find truly terrifying. What the artist has captured there is the nearest I have ever seen to pure, undiluted evil."

"I think I would rather take on the eight-legged sea monster than that. Not that I am over-keen to take on either you understand."

"I know what you mean, my friend," I agreed. "I think I would sooner do battle with anything other than this creature."

Sydney was looking at some of the other strange creatures illustrated in the book I had borrowed. Some of the colour plates in particular were little masterpieces in their own right. The use of colour and artistic license had produced some breathtaking images. I could tell that Sydney, like myself, was immediately enchanted by the pictures. He found even the drawings and sketches fascinating.

"Do you seriously believe there to be any truth in all this rubbish?" he asked without conviction.

"Usually, Sydney, you will find in any research into legend and folklore that a great deal of mythology and superstition is clouding the truth. That book, for example, was, I think, scribed by an order of ancient monks, probably only a few hundred years after the birth of Christ. I am not even clear how Christianity had found Heffen so far back. Such work as this, however, is most often born out of something real, Sydney," I said. "It's just that through the telling and retelling of these tales, they will no doubt have become exaggerated."

"I hope to God that Efulric the Apprentice is exaggerated," replied Sydney. "Surely a serious scholar, an educated chap like yourself, doesn't believe any of this mumbo jumbo, do you?"

I smiled sadly at him and gestured back to the book. "Try, I think it's page three hundred and six," I directed.

Sydney Greenburgh looked puzzled. He flicked through the thin pages searching for the page I had suggested. It would have been wonderful to be able to preserve for posterity the expression on my companion's face when he found the drawing I had directed him to.

"Mable!" he gasped, looking at the pen-and-ink sketch which bore an uncannily strong likeness to the beast we had encountered in the jungle.

"Would you not have thought that thing, whatever it is, to be a most fanciful notion, Sydney?" I smiled. "That is, if one had not just recently tried to eat you."

Sydney looked at me, perspiration forming on his forehead. He pushed his thick black mop of hair out of his eyes and blinked at me. "Yes, but it is sort of an animal, old boy," he argued, without any conviction. "They must have made up this Efulric. I mean, there are no such things as demons, or their apprentices for that matter."

"I think you are probably right, Sydney," I agreed calmly. "A lot of artistic licence has been used here. Except, that is, those eyes."

"Eyes?" questioned my friend nervously.

"Nobody could have made them up, Sydney. They are more frightening than anything a man could dream of in his most appalling nightmares. The artist saw those eyes. They probably haunted him to his grave, but he did see them, I am quite sure of that."

Chapter 9

Richard Boscastle could not believe his eyes. It was impossible for anyone to get within 500 yards of his rundown and desolate ranch, and yet there she was. Nobody should be able to enter his home without at least setting off a dozen or more alarms. In the room where he spent almost all his time nowadays, a series of about fifty small bells had been set up. These were reminiscent of the kind of system that might be found in the servants' quarters of a large house. Instead of indicating where in the house service was required, Boscastle's system had been cleverly set up to indicate whereabouts, in the house or grounds, an intruder might be lurking. It was inconceivable that anyone could have crossed his land and entered the house without ringing at least some of the warning bells.

The system was, the old man was grudgingly forced to admit, not foolproof. His well-armed guards would frequently be sent out on a fool's errand. Boscastle would simply remind himself that nowadays one couldn't be too careful in the protection of one's most precious possessions.

Usually the culprit was nothing more than small vermin. A rat, rabbit or fox could so easily trigger one of the bells. Sometimes the perpetrator would be a larger animal, such as a monkey, or even a wild cat. However, the cleverer animals had learnt to avoid coming to close to the ranch because of all the deadly traps Boscastle had ordered to be dotted around his estate.

There were hidden ditches full of sharpened spikes, wires across paths that triggered a volley of spears or arrows. There was almost no kind of trap ever thought up by man that Boscastle had not employed somewhere around the perimeter of the ranch. Added to all the alarms and traps, Boscastle's guards were generally accepted to be amongst the best on Heffen. Indeed, almost all of Boscastle's substantial private income was spent on defending his equally substantial collection of precious stones, fine art and exquisite furniture.

The only successful invasion at the Boscastle ranch house, in fact, was a particularly nasty strain of termites that were gradually eating the once imposing wooden building. Even Boscastle had come to think of his crumbling home as impregnable. So how the girl had got into his private quarters, without setting off any alarms or becoming impaled on either a spear or a spike, was a mystery as well as a shock to the old man.

He reached shakily for the pistol on his lap.

Advancing years had taken their toll on him physically. His mind, however, was as sharp as ever. Prudence Fairweather did not have to move very quickly to press her sword to his throat before his arthritic hands could grasp the pistol.

"I was thinking, Uncle Richard, how nice it might be if I dropped by for a chat." She smiled sweetly at Boscastle, who was sat in his bath chair, shaking with a mixture of fear and anger. "I don't suppose you get very many callers these days," Prudence continued. She leaned forward and removed the pistol from his lap. "You must get very lonely here all on your own. To tell you the truth, Uncle Richard," the tall girl whispered loudly into his ear, "I think it's probably all the nasty little traps that put people off popping in to see how you are."

Boscastle was sweating heavily. All his life, security had been of paramount importance and yet somebody had just walked in as if there was no security. Suddenly, everything he owned was vulnerable.

"Who are you and what do you want," he demanded. "I do not welcome visitors here. I shall call the guard."

The room was dark and gloomy. There was an overpowering smell of damp and dry rot. It was difficult to walk on the floor without finding creaky and uneven floorboards. The large sofa and a big high-backed armchair were covered in threadbare material in a simple green and red floral pattern. They gave off a damp and musty odour. Despite the gloom and his failing eyesight, Richard Boscastle knew exactly who the intruder was.

"Calling the guard would be just a teensy weenie bit of a waste of energy, Uncle Richard," Prudence told him sweetly in a tone that suggested she was more concerned about his health and well-being than she truly was. "Some friends of mine have arranged to entertain them for us, so that we aren't disturbed," explained his late friend's little princess. She stood up again and sauntered over to the large fireplace that dominated the room. The fire had not been lit for a long time, even though the evenings were now quite cold.

"I have heard of your new-found notoriety, Mistress Prudence," said Boscastle. "Your father, I am sure, would not have approved. Now, child, you presumably must have a reason to break into my home uninvited." Boscatle stared at the child through piggy eyes. "Surely you are not now reduced to thieving from your father's old friends?"

"You were a close friend of my daddy, Uncle Richard. He would have expected me to keep an eye out for you, wouldn't he?"

Prudence took hold of the bath chair and wheeled him over to the fireplace. She might be tall and slim, with voluptuous curves and long shiny auburn hair; however, Boscastle recognised much of her late father in her, even if the old man's curves had been rather less attractive. Mostly he could feel old man Fairweather's incorrigible and sometimes quite irritating sense of fun. Prudence spun the bath chair round to face her and leant over close to the crippled old man.

"You know what happened to my daddy too, Uncle Richard, don't you?" She pushed the bath chair away from her. "It's a rhetorical question, you don't need to answer," she added sulkily.

"Do you ask yourself often what would your old father might think of you now, girl? A thief, a murderer and a pirate who will no doubt, sooner or later, find herself dancing at the end of a rope."

Prudence laughed. "There are many out there who think it is you, Uncle Dick, who should be swinging from the gallows." Prudence sprawled back on the musty couch. "There was evil about then." She sat forward to adjust her long black cloak. "I think you know it was that evil that brought about the murder of my family and your beautiful wife."

"Superstition and poppycock," muttered Boscastle.

"And," Prudence ignored him completely, "I think you were touched in someway by this evil. Someone sold their soul to this particular devil and I need to know who."

Boscatle began to sob. Prudence could feel his fear. She knew at once that she could not hope to compete with whatever it was that had filled him with such terror.

"Your father was a good man you know, Prudence," he told her, after he had recovered a little. "Had it not been for his kindness, I could not have settled here with my young bride. I wished him no harm, you know that. I am, on the other hand, not a good man like your father was. I am easily afraid. I covet wealth, success and pretty things too much. Your father did not need to die."

"Yes, he did, because my father would not subscribe to the work of the devil," said the girl bluntly. "That I understand already. What I do not understand is where you and others stand in all this."

"Why ask me? Why not ask the man who killed him, Prudence? You were there, you saw what happened, or has the child in you driven it from your mind?" Boscastle forced a weak laugh. "There is much I have tried to force from my mind, believe me, child."

"I know the man who killed my father and some enchantment protects him and others from harm. No doubt you are already aware of that, so tell me about this powerful magic, Uncle Richard, tell me what it has done to you."

"Believe me, child, you do not wish to know." Boscastle wheeled himself back to the window. "Even you cannot fight the devil itself, Prudence Fairweather. Your father thought he could and he died."

Silhouetted against a moonlit sky, Boscastle's eyes glinted as he turned back to face Prudence. There was something in them that sent a cold chill running through her veins.

Prudence got up again and flung open the doorway into the old hall. Water now seeped through the beautiful wooden ceiling. The staircase where Boscastle's young bride had died violently all those years ago, now rotting and covered in cobwebs, stood as a stark reminder of that night.

"You could do with a housekeeper," Prudence told him cheerfully.

She looked around the hall and then returned to Boscastle's room, cluttered with clumsy furniture and a large bed. "I sort of came to terms with what happened a long time ago," Prudence said. "I wish it hadn't happened, but it did. I have a good time now and have made many good friends." Prudence walked over to the window and looked out into the blackness. "I do not seek revenge, Uncle Richard, on you or anyone for that matter. I know that might come as something of a surprise to you. Our esteemed governor doesn't believe me either." For a moment Prudence was quiet, lost in thought, still staring out into the silvery night. "I am not the first to realise that whatever that dark malevolence really is, it's back, Uncle Richard, and right on cue. From what I can tell, I am not the only one who knows this by any stretch of the imagination."

"I am a lost cause." Boscastle wheeled himself over from the window, stopping next to Prudence. "I have done bad things for which I can never hope to receive redemption. People I classed as my friends now want me dead, not to mention my enemies, who always have. Even my body is broken, and believe me, there is nobody on earth who can fix it this time." Boscatle was becoming upset. He paused for a moment to recover his composure. "I never considered growing old. Do you know my mind is still as young and alert as it was when I was a young man? It would seem that my body is the one possession I could never protect."

"And your wife?"

"I suppose I killed her," he answered wistfully. "I don't remember doing it, but I know that I wanted to. She was going to leave me you see."

Prudence could tell that Boscastle was speaking the truth. She could not help feeling sorry for the old man. It had been greed that had brought him to this pitiful state. Boscastle reached up from his bath chair and grabbed the girl's arm.

"So as I say, I am a lost cause. There is no hope for me, and I neither need nor deserve your pity. You have everything to live for, Prudence Fairweather. You tell me that you have a good ship and a good crew. Leave these islands; get away before it is too late. You are a beautiful and clever young lady. The combination of that and your father's undeniable charm and wit makes you unstoppable. You got your charm from your father, but not your good looks. Let's face it, he was no oil painting."

"Oh, I don't know, Uncle Richard, I have a couple of nice ones."

"If you have any paintings of your mother you will understand who gave you your good looks. She was a very beautiful woman your mother, not like that ugly oaf of a father you were lumbered with. I was fond of both your parents, Prudence, and they were kind to me always."

Prudence smiled and firmly removed the old man's swollen hand from her arm. "I think my father claimed to be ruggedly handsome." She laughed. "So what exactly would I be running away from, Uncle Richard?"

"Ask yourself, Prudence, does the little princess have her father's iron will?" Boscastle looked into the pretty girl's eyes. "Just go as quickly as you can. If you stay, you will come up against an enemy who is too awesome even for Prudence Fairweather to fight. It would break my heart to see it kill one more Fairweather."

"Trouble is," said Prudence softly, more to herself than to Boscastle, "I know you are right. I need to take my companions and point the *Albatross* in any direction and then put a hundred leagues, or maybe more, between us and the Heffen isles." She walked back to the door. "Only something inside of me, something else I can't fight, is stopping me."

Deep down inside, she wanted Boscastle to admit to her that he had shot his wife in cold blood. Just another possession he could not protect from others without destroying. Perhaps if she heard him admit his guilt, she would no longer feel quite so sorry for him. Prudence turned to leave.

"By the way," Boscastle steered his chair round with surprising agility to call her back, "have you found the government's new demon hunter yet?"

"What do you know about that?" Prudence was caught off guard for the first time, which pleased Boscastle.

"Believe me, not much." Boscastle laughed for the first time since Prudence had arrived. "I do not enjoy the privileges I once did," he pointed out. "All I do know is that whoever it is has arrived on Heffen to track down this evil that you talk about." Boscastle laughed again, although it was very much a forced laugh. "Still, if this demon slayer is as good as the last one they sent, there is no hope for any of us." Boscastle leaned forward in his chair and grabbed hold of the girl again. "If you aren't going to run, you will have to deal with this man sooner or later. We all know how dangerous outside interference can be. Word is he came in on the *Wild Swan*, but I doubt if it was only the British government who sent him."

"Who else would send for such a man?" demanded the girl.

"You really don't get it, do you?" Boscastle chuckled. "And your father thought his little princess was such a bright little girl." The old man had Prudence's arm in a vice-like grip now. The pirate winced and tried to free herself from him. Her arm was starting to go blue. "It is not only the good guys who think they can defeat this evil, Prudence," Boscastle continued, oblivious to the discomfort he was causing her. "Trouble is, they have it just as wrong as you. Nobody can defeat it. Your good father proved that to us all in spectacular fashion."

"How did it go?" asked Arthur.

He had guided Prudence and Harry, with some speed, back to the coast. To visit Boscastle, they had taken a small dinghy round the headland at the top of the northern island. In doing so, they had been forced to sail too close to Burleigh's private villa for comfort. Prudence was not ready for a showdown with Sir John just yet, although that day would come.

There had really been no choice going so close, as a mountain range separated all the safe landing places from Boscastle's ranch. It was downhill and mostly open ground back to the sea. Consequently, there was almost no cover and the three pirates felt very exposed. They had said little to each other since making their escape from Boscastle's rundown establishment.

"To be honest, I didn't get much out of him I didn't already know. He's scared though, very scared," replied Prudence.

Prudence remembered what being scared was like. She had been protected as a child. She was the youngest, which gave her some advantage over her brothers. She was also a young lady and the apple of her father's eye. Old Man Fairweather had perhaps been a little overprotective.

There had been a sense of foreboding for some weeks. That dreadful night ten years ago would always haunt her dreams. The cluster of outbuildings was already engulfed in flames. Some collapsed; others remained standing, stark, black skeletons, smouldering in the waste ground that had once been such a happy place. The elegant house that would not have looked out of place in the better residential parts back home was already alight. Prudence's father had been so proud of their home. The dream of a lifetime he had built for his family.

People were running in all directions, consumed with fear and panic. In the confusion, the terrified young girl was able to escape.

There were men after her. Some of the same men who had killed her mother and father. She had left with nothing, although she clutched to her a small and beautifully carved musical box her father had made for her. She had to have something to remember him by. The frightened child ran as fast as she could for the cover of the forests. She was little more than a child. Physically she had been transforming, rather too quickly her father thought, from his pretty little princess into a shapely and beautiful young woman.

The men were catching up, and Prudence was well aware that they were not taking prisoners. She could not, however, run much farther.

The combination of fear and adrenaline was making her feel dizzy. She dare not stop for long enough to see how close behind they were. She could sense that they were close.

It was then that her foot caught the trip wire. This stretched along the ground low and well hidden. Prudence was slightly off balance and she was hurtled forward, rolling down into a ditch full of foul-smelling water. The volley of spears that the wire had fired took out all but two of her pursuers. The two able to keep going plunged screaming into one of the hidden pits where they were impaled on spikes.

Prudence was frozen in terror. She knew at once that she was in an area covered in mantraps. She also knew where she was. Richard Boscastle was a man she had always liked. Her father and Boscastle had been good friends. She remembered, however, her father explaining to her mother about the way that Boscastle had turned his place into a fortress. After awhile, the girl began to move very slowly and carefully, looking for any clues as to the whereabouts of the next trap.

After she had gone just a little way, she heard the sound of a man groaning in pain. Prudence still could not explain why she went to find the man. He had put his foot into one of those cruel old-fashioned traps used to snare small game. His ankle looked to be in a mess. Prudence was not used to the sight of blood, although she had seen far worse that night.

The two together managed to free the man's ankle from the trap, and Prudence used a part of her petticoat as a bandage. The man she rescued was slightly familiar. At first she could not recall where she had seen him. So much had happened that night and she wanted so badly to cry. Only for some odd reason she couldn't.

"Who are you?" she asked. Her voice echoed around in her head as if it wasn't hers.

"You may call me Douglas, child, and I am extremely grateful for your help." Douglas was close to fifty years of age and was wearing what had once been a finely tailored suit. He had a kindly face, which not surprisingly was clouded by fear. "You have without doubt saved my life, young lady." The man paused to study the girl's dirty face. "Are you not Old Man Fairweather's lass?" he asked.

So that was where she had seen him. He had called the other day, and he and her father had been locked away for hours in the study. After the man had left, Father had been in an odd mood. He had described his visitor as an old friend from London.

"I think my parents are dead," said Prudence in a hoarse whisper. Still she could not find it in her to cry.

"Do you know how I get back to the sea?" asked Douglas. "I have a boat waiting to take me off the island. If I don't escape, I am a dead man."

"I know the way like the back of my hand," answered the girl. "Mother used to despair of my tomboy ways." She fastened the bandage on Douglas's ankle as tight as she could. "It will be dangerous out there now."

"I do not ask you to come with me for my sake. If what you say is true, I can get you away from here to a place of safety. The boat, however, will not wait for long. I do not wish to frighten you, child. There are terrible things happening here on Heffen and I am very much afraid they are going to get worse. Someone has failed me terribly."

"You mean my father, don't you?"

It was at that moment two men looking much like pirates entered the clearing. One was tall and broad, with most of his teeth missing. The other was older, with a shaved head and a large scar down one side of his face.

"It's our lucky night," said the one with no teeth.

"What is the price for this pretty head I wonder?" asked the scar-faced one. There was a heated argument over the ethics of beheading the girl or shooting her first. They decided to shoot Douglas at point-blank range and then have some fun with the girl. The toothless man then suggested that Douglas might like to watch them having a little fun with Prudence before they killed him.

The taller man stepped forward and ripped the front of her dress away. Prudence brought her knee up into his groin. The other man raised his gun to shoot her.

"No, leave it." The tall man grinned, showing all three teeth he had left in his ugly head. "I like a bit of fight in them." He laughed grotesquely. Then something fell from high above in the tall trees.

It was a man, tall and wiry with the face of a rat. Dressed in a striped top and dirty leggings, he swiftly despatched the two assailants using a pair of vicious-looking long daggers. With the advantage of surprise and speed, the two men died almost instantly and as silently. The ugly man then turned and bowed to Prudence and Douglas.

"Good evening," he said, bowing again. "Your father and I were not in truth friends, Miss Fairweather." He carefully wiped his long blades clean. "He did not approve of my thieving ways," he explained. "I do, however, owe him my life and I promised him I would return that favour one day." The grin had gone from his face. "Sadly, I was too late to save your father. I am sure, in any case, he would have much preferred that I saved his little princess. My name is Arthur."

Prudence was silent for some time. Douglas had his arm around her to comfort her.

"Who are you?" demanded Arthur, wiping his huge nose with his sleeve.

"My name is Douglas. I am from England and I need to get back to my ship. A great deal may depend on it." He looked tired and weak from loss of blood.

"I will take you somewhere where you may both rest," Arthur decided after a moment's thought. "There is someone else I need to see safe for, I confess, selfish reasons. Although why I should bother myself on another person's account when they are so cruel to me I do not pretend to understand."

Douglas began to protest, but the beak-nosed man ignored his protestations and carried on.

"When you are rested, sir, I will take you and the young lady safely to your ship." He was grinning again now. "Of course I owe you nothing, Douglas, or whatever your name is, so I will need to charge a small price."

"But I have nothing," protested the ragged gentleman weakly.

"And I have less than nothing," mumbled Prudence to herself. She held her ripped dress over her bodice and stared blankly across the clearing. Even now the tragic events of that night seemed unreal to her, a bad dream from which she would soon wake up. A dull aching somewhere deep inside her soul told her that this was not a nightmare and that there was no waking up from this.

Arthur led them through a thick part of the jungle, pointing out various traps. "We can use Mr Boscastle's excellent defence system as our own. Here is a good place to rest."

The greenery was dense at this point and at first they could not see what Arthur was pointing out. A massive tree stood in the centre of the wilderness. It was a venerable old thing, part dead and part still living. Prudence had been here before, and always thought this monstrous thing quite odd. The ancient trunk itself was at the very least a good twenty feet in diameter. The centre of the trunk was hollow. Inside it there was room at a squeeze for a dozen or more men.

"I should be back soon," whispered Arthur. He handed them each a pistol. "Just in case," he explained. "If I am not back in a couple of hours, I am afraid you will have to get yourselves to this ship you speak of." He looked at Douglas. "I am usually, although sadly to my great cost not always, a good judge of character. You look a decent man to me." He laughed. "Although you clearly did not dress for a night in the jungle."

Arthur paused for a moment, as if considering the rashness of his actions.

"If I do not return, look after the child if you can."

"I can look after me," said Prudence sulkily. "Let's face it, I am going to have to now, wherever your ship takes me, sir."

"You haven't told me your price yet, friend," pointed out Douglas weakly. "I have already told you I have nothing."

"A free passage out of here for the friend I am going to save." Arthur looked sad for a moment. "Assuming, that is, that she will take it."

Prudence remembered waiting in the hollow of the tree for Arthur to return. She remembered that this was no ordinary tree. Her companion was ill and had become feverish. She remembered wondering if this kindly man was going to die too. She remembered being thankful that this was no ordinary tree.

She remembered crossing those same open fields towards the coast.

There were hostile patrols everywhere. Like now, ten years later, there was nowhere to hide.

Harry had stopped by a clump of rocks that offered some cover. "You ok, Prudence?"

"She's remembering, Harry, you insensitive moron," said Arthur grimly.

"You don't have to be a pig ugly oaf like you, Arthur, to realise that."

"You were the one who could have talked her out of this foolhardy escapade. But no, just when you have one chance to be useful in your long sad life, you go and blow it."

"Are you two trying to draw attention to us, perhaps to add a bit of spice to the day maybe? Or are you both just complete idiots?" demanded Prudence in a whispered rebuke.

"He started it," grumbled Harry.

"You started it by being born."

"At least I was born."

"Gentlemen, please." Prudence glared at them angrily. She knew, however, that the two men argued even more than normal when they were worried.

"That's the road down there," pointed out Prudence. She recalled quite clearly that the road was very close to the coast.

"We are almost home from here," observed Arthur, grinning at the others.

"I don't want to go home yet," said Prudence flatly. Her two companions stared at her in horror. They were not, however, surprised.

Back in his rotting fortress, Richard Boscastle sat in his bath chair staring out into the silvery light that mixed with the numerous torches to illuminate the compound. He was reflecting on the visit from the pirate girl.

When they had moved here and befriended the Fairweathers, the child Prudence had been little more than a toddler. The old man had been proud of all his children. Prudence was, however, very special.

Fairweather's little princess.

A noise behind Boscastle made him jump. The silhouette of a woman stood naked in the doorway, illuminated by the bright lights from the hall. He knew instinctively that this was no intruder. He swung the bath chair round to face the door.

"Is that you, Patricia, my dear?" he said.

Henry Jessop stood looking at the governor's palace. It was arguably the finest building on Heffen. Some might argue a preference for the classical lines of Heffen Library, whilst a few would secretly covet the gothic splendour of Burleigh's grotesque mansion. Jessop believed that the governor had got it right. The palace, built of brilliant white marble blocks, could be seen from a ship many leagues out at sea, the golden domes glittering in the hot sunshine. Standing as he was on the geometrically perfect drive, surrounded by impeccably manicured lawns, Jessop felt very small.

Facing the grand steps, he took in some of the best topiary he had ever laid eyes on. The theme was of birds. Some stood at least twenty feet or more from the ground. Each one was a perfectly shaped replica. Collectively, along with the immaculate gardens and the grand palace, they helped to create an effect that was both bizarre and quite definitely surreal. Inside, the floor of the grand entrance hall had a similar pattern to the stone work as the drive outside. The vast marble walls dripped in gold and precious stones.

"He will see me, I promise you. Just tell him Henry Jessop has returned." Jessop did not feel as confident as he sounded as he handed a small leather wallet to the officious young man who was blocking his way to the governor. "Official business, youngster," he said casually. "Now please hurry up. I am, after all, a busy man."

The young secretary eyed up Jessop with considerable doubt evident in his expression. The man who was demanding an audience without an appointment looked, to say the least, rather down at heel.

Nevertheless, he bustled into the governor's large and stately office and handed him the leather wallet. Before he had chance to say a word, Silas Raines looked up angrily at him.

"You better show Mr Jessop in," he said softly. The governor sat down again and, picking up a long quill, continued with his work.

Unseen to Jessop, he had been followed from his digs, through the golden gates and along the grand tree-lined drive to the palace. Even as he was shown into the governor's office, a small man in a dark frock coat was watching him.

"It begins," said the little man. "They start to come back like moths to the flame."

The naked body was of a man. It was difficult to put an age to it. The cadaver had a shaven head, was quite muscular in build, but was not very tall. There was no wound on his body that anyone could see. His face had, however, been frozen in a moment of pure terror.

The dead man had been washed up onto the sand in a small cove not far from where the *Albatross* was sheltering herself from prying eyes. The body had been found by a group of local fishermen. They had told someone of their gruesome discovery. Word had in this way reached the *Albatross*. Concerned that it might be one of their own scouts, Monkey had put together a small landing party to investigate. Meg had insisted on coming too.

There seemed to be no one about that evening as a few of the men pulled the boat onto the beach. It was, in any case, a deserted part of the north island where few, other than pirates and fishermen, would ever go.

The dead body, Monkey guessed, had been deep underwater for a few days, for it was remarkably well preserved. There was a mark around the corpse's ankle indicating that he might have been deliberately weighted down. Somebody, it seemed, would have preferred that the body remain at the bottom of the sea. The dead man's grey face stared wide-eyed up at them.

"I wonder what scared him so much?" Meg shivered. "Any idea who he is?" She looked at Monkey, who in turn looked at the rest of the landing party. Everybody shook their heads.

"Well, I don't know him," said Monkey. "He doesn't even look familiar like some people do."

"Some people being Captain Jakes you mean?" suggested Meg, walking round the body in circles.

"Do you feel that too?"

"No, but I could tell you did." Meg knelt down to examine a small tattoo on the man's shoulder. "If Arthur was here, he'd be able to tell us something about that," she said. "He reckons that he can never remember a face but almost always remember a tattoo." She took a pencil and a scrap of paper and began to sketch a rough drawing of the mark. It was a stylised picture of what looked something like a crucifix on which there was a pattern.

"Maybe he was this government agent," suggested Monkey.

"It would not be unreasonable to think that, but equally he could just be some drunken sailor," pointed out Meg as she worked. "Whoever he was, someone got to him before we did," she observed, not looking up from her task. "There, what do you think?" She held up her rough but surprisingly accurate sketch of the dead man's tattoo.

"Not bad, Meg. You obviously have hidden talents." Monkey looked genuinely surprised by the slim girl's efforts.

"You better believe it," she replied, running to keep up with the big man. "Give me the opportunity and I will prove it to you, sailor. You gorgeous man," she said to herself.

"Sorry, did you say something?" Monkey had stopped near the boat.

"I said, have you had the opportunity to think where you saw Captain Jakes?"

"You know you can remember your life before Prudence rescued you," said Monkey. He turned to the crew who had collected round. "We have no idea who he was. Possibly our spy from England or as Meg says could be just a sailor who's fallen overboard. Whatever he was, he deserves a decent burial." The men nodded and, grabbing a couple of long-handled spades from the boat, they went back to dig a hole for the dead man. Turning back to Meg, Monkey went on, "I remember nothing before Harry found me."

"Believe me, Monkey, there is plenty in my life before I joined the *Albatross* that I wish I could forget," said Meg sadly.

"Maybe that is what I have done," agreed Monkey. "Blocked out everything because of something that's happened. On really bad days I don't feel part of this at all." He gestured at their surroundings. "For the first time ever, Meg, I recognise something. I am sure Jakes is from my past, but I still don't remember where."

Meg put a hand gently on one of Monkey's huge muscular arms. She knew they had found Monkey as a boy, somewhere out near the reef. It was the crew of the *Albatross* who had rescued Monkey. Harry had adopted the lad, although he pretended he wanted nothing to do with him.

"I wonder what would have happened to me if Harry hadn't come along?"

"I've always thought Harry was far too nice to be a pirate." Meg smiled.

"I always got the feeling that he had a previous life like I must have done," went on Monkey. He was sat on a rock, looking out towards the *Albatross*. Clothed in little more than a loincloth, his bronzed body looked as perfect as anything ever could to Meg's eyes. "I think he had a family once, a son and a daughter perhaps, although he only ever talks about them in his sleep. I was probably a substitute for the family he misses so much."

"Did they die?"

"I don't know, Meg, but I am sure I once overheard him say he might have grandchildren."

"It's strange, isn't it? Harry is so full of tales of his exploits and yet he never talks about his family." Monkey smiled. "I wonder if it's guilt sometimes. The way he talks in his sleep, he is always apologising to someone. I'm pretty sure Prudence knows the truth and Arthur."

The sun was setting over the quiet cove. The clear blue water lapped onto the beach and splashed over the rocks. It was a calm night, still quite warm, although when the sun finally went down there would be a chill in the air.

"I think you and I are his family now," he said. "And Prudence, too, of course."

"It is so beautiful here," said Meg softly. She looked into the rich red sky splashed with so many other colours and even more different shades. Purples, blues, yellows and greys were all splashed across the horizon in a breathtaking display of such intensity that it seemed the heavens might be on fire.

"Beautiful," agreed Monkey who was deep in thought. "Something is never quite as it should be though. I can never fathom exactly what that something is, or why it isn't right."

When the men had buried the stranger's body, they all stood round whilst Monkey rather awkwardly said a few words. Having given the unknown man a proper burial, Monkey returned to his rock.

Meg sat next to him and they watched the sun set over the hills. For ages they were both still and silent, marvelling in their almost perfect surroundings. The sea had turned inky black with ripples of dark red and orange. As the sun finally disappeared, the moon sent shafts of silver light to dance on the surface of the water. As the air grew cooler, Monkey put his arm round Meg to keep her warm.

"Everything is going to be ok, isn't it?" asked Meg.

"Course it is," replied Monkey unconvincingly. "Course it is."

Chapter 10

The apprentice Efulric is the most concentrated manifestation of evil ogres. These monstrous beings are too hideous in appearance for readers of these notes to begin imagining. If freed from their dimension, they shall cover our world like a plague of locusts, devouring everything and everyone in their path.

For now, and perhaps for centuries to come, Efulric is trapped inside our dimension. So too is its guardian angel, which will settle in unwilling hosts, unnoticed by our world. Unnoticed until the time comes when the hidden key empowered by avarice, greed and hatred will open the gates of hell and unleash the full extent of Efulric's evil onto a defenceless world. It will be the most terrible event in the history of mankind. It is doubtful any of our descendants will survive this holocaust. Mankind will surely end unless Efulric the Apprentice is stopped.

I am endeavouring to find a way to destroy the Fault. This can be the only way of preventing Efulric from opening the gates for his terrible army to descend upon us. How the creature Efulric himself can be defeated I know not. I am personally of the strong opinion *that he may be indestructible. Until the time I speak of, the creature will lead a quiet life, feeding on the sins and avarice of others. You will know when the time is almost upon you. Treat my words as some foolish superstition and the world will pay a heavy price.*

—Taken from the original manuscripts of a forgotten explorer who claimed to have transcribed the actual words of the pirate Francis Gabrielle

I had not been able to stop thinking about the pirate Prudence Fairweather. I longed to see her again, although I doubted very much if she had given me a second thought. The beautiful pirate would, without doubt, have plenty far more suitable admirers amongst the cutthroats and villains she kept company with.

I had tried to distract my attention from this hopeless cause by concentrating on researching further into the mythology of these strange islands. I was, for some inexplicable reason, convinced that it was in the legends of these islands I would find the reason for this sense of impending doom. To further my studies, I had also decided that Efulric the Apprentice was most worthy of my attention.

For one thing, this demon appeared in almost every book on local legends and mythology I had looked in. If some of these fanciful accounts of the creature had any credence to them whatsoever, then there was also compelling evidence to suggest that Efulric was about due to stage a big comeback.

Francis Gabrielle seemed to believe that there was truth in the legends of Efulric. He wrote about the Apprentice demon at some length. I had found a great deal in Kidner's office from various different scribes, all mostly written around Gabrielle's time. These described in some detail the pirate's beliefs and fears.

He described the Apprentice as leader to a monstrous horde of demons. The devil's army waiting to invade our world. I showed some of these notes to Sydney, who treated them with the very disrespect that Gabrielle warned against. Professor Kidner, on the other hand, looked frightened when I mentioned the name of Efulric.

I could find no trace of any of Gabrielle's own notes, although I did find some perfectly preserved manuscripts by the young playwright William Shakespeare, including at least one unpublished work!

Despite all the warnings of demons and holocausts, life went on as normal. Burleigh continued his evil trade in human flesh unchecked. The governor continued to hoard his gold, ruling for the benefit of the few at the considerable expense of the majority.

I continued to teach my charges. I found them becoming more and more responsive to my lessons. They both had enquiring minds and were eager to learn. Rupert often needed reassurance that Prudence Fairweather was not about to grab him from the shadows. In other ways he grew in confidence with every day that passed. I tried to explain to him that the pirate woman meant him no harm. Not surprisingly, I suppose, he did not believe me. As there was a real threat to his life, I took comfort in the fact that at least he would remain vigilant. When my spirits were low, it even occurred to me that maybe I was wrong, that Prudence Fairweather was the killer, as proclaimed in thousands of notices posted all over Heffen.

I was certain that the small man in the frock coat and hat we had come across in Heffen Library was a potential threat. If he was the killer who had replaced Skeet, and I strongly suspected that to be the case, then it made no sense. Why had he not killed Rupert when he had the chance?

The feeling of impending catastrophe that had affected almost everybody had been lifted at least temporarily. There was a tangible feeling of excitement and anticipation with the approach of the grand ball, due to take place at the governor's palace. The palace still wasn't finished. Some estimates claimed it could take up to another ten years to completely fulfil Silas Raines's dream.

Preparations for the ball were well advanced. Mrs Moffat was now in permanent panic trying to deal with all the extra staff and extra slaves brought in to help with preparations. It was during all this activity that I came to realise just how many society folk there were on Heffen. This was truly a place of contrasts. Society in Heffen was divided into three main groups.

The rich immigrants living on Heffen were mostly English, but with a good cross section of other nationalities from all corners of the globe. The ordinary local people, that is the natives of Heffen, lived in stark contrast to the lavish decadence of the new residents. Few of them had any money or position in modern Heffen society, unless they had married into it. Major Baldock had not been the only Englishman to fall for a beautiful native girl.

Then there were those who had nothing, not even their freedom. The colourful comings and goings of tradesmen, explorers and seafaring men to be found around the harbour and dealing rooms completed the picture of this most cosmopolitan of places.

I was in the small classroom one day with Victoria and Rupert. We had been exploring England, Wales and Scotland in some detail. The children wanted to know more about the island where they came from. It was easy to forget that Rupert and Victoria were such a long way from home.

We were deep in discussion about developments in agriculture when we received the most unexpected visitor.

"Please, Mr Anders, don't let me disturb your lesson," insisted the governor. He was, as always, immaculately turned out. "It's a mad house downstairs, what with all this preparations for this wretched ball. I thought I would find sanctuary somewhere in the palace." He smiled his broadest smile reserved for small children, public meetings and hangings. "I will just sit at the back here and join in if I think I know the answer."

The governor squeezed between the astonished children to a desk in the corner at the back of the room. Although not a tall man, Silas Raines had become quite plump through years of good living. The chair he perched precariously upon was far too small for him. In truth, he cut a comical sight as the chair groaned and sagged beneath his weight. From where he sat, there was a good view through the small window of part of the immaculate palace grounds. Unbelievably, a large group of slaves had been brought in to tidy up the already spotless gardens.

"We were talking about England," I explained nervously.

"Good," retorted Uncle Silas. "Do you know, I haven't been home for a very long time. Sometimes miss the place too."

The lesson continued, becoming more specific to the children. After an initial reluctance, the governor seemed happy to tell the children about their grandfather Charles Raines.

"What was he like?" asked Victoria. "Mother would never talk about him."

"Well, let me see." Silas took a deep breath. Even he thought it best to try and hide the deep resentment he felt for his father. "He was what you would recall larger than life, tall some might say. Not particularly good looking, although he considered himself handsome. Oh, and he was a great storyteller."

"What happened to him, sir?" asked Rupert.

"Not sure really." There was a note to the governor's voice that convinced me that he was lying. "Of course, your mother and I were only young when he left. I am not certain, but I think the pirates got him in the end."

"Pirates got our father too," said Rupert.

"He went out without his lucky charm one day," explained their uncle. "I know it sounds stupid, but it protects us." He chuckled in a good-humoured way. "I have one, and if I am not mistaken, Rupert my dear child, you have your father's. Take my advice and keep it with you at all times."

"In case the pirate tries to kill me, Uncle?" asked the boy.

"Exactly that, my boy," enthused Uncle Silas. He took his pocket watch out and examined it closely. "Unfortunately, I have a meeting I must attend. Sadly, I must take my leave." He got up to go. "Forgive me if I have disturbed your lesson, Mr Anders," he said. The governor tucked his watch back into another of his colourful and stylish waistcoats. His grey hair was, as always, oiled back. He looked over tiny wire spectacles at the children.

"The children seem to be both happy and successful at their studies. I congratulate you, Mr Anders." He patted my back, shook my hand and left.

That evening, I decided to return a couple of the books I should not have borrowed to the library. This time I went on my own. The palace security alone should keep Rupert safe. I had, however, instructed Mrs Moffat to keep an eye on the children. As I also realised how distracted she had become with matters pertaining to the grand ball, I borrowed Odi from Simms as extra insurance.

There were a few people left in the great circular hall. Just a handful of slave boys fetching books. I glanced up at the walkways criss-crossing above me and could feel the panic well up inside of me. Part of the intricate network of bridges was still missing, although for some reason, it did not seem to inconvenience the boys in their work.

Professor Kidner greeted me with more of his old warmth. The tall thin man still seemed very troubled and not a little frightened about something. I asked him again if he had come across any other notes on the destruction of the Fault. There was something in the way Kidner looked that brought to mind the plate of ash on his desk.

"You can work in my office as late as you wish, Mr Anders," he told me. "There is a side door at the end of the corridor beyond which is a path directly back to the palace."

Once Kidner had gone, I began to look for further references to Efulric the Apprentice. I had not paid any attention to time nor to the presence of anyone else in the vast library. I wondered in passing if Joseph had found his hairy mammoth yet. Heffen was already beginning to teach me that not everything could be explained in a rational way. Perhaps he would find it after all.

The professor had also found me a large jug of local wine to wash away the dust that collected in every part of his untidy office. In places it was more than an inch thick. I managed to drink only a single goblet of what was, to be fair, a very fine red wine.

So engrossed was I in my research, I had quite forgotten what hour it was, or even to take a drink. I was tired now and the hour I thought must be very late. The office was quite dark. A candle on the desk and an oil lamp on the fireplace were all that lighted my studies. Some light still burnt in the corridor outside. I poured more of the very drinkable wine and leaned back to admire the portrait of Prudence Fairweather gazing regally down from above the fireplace.

I must have sat looking at the picture for ages. Although poorly illuminated by the flickering lamp on the mantle shelf, this somehow gave the picture an eerie lifelike quality. I raised my glass to the pirate.

"Wish I could get you out of my head, Prudence Fairweather," I said softly. "Anyway, your very good health."

"Pardon me, sir, but are you, Mr Anders?" I turned to see the bulk of a large man silhouetted against the light from out in the corridor. I cannot swear to this, but I thought I glimpsed a much smaller figure to his side. I could smell the big man and it was a foul stench. I could also sense something else indefinable. It was like breathing in a cocktail of fear and despair.

The monster of a man stepped into the light. He looked as hideous as he smelt. His eyes were set at a different height from each other and seemed to look in different directions. His mouth was so hideously deformed that it hung limp and caused him to persistently salivate.

"Nothing personal, Mr Anders, and no hard feelings," he continued with a very pronounced lisp, "but I have to kill you."

As if to emphasise his point, a man of few words, but plenty of spit, he drew a large curved sabre. Although I felt fear choking me, I threw myself backwards as the sharp blade smashed into the desk where my head had just been. While he wrestled to pull the sabre out of the desk, I had got to my feet. Snatching the lamp from the mantle shelf, I hurled it at his face. He screamed in pain and anger. At the best I had only slowed him down. I ran out into the corridor, past my attacker, who was screaming with rage. Another figure blocked the exit, sword drawn ready. My heart sank. To run in the other direction would mean being trapped in the darkness of the main hall.

"Get down, Mr Anders," ordered a familiar voice. I obeyed, dropping to the floor. I felt the sabre scythe past the top of my head by little more than an inch.

"I didn't think he was in need of a haircut myself." Prudence Fairweather was not looking at me but at my assailant. "You, on the other hand, my wretched creature, are much in need of extermination." The fight that followed was short. There was the echoing sound of steel hitting steel as the giant launched a vicious and powerful attack on the girl. I was on my feet, terrified but ready to help.

"No heroics are needed, Mr Anders." Prudence seemed to have sensed my intentions. I could see that despite this man's brute force, the pirate girl's skill made her more than a match for him. Sensing this himself, he used his strength to send Prudence flying across the corridor. In the couple of seconds that action bought him, the giant ran down the corridor towards the only exit. Prudence was after him quickly. It took, however, a valuable few seconds for her boots to grip on the slippery floor, by which time my attacker had disappeared into the night.

"It seems you have made some enemies, Mr Anders," she said. She was leaning against the wall, trying to catch her breath.

"I don't know why," I protested. "I have done nothing I am aware of to cause that much offence since I came to Heffen." A small fire was still burning in Kidner's office from the oil lamp I had thrown. Prudence used her cloak to kill the flames.

"That wine you were drinking looked good," she suggested, "if only for medicinal purposes." She laughed and poured us both a goblet full.

"You were watching me?" I said incredulously.

"Only for an hour or two." Prudence smiled and handed me the wine. "You were using the books I wanted to look in," she added sulkily. "I thought I might as well hang on until you had finished. I don't get to come to the library that often to be truthful." Kidner's office had become quite smoky, but as far as I could see nothing important had been damaged. I was still trembling from the attack but was trying desperately not to show that to the pirate.

"I wasn't to know how long you would have your head in the books of course," she went on. "In the end, I gave up and left. Only just after I came out, the smelly ugly one came in."

"Did you see another chap with him? Not a very tall man?" I asked. I was hoping and praying that Prudence had left before I had toasted her picture.

"I don't wish to be rude, Mr Anders, but I don't think they thought it would need two."

"I am sure I saw another man," I insisted, almost to myself. "A smaller man, next to the big chap with bad breath. He was here in the library the other day."

"He was alone I promise you," the girl reassured me. She sat down on the desk next to me. "So what have we been reading then," she asked, picking up one of the volumes from the desk. "Thought you were a bit long in the tooth for fairy tales," she added with one of her sweetest smiles.

"Ever heard of a chap called Efulric?" I asked. "Or Efulric the Apprentice to give him his full title."

"What's all this research you're doing for?" Prudence asked, flicking through another book which she had leaned across me to retrieve.

"To be honest, I started out with the intention of writing a book all about the Heffen islands. I wrote quite a lot about Heffen in an earlier work, but now that I have been here, I thought I could make a better fist of it."

"So what's changed? I can tell by your tone something has." Prudence leaned across me again to top up my wine.

"Just a feeling to be honest, that's all," I said. "A feeling that something is about to happen. Something very bad and quite beyond our comprehension." I looked at the beautiful girl sprawled nonchalantly on the desk. "I thought perhaps we ought to try and stop it," I added.

Prudence spat out a mouthful of wine. "And what makes you think that plain old home-loving Thomas Anders could stop something like you describe," she demanded, wiping the spilt wine from her cleavage with what could well have been a priceless ancient scroll.

"I don't." There was a note of hurt indigence in my voice that made Prudence laugh.

"Oh come on, Thomas, don't go getting all offended on me." She laughed. "You must admit you don't look the type to take on a powerful and indestructible, red-eyed, horned demon spirit single handed. That dribbling creep with no brain nearly took you out ten minutes ago. Believe me, my friend, he wasn't even a third-rate assassin."

"So you have heard of Efulric," I observed calmly. "You describe him well, especially as you don't apparently read fairy stories."

"Know about Efulric the Apprentice?" She started to search the drawers and cupboards in Kidner's jumbled-up office. "Is there no more wine in this place?"

It was my turn to smile. "First thing Odi did for me was find Kidner's secret liqueur store." I got up from the chair behind the desk and went to one of the cupboards. I was still a little shaky and knew deep down that Prudence's remarks had been right. I brought two bottles back to the desk. Prudence, in a very unladylike way, pulled the cork from the first bottle with perfect white teeth. She spat it out into a huge mound of papers in a dark corner of the room.

"Tell the boy Odi he can have a job on the *Albatross* whenever he wants," she said, savouring the bouquet of the newly poured wine.

"I'll tell him," I promised.

"Actually, you shouldn't feel too bad about what I said before," she continued. "You see, there is only one person who has the power to stop Efulric the Apprentice and all his marauding army of hell demons."

"Do you know who?" I asked.

"Me," she said flatly.

"Why you?"

"I don't know why I am cursed in this way, Mr Anders, I just know that I am." She took a long swig of her drink. "There are demon hunters, of course, but apparently old Efulric is pretty much immune to them."

It was my turn to drain my goblet and immediately refill them both. I scratched nervously at two days' growth of stubble on my chin.

"How are you supposed to defeat an immortal demon and the hordes of hell?" I asked after a moment's silence. "Forgive me for asking," I added, "but the slaying of impossible mythological demons has always been a particular interest of mine."

Prudence grinned and her nose wrinkled in such a way that it would melt the hardest heart. "You think you are a very funny man all of a sudden, Mr Anders," she observed coolly. "The point is, whilst I am sure the responsibility is mine, nobody has got round to telling me just how I'm supposed to kill the bloody thing yet." She was toying with the goblet in her strong slender hand. "That's why I came here tonight, to try to find out more about Efulric."

"If he exists," I said.

Prudence sighed. "Oh, the Apprentice exists, Thomas Anders, I promise you. I have seen him, or at least his spirit." She drank down her wine and held her goblet out for more. "I think you must have realised by now that I am not easily scared." Her beautiful big brown eyes spoke for themselves. "I have never felt such fear and would prefer never to again. I had a choice once and I still have. I could take the *Albatross* and run as far from here as the wind will take us."

"Why don't you?" I asked innocently.

"To be honest, I have no idea. I enjoy my life very much. I love parting unpleasant people from their wealth and freeing a few slaves here and there." She reached out and touched my hair with her hand. "Please do not think that I pretend to do great good. If ever I do some good it's usually by default and always to salve my conscience. I am a pirate and, most of the time, proud to be one." She got up and walked to the door. "It might be a good idea if I was to walk you home," she suggested.

I must have looked almost offended by the idea that I might need her protection. In truth, I am absolutely sure that I did.

"Please don't give me that hurt look again," she said, walking seductively back over to the desk. Leaning forward, she tickled the end of my nose with a long slender finger. "First of all, we now know somebody wants to kill you," she whispered. "And anyway you haven't told me why you can't get me out of your head yet." She gave me a tantalising little peck on the cheek. "Do you really think the painting is a good likeness?"

I could feel my face going as red as a beetroot.

Once out in the cool night air, we were silent for a while. I had not attempted to answer her question of course.

"How do you know you have the task of killing Efulric?" I asked slowly.

We found a place to sit in the silvery moonlight that overlooked the sleeping town. A few lights still moved down in the harbour, as if to prove that this was one place that never sleeps. The masterpiece of reclusive architect George Mansfield dominated the scene before us. The ivory white building took upon it an almost ghost-like aura in the silver moonlight. Torches burnt all the way along the walls, adding flickering patterns of colour which washed over the ivory sides of the remarkable monolith.

Prudence told me of her escape from her home on the night that she saw her family massacred. She told me of the man called Douglas and of Arthur leaving them hidden in the trunk of the old tree.

"The man who called himself Douglas was very ill, feverish. I thought that he was going to die. I had already seen too much death that night and I did not think I could stand to watch one more good and kind person dying. I did not know this man. I had no clue as to why he was in the forest that night. I felt sure for some unaccountable reason, however, that he was a good man.

"I also said before that nothing much scares me. I suppose that isn't exactly true. As a child, I never liked the dark. I could imagine all sorts hiding in the shadows. The tree trunk was very dark. I found a candle and decided to risk lighting it. I had some dry tinder. It was then I began to realise just how strange my surroundings were. It was much larger than I expected. Thin roots grew up the sides, intertwining with each other to form elaborate patterns. These carried on to form a high ceiling over us, as grand as I have seen in any building. There seemed to be dark corridors leading away from this strange hallway.

"Am I boring you?" she asked.

"Not at all," I said. "Please continue."

"Then there was the music. At first I thought it was my musical box."

"Your what?"

"If you don't want to listen, just say so."

"Sorry."

"I had a little wooden musical box with a ballerina who danced. It was my mother's I think. I took it with me when I ran from the house. The music was very similar to my music box, soothing, hypnotic and very beautiful. My heart had been broken that day and yet it almost felt that this music had the power to mend it. Then I spilt hot wax on my hand and dropped the candle, which promptly went out of course."

"And you were back in the dark you dislike so much," I said

"Were you there? I hadn't realised," snapped Prudence sarcastically.

"Sorry," I said again.

"You want to tell the story?"

"No, please carry on."

Prudence glared at me and then recommenced her account. "It wasn't dark at all. There was a strange bluish-white light that glowed from the walls. It was then I saw her. She was sat at the far end of this vast chamber."

"Saw who?" I asked without thinking.

"If you would stop interrupting, I might consider telling you."

"Sorry."

"You said that before, but you are still interrupting."

"I won't again."

"Promise?"

"Yes, I promise."

Prudence looked at me. The silvery moonlight bathed her soft olive skin. "I have never told this to anybody before," she said quietly. "Not even Harry."

"Please go on," I begged.

Prudence continued her strange story. "She sat motionless looking directly at me. She was hard to see because she blended in with her background so well. She was tall I would say, and I think she was beautiful in a very formal way. Her clothes were the same colours that were in the wall of roots. Countless shades of brown and grey made her melt into the organic wall behind her."

Then Prudence slipped into an account of what happened.

"What is your name, child?"

"I am Mistress Prudence Fairweather, my lady." She leant forward, her clothes rustling like dry leaves.

"And why do you trespass in this holy place, Mistress Prudence Fairweather?" asked the woman. Her face was mottled in greys and browns.

"I did not mean to trespass, my lady," I assured her. "My companion here is ill, there are people trying to kill us and your tree looked warm and safe."

"I expected you to be older than you are," she said. I sensed an air of sadness in her voice.

"You expected me?" I asked.

"I wasn't sure you would survive, child." The beautiful face smiled down at me. "With all my hundreds of years and all my wisdom, you would think that I would have known better than to doubt you, Prudence Fairweather."

"My parents are dead," I said weakly. "And my brothers and all the people I knew and loved. They have been slaughtered and I don't understand why."

"Your father was a good man. He stood against evil." She floated towards me, her body now a thousand shades of greys and browns that changed constantly. There was also a kind of transparent quality to this strange apparition.

"And evil won," I said. I knew that I sounded like I had lost all hope.

"It is hard for you to understand this now, child." I could touch her now. I was surprised my hand didn't go through her. The delicate hand that touched my cheek was warm and comforting. "You have suffered a great loss." She wiped one single tear from my face. "You mustn't be afraid to cry, Prudence." Then she held me warm and safe whilst I cried. I do not remember how long I cried, but it must have been a long time.

"Your father knew the sacrifice he made tonight. He had faith that although the price was higher than any man should be asked to pay, he would deal a cruel blow to this malevolence that would consume us all. The demon's name is Efulric the Apprentice and he controls some of the armies of hell."

"And my father killed him?"

"Your father set back the demon's plans. It is to his last born the task of killing the Apprentice Efulric and saving our world falls."

"But that is me." I looked up into her eyes.

"You must choose, Prudence Fairweather. You could leave these islands very soon and live a long and happy life, although you may never know what it truly means to love someone. You have already been offered free passage. I know that. The pain you feel now will gradually heal. You are strong and you will do well in the world you choose, wherever that turns out to be. You will not be punished, nor will you feel any guilt or remorse should you choose this path. Or you can stay and live in the shadows you have always been afraid of. You will be an outlaw and even your own blood will hunt you and try to kill you. One day you must face this demon, Prudence. The enormity of its power is unspeakable and yet he fears you, child."

"Will I live a long and happy life if I choose the second path?"

"I do not know the answer to that question. I know that you will live what life you are given to the full. Efulric is powerful and like all demons he has a guardian who will also be both cruel and devious. This guardian may even take the form of a friend and use both fear and guile to try and destroy you for its master's sake."

"I don't know what to do, my lady," I cried, holding myself tight to her warmth.

"Only you can decide that, Prudence Fairweather," she said softly. A shimmering hand stroked my hair. "Now sleep, child. I will take care of your companion."

"But I am alone now, I have no one. All my family are dead, all my friends are dead. What threat am I to this demon alone?" I was strangely relaxed and close to sleep. This strange creature was so warm and so comfortable. I felt secure when a few moments before I had felt I could never sleep again without reliving the horrors of that night. As I fell into deep and peaceful slumber. I remember her last words to me.

Prudence waited a moment for me to interrupt, but I didn't.

"Prudence Fairweather," she said in an oddly stern but also reassuring way, "you will never be alone except of your own doing. You have already made two friends who will both become extremely important to you."

"That's all she said?" I felt Prudence had not quite told me everything.

"She did say I would make lots of friends," she gave me a gentle smile. "In the morning I woke and we were in a tree trunk. It could have been a dream, but I doubt a dream would have fixed Douglas's ankle, or given him back all the blood he had lost. The wound had healed, the bones mended and the swelling gone. So had his fever. It wasn't easy for him to cope with that, so I didn't bother telling him what had happened."

"Why didn't you get on the ship with, Douglas?" I asked.

Prudence started to laugh. "Do you know, Thomas Anders, I have asked myself that question a few times over the years and I still have absolutely no idea."

The first evidence of sunrise was starting to appear on the horizon, turning the sky from coal black to a watery blue, flecked with splashes of pinky red.

"It will be light soon and we are uncomfortably near the palace gates," I pointed out. "Should you not be disappearing back into the shadows?"

"You still haven't answered my question, Thomas Anders."

"I haven't?" I had hoped that she would not pursue this.

"No, you haven't." She stood tall and statuesque, her long legs a little apart and her hands on her hips. "And I am not disappearing into the shadows until you do." She was mocking my discomfort, my face now almost as red as the dawn sky had become. "If I am to hang today, Thomas Anders, may it be on your conscience."

"I think I have fallen in love with you, Prudence Fairweather." My heart was threatening to jump out of my mouth and my legs trembled. An ugly assassin was far less frightening than this. "It is not love as I imagined it nor thought I might have experienced before. It is consuming me. I just want to be with you, to talk with you, to dance with you." I sat back down on the rock.

"Thank you for your honest reply, Mr Anders." She walked over and kissed the side of my face. "You're right though, it's time that I disappeared into the shadows."

Before I could say anything more, she had gone. I spent a long time looking for her. The sun had climbed quite high in the sky before I gave up and set out with a heavy heart towards the palace gates. Prudence Fairweather was very good at hiding in shadows.

Chapter 11

I crept silently into the back kitchen. My hope was that I would be able to sneak up the back stairs to my room, unseen. Moving silently across the well-scrubbed stone floor and out into the small hallway, I skillfully avoiding the squeaky floorboards that led to the stairs and safety. Just as my foot touched the bottom step, there was a loud and disproving cough from behind me. Mrs Moffat was stood, arms folded across her chest, glaring at me.

"I have been worried to death about you, Mr Anders. Where in the Lord's name have you been, young man?" she demanded. Her eyes took in my torn jacket and dirty trousers. I was probably also a little inebriated. A direct result of the large quantity of wine we had liberated from poor Professor Kidner's hidden store.

"I have been at the library," I explained, trying very hard to sound sober. "I lost track of time," I added.

Mrs Moffat looked just as angry.

"I got attacked by a big man who dribbled," I told her. "He had a very big bottom lip and a very big sabre." I held my hands out as a fisherman would, if trying to explain the size of the one that got away.

"I suggest that you go to your room and get yourself cleaned up, Mr Anders," said Mrs Moffat firmly. "Lessons start in less than one hour." The housekeeper still looked very cross. "You ought to be ashamed of yourself, young man," she scolded me.

"I might have had a glass or two of the good professor's excellent vintage, Mrs Moffat," I confessed, staring bleary eyed and foolishly defiant in the Irish woman's angry glare. "In fact, I may have had two too many," I added even more stupidly.

"Rupert and Victoria will be down in a few minutes. They look up to you, Mr Anders. I suggest you go upstairs and get yourself cleaned up."

"I confess, Mrs Moffat, that I am not feeling wonderful this morning."

"It does you no good, excessive drinking, it does not. Mr Moffat used to drink to excess before he discovered temperance." Mrs Moffat smoothed her hands down the front of her white apron, as she always did when upset or put out. "Mr Moffat was a nice man when he was sober, but not nice at all after a few drinks."

Even a little drunk, I could see that Mrs Moffat was becoming upset. "Please forgive me, Mrs Moffat. The last thing I would ever wish would be to cause you any offence." I bowed slightly. "I will go and clean myself up as you suggested."

I was glad to get to my room. I had a dreadful headache and my mouth was dry. I imagined Prudence back on board ship telling everybody how the foolish teacher from England had taken her flirting seriously. Whilst full of wine, he had declared undying love for her. I could hear the laughter.

Simms knocked on my door a little while later. I had persuaded myself by this time that I might see Prudence again. She must quite like me to go to the trouble of saving my life, if only as a friend.

Simms looked as immaculate as ever. He stood almost to attention, dressed in a perfectly laundered white frilled shirt under a long black coat and light grey pants.

"Mrs Moffat was a little worried about you, sir. She asked me if I could mix up some of my infamous concoction." Simms proudly handed me a glass of muddy coloured liquid with something yellow floating in it. "You need to drink it down in one, sir," he explained without any trace of emotion. "I must confess it does not, shall we say, have a particularly nice taste. It will, however, hopefully make you feel better, if you can keep it down that is."

I have never tasted such a foul and unpleasant drink. It was on its own an excellent deterrent for alcohol abuse. However, not long after I had partaken of this foul concoction, I started to feel a good deal better in body, if not in mind. I doubted Simms had any ancient remedy to cure that.

Having washed and shave and changed into fresh clothes, I returned to the kitchen, still feeling extremely delicate. Although Simm's evil potion had helped, any sudden movement had the effect of making me feel most unsteady on my feet.

In my mind, I went over and over the last few minutes I had spent with the pirate girl. What I would give to take them back. The wine, perhaps also the adrenaline and of course the beautiful sunrise, had all helped to free my inhibitions, just for long enough to blurt out my innermost private thoughts.

How could I ever face her again without showing my embarrassment for such juvenile and inappropriate behaviour? What I would give for just a little part of Sydney's skill and confidence with the fairer sex. I did, however, recall with some satisfaction that Sydney's infamous charm had not it seemed worked well on the pirate either.

Then I remembered the story she had told me. I could not believe I was worrying about my behaviour, or about making a fool of myself. It would mean little to a girl who had lived through as much as Prudence had. She had told me of her terrible destiny. She had told me things she had told nobody before. I was letting my heart and my desires rule my head.

My mind wandered back to the haunting tale Prudence Fairweather had told me. Despite the fantastic and unlikely nature of the events she had described, I never for a moment doubted the truth of her story. I was sure that, despite having no reasonable explanation, the experience had been told to me precisely as it had happened. If I accepted this story as fact, without question, then logically I must also accept the existence of hell demons.

That thought in turn led to the undeniable conclusion that Efulric the Apprentice himself must exist. Added to all this was another minor detail that had slipped my mind. So besotted had I become with the pirate, I had forgotten that somebody was trying to kill me now.

I sat down to a large helping of Mrs Moffat's thick and lumpy porridge. She had decided that I needed an extra large helping to aid my struggle with the day ahead. Just looking down at the huge portion in the bowl on the table, I felt ill. Mrs Moffat's famous oats served only to reinforce my conviction that I would not make it through the day.

The famous architect George Mansfield had known exactly what was in Sir John Burleigh's dark and shadowy mind when he had designed his folly. A bleak and foreboding sky began to move over the farthest tip of the northern island. This was indicative of the imminent arrival of one of the freak storms that acted as a precursor to the rainy season.

Beneath the black swirling clouds, Burleigh's dark palace rose in savage magnificence from the rock on which it had been built. Sparse trees scattered around the great mansion bent in the strong wind which rattled the windows in their frames. A fork of yellow lightning seemed only just to miss the great gothic tower of the west wing. A second fork of lightning turned the monstrous building momentarily white. The hideous gargoyles seemed to leap from the walls.

Inside this nightmare, in the stark hall with a high stone vaulted ceiling, Burleigh sat in a comfortable chair by a huge open fire that bathed the cavernous hall with dark orange light. Torches burnt at strategic places around this cold, austere place.

The only other furniture consisted of a large table and chairs on which the carpenter had carved intricate and detailed patterns that included serpents and gargoyles. The wind battered against the windows, and the thunder rumbling in the darkness outside echoed around the vaulted roof.

It was a far cry from what had once stood here. Once in awhile,

Burleigh thought he heard music. There was not just one type of music, but different styles, coming from different places. Other visitors would raise an eyebrow at the sound of happy laughter, faint but definitely audible. Some days there would be the smell of baking, and yet the ovens in Burleigh's gloomy kitchens had never been lit.

These apparitions seemed to be getting worse. The night before, Burleigh had been woken by a terrible storm. He lay in his great four-poster bed listening to the rain lashing against the window. The terrible draft that came from somewhere in the attic conspired to make everywhere in the house permanently cold. It also made the single candle on the dark mahogany dresser flicker and die.

The mansion had more than twenty bedrooms, but Sir John Burleigh lived alone. Few visitors chose to stay at Burleigh's monstrous folly. He could hear a sound coming from below. For a little while he convinced himself that the sound was only his fanciful imagination. At last he could stand it no longer. Pulling on a long grey-checked housecoat and slippers, Burleigh relit the candle. He slipped quietly out of his room onto the landing.

Lightning momentarily illuminated the hollow casing of a black knight standing to attention as he had done for centuries probably. As heavy rolls of thunder rumbled across the great house, a large and ugly black crow screeched from his perch high in the vaulted ceiling and flew to a window ledge. Here the grotesque creature began to prune itself, silhouetted against the church-like, leaded window.

The wind howled around the high buttressed roof. At the top of the great staircase, Burleigh gripped the carved wood banister rail and looked down into the hallway. There were children playing on the stone floor. At first the only light seemed to come from the single candle flickering in his trembling hand. They all looked up at Sir John Burleigh and began to laugh. He realised that some light also emanated from the children themselves.

There was a loud crash of thunder and the candle went out. For a moment, Burleigh struggled in the pitch black to re-light the candle. When he had done so, he went carefully down the stairs into the hall. It was quite empty, except, that is, for an object moving in the shadows.

Burleigh, his heart pounding, moved slowly forward. He could still hear the children's defiant laughter mocking him. The light from the candle shone onto a child's rocking horse, still rocking to and fro, then that too faded into nothing.

Sir John's first visitor the following morning was the assassin Peckham.

"I must object strongly to you summoning me again, Sir John. These are small islands and people talk."

Sir John laughed at the little man's concern. He rose from his chair by the blazing fire and helped himself to a long thin black cigar. This he took from an ornate wooden box shaped a little like a tiny coffin. He lit the cigar from the steel grey candelabra that formed the centrepiece of the table.

"Few ever come here, Mr Peckham, although I am expecting a visit from the governor."

"He of all people must not see me, Sir John, even if he is helping to fund my payment." As always, Peckham was dressed in black and grey and carried a small case.

"I wanted to ask you, Peckham, why you did not kill the boy the other day?" He paused to re-light his cigar and inhaled a lung full of strong and foul-smelling smoke. "By all accounts you had the ideal opportunity and yet the boy lives."

"It was not the appropriate time," replied Peckham with half a smile on his deathly white face. "If you pay for a professional to do a job for you, Sir John, you must also learn to trust his judgement."

"You would not, by any chance, be doing a little moonlighting, Mr Peckham?" demanded Sir John. He was outwardly as calm and unruffled as ever. Closer inspection of the cold and calculating man might have detected an uneasy edge hidden beneath the immaculate exterior.

"If you mean the clumsy attempts to kill the new teacher man then you insult me, Sir John. Although I would not expect you to grieve much at the passing of this fool Anders."

"He is of no consequence," said Burleigh. "Although he does have a habit of getting in the way. I suppose it would have been fitting for such an inconsequential man to have an appropriately inconsequential end." Burleigh stood by the fire and lifted his coat tails. "What about the pirate woman!" Peckham could feel Burleigh's fear even just speaking of her. "I would be pleased by reports of her tragic and untimely death, Peckham."

"It is not she you need to fear, Sir John, although I understand you fearing her," he acknowledged graciously. "I am a little wary of her myself," he added, his voice for a moment sounding cold and dispassionate. "We all have our potential nemesis and yours may well be Prudence Fairweather."

"I fear no man and certainly no woman," retorted Burleigh angrily.

"Then you are a fool, Sir John," said Peckham softly.

"I have hired you to do a few little jobs for me," pointed out Burleigh coldly. "I have not asked for, and do not value, your opinion."

Peckham gave Burleigh a cold smile. The smallness of the man was emphasised by the tall and debonair figure of Sir John towering above him. Nevertheless, Burleigh felt intimidated by the little man. This made him feel very uncomfortable. He was used to intimidating others, not feeling threatened himself.

"I promise you, Sir John, I have the situation under control. People will die when it is right and timely that they do so."

In the dark shadows on the first landing by the grand staircase, two men, hidden from view, listened to the conversation below.

"What did he say then?" whispered Harry.

"Have you considered getting your ears washed out, you deaf old bastard?" suggested Arthur.

"At least I am not an ugly old bastard like you," hissed Harry.

Down in the hall, one of Sir John's footmen entered.

"His Majesty's Governor to the Islands of Heffen awaits your pleasure, Sir John."

"This could be interesting," observed Arthur from the shadows.

"He does seem to be getting some interesting guests today," agreed Harry. "Are you not glad we dropped in now?" he added, with the smug look of a man whose idea had been proved to have been a good one.

"This place gives me the creeps," moaned Arthur. "Can't you feel it, you insensitive oaf? It's everywhere. I can't stay here much longer or I swear I shall go insane."

The little man made it very clear to both Burleigh and their unseen observers that he had no desire to meet the governor. Sir John summoned a rather comical-looking footman in a bleached white wig and matching tights. These were topped off with a smart mid-green waistcoat of almost military style.

The footman was directed to show the little man the rear exit through the kitchens. Peckham, still clutching his little case, was ushered out. As he was directed towards the servants' door, the little man turned momentarily and looked up towards the balcony. The strange saucer-shaped eyes peering out of the pallid face seemed to be looking directly at Arthur and Harry. It was as if the little man knew that they were there. His face remained expressionless and he turned to follow the footman out.

"Sir John, it is good to see you." The governor beamed his warmest smile. The shorter and rather portly man was as always impeccably turned out. He wore a green frock coat over a mustard yellow waistcoat. He was once again examining his pocket watch. "I have had the most dreadful journey, Burleigh," the governor told him with surprisingly good humour. "It works up quite a thirst in a man," he added with a big smile and a sparkle in his sharp eyes.

"I would have happily come to see you and saved you the tedious journey, Governor, you know that," said Burleigh smoothly. He indicated for refreshments to be brought in.

"Nonsense," exclaimed Silas Raines. "They are completing preparations for the grand ball at the palace, and frankly, Sir John, I was glad to get away from the place. Anyway, you look tired, have you not been sleeping well?"

"I had a disturbed night because of the storm, that's all," explained Burleigh.

"Really, how very odd," replied the ebullient governor. "Your footman was just telling me that the night was fine here and that the storm was only now getting a hold."

Sir John Burleigh looked uncomfortable for a moment. "I must have dreamt it then," he said slightly awkwardly.

"Just a couple of things I wanted to talk about," the governor said. "I thought you might be interested to know that I had a visit from Henry Jessop."

"Jessop back on the island." Burleigh was obviously surprised. "I thought I told him never to return," he said. "So I wonder, does our friend still have the ear of friends in high places? The British government for instance? I have begun to fear our very special assassin might be playing a double game. I know for a fact he, too, has good connections with some very important people in England. I am not very keen on the idea of a government agent in our midst, Governor."

"Jessop is a rogue, you know that better than most surely."

"Ah yes, Governor. However, being a rogue does not necessarily preclude a person from government work of this nature."

"There is absolutely no evidence that Jessop is their man," pondered Silas Raines. "I asked him, of course, but he wasn't going to tell me, was he? As a matter of fact, he insists that he's experiencing bad times. Going on his general appearance, I could be disposed to believing his story." Raines's high forehead furrowed into a frown. "If your man, what's his name, is working for the British government then that's a pretty difficult situation, Burleigh."

"Not much we can do about it, Governor. His kind of specialist doesn't grow on trees. Shall we just say I am keeping an eye on the situation." Sir John smiled. "You said a couple of things, Governor?"

"The other thing was that I wanted to remind you of our plan, Burleigh," explained Raines, looking at Sir John through narrowed eyes. "We have no choice but to do as we are asked, you agree?"

Burleigh began to laugh. "I have told you, Governor, this man we have hired, double dealing or not, is a specialist. I have fully checked his credentials and there is no doubt he has been able to complete similar tasks with a one hundred percent success rate." He paused to supervise the arrival of food and drink. Once all the food had been placed on the table, the two men began to help themselves. It was plain and simple fare. There was pork, venison and beef with large cobs of bread fetched in from a local smallholding. All this could be washed down by jugs of strong ale that made the two watching pirates' mouths water.

"They will hear my stomach rumbling with hunger and then the game will be up," moaned Arthur.

"With a bit of good fortune they might mistake you for an oversized rat," replied Harry. "It would be an easy mistake to make."

"Why can't I meet this man who can achieve the impossible?" demanded the governor through a mouthful of pork, bread and ale.

"He is keen that he is known to as few people as possible," explained Burleigh. "That is, I suppose, understandable in view of his line of work."

"I would never have known where to find such a man, Burleigh. I take my hat of to you for that." "I mean, who ever heard of a genuine bona fide demon killer?" he added.

"Exactly, Governor, and as I know of no others, if he turns out to be double crossing us, we will just have to deal with him after he has killed Efulric."

My mood did not improve as the day went on. Victoria and Rupert had both decided to be particularly difficult. On more than one occasion, I exploded with anger, reducing both my charges to floods of tears. As a consequence of this, I ended up feeling as if I was now failing at the one thing I was any good at.

As we were coming ever closer to the grand ball, there were more and more people rushing up and down the corridors of the palace. It was becoming increasingly unclear what useful purpose many of these people served. Major Baldock had increased the number of soldiers, both inside and outside the palace, almost fourfold. These extra security measures further added to the chaos.

There was an orchestra practising in the annexe to the grand ballroom. A string quartet was scraping away in the main reception room, and a military band, making an even worse racket, in the hall or courtyard depending on how wet it was. For some inexplicable reason, there had been added to all this cacophony of sound the bizarre sight of a lone bagpipe player.

There were men with hammers everywhere. People screaming orders at their subordinates. This was a bad day to have a bad head in the governor's palace. Sydney Greenburgh called to make my day even worse. He had dropped round to tell me that he had asked a young lady if she would do him the honour of accompanying him to the ball. The lady in question, who was according to Sydney more beautiful than the most beautiful girl in the world, had said yes. My foppish friend did not mention what her husband looked like.

I told Sydney about the man with the deformed lip and mentioned that I had bumped into Prudence. I was perhaps a little vague about exactly what happened, concentrating more on the quality of Professor Kidner's wine cellar. I did not tell him any of Prudence's story. After all, she had told no one else but me. I also decided not to mention my clumsy declaration of love for the pirate. It would have only earned me a lecture on the correct way for a gentleman to woo a lady.

Sydney was, to be fair, concerned for my safety, and clearly thought I should report the matter to our old school chum, Major Baldock. I, in turn, was not keen on the idea, as I did not wish to draw attention to Prudence or myself. The idea of discussing my theories regarding the legendary demon Efulric the Apprentice with the major, who I remembered from school as being a dull and unimaginative chap, did not appeal much either.

The annual grand ball was continuing to lift everybody's spirits, except perhaps mine. In the afternoon, I took Victoria and Rupert for a walk in the palace grounds. This seemed a safe enough course of action. Palace security was always good and, with the impending arrival of important foreign guests, had become even better. It was an opportunity to get away from the mayhem inside.

The corridors were choked with people colliding with each other and a complement of fully armed soldiers. I had noticed Major Baldock checking his troops, but he had not appeared to recognise me. He had been Sydney's friend more than mine. Baldock had, like Sydney, been a good and competitive sportsman, both in school and out!

We had reached the entrance to the maze when I saw a man of medium build, in a tall hat and top coat, take a whip to one of a group of young black slaves. I am ashamed to say that my first reaction was to try and hide this horrible sight from Rupert and Victoria. I was, however, too late. Victoria began to scream and point. Rupert was tugging on the sleeve of my coat.

"That man is hitting Odi!" he shouted. I ran the short distance, pushing my way through a small group of workers, and grabbed the man's arm as he swung the whip back.

"That will do, sir," I said, taking the whip out of the surprised man's hand. He was a cocky young man who, like most bullies, cowered back. Victoria had run to Odi.

"Is he ok?" I asked. My eyes were fixed on the supercilious slave driver.

"No, he's not," sobbed Victoria.

"I'm ok, Mr Anders, sir," said Odi. There were tears running down his cheeks, although he was trying hard to smile.

"He's a worthless bit of shit," said the young man. "What you getting so worked up about!"

I hit him quite hard, hard enough to really hurt my hand. Despite the searing pain in my fist, it was the first time that day I had felt good about anything.

"Thomas Anders!" shouted a voice behind me. I looked round to see the major approaching.

"He hit me, Major Baldock," said the bully, pointing a bony finger at me. "I think he's broken my jaw," he added, feeling his stubbily chin carefully, as if checking for exactly where the fracture might be.

"I have told you before, Mr Brunt, I do not care to see people taking a whip to a slave. In any case, it is the governor's express wish that such punishments should not take place in the grounds of the palace."

Baldock paused and looked at me. "I am sure Mr Anders might consider not reporting this incident to the governor." He looked at me questioningly.

It must have been well over ten years since I had last set eyes on Philip Baldock, and his appearance had changed very little. He had kept his boyish good looks, although his hair was beginning to recede a little and he had a few grey hairs.

"If Major Baldock wishes and if Mr Brunt gives me his word that this will not happen again, the matter could quite easily be overlooked."

"My word as a gentleman," Brunt assured me without the slightest trace of sincerity in his tone.

"Then it is agreed," decided Baldock cheerfully. "Now leave us before I change my mind, Brunt."

Brunt turned to walk away, passing close to the still trembling Odi.

"They won't be around to protect you all the time, nigger boy," he hissed in Odi's ear.

Odi said something back to Brunt. I could not quite hear what he had said. It sounded like some unrecognisable foreign tongue, one I am not familiar with. Whatever it was Odi said, the bully looked even more scared than before. He melted quickly into the crowds.

It was pointless for Baldock or me to do or say any more. There was little doubt that Brunt could have had Baldock arrest me for common assault. I was fortunate to get away with nothing worse than a very sore hand. Baldock had completely fabricated the claim that the governor objected to the public flogging of slaves. In truth, he had no idea what the governor's stance would be on this issue.

"So how are you, Philip?" I asked. "I heard you had settled on Heffen."

"Unless I am ever posted, Thomas." Baldock smiled awkwardly. "I used to worry about that, but the governor assures me that as long as he is in charge I will be required to serve here. So what the hell are you doing here? You're not this British agent everybody seems to be expecting?" Baldock looked a little worried by his own question.

"Did this particular spy take out advertising space with Reuters to announce his arrival?" I asked. "Only everyone I talk to seems to be expecting him."

"We are all a little on edge, Thomas, that's all. Is the slave boy ok?" Baldock asked, changing the subject and choosing to ignore my observation.

"His back is a mess." I looked at the child resting against Rupert and Victoria. "I will get him back to Mrs Moffat, if that's all right with you, Philip."

"Yes, of course it is," he said quickly. The soldier looked uneasy in all his finery, brasses polished to excess, and his long leather boots shined up like mirrors. The jet-black footwear contrasted well with immaculate ivory white trousers and the scarlet tunic. I started to walk back towards the palace.

"Did Sydney tell you we had bumped into each other?" Baldock caught up with me and fell into step in fine military tradition.

"You'd had a little farceur that day, Sydney seemed to think."

Baldock smiled. "Well, I was always getting into punch-ups at school, so that is nothing new." The major looked at me disapprovingly. "I don't recall you ever hitting anybody, Anders. What is going on with you? I remember you always had the ability to talk your way out of trouble. Used to admire that. All Sydney and I ever did was scrap with people over women."

I pushed some of my mop of unkempt hair away from my face. It had started to turn quite breezy and was raining again. "Nothing to admire, Philip. I was always afraid if I hit somebody, they would hit me back, only much harder. Anyway, I'm not sure how you talk an animal like that into treating his fellow human beings with respect," I said. "No, our friend Brunt managed to get me angry enough to forget for a moment what a coward I am."

Baldock's expression changed noticeably at the word coward.

"I know you soldier types do not approve of cowardice, Philip," I said. "I am probably being a little hard on myself."

We had reached the driveway, with its perfectly geometrical paving stones. The oddly unreal hedges that formed the large maze loomed up to our right in the greyness of a wet evening. The wind, now even stronger, gave life to the topiary birds formed from similar hedging to the maze. Despite the drizzle, a group of finely dressed men and women were playing croquet on the main lawn, directly in front of the marble palace. Its ivory white walls shimmered in the lights of more than a thousand torches.

"My fight was with Sir John Burleigh," said Baldock flatly. "It is the evil of that man which spawns lowlife like Brunt. Thomas, Sir John is one of the most despicable men alive today." We had stopped near to

273

the grand stairway leading up to the front entrance.

"Are you not the law in these parts, Baldock?" I asked. "From what you say, this Burleigh would be better clapped in irons."

"Sir John has friends in high places. He is protected from any harm, protected in ways you wouldn't understand. There is nothing I or indeed anyone can do. If I was you, Thomas, I would seek out old Greenburgh tonight and buy passage back to England on the next ship to leave Heffen."

"Friends in high places," I repeated Baldock's words. "You mean friends in government and that means the governor of course."

Baldock laughed. "Burleigh does not limit himself to worldly alliances, Anders." The major could not hide the fear in his eyes. For a moment, our eyes were locked on each other. I turned to watch a tall lady in a tall hat, matching elegant cream blouse and long tight skirt take her croquet mallet and smash her opponent's ball out of her way. The action appeared to be completely out of character for this elegantly demure figure.

"He's made a pact with the devil," said Baldock bitterly.

A team of more than thirty people had all but stripped the *Sally O* of fixtures and fittings. Large areas of timber on the hull had already been replaced. The damaged mast was to be replaced by a new one. This was nearing completion.

Many of the people working on the dismantled schooner were islanders. Their special crafts had been passed down from generation to generation. Since the settlers had first started coming to Heffen such skills had become less and less in demand.

Although most of the slaves passing through were taken from places a long way from Heffen, if Burleigh found a consignment was particularly down in numbers, he would arrange for a similar number of islanders to be added to the cargo for the journey on to the Americas.

The governor had ordered the military to turn a blind eye to this practice, which was otherwise quite illegal. This is to say, nothing of it being totally against the spirit of the treaty between the people of Heffen and the British government. Such actions lead the natives to distrust the English and increasingly to despise them.

Captain Jakes sat on the dockside, watching his ship being transformed from a leaking tub to a fine seaworthy craft. He marvelled at the skills of the native craftsmen. Olive-skinned men, mostly clothed in little more than a loincloth, worked through the blazing midday sun, cutting, shaping, treating and fitting replacement sections. Others skilled with a paintbrush were transforming the careworn vessel to her former glory.

"Your ship will be as good as new when they've finished, Captain." Meg sat down next to him on the rock. Monkey had wandered down to chat with some of the men.

"What is he saying to them?" asked Jakes. The big man had been persuaded to take off his uniform. He sat in a baggy white shirt, open almost to the waist. His long and curly, silver grey hair was complemented by a similarly hairy chest.

"Prudence wants your ship fully seaworthy as soon as possible," explained Meg. "As it is, even at the speed they're working, it's going to take a few more days."

Monkey walked over to join them. Meg hungrily admired his rippling muscles as he walked back up the pebbly beach. He made her slim and lithe little body go all goose-pimply. She hoped that nobody had noticed but was pretty sure that Jakes had.

"Another week at sea, Captain, and the good *Sally O* would have most likely sank without trace," Monkey said cheerfully.

"She looked worse than she was," lied Jakes. The even bigger man, the giant Joshua, had walked down the beach to join them.

"Hey, Monkey, Joshua is bored!" he shouted.

"Like Prudence says, they're like children these two," Meg told Jakes.

"You need to work some of the fat off you, Joshua," suggested Monkey. "You are spending too much time doing long division sums for Prudence."

"I am in far better condition than you are, lad," replied the giant. "I just happen to have a few brain cells as well."

"Joshua is a clever boy," Meg told Jakes. "Only like all you blokes he feels the need to flex his muscles now and again." Meg jumped up and drew a large circle in the sand.

"Right," she said, commanding the two men to order. They obeyed at once, despite her already diminutive stature being exaggerated, standing so close to such tall men. "You know the rules. First one to put a foot out of the circle smells."

The two men were almost equally matched. Joshua, the older of the two by little more than two summers, was also the larger by almost a foot. Monkey had compensated by building up the muscles in his arms and legs even more than his opponent. Both had worked hard to build their bodies to almost physical perfection. Now they stood facing each other.

Muscles rippled in their arms and legs and then tensed as they braced themselves against each other. Both men put enormous effort into the struggle that followed. Perspiration trickled down their massive arms and legs. Bare feet sank into the soft sand as each tried to at least hold his ground. Many of the people working on the *Sally O* came to watch, along with a motley selection of pirates.

"Does he remember nothing from his childhood?" asked Jakes.

"Not much," Meg answered. "This isn't good for a girl, all these naked sweaty bodies you know."

Jakes looked quite shocked. His weatherbeaten face took on a most comical expression which made Meg giggle.

"I'm sorry, Captain," Meg made herself stop laughing at the look on Jakes's face. "It's Prudence's fault," she added. "She has no sense of decency or decorum." Meg gave up the struggle and exploded into hysterical laughter.

Jakes looked at the diminutive and innocent-looking black girl and began to smile himself. He wondered how this pretty girl was able to have so much laughter in those beautiful, big eyes after all the terrible things that had happened to her. As for the man she was so obviously besotted with, he wasn't absolutely sure, but he thought he knew who he was now. Whatever terrible things Monkey had suffered in his past, his mind had blocked out completely. These people made him feel very relaxed and a little humble.

He was laughing too, although he had no idea what about. Monkey blamed the noise the two of them were making for causing the break in concentration that sent him over the edge of the circle first. Jakes felt almost guilty, until Meg reassured him that Monkey always lost.

"They could have still been there well after dark though," she said.

Jakes smiled. Nobody could blame him feeling a little protective towards the lad, because Jakes was now absolutely certain he had found his son.

Mrs Moffat was horrified when she saw what had happened to the little boy. The little Irish woman scurried around her back kitchen muttering blasphemies to herself whilst preparing the boy soup. This was her remedy for almost all ills. She was clearly very angry that anyone could do this to anyone, never mind to a child. Despite her anger, she had been very gentle with Odi whilst washing his wounds and putting on some strong-smelling ointment from her first aid box.

"You will be right as rain in a couple of days," Mrs Moffat told him.

Odi was a survivor and a free spirit, but I was very much afraid that this man Brunt might have knocked that out of the lad. The look on his face was difficult to read, unlike his normally cheerful and cheeky countenance. It could have been hate, perhaps fear, or maybe anger.

Rupert and Victoria were fussing about him almost as much as Mrs Moffat was.

"Was the man with the whip one of Prudence Fairweather's men?" asked Rupert. "Maybe it was me they were after really," he added hopefully. The child was keen to prove to me that the pirate was out for his blood. I found myself wondering how you would explain anything about what had happened to a small child.

"It didn't used to be like this on Heffen. Not when we first came here it wasn't," Mrs Moffat said. "It feels as if bad things are happening everywhere. Mr Moffat said it was happening, and I took no notice. I thought it was the drink talking." She paused and looked at Simms and me. "He was always telling everyone who would listen that the devil was at work on Heffen."

"Did you believe him?" Victoria asked politely.

"Nobody believed him, my little pet, nobody, especially not me."

I took Simms into a corner of the kitchen. "I am concerned, Simms, that this coward Brunt might try to beat the boy again, when there is nobody there to prevent it."

Simms nodded. "I was just nipping out for a little while, Mr Anders. I will give your concern the most careful consideration." He gave me a rare smile.

"If Odi slept in my room, I could protect him from the pirates," suggested Rupert, who was not feeling quite as brave as he was trying to sound.

"That's a very good idea," agreed Victoria. "In fact, by Rupert's standards, it's an incredibly good idea," she added with a haughty smile.

For the first time for ages, Odi managed a smile.

Chapter 12

The evening of the grand ball had at last almost arrived. For the last two days, any attempt to teach the children had become an increasingly impossible task. Apart from the level of noise and number of people squeezed into the palace, the children were now very excited themselves. There was no doubt that the forthcoming ball had lifted the spirits of most of the people on the island.

There had been some concern, after a few days of light showers, that the rain would come early and wash out the governor's parade. This took place every year as a precursor to the grand ball. All the common people of the south island and quite a few from the north would line the road leading to the palace to catch a glimpse of the many fine carriages. These would be purveying the extravagantly clothed guests to the biggest event in Heffen's social calendar.

Torches were lit all the way along the twisting road from the harbour. The governor had, as was the custom, lent his official carriages to carry the most important guests from their ships. Officially the most important of these guests was the British ambassador, who was, we were told, accompanied by a gentleman travelling incognito

Local gossip insisted that this was probably a less than savoury member of our Royal family, who was said to come every year, health permitting. Others talking in dark whispers behind closed doors claimed that the British government had sent a demon hunter with the ambassador.

Other guests included a member of the Spanish royal family and envoys from France, Portugal and the Americas. There was a Mandarin, a sprinkling of clerics and politicians, together with an Arabian prince, who alone had an entourage of more than a hundred. There was much talk about the arrival of Lady Catherine Ridley, the Countess of Thorn, said to be a very close friend of the governor and the widow of his predecessor.

I had done my best to clothe myself in a more than presentable style, as befitted such an important event. I wore a cravat which I was convinced had developed a mind of its own. The dammed thing was dreadfully uncomfortable to say the very least. My jacket and trousers were too fancy, not to mention a little tight for my liking, but nevertheless appropriate for such a flamboyant night.

Victoria had on a pretty lilac dress with a large bow at the back. Mrs Moffat had taken ages to do her hair. Victoria did a few twirls and even Rupert conceded reluctantly that his sister looked lovely.

Once the three of us were ready and Victoria had made me let her comb my hair, we reported to Mrs Moffat's back kitchen for final inspection and approval. I was feeling very nervous about the evening. As a general rule, staff are not invited to the grand ball. I suppose I had been invited simply to look after the children, or perhaps for my work in studying the history and geography of the area.

Mrs Moffat stood, arms folded across her chest, and examined each of us in turn with her critical eye. She went over to Rupert and retied his tie and straightened his pants. She curtsied to Victoria and whispered, "You look perfectly beautiful, my lady, you do that."

Victoria curtsied back and giggled.

"You will have to make sure she is chaperoned at all times, Mr Anders, for there will be a queue of men looking to dance with this beautiful young lady, to be sure there will."

"Just as long as she saves one dance for me, Mrs Moffat," I said.

Mrs Moffat had reached me. "For goodness sake, what on earth is going on here?" she demanded, tugging at my cravat.

"I am not very good with stuff round my neck," I said. "I think I must have been hung in a previous life."

"Just as long as you're not hung in this one," replied Mrs Moffat sternly as she retied the offending cravat. She stood back to admire her work. "You'll do," she decided.

"Thank you," I said, still unsure I would not be far better retiring to my bed with a good book.

"If I was quite a lot younger than I am and lucky enough to go to such a grand event as this, Victoria, I know who I would like to dance the night away with." She gave me a strangely soft look. "I once had a man who looked a little like you, Mr Anders. Maybe he wasn't the most handsome man the world has ever seen. Still, he cleaned up ever so nice like you do." For just a moment, Mrs Moffat was still and quiet, then brightening up again, she said, "If you are taking the children to watch the governor's parade, you should be going or you will miss it. Now that would be a terrible shame now, would it not?" She began to shoo us from her kitchen. "Come on, be off with you now," she said.

Mrs Moffat was right about the governor's parade. It was as outrageously breathtaking an event as it was intended to be. One of those very special occasions in life filled with such colour and pageantry that neither the children nor indeed I will ever forget.

We had a grandstand view from one of the private balconies that overlooked the winding road from the harbour, as well as the road north. Beyond in the distance we could see the harbour itself. Sunset was coming earlier at this time of the year. Today had been as hot as ever, although as the sun had gone down, it had become noticeably cooler. This had not put people off lining the roads up to the palace. I could feel the excitement and anticipation of thousands of men, women and children waiting for the spectacle to unfold.

At last Major Baldock rode into view on a magnificent white stallion. He was even more immaculate than usual, if that was possible. Turned out in his best dress uniform, the tunic a rich, dark blue, unique to the Heffen guard, the major ordered his equally well turned-out soldiers over the head of the hill. A sea of blue tunics and shining brasswork surged towards us, marching in perfect time.

Behind them came the military band, whose cacophonous racket had been driving me insane for three weeks now. I had to concede that they sounded good and looked even better in their smart blue tunics, marching in perfect step.

Behind the soldiers came the entertainers. This colourful band of circus folk was led by a group of men on stilts. These men, walking with slow military precision, towered above their audience. Mixed amongst them were fire-eaters, jugglers, tumblers and jesters in glittering outfits that sparkled in the light from the torches that lit their way. Magicians and fortune-tellers mingled in the crowds to work their clever spells and share their own perceptions of the future.

Behind the acrobats were the elephants. A dozen of these massive beasts moved slowly along the road, trunks linked to the tail of the animal in front. I thought of my brother searching the Amazon for the elephant's ancestors. These were not hairy mammoths, but I wondered if I might have got closer to one than my poor brother ever would. Tall, slim and beautiful men and women in figure-hugging leotards posed on the backs of these mighty beasts.

More jugglers followed. Some stood on the backs of jet black or pure white circus horses that pranced proudly along the road, plumes of silver and gold blowing in the light breeze. After them was the entertainer's own band. A motley group of hobos and misfits led by a red-nosed clown with a great base drum strapped to his front.

With baggy trousers and a painted grin, the jester had a supposedly comic appearance, although the drawn-on smile for me had more of a look of evil. A momentary reminder in all this noise and pageantry of the awesome powers of darkness I sensed all around us. Through this celebration of colour and spectacle, it lurked somewhere in the darkest shadows, waiting patiently for the moment to strike.

The sound of the band was worse than the military's rehearsals had ever been. Nobody in the vast crowds enjoying all these wondrous spectacles cared if the players were in tune or not! They received the same level of noisy appreciation as anyone else.

Then came the guests from various parts of the two islands. The procession of fine carriages was led by the governor. Silas Raines waved to the people of Heffen from his golden, jewel-encrusted coach, pulled by six black stallions. His companion was the mature and handsomely beautiful Lady Catherine Ridley. She was smiling, too, and waving a golden-gloved hand regally at the populace. For the first time, however, the cheering had subdued, and there were a few open murmurings of discontent amongst the crowd.

Simms had entered the balcony behind us, looking as poised and unruffled as he always did. "Lady Catherine Ridley is a most beautiful woman, don't you think, Mr Anders?" he said.

"Beautiful maybe, Simms," I agreed, "but as cold as ice."

"Odd you should say that Mr Anders," observed Simms. "She was often referred to by the populace of Heffen as the Ice Queen."

Beyond the governor came the carriages of many island socialites. Boscastle's coach was functional and clean, Burleigh's shiny black. There was one small carriage that would have looked more in keeping in a funeral procession. Built with a strong resemblance to a hearse, it was small and black, with a dull shine to the paintwork. Just two smallish black horses pulled the carriage, which had large heraldic crests on the doors.

On the great marble stairway leading from the immaculate garden to the entrance of the palace, the lone bagpipe player, in full Highland costume, played his lament. The crowds had fallen silent. There was no other noise except the occasional snort from a horse.

"I came to tell you that your friend Mr Greenburgh and his young lady are here, Mr Anders," explained Simms.

"I understand the bagpipes now," I said quietly. The Highlander had stopped playing. He stood absolutely motionless silhouetted against the bright silver light of a full moon. For a moment everywhere was silent, and then the crowds began to cheer again.

Odi's back healed remarkably well. The physician who Mrs Moffat had both arranged and paid to attend to the boy expressed some surprise at both the speed of his recovery and the apparent lack of any permanent scaring. Indeed, it required quite close inspection to notice any marks on his body. I feared that instead the damage was inside his head.

He had lost his perkiness and got on with any work given to him quietly and without either argument or good humour. He had noticed the man, Brunt, a few times. Odi, however, had been moved to a different part of the palace and so, in theory at least, would not for now work under this man's jurisdiction. He knew, however, that this could only be a temporary arrangement. Indeed, two of Brunt's men had already managed to tell him that he had a beating to finish. Brunt himself seemed almost as frightened of something as the boy was of him.

During the few days leading up to the night of the grand ball, Odi had, like all the workers on the estate, been very busy. Nevertheless, his eyes were always searching for danger. Odi understood what it was like to be a slave. Although his friends had been kind, he felt there was little more anybody could do to protect a slave boy. The little black lad felt both lonely and very scared.

As the parade was beginning and the free people of Heffen were crowding the roadside to enjoy the festivities, Odi had been told to clean out one of the stables behind the palace. He would have liked to see the parade, particularly the elephants. There were none of these fine animals native to Heffen, and Odi had only ever seen pictures of them. Something else moved in the darkest corner of the stable, and once again the child's terrified eyes searched the shadows.

Waiting on the road to move off into the parade, Sir John Burleigh, dressed finely in silk shirt and shimmering grey silk suit, held a gloved hand to his thin mouth. He looked coldly at the man Brunt, who stood cringing before him.

"I have enough problems presently, Mr Brunt, without hearing that a nigger boy has been saved from a beating. Such things will bring nothing but trouble. It is bad for business, Mr Brunt." He beckoned Brunt closer and two burly men helped the frightened man to comply.

"So I would like a message sent to me at the ball. Just a short note, nothing too elaborate you understand. I simply require confirmation that the child has been flogged and then hung. It will serve as an example to anyone who considers meddling in my business."

Brunt nodded his agreement to Burleigh's instruction. He was too frightened to make any audible sound. Somebody came to tell Burleigh's coachman that the parade would be moving off shortly.

"If I don't feel that this message has been received by everyone, Mr Brunt," Burleigh smiled in his unpleasantly, inhuman way, "in the unlikely event that you fail to convince me, Mr Brunt, I am afraid you will be hanging next to the slave, which would not only be terminal, but ever so embarrassing for your family." He continued to smile humourlessly at the cowering bully. "I am confident you will not let me down," he said smoothly and nodded to two of his private army to escort Brunt away.

"I never wish to put unfair pressure on my employees, Mr Brunt, so I have arranged for the child to be alone in one of the stables at the rear of the palace. With all the noise and jollity, nobody will hear his pathetic screams." Sir John's carriage pulled away into the long procession, heading slowly towards the palace. "I would have liked to hear the screams myself, Brunt," he called back. "Sadly, duty calls."

Brunt watched the shiny black carriage join the long procession.

Sydney Greenburgh was the perfect example of suave sophistication. He oozed a combination of opulence and elegance far above his station. His finely tailored, rich velvet suit combined an air of flamboyant charm with a clever note of respect for the importance of this event. To put it another way, Sydney's expensive garb was just inside the boundaries of good taste. Although admittedly only just!

I had always envied Sydney his confidence and his dress sense. The girl draped over his arm was, at the very least, almost as beautiful as he had claimed. She was quite small, slim and shapely, with the familiar smooth golden brown skin of an islander. Her obvious good looks were complemented by a stunning off-the-shoulder full-length gown in glittering white gold.

"You know, I never thought," said Sydney in a patronising way. "I could have got her to bring a friend for you, old chap, couldn't I?"

"She's very nice, Sydney," I said. "But no thank you. I am perfectly capable of finding my own woman."

"No, you're not, old man," protested Sydney. "I mean, just take your recent track record. Of all the beautiful girls on Heffen to pick from, you choose a pirate. A girl, who even if she was to fall for a respectable and learned type such as yourself, will almost certainly be hung before you have chance to sire any little pirates."

"Keep your voice down, Sydney. Please remember the children," I begged him.

"Tell me you have forgotten her, Thomas old chum, please?"

"You should be going down and joining the queue," Mrs Moffat told us, rubbing her hands down her apron.

"Bet you wish you had got an invitation, Mrs Moffat?" said Sydney cheerfully.

"There is a man out there somewhere who maybe owes me one more dance."

Odi had been working hard. He could hear the noise of the crowd now. He even thought he heard one of the elephants trumpeting. Going on the rehearsal at the palace, it was probably more likely the second trumpet player in the military band. A thin sallow-faced youth who sounded always to be in a different key from the rest.

Odi thought of sneaking out to have a look, but the thought of another beating was a large deterrent. Then the shadow of something or someone did move in the darkness. Odi caught only a glimpse, but he was sure he was no longer alone in the stable. The evening was becoming quite cool and the small boy was shivering with cold and fear. The one lamp threw out a weak yellow light across the floor towards the door.

"Who's there?" stammered the boy. "Please tell me." He looked wildly around him, and as panic began to take over, he bolted for the door. The door slammed shut just before he reached it.

"Here then, we have an example of shutting the stable door before the child has bolted." Prudence Fairweather was leaning against the wall by the door, mostly in darkness. The tall woman wore a full-length vermilion cloak with the hood up. Odi recognised the notorious pirate at once.

"Please don't hurt me," mumbled the frightened child.

"As I recall, Odi, the last time we met, I offered you a job. I am only here to insist that you take my offer." She knelt down in front of the child and held out her arms. "We can haggle over pay and conditions later, can't we?"

Instinctively, Odi knew he was safe. Shyly he stepped forward and she hugged him to her warm body. Odi was crying. It had been a long time since he had been held like this, a very long time.

"Quiet, he's coming," whispered Prudence. "Trust me, Odi," she added and she seemed to melt into the darkness before his eyes.

The door of the barn swung open, and Brunt stood in the watery light, smiling at the boy. He slowly and deliberately bolted the door, although Odi could see his hands were shaking. The bully pulled a whip from his inside coat pocket and moved towards the child.

"Teacher man got me into some bad trouble, stopping you get the beating you deserved. He did you no favours, nigger boy. I have to give you a good beating, only now, I've then got to string you up as well, you filthy little urchin. Nothing personal," he rambled on, "but I have to report the deed done to Sir John at the palace."

Odi was fascinated by the fear in Brunt's eyes. "Why are you frightened of me?" he asked innocently.

"Frightened of you? I am not frightened of no nigger boy," lied Brunt.

"Yes, you are," insisted Odi.

"What about me, Mr Brunt? Are you frightened of me?" The pirate made Brunt spin on his heels.

"Do you think some girl is going to stop me?" Brunt struggled for the pistol in his belt. There was a strange sense of relief in Brunt's manner as he pulled the pistol from his trousers.

"She's not some girl!" yelled Odi from behind him, suddenly feeling braver again.

"Well said, child," encouraged the pirate. "You tell him who this girl is, if you like," she added, starting to circle the frightened man. She moved like a cat stalking its prey.

"That's the pirate Prudence Fairweather, Mr Brunt, sir." Odi got some satisfaction from the terror in the bully's eyes. Prudence Fairweather stepped into the pale light.

"I suppose it is pointless to ask if the boy may leave before I kill you," she said coldly. "I doubt you would agree, only let's face it, your screams of agony are hardly going to be suitable for a boy of such tender years."

Brunt was trembling with fear and already begging for his life.

"Get out," hissed Prudence. "I am not sparing you, Brunt. It would be kinder to kill you now, and I would if the boy wasn't watching. At least the longer you live, the more your nightmares will grow."

Prudence walked up close to the man. "My people will be after you, the anti-slavers will target you, your employer will no doubt wish to make an example of you. If all that fails I know a nice little hell demon who will just come along and gobble you all up."

Brunt ran in terror out into the stable yard. He kept running until he was lost in the crowds still being entertained by the acrobats, clowns and men on stilts. Nobody would ever know exactly who killed him. There were without question quite a few of Prudence's buccaneers mingling with the revellers. It was also obvious to Burleigh's men that Brunt had failed. There were plenty of others in the great gathering that night who would rarely ever consider violence to be a solution, but were prepared to make an exception in Brunt's case.

The fortune-teller was barely five feet, slim and had very rich and quite beautiful dark chocolate-coloured skin.

"Tell your future, sir?" she said sweetly. "Generally speaking, people who can take a whip to a child or call him rude names 'cause his skin is a different colour, well, they kinda die young."

Brunt screamed and backed away from the girl. Someone somewhere must have pushed him. Helped him fall. The elephants nearly trampled over him, oblivious to his screams. The biggest bull elephant was coming at him now. Brunt was sure, in the last moments, if he would ever be sure about anything, that there was a small black boy riding the beast. He was convinced that the little boy laughing at him was the child he had been supposed to beat and hang that evening. He rode the elephant with amazing skill, thundering down on the hapless man.

It was impossible that Odi could have been riding the bull elephant. He was with Prudence Fairweather. She was going to take the child to a safe place and give him his freedom. Brunt didn't know that and he never would. He was sure it was Odi; however, before those thoughts could move to any logical conclusion, the great bull elephant crushed him into the dirt. He lay still, broken and bloody. Brunt would never bully anyone ever again.

"Now you know how good I am at telling the future," Meg said to his crushed remains when they found him a little later that evening. "Please tell your friends about me." Meg threw the playing cards she was holding over the carcass and, smiling at Arthur and Joshua, mingled back into the crowd.

"Right you." Prudence picked up a bag from by the wall of the stable and looked at Odi. "What I need is somewhere to change, young man."

For a moment, Odi's eyes were staring blankly out, as if he was in some faraway place. A faint smile flicked on the little boy's lips. "He only gets what he deserves," he said.

"Yes, Odi, that's right," said the girl, taking hold of his hand. There were tears forming in the small boy's eyes.

"Come on," Prudence said softly. "I have an important date."

In the shadows of the stable yard a tiny child-like figure watched the stable from under a black hooded cloak. The face remained hidden in the darkness. Blood red eyes scanned the stables.

It had seen Prudence Fairweather, watched the way she moved. She was, it thought, a worthy adversary. Efulric was not worried. She was only mortal and could never hope to fight such strength, even more so much guile.

It did not fear her, because the creature already knew that the one who loved her was going to destroy her. The Apprentice had no understanding of love, but was glad of it now. It had, however, seen something that night that had alarmed it. Efulric must speak with its protector. The creature was clearly not doing its job very well.

For a moment longer, the demon enjoyed the feeling of the young shell in which it had taken temporary residence. A moment later the creature had gone. The body of a slave boy lay dead where moments ago the demon had stood. A repugnant smell hung over the place. It was still there long after the boy's body had received a proper burial, and would most likely still be there when the body had long since become dust.

Chapter 13

"Count and Countess Marios, from the Marios Estates, in the northern island." Simms was in his element as he announced the long queue of guests into the grand ballroom. It was not difficult to understand why the grand ballroom was so described. To begin with, it was a huge auditorium which led from a much smaller, although equally ornate, reception room. It had a high ceiling on which classically painted murals of naked men and women cavorted amongst cotton-wool clouds.

Around the sides were planted tall palm trees, amongst which long tables were set ready for the banquet to be served. The dance floor was in the centre of a beautiful flower garden. This was not only pleasing to the eye, but gave off the most wonderfully perfumed aroma.

This stunning arena was accessed from small bridges over clear running water in which large golden fish swam up and down. Other smaller fish played in the waterfall that cascaded down the mighty rock face. This had been constructed especially for this year's ball. A twisting pathway led through the rocks to the gardens outside.

The ballroom had been decorated in black and gold drapes. Crystal glass chandeliers hung low from the roof. Candles lit the tables, and a mixture of torches and lanterns were strategically place around the walls. At the far end of this colossal place was the stage, on which a mixed bunch of musicians were playing a selection from the classics. Their military-style garb complied with the black and gold theme of the evening.

As hundreds of splendidly dressed guests filled up the grand ballroom and began to mingle, a cacophony of colour blended into the regal surroundings, combining to give a most memorable spectacle indeed. It was hard to believe that so many wealthy and important people lived on Heffen. The women all wore truly fantastic gowns, often quite revealing and always blatantly expensive. Many of the men wore military dress. It was doubtful that more than about a tenth of those so attired had ever actually seen any military service.

Many of the younger men had probably paid even more for their foppish but fashionable attire than their womenfolk had. A large number of them had shipped in at enormous cost the latest London and Paris fashions. At the top table, Silas Raines, governor to the Heffen islands, entered from by the stage to a drum roll and cheers from the guests. Lady Catherine Ridley, Countess of Thorn, was by his side. The tall, slim and handsome woman made the plump governor look even smaller than he actually was. Her gown was gold and shimmered and glittered in the flickering lights of lamps, candles and torches. It was of full length and tight to her hips and very low cut to reveal Lady Catherine's much more than adequate cleavage.

The children were understandably overawed by their surroundings. They must have wondered, even if only for a moment, why a world that permitted the existence of workhouses could also sanction such tasteless opulence as this. Simms had given them a cheerful grin and a wink of the eye when nobody had been looking.

"This is incredible," observed Sydney, pulling out a chair for his latest conquest to seat herself on. I found myself hoping perhaps a little cynically that the lady's husband had not had a separate invitation to the ball. Or perhaps if I am honest I was hoping he had!

"I think there are quite a few unattached ladies here tonight,

Thomas," he went on to point out. It was true. There were some very attractive women at the governor's ball.

"Sydney, you have brought a very lovely young lady with you," I whispered. There was a note of despair in my tone. "You can't possibly start admiring others. That would not be exactly gentlemanly, even by your standards."

Sydney laughed. "I don't know, old chap," he said. "Only I was thinking of you not me."

Professor Kidner had spotted us. It probably was not difficult, as it seemed that Rupert and Victoria were the only children that had been invited.

"Mr Anders, good to see you," fussed Kidner, who despite having obviously gone to a great deal of trouble with his wardrobe, still looked as unkempt as ever, in what appeared to be a hand-knitted suit. He nodded to the children. There was a big grin lighting up his face, although as always the thick glass in his spectacles served to hide most of his expression. He did, however, look tired and a little more confused than usual. "Wonderful, isn't it, don't you think, Mr Anders?" he enthused. "Now here is something to write about in your book."

"The parade, this place, it is truly fantastic, Professor," I agreed.

"I trust young, eh, what's his name, has recovered from his experience the other day at the library?"

"Rupert is fine, Professor," I assured him. "Have you seen the strange little man at the library again?"

"Unfortunately, I do not recall your funny little man," explained Kidner strangely. "I was perhaps a little late on the scene," he added lamely, as if searching for a reason.

Some of the people near to us had made way for an old man to hobble slowly past on two sticks. He irritably brushed away any help offered.

"I can manage, I am not a complete cripple yet." He paused on reaching Kidner. Recognising the professor had given the elderly gentleman an opportunity to rest on his sticks. "Professor Kidner, isn't it?" he gasped, wiping sweat from his lobster red face with a large handkerchief. "Are you not going to introduce me to your friend?"

"This is Mr Anders, a teacher from England." I got the impression that Kidner did not approve much of this man. "He is tutor to the governor's wards."

"Not the spy everybody seems to be expecting then?" Boscastle gave me an odd look. "No, wait a minute, I know who you are. Mr Anders did you say your name was? You are the chap gave that slaver a bloody good and well-deserved beating, aren't you? My dear old friend Fairweather would have been proud of you," he added, smiling at me.

"The story has become slightly exaggerated in the telling, sir, but I confess, I did strike the man, although only once."

"There are so few of us left on Heffen who oppose this foul trade, Mr Anders. Be careful, though, young man. You will have made yourself a few enemies by your actions." It was at almost exactly that moment the broad grin on the old man changed to one of twisted hatred. If Sydney had not moved with surprising speed, Boscatle would have without doubt fallen. Sidney dived from the table, catching the old man, and only just managed to lower him onto a convenient chair without falling with him.

Boscastle offered no thanks. His face was even redder and horribly contorted into a mask of blind hatred. For a moment I thought his wavering stick was pointing at me.

"What the hell is that bastard doing here?" Boscastle spat the words out through clenched teeth. I was sure he would give himself a serizure at any moment. The man he was pointing at was of a similar build to Sydney. He also had the same ageless charm that Sydney had. Unlike my friend and companion, there was something sly, even sinister, about this man.

Major Baldock had rushed from his graceful wife's side to attend to the emergency. "Richard, calm yourself," he said to the old man, who would surely burst a blood vessel at any moment.

"Did he become so angry before he shot his wife dead, in cold blood, do you suppose, Major Baldock?" asked the stranger. "Forgive me for asking, but what with you being in charge of the coverup, I thought you might know." Henry Jessop sauntered over to Boscastle. "You should have been hung a very long time ago. Only the major here wanted a nice big house for his wife and kiddies."

Boscastle lurched at his accuser, and once again Sydney prevented the frail old man from falling on his face. Another man had walked over to investigate. I had no need of an introduction to this suave and coldly handsome man. I knew at once who it was who took charge of the situation.

"Jessop, I understand our honourable host invited you on a promise that you would behave yourself." Burleigh's tone was smooth, but menacing. "Now go to your seat or leave. The choice is yours." He turned to address Baldock.

"Major, I am quite sure Mr Jessop realises he was out of order in his foolish accusations, even though your handling of the situation could have perhaps been a little less clumsy, to say the least. Now why don't you run off back to your lovely wife before I mistake her for one of my girls I have brought with me tonight to give pleasure and entertainment to some of the governor's important friends. Maybe you would like to try one yourself. The governor is paying I understand."

I caught hold of Baldock just in time to stop him going for Burleigh. He turned to me and a smile played on his thin mouth. "Mr Anders," he whispered, "I am grateful to you for restraining Philip. He can be somewhat impetuous at times, don't you think?" He leaned across and spoke into my ear. "Lashing out at people is both foolish and irresponsible, don't you think, particularly for such a learned man. I do not take kindly to my employees being prevented from carrying out their duties, especially when those duties involve making an example of some little nigger boy. Now I know you are new around here and one must make allowances, but please, in the future, bear the consequences of your actions in mind. Even I sadly could not protect the child from the rage of his handler."

He turned to walk away and then stopped. "It is always a shame when a child has to die, Mr Anders, even a nigger child." He turned to look down on Boscatle with disdain. "And you, Richard, you sad old cripple, take my advice and stop clinging onto life so much. You are becoming a bore. Do us all a favour and die." The smile remained as Sir John Burleigh fixed his eyes on mine.

"You could find yourself dying prematurely if you interfere in my affairs again, Mr Anders, but I am sure I have no need to worry on that score. Oh, and the governor will need a new boy slave. I have a few strong young ones in stock. Why don't you come and choose? It will be on the house of course."

The crowds who had stopped to watch moved on. Henry Jessop had melted into a group of revellers. Baldock, Sydney and I helped Boscastle back to his feet. Despite Boscastle's protests, the major insisted on taking him to his seat. Simms had come over to help. He grabbed me by the arm.

"Master Odi is quite well, Mr Anders, sir," he whispered.

"Are you sure?" He had seen how upset I was looking. I had been unable to utter a word to the abominable Burleigh.

"Unfortunately, for some unaccountable reason, sir, Sir John must have received the wrong message. I will reprimand the offending member of staff, of course, but I blame myself really." He smiled, bowed stiffly and went about his duties.

As I turned back to see what the children were doing, I caught site of a figure by the doorway to the garden. He wore a bowler, black tailcoat and pinstriped pants. I couldn't make out his face properly, although he looked to be staring straight at me.

"I bet you that she's our spy, our demon hunter," Kidner said to Sydney loudly. "That bloody woman with the governor. She must have a reason to return here. I doubt even she has the nerve to come back to Heffen without one."

I turned back to look at the doorway, but the sinister little man had vanished.

Kidner was, of course, referring to the countess. Her presence seemed to dominate the governor, all his important friends and honoured guests. She was first to dance. An elegant slow formal dance with the governor as her partner. The portly man's girth was held in place by a sparking gold and black waistcoat, from which dangled a long golden chain.

Victoria finally persuaded me to dance with her. Rupert had very sensibly refused to go anywhere near the dance floor. Sydney now had eyes only for his beautiful companion and so far there had been no sign of any angry husbands. My meeting with Sir John Burleigh had done nothing for my evening. There was no question that this man terrified me. Never had I met anyone who enjoyed being so transparently evil. I wondered what he would do when he found that Odi was safe. There was no doubt he had arranged for him to be killed and for me to know that he had.

I confess I took some pleasure in imagining his displeasure, as well as being scared as to what his reaction might lead to. The spectacle and mood of the grand ball soon lifted my spirits. Victoria found my lack of dancing skills hilarious. It is to my great shame that a ten-year-old girl was trying to teach me some rudimentary dance steps when she could stop laughing at me for long enough. I was honoured to have such a charming partner and I was having fun again too.

We had returned to the table after a particularly vigorous dance that had left me breathless and poor Victoria's shins covered in bruises. I was still full of food from the mouth-watering spread that had been placed before us earlier. Cooks from every conceivable nook and cranny around the globe had contributed to the banquet spread out before us. The contrasting tastes and smells from countries as far flung as China and South America seemed appropriate for such a cosmopolitan place as Heffen.

Any guest feeling homesick had a good chance of finding something pretty close to home cooking, for there was a choice of delicacies probably never assembled under one roof before. The skilled use of herbs and spices made the food taste delicious. The blend of different aromas from different parts of the world, mixed with the scent from the brightly coloured floral arrangements decorating the ballroom, infused the air with an unusual but pleasant perfume.

"Good evening, gentlemen." I looked up to see Silas Raines beaming warmly at Sydney and I. "I trust you are enjoying my little party, my friends?" he asked. It was a rhetorical question. It would never occur to Silas Raines in a million years that anyone might not be enjoying themselves. "I think it is going particularly well this year, don't you?" The governor was genuinely excited. He slapped me on the back and gave me no time to explain that this was my first ball and therefore that I was in no position to compare.

"Almost everybody who is anybody is here tonight," Raines flamboyantly gestured about with obvious pride. He leaned forward to whisper, as if he was taking us into his confidence. "There is one guest, I might add, I would not in a million years have expected here tonight." He turned to find the handsome countess, Lady Catherine, now stood by his side.

"Please forgive my rudeness." He became slightly flustered. "Lady Catherine Ridley, this is my wards' tutor Thomas Anders."

"It is wonderful to meet you, Thomas," she purred disconcertingly. "And these are the lovely children you told me about, Silas my dear?"

Rupert cowered back into his chair. He was enjoying the spectacle of the night. The boy had also eaten more than his fair share of the food. Despite Rupert's sterling efforts, there would probably still be enough food thrown away at the end of the night to feed the whole of Heffen for a week. He found the tall and overpowering woman as intimidating as I did.

"I am so sorry about the spot of bother earlier," apologised the governor. "I'm afraid there is bad blood between Jessop and Boscastle from a very long time ago. I should have done more to keep them apart tonight, very remiss of me. I do hope it has not in anyway spoilt your evening."

"Really, Silas, you do go on so," scolded Lady Catherine. "You look very pretty, Victoria my dear, and you dance beautifully, despite the inadequacies of your partner." The very beautiful countess looked at me and smiled. I was then quite sure I did not like her.

"I suppose, Master Rupert, you would not consider a dance with me?" she went on. Rupert cringed into his chair.

"Never turn a pretty lady down, lad," urged the governor.

"We haven't been able to get Rupert onto the dance floor, or anywhere near it for that matter. I confess, if this pretty young lady had not been so insistent, I would probably have not been near it either."

"Perhaps you have no one you wish to dance with, Thomas." Lady Catherine was looking at me strangely. "No, I see now. You have someone you very much wish to dance with, only she is not here."

"Bloody odd, the way she can do that, Mr Anders," exclaimed Silas

Raines. "Unnerving sort of a gift. You can never lie to Lady Catherine. Believe me, I have tried and failed a few times." He laughed heartily and slapped me on the back again. "So why didn't you bring her tonight?"

"It is painful to talk about, sir," I said. "But the lady you speak of does not return my affection, and in any case, it is a long way to England from here."

"I made the journey, Thomas," pointed out the countess. "A girl not prepared to make such a journey to be with you, Thomas, is a fool. Especially if a long journey isn't absolutely necessary." She turned to the governor and smiled down on him. "Your adorable young nephew will not dance with me. I should need shin protectors to dance with his positively delicious young tutor. I'm very much afraid that you will have to dance with me again, Silas, my little pet."

We watched the dreadful countess escort the governor back to the dance floor. For the first time since arriving on these picturesque islands, I felt just a little sorry for Silas Raines.

"Oh, Anders," he called back as Lady Catherine dragged him over one of the little bridges. "Sir John has provided some lovely ladies for my friends' pleasure later. Feel free to come and choose one. I will, of course, cover any cost involved."

I could not think of any reply that would not have been extremely disrespectful to my employer. I thought it wiser to simply ignore his generous offer.

The British ambassador was a big man and his grand uniform suited him well. He stood on one of the terraces and looked around. For a moment he did not notice the small man in the pinstriped trousers.

"So you're Peckham?" he said gruffly. "Forgive me, I expected a slightly taller man."

"You have a problem with size?" Peckham asked in his broken accent, apparently unable to understand this.

"Not at all," blustered the ambassador, who was keen to get out of the cool night air and back to the dance. "Burleigh said you were not keen to be seen. How the hell did you get in here anyway? Security is tight here tonight. They reckon that absolutely nobody could get in here without a personal invitation from the governor." He was looking forward to having fun with one of the slave girls Burleigh always found for him on his visits. He could indulge himself here in ways that would be impossible at home.

"Let's just say I have my ways," said Peckham smoothly.

"Admiral Samuel Gilding will be at your disposal within the week," said the ambassador.

"Yes, but is he any good?" demanded the little man. It seemed odd that one so small could intimidate one so large, but there was no doubt that the little man frightened the ambassador.

"His record for ridding our waters of pirates is second to none, Peckham" he assured him. "Admiral Gelding is a cruel and ruthless man. Exactly what you asked for as I recall. In any case, you know yourself the reputation of this man. Surely that is why you requested him."

"Good," said Peckham quietly. "Yes, that is exactly what we wanted."

Many of the pirates were mingled into the crowds that thronged the streets of Heffen, soaking up the atmosphere and enjoying the noise, the roadside fairs and colourful entertainment. Here and there they came across someone cooking a whole ox on a big spit over a massive bonfire. Or roasting chestnuts over hot ashes. There were plenty of places to purchase countless varieties of locally caught seafood. Cockles, mussels, squid and octopus were on sale, not to mention sardines, tuna and swordfish, as well as the inevitable shark steaks. Stalls where you could buy a mouth-watering variety of locally grown fruit were also common.

The air was filled with the most incredible cocktail of smells. There was the rich odour of meat and fish being slowly barbecued. This mingled with the smell of the roasting chestnuts and fresh fruit which seemed to be wrapped up in a thousand different spices.

It was a bizarre place to be on a dark and cool night, Jakes told himself. He had decided to come when Meg had invited him. For one thing, Jakes was one of the few men alive who actually liked the local ale. He had also decided that if he drank enough of this filthy brew, it might give him enough courage to go and find his woman, and perhaps ask her for one more dance. He needed to tell her what he was now sure he had found out.

Sadly, Jakes was so much in love and so frightened that it would probably take more beer than there was in the whole of Heffen to give him the courage he needed.

"You ok?" asked Meg.

"Yes, fine," confirmed Jakes distantly.

"Go tell her, you daft man," urged Meg.

"You don't understand. It has been too long, so much has happened." The excitable crowds were jostling Jakes, pushing their way through the solid mass of people towards one of the many food stalls.

"At least you would know where you stand," argued the black girl, clearly frustrated by the man.

"So you will tell Monkey how you feel about him tonight?" said Jakes, unable to hide the triumph in his eyes.

"That's different," protested Meg, blushing a little.

"Is it?" The captain smiled smugly. "At least you would know where you stand."

"Point taken," grumbled Meg sulkily.

Any further discussion was at this point interrupted by the arrival of Harry and Arthur, who were pushing their way through the crowd towards Meg and Jakes. They were, as usual, engrossed in argument. Harry, however, seemed both very angry and a little quiet.

"Listen, you stupid numb-brained old fool," Arthur was shouting at Harry as he tried not to lose him in the crowd.

"Get lost, you ugly rodent-like lowlife," Harry shouted back.

"Are you two trying to draw attention to us," demanded Meg. "Roll up, roll up, folks, catch yourselves some off-duty pirates."

"She's come back." Harry could not hide the venom in his voice.

"She has come back and now I have to kill her. Unless you feel the honour should be yours, Arthur."

"I have as fair a claim as you, old fool, and would, I feel certain, gain a good deal more satisfaction from the task as well as complete it far more efficiently. Although that goes without saying."

"Who has come back?" asked Meg. She was clearly confused.

"Lady Catherine Ridley," said Arthur flatly. "And for once the stupid old bastard is probably right. One of us really ought to kill her."

Simms was standing by our table again, elegant, impeccable and imbuing a sense of calm efficiency as he always did. Despite the dreadful injuries my clumsy footwork had caused her, Victoria was begging me to have one more dance before they had to go to bed.

"Forgive me, Mr Anders, sir," he said in his most formal manner. "There is a young lady on the table next to the top table who tells me that you marked her card and yet have not so far this evening danced with her, sir."

"I have marked no ladies' cards tonight, Simms."

"I confess I wondered that myself, sir," he agreed. "I was wondering if Mr Greenburgh may have intervened on your account. I did hear him threatening to do so, sir."

"Apologise to the lady and tell her it is all a mistake," I said coldly.

"Forgive me, Mr Anders, but I am a little bit more than a mere messenger boy, and as a matter of fact, I also happen to be particularly busy. If you feel the need to continue being so rude, then I am confident that the lady in question will get the message, sir." He turned to Victoria and gave her his most charming smile. "I can only deduce that she cannot have seen him dancing, or she would surely not have entered into this complicity with Mr Greenburgh, would she?"

Victoria giggled and gave me a very sheepish look.

"I will see Master Rupert and Mistress Victoria home for you, Mr Anders." He bowed and the children followed him, almost without argument. I sat alone at the table, watching the other guests. Most were now getting quite drunk. I was glad the children had gone. I was annoyed with Sydney, although I knew he was desperately keen to distract me from the pirate.

A string ensemble had replaced the full orchestra. Their music I found quite soothing. The top table was almost empty of its guests now. I could see no sign of anybody waiting to be asked for a dance.

I decided that it had been a long day and I should retire myself.

"You did say you wanted to dance with me, Thomas Anders. So does a girl have to wait all night?"

Prudence Fairweather stood, looking breathtakingly beautiful, in a long burgundy gown that hugged the contours of her fulsome figure exactly as it was supposed to do. The gown was cut low and worn off her broad shoulders. She had a pretty lace shawl thrown about her.

I stood open mouthed, and probably drooling, at this vision of loveliness. Even her rich and shiny auburn hair had been done especially for the night.

"I don't scrub up too bad when I make the effort, do I?" Prudence smiled cheekily. She spun slowly round as if to offer my eyes further proof of that.

"Are you fishing for compliments by any chance?" I asked.

"You wanted to dance, you said, so here I am." Prudence walked up to me. "Of course, if they see you dancing with a wicked buccaneer such as Prudence Fairweather, they will probably hang you." Prudence paused and walked round me a couple of times, pretending to be deep in thought. "There is another tiny problem, Thomas, I am just a little scared. No, more than scared. To be honest, I am actually terrified."

"Of what?" I asked.

"I have never considered myself to be a coward, Thomas, ruthless pirate and cutthroat that I am. Having seen what you did to that poor sweet child on the dance floor earlier, I came so very close to running. I can deal with the palace guard, hopefully defeat flesh-eating demons, but frankly, Thomas, I doubt I will ever be able to teach you how to dance."

"I am not a very good dancer," I confessed. "I seem to have little control over what my feet do."

"Just remember," whispered Prudence, putting her arms around my neck, "that I am not a defenceless child." She was breathing on my ear. "Do that to my shins and I'll probably kill you." We had moved out onto the dance floor. It was a slow waltz. Our bodies were pressed close together. Her eyes were fixed on mine.

"Do you make all the men you dance with this nervous?" I asked.

"You're nervous?" Prudence smiled. "I'm the one who should be nervous, the way you dance."

"Well, yes, I am nervous actually. For a start, Baldock's guards could arrest me for cohorting with a very bad person."

"And I am a very, very bad person," purred Prudence, her lips almost touching mine.

"And if Baldock's men don't get me, I am bound to step on you sooner or later, and then you are going to kill me."

"Would you like me to melt away into the night?"

"That's what I am most nervous about," I answered very quickly. "I'd sooner be hung, if that's ok with you."

"Ouch," complained Prudence as my foot struck her shin.

"Or murdered by a beautiful pirate," I added ruefully.

"Oh yes, that reminds me. I was going to ask you about that," said Prudence. "Do you really think I am a beautiful pirate?"

"You're fishing for compliments again," I pointed out, a little more confidently this time.

"Look, I'm in the middle of a dance floor, in one of my archenemy's homes, currently under the guard of almost the entire British garrison. All because you wanted a dance, Thomas Anders. So I don't think it unreasonable to fish for the odd compliment."

"Well, you are definitely the most beautiful pirate I have ever met," I conceded. "Although, come to think of it, most of your crew was pretty ugly as I recall. So to be fair, you don't have a lot of competition."

Prudence smiled. "You're getting just a little too brave, Thomas Anders." She paused as her lips made contact with mine. It was a deeply sensual kiss that sent little shivers of ecstasy rippling through my body.

"If you want another kiss like that one," she said, "you will have to catch me first." Prudence laughed and, breaking free from my embrace, ran outside into the gardens. Her long, figure-hugging gown, despite having a long slit down one side from her thigh to her feet, did not, however, prove easy to run in.

Despite this impediment, Prudence managed to keep just ahead as we ran through the gardens. A handful of soldiers, sober and on duty, took little notice of the most wanted outlaw on Heffen as she ran past them, laughing and shouting back insults at her pursuer's level of fitness.

"Good luck, my friend," one of them called out to me. "That one looks well worth catching."

Prudence had run into the maze, and without thinking, I ran in after her. For a while, I ran up and down different paths, trying to find her. After a time, I realised that I had also lost my way back out. I reached yet another dead end and, pausing to catch my breath, began to consider how to find my way back out. I do not feel comfortable in confined spaces. The towering hedges began to feel as if they were closing in on me.

"You are not lost, are you, Thomas?" Prudence stood at the entrance to the short dead end, smiling in the moonlight.

"You know full well that I am lost," I said.

She walked up to me. "I know the way out, so I suggest you don't lose me again then."

"I don't want to lose you again," I replied honestly.

Prudence laughed. "Perhaps we should stay here for a few minutes, whilst you catch your breath."

"Wasn't coming to the dance a little dangerous?" I said, sitting down on the grass and ignoring her last comment. Although it was true, I was puffing a bit. Prudence kneeled down next to me with some difficulty. Her gown had a satisfyingly inhibiting effect on her movements.

"I couldn't get trussed up like this too often," she complained, hitching up the front of her frock. This had become so dangerously low that her breasts looked like they would spill out at any moment.

"You do look lovely," I said, feeling myself reddening slightly with embarrassment.

"That's probably why I came," she decided. "It's a very long time since a man has bothered to tell me that I look lovely. It's nice for a girl to be told that from time to time, even if it isn't true."

"I can't believe that. Your crew must be blind."

"It's my own fault. I do my best to avoid becoming involved," she explained. "Being a pirate is complicated enough, without trying to form meaningful relationships with people. You have pretty well worked out for yourself that we have some kind of an Armageddon situation rapidly approaching."

"Efulric the Apprentice is not a figment of our imagination then?" It was a rhetorical question. "I don't know why people find it hard to believe in demons. I, for example, like many others, often say little prayers to God. If we believe in God, then most likely we ought to believe in the devil."

"You pray much?" asked the pirate.

"Usually I'm looking for a favour, probably only something small, well, small to God anyway. You know the kind of thing. I might ask him to look after Mama and Papa and all my brothers and sisters. I've got lots of brothers and sisters, including numerous adopted ones, so I suppose that's quite a lot to ask. Perhaps I would seek some help to get me through a particularly difficult day. I might beg him to get my class to be less troublesome for example, if it wasn't too much trouble."

"I haven't prayed since the night my family was murdered." Prudence looked as if those beautiful brown eyes might fill with tears. "I prayed that night, I prayed very hard, but your God didn't hear me. Fat lot of use he is."

"Listen, I hate people preaching at me about anything. That is why I didn't follow in my papa's footsteps as everybody expected me to. Before you write God off though, are you absolutely sure that he didn't answer your prayers? Somehow, you survived that terrible night one frightened young girl. What odds would a betting man put on that? Something protected you until you found help. Maybe because you are the only living person in the world who has the power to slay this demon."

"I am going to have to watch you, Mr Anders, or I could end up doing something very stupid. As for Efulric the Apprentice, I may be the only person on earth who can stop it, but I don't have the faintest idea how."

"You have to destroy the Fault," I said bluntly. "Only there is a problem. Gabrielle, it is said, wrote in his own hand detailed instructions on how to destroy it. Until a few days ago I was sure that those notes were in the library. Now I am afraid they have been destroyed. It looks to me like Professor Kidner burnt the documents in question himself. If he did, then for some reason he has destroyed the only copy of Gabrielle's instructions known to exist. He will be aware of that."

"That's why I came to the library the other day. I knew about Gabriel's instructions. I had hoped to find them," Prudence explained. She frowned. "Professor Kidner is one of the few decent people left on Heffen, who hasn't become an outlaw, that is. The professor will understand how important Gabrielle's notes are. I find it hard to believe he would destroy the only possible salvation of our world, for any price," she added.

"You're probably right," I conceded. "I don't know him well, but he seems very frightened about something though."

Prudence Fairweather was shivering.

"We better go," I said. "You're getting cold and I need you to get me out of here."

"You could warm me up for a few minutes." Prudence almost fell onto me, and I put my arm around her. I was shaking a little.

"What about that other kiss?" I asked apprehensively.

"You didn't catch me."

"Well, if I didn't catch you, what are you doing in my arms?"

Prudence Fairweather thought through the logic of my argument. "Probably waiting for you to shut and kiss me, Thomas Anders," she said.

A number of late revellers were gathered around, staring into the clear waters of the indoor lake that circled the dance floor. Most of them were quite drunk, the palace wine cellars having been seriously depleted during the evening. They were not staring at the big golden fish swimming close to the surface. The focus of everybody's attention was the dead body lying on the bottom. The cadaver's mouth was open wide, and his dead eyes stared blankly back at the onlookers.

Major Baldock pushed through the small crowd to the water's edge. The string ensemble continued to play soft and romantic waltzes. His beautiful wife Mia, her stunning figure wrapped in a skin-tight gold and silver gown, followed him. She had sat in shadow most of the night. Some of the other guests were sure they recognised the beautiful Mrs Baldock from somewhere.

"She must have that kind of face," decided one rather plump lady also wearing a skin-tight dress to dramatically less effect. Her husband hadn't been looking at her face!

Baldock was studying the corpse.

"Is he dead?" shouted one of the guests.

"Unless he's grown gills he is," said another.

"What a shame, Major." Burleigh gave the soldier a watery smile. "I'm afraid you're never going to get the chance to hang him now."

The major stared gloomily at the contorted face of the corpse, the fish swimming around it as if investigating why it was in their pond.

"Looks like something's scared him to death," observed another onlooker.

"He's some old guy, probably had a stroke or something," shouted someone else.

Major Baldock was kneeling by the edge of the pond, deep in thought. It could have been a stroke, or a heart attack perhaps, but what was the crippled Richard Boscastle doing so far from his table? How had he got himself over the steep bridge towards the exit? There was no doubt in Baldock's mind; Richard Boscastle had been murdered and he was certain he knew who had ordered this. Once again he could see no way of bringing the perpetrator to justice.

Chapter 14

*H*effen's splendid library was quiet the following day, as I expected it would be. With the exception of a large contingency of slaves and their handlers, almost everybody in Heffen was on holiday. I am sure many of the governor's guests would wake today with a very bad head. The common folk had partied late into the night as well. On the streets and around the harbour there were raucous celebrations going on everywhere.

Keeping with tradition, a huge display of fireworks lit the skies over the south island, courtesy of the Chinese delegation. With many loud bangs, the pyrotechnics used the star-lit heavens as their canvas on which to paint patterns of shimmering multi-coloured lights. Explosions of fire danced across the clear night sky. Complex designs would gradually build to a crescendo, then explode with a blinding flash and a deafening bang into a thousand falling stars.

Prudence and I walked down the hill towards the harbour, hand in hand. On our way, we passed a multitude of good-natured and drunken revellers. Some offered us a share of their remaining drink. Others told me how lovely my companion was. I could not disagree, and Prudence positively revelled in the compliments paid to her.

"Armageddon or not, I have had the best evening I have ever had," I said.

Prudence smiled. "Don't expect too much from me, Thomas Anders, will you?" She put her arm around my waist. "I have some good friends I admit, but I have looked out for just me for too long to be able to change much. I don't shirk my responsibility for others, but they don't involve any kind of relationship."

"What are you trying to tell me?" I must have looked pathetic.

Prudence burst out laughing. "I don't think I have ever met anyone like you, Thomas Anders, except now you come to mention it, there is a little bit of my father about you." She stroked the side of my face gently.

"I don't think you did mention it. Do I take that as a compliment?"

"I don't mean you look like him. Father was a big clumsy oaf of a man. I think it's got to do with your inability to walk away when even you know you should. Father was a very stubborn man."

"I'll take that as a compliment then," I said.

"It was meant as one," admitted Prudence. "You know, if things get as bad as I think they might, I may need a favour." She fluttered her eyes at me in a deliberately obvious attempt to get me off guard. "There are, as I said, a couple of people I promised my father I would protect."

"Who?"

"You don't need to know that yet. If something happens to me though, you have to get them off Heffen. I am having some of the leaks fixed on the *Sally O*. She is a fast little ship and Jakes will be at your disposal."

"But I couldn't leave you here," I protested. "We will find away to blow up the Fault and kill the spirit of Efulric the Apprentice, or whatever its name is."

Prudence laughed. "I doubt it would appreciate you forgetting its title, Thomas," she reproached me. "Efulric is very strong and very cunning. It is a terrifying adversary, because it is not just pure evil, with hopefully exaggerated magical powers, but also according to all that I have read, the Apprentice is a particularly bright demon."

"And we can't see the thing either," I added bitterly.

310

"The creature feeds off evil. I'm sure of that, and as we approach the time, it will need more and more power."

"Which presumably means more and more evil," I said. "This sense of doom is really a sense of evil, terrible evil, like Sir John Burleigh, and our governor. That is what Efulric is feeding off, isn't it?"

"Yes, I think so," the pirate agreed. "But don't you see, it isn't enough. So it brings bad people back to the island. Why do you think Lady Catherine Ridley has returned? Trust me, the Countess of Thorn can make Burleigh seem like a pussycat. The trouble is that Lady Catherine has the ability to bring out the evil in all of us."

"Meaning even more for this thing to feed off of," I said. "Efulric is arranging his own feast. If you killed one of them, let's say Sir John, would that not reduce Efulric's power?" I looked at Prudence questioningly.

"Please pay attention, Thomas. I did say we were dealing with a very clever demon. All his servants are, it seems, protected from physical harm. I have killed Sir John Burleigh at least once. The bastard just won't die."

"You mean he is invincible, indestructible? I am only just getting the hang of demons, and now you want me to believe Burleigh can't be killed?"

"Thomas, I put a sword through his heart only a few months ago. He is the better skilled of the two of us with a sword. He got careless; I got lucky."

"I suppose you would tend to be a little careless if you had become invincible," I pointed out. "So where is Efulric now?" Another great explosion of fireworks sent a cascade of reds, greens and yellows spiralling down from the sky.

Prudence sighed. "The true answer, Thomas, is I don't know. Its spirit has been trapped in our world, so I don't think the creature has a physical form of his own. It uses the body of a child, mostly young slaves, to sustain life and provide his earthly manifestation. The creature can only sustain this for short periods. It may well have by now found itself a host and will have spent most of the time since then dormant inside this unfortunate person."

"Can we not find who this poor unfortunate is and mount a rescue?" I suggested optimistically.

"If you had been more thorough in your research, Thomas Anders, you would know that the demon's host must be a willing part of all this. Indeed, he or she must invite the demon in, if you understand me."

I shuddered at the thought, understanding exactly what Prudence meant. The very idea of such a bonding filled me with revulsion that made me feel sicker than the *Sally O* ever would.

"So you are the only person who can actually kill this monster," I said. "But that doesn't mean others can't help, if they want to."

"Actually," Prudence was still looking at me with laughter and warmth in her big brown eyes, "it is possible I am not the only one who can kill it, you know. Harry and Arthur dropped in on Burleigh the other day, uninvited of course. I think from what they overheard, Sir John and your employer have hired in a bona fide demon killer."

"I have heard of such people," I conceded, "in past research, but could one of these demon hunters really kill the spirit of a demon? I understood a demon hunter helped to locate the prey, not kill it."

"I don't know, Thomas. I have long since accepted that Efulric is real. But until recently, I thought that demon hunters existed only in ancient stories. Burleigh and the governor, however, believe that they have a real-life demon killer. They also think he might be an agent sent by the English parliament." Prudence paused to push some hair from my forehead. "That would make sense, because I was told on reliable authority that the English were sending such a person." She smiled. "Look, I have to go. The ball gown helped me blend into the night, but it is almost daylight."

"Will you meet me later at the library? I would imagine that there will be very few people around today. Maybe between us we can work out how you kill this thing."

"Go to bed, Thomas Anders," she whispered, leaning forward to kiss me. For the third time that night, I held the pirate girl in my arms. I wanted so much to tell her how much I loved her. How much I wanted her. I knew this was not the time. She put a finger on my lips, almost as if she could read my thoughts.

"I will see you later," she said, grinning broadly at me. Prudence's ability to vanish was something that had no doubt kept her alive and safe over the years. I turned and began the long uphill walk back to the palace.

I had slept for only a short while. My mind was too busy trying to cope with everything that was happening. Most people, when presented with the distinct possibility of demons existing, would have some trouble assimilating such a concept. True, I did have a slight advantage in that I have always had an interest in stuff that sometimes cannot easily be explained.

From my studies, I suppose I had learnt not to dismiss anything just because it couldn't happen. I had, of course, never seen a real-life demon, but then I had never seen a real-life pirate either. Because of my somewhat parochial existence until recently, I had not seen the sunset on a tropical island, or felt the heat of a tropical sun. I could never have imagined how claustrophobic the hold of a boat is, or just how awesome Mother Nature can be. I found it less surprising to discover how cruel my fellow humans can be. Sadly, this alone would seem to be a universal problem.

Efulric existed, feeding on the evil that plagues our world. I could feel its power and I could feel just how clever it was. Then there were my own demons to deal with. Here on Heffen, I had found the girl I wanted to spend the rest of my life with. Unfortunately, Prudence was not the type to settle down, raise children and enjoy polite society. The bitter irony was that it was this free spirit with which I had fallen so in love. The very reason I would probably lose her.

Only Mrs Moffat was up when I came down to the back kitchen. As usual, she made me have a large bowl of lumpy porridge, which I really didn't feel like. The Irish housekeeper would not even consider the idea of anyone starting the day on an empty stomach. I had got back to my room just after dawn. Bathing and changing out of my formal wear, I checked the children, who were both still fast asleep, before coming down to breakfast. Rupert might have been having a nightmare. If he were, it would be about pirates, not demons thankfully. I did not feel particularly tired after such a long night.

"I shall not disturb the children," she said when I had told her they were still sleeping. "They had a very late night, although I know someone who was much later still." She raised one eyebrow at me, as she did when convinced some terrible sin had been committed. "I failed to see why you bothered to come home at all, Mr Anders."

"Got to go," I said, shovelling in the last mouthful of porridge and preparing to beat a hasty retreat. "I think I'll go and have a good rummage in the library today with the children having no lessons," I said, my mouth still full of porridge. I felt more like battling demons than Mrs Moffat. I would have at least some chance of winning.

So there I was sat in an almost deserted library, searching book after book for more information on Efulric the Apprentice. The rest of Heffen was no doubt sleeping off the heavy excesses of the previous night. I found some reference to the spy that everyone was talking about. There were numerous mentions of a prophecy which claimed that this spy, in truth a demon hunter, would be sent across the seas to save the world.

> The demon hunter will travel thousands of leagues from a faraway place to seek out the demon apprentice, Efulric. He will be overcome by the overwhelming presence of evil. Infected by fear and lust, this spy will fail terribly in his task. As a result, he will be indirectly responsible for the death of one of Efulric's most feared enemies. Only in death will he make amends for his failure.

Sydney walked into Kidner's untidy little study.

"You couldn't sleep either, old boy," he croaked wearily. "That girl I was with last night, Thomas, she was fantastic. I had only just escaped the filly for a rest before the little minx killed me." He grinned, an action itself apparently too energetic for poor Sydney. "Mind you, it would have been a bloody good way to go," he added.

"Are you a demon hunter, Sydney?" I said, hoping desperately to avoid a lurid and embarrassing account of Sydney's latest sexual exploits.

"No," he answered indignantly. "I don't even believe in the bloody things. I think you're all mad frankly."

"Ah well, but you would say that if you were a demon hunter, now wouldn't you?" I pointed out. Sydney eased himself into the nearest thing to a comfortable chair in Kidner's office and scowled at me.

"If I was, would you promise not to tell?" he asked.

"Promise," I said. We continued to study various volumes for inspiration.

"What the hell is this?" mumbled Sydney.

I looked up from a piece about mystical keys releasing demonic hordes. "What?" I enquired.

"Just exercising my incredibility threshold, old boy," explained Sydney with absolutely no conviction whatsoever. "It's just more twaddle, I'm afraid, Thomas."

I sighed and put down Kidner's magnifying glass. "Tell me anyway," I suggested.

"It says that the satanic demon's spirit shall rise and feed on the blood of others. We are not looking at, what do they call those blood-sucking things?"

"Vampires," I said, "the living dead. No, I don't think so. It's probably a reference to the suffering. Efulric feeds on bad things."

"I hope you're right." Sydney sounded more and more concerned. "Not that I believe in all this mumbo jumbo you understand," he added unconvincingly, feeling his throat for bites.

"So is that it?" I must have sounded a trifle disappointed. We had been wading through volume after volume and had learnt very little more than we already knew. "Nothing," I added.

"Not that I can see," said Sydney, but as he answered me, I could tell something else in the passage he was reading had caught his attention.

"Hang on. This is odd after what you were saying earlier."

"What, Sydney?" I was becoming a little exasperated. I had found no knew reference to the Fault. Nothing whatsoever on how to destroy it. The best I had found were a couple more scribes who supported Gabrielle's theory that the Fault must be destroyed. Perhaps, not surprisingly, I could find anything that told us how to do this.

"There is all the usual rubbish that goes on about the fact that good will or won't withstand evil, depending on how optimistic the author is," continued Sydney. "The price may be high, the sacrifice may be great, but the good in heart shall overcome their fear and weakness and make the ultimate reparation. You know the kind of thing."

"And this is odd, Sydney, because?" I interrupted.

Sydney glared at me, brushed his hand though his hair and continued. "No, that's not the bit I thought was odd," he explained irritably. "This bit here is the odd bit." There was a silence whilst Sydney started reading to himself again.

"Sydney." There was a good deal of menace in my voice.

"What? Oh yes, it says that the demon hunter sent by the people of Britannia will make a terrible mistake. As a result of this, it, well, it seems to be suggesting that the satanic beast may well prevail."

"Let me see that, Sydney." I leaned over and grabbed the book from him.

"Of course it would help if we knew who this demon hunter chappy is, wouldn't it?" He leaned right back in his chair.

"We do know who the demon hunter is," announced Prudence from the doorway. "I thought Mr Anders would have mentioned that."

Sydney fell backwards off his chair into a great stack of papers. These went flying in all directions. In a moment of priceless comedy that would have done credit to the best-staged farce, Sydney attempted to save himself. Instead, he brought most of the cluttered contents of the desk on top of him. He was deeply offended that both the pirate and I thought this very funny.

"I knew about that too," admitted Prudence, pointing at what Sydney had just read out. "Why do you think I was so keen to find the spy from England?"

"And you know who it is?" Sydney dug himself out of the mound of scrolls and parchment. He was muttering oaths under his breath about the lack of sympathy, or concern, he had been shown. "And they never bother to tell me anything nowadays," he grumbled, trying to brush hundred-year-old dust from his bespoke jacket and pants.

"The little man in the bowler hat and frock coat is our demon hunter," I said. "A couple of Prudence's people overheard him discussing their plans with Sir John Burleigh."

Prudence pulled up a chair and sat down. Her hair had already reverted to its wild and tangled natural look. She put her feet, contained in long black leather boots, on the table and closed her eyes.

"I am still very tired," she complained. "Due no doubt to the very late night I had, Mr Anders."

"I think I should be getting along," decided my companion, realising he was in danger of becoming a gooseberry, or judging by the colour of his fashionable attire, a lemon. Feeling his posterior cautiously, Sydney winced in pain. I pride myself on my ability to recognise an example of Sydney's overacting when I see one.

"Sit down, Sydney," commanded Prudence without opening her eyes. It would be a much braver man than Sydney who would argue with this command.

"I thought I was being, well, you know, a bit of a gooseberry if you get my drift," stammered poor Sydney.

"Mr Anders and I were not planning to have wild sex on the desk just at the moment, were we, Mr Anders?" Prudence opened one deep brown eye and looked wickedly at me through it.

I was shocked by her openness. Seeing Sydney red faced, and savouring the delightful fact that he for once was speechless, was a joy I cannot adequately express in words.

"In any case, I haven't quite decided if I'm going to let Mr Anders have wild sex with me yet." She looked at me now with both eyes fixed on mine. "I probably might, but not on this table, or even in this library. I was thinking of somewhere a little more romantic. Don't you agree, Mr Anders?"

My mouth opened and shut a couple of times like one of the big golden fish in the ballroom pond. The only sound, however, that managed to escape was a strange stifled gurgling noise.

"Now listen, boys." Prudence sat forward in the chair. "We have had no luck whatsoever finding Gabrielle's notes on how to blow up the Fault. Mr Anders is desperately keen to be heroic in the vain hope it might impress me enough to fall into his arms. Then I am led to believe from various reports that you are both very learned men." Prudence looked at the two of us as if waiting for an answer.

"Thomas got better results," Sydney said. "I probably spent too much time, well, you know."

"No, Sydney, do tell me." Prudence gave him a look of mock innocence.

"Sydney was more on the science side, mostly biology," I explained. "Quite a lot of hands-on practical experience."

"I want to go and examine the Fault," announced the pirate. "I thought perhaps you two could excuse a couple of days absence on research for Mr Anders's book."

"Isn't the Fault kind of a dangerous place to take a boat?" inquired Sydney, who was now looking very nervous.

"It's a ship, Sydney, not a boat," Prudence corrected him.

"I think what Sydney means is that if we are going to start taking local legends seriously and treat them with some respect, it follows that we should be wise to remember that many ships and many crews have gone missing in the mists around the Fault."

"Gentlemen, the secret of sailing safely through the reef and the Fault, for that matter, are known to very few. I give you my solemn word that you shall have the best navigator in these waters."

"Dare I asked who?" I ventured at this point.

"Did you know that there are probably only three or four people alive today, outside of a handful of islanders, who can sail a ship through Gabrielle's Reef?"

"That's the reef," pointed out Sydney sulkily. "What's that got to do with the Fault?"

"In theory, if the knowledge of the reef has been passed down, then the knowledge of the Fault has been as well," Prudence pointed out patiently.

"Not over-keen on the word theory. Not in this context anyway. Don't you agree, Thomas, old chum, or are you so besotted with this creature that reading the small print is out of the question?"

Prudence smiled sweetly at Sydney. "Would it ruin our friendship, Mr Anders, if I had your friend strung from the main brace?"

"Only should it prove to be a far too merciful end to such a sad and sorry existence," I replied, glaring at Sydney. "Although he does make an interesting point here, Prudence. A theory is usually a concept that has, up to that point in time, never been actually tried. What I suspect is perhaps alarming my pathetic friend here is that theories can, once in awhile, prove to be wrong."

"Only little ones," argued Prudence. "And not very often," she added for extra reassurance.

"But nobody has sailed the Fault before?" I pressed.

"Of course they have," answered Prudence crossly. She kicked away her chair and walked over to her portrait above the fireplace. "Just not for a hundred years or so," she conceded sulkily.

"Now you heard that, Thomas?" Sydney was becoming animated.

"Prudence has a point, Sydney. Within your scientific knowledge and my own geological studies lies our best hope of finding a way to close down the Fault. We have to take a look."

"Then we are agreed," said the pirate.

"I haven't agreed to anything," complained Sydney bitterly.

"There is a bright side to everything, Sydney," I told him.

"Well, I'm sorry, but I don't see it," he replied grumpily.

"If we get sucked into the mysterious fog, never to be seen again, then all those angry husbands will never be able to find you."

"Very funny, Thomas," muttered Sydney despairingly.

"Who has this knowledge, Prudence, apart from your pirates?" I asked.

"Thomas, the word knowledge is to suggest that they know what they're doing. A much better question would be who has this theory," complained Sydney.

"Captain Cornelious Jakes." Prudence smiled. "But in his case, believe me, it really is only theory. I doubt he could even remember how to navigate the reef, never mind the Fault."

"Please tell me he isn't the person you have in mind to navigate," begged Sydney. "Only I for one thought our safe arrival in Heffen Harbour to be certain proof that Thomas's papa is right and that there is a God after all."

Prudence laughed, came back over to the desk and sat down again. "I will be navigating us, Sydney. Do you have a problem with that?" She

319

glared at the man in such a way that if he did have any problems, he would have to be both very brave and very stupid to raise them now.

"When do you want us to go on this trip?" I asked nervously, remembering just how much I hated being on boats.

"Very soon," answered the girl without thinking. "We need to take a look before the rains come. I will send a boat to collect you first light tomorrow. You have no lessons on a Sunday, Mr Anders, do you?"

"I am normally expected to take the children to church," I pointed out. "Anyway, isn't somebody still trying to get to Rupert?"

"I will continue to protect the child for you, Mr Anders, as best as I can. There is someone else who would never forgive me if a child were to die at the palace. I think the people I have watching over your charges are better equipped than you to keep them safe." Prudence stood up again and ruffled my sulking friend's hair. "See you tomorrow, Sydney." She leaned forward and gave me a brief kiss on the lips. "Sorry to put you in a ship again so soon, Thomas Anders." She smiled and walked to the door.

"I have a very good example of a theory that was extremely floored, Miss Fairweather," stammered Sydney. "For a long time, it was claimed that the world was flat and if you kept on sailing, eventually you would fall off the end."

Prudence gave Sydney a look of grave concern. "You mean that isn't true, Sydney?" she gasped in mock surprise and then she was gone.

The governor sat bleary eyed in his office. His chair was positioned so that he could look out over his normally immaculate grounds towards the north island. The mountainous volcanic rock, Niridia, was not visible from here. Beyond the northern hills, he could just make out the acrid black smoke that leaked from its summit. It was a salutary reminder that Niridia was still very much active.

On that morning, Silas Raines was more concerned at the state of his grounds. The governor disliked untidiness of any kind. The palace gardens had taken on the resemblance of a battlefield. Bottles, glasses, uneaten food, and discarded clothing covered the usually immaculate lawns. Already a contingency of slaves was busy restoring the grounds to their normally spotless condition. Many more were doing the same within the palace.

Outside the side entrance, wagons were being filled with stone from the large indoor rock face that had been constructed in the grand ballroom. It had been built at enormous expense to serve only for the one night. By tonight, there would be little evidence left that the biggest event in Heffen had been in full swing less than twenty-four hours earlier.

The door opened and Sir John Burleigh entered.

"Good morning, Governor," he said with shallow warmth to his tone. "I trust you slept well last night." He smiled knowingly. "I mean eventually, Governor," he added smoothly.

The governor looked coldly at Burleigh but said nothing. Instead, he reached shakily for the coffee, poured out next to him. He took a mouthful, grimaced and swallowed. "Cold," he spluttered in way of explanation. "I will send for fresh."

"Don't worry on my account, Governor," Burleigh insisted. "I have already breakfasted. I just thought I should drop by and see you before I take my leave."

"I thought it went well last night," said Raines.

"Absolutely, Governor," agreed Burleigh with overplayed enthusiasm. "I am afraid that the bill will be a little more than I had anticipated."

"Let me guess, the British ambassador again?"

"I have people clearing up his mess, Governor, but I have lost three of my best-looking girls from stock and that costs me money."

"He is a vile man," muttered Raines, swallowing another mouthful of cold coffee.

"However, he has been of considerable use to us over the years, Governor. So it is probably a little late to become squeamish or moralistic, don't you think?"

"Just send me the bill, Burleigh. I do not, however, need to know the details," pointed out the governor. "Has Boscastle's body been removed from my ballroom?"

"On its way back to his seedy little ranch I believe. I have taken the liberty to suggest to his staff that Richard should have a quiet burial with the minimum of fuss."

"I think it unlikely that I shall attend," muttered Raines.

"I did happen to mention that, unfortunately, our governor's commitments were such at the present that it would be very unlikely he could be present at the ceremony. I said that you would probably send a wreath. I trust that was in order."

"Will you go?"

"Yes, I think I will. I quite enjoy funerals." Burleigh smiled. "And anyway, Catherine has her heart set on it."

Silas Raines smiled for the first time that day. He opened a small well-concealed drawer in his desk, from which he took out a small package. This he then carefully opened to reveal a small wooden box with an even smaller key that hung from a golden chain around his neck. Inside the box were three irregular-shaped pendants.

"I was afraid there might have been a living male with a greater claim than I on this beautiful thing," he said softly, holding one of the pendants up to the light.

"He was your bastard uncle for goodness sake, Raines. Your grandfather was not quite the pious, clean-living man he liked people to believe. I checked long before we persuaded the old fool to bring his young bride to Heffen. I am afraid poor Richard had no other living relatives." Burleigh rose from his chair. "Sometimes you worry too much, Governor."

"I did not become governor of these islands without a certain amount of worrying," he snapped back, pulling the large vermilion chord next to the flag of Heffen to call for service. "I worry that the coffee is cold for example." He flung his cup across the room, shattering it against the wall. "It is a shame Richard couldn't have just died without our interference. God knows the man cannot have had long to go."

"All the same, Governor, Peckham did a good job with Boscastle, I thought. Considering he specialises more in demon slaying," observed Sir John.

"I hope he is as good as you say, Burleigh, for if he fails, we are all finished. You, me, the people of Heffen, the whole dammed world is finished." Raines paused to study his fob watch. As almost always, he had no interest in determining the time. "I will give this Peckham credit where credit is due, Sir John. He gained entry to the ball, despite all my security, and murdered Boscastle in full view of everybody. Apparently no one saw anything."

"You saw him, Governor, though. I saw you greet him, shake his hand warmly like you would an old friend."

"That is what governors do, Sir John. I greeted everyone in that way and everyone was accounted for. You must be mistaken."

Sir John Burleigh frowned. For a moment he seemed surprised by Raines's last comment. Then he forced his narrow grey lips into another humourless and insincere smile.

"Peckham has had another rather good notion, Governor," he said carefully. "He has persuaded the ambassador to loan us Admiral Samuel Gilding and the *Serpent King* of course, just for a couple of months or so. It will clear our waters of pirates. The problem is already getting really out of control."

The governor was noticeably thrown by this latest piece of news. "Not him, Burleigh," he said, rising from his chair in obvious alarm. "Have you any idea what you are unleashing upon us all?" he demanded, now quite red in the face. "You would no sooner let our British ambassador take our daughters for a walk in the park, then let this man loose again on these islands. He gets his kicks out of other people's suffering. He likes nothing more than to torture people. I have heard it said that he can take days to kill a man."

"Perhaps not as subtle as Lady Catherine then, but then you seem impervious to her darker charms if I may say so, Governor," said Burleigh slyly. "Gilding has, however, earned himself an excellent reputation for killing pirates, and you always knew he must return one day. Why should we mind if he enjoys his work?" There was a sharp knock on the door and Simms entered.

"Yes, Governor," he said, stiffly bowing slightly as he spoke.

"I want hot coffee, Simms," he barked at the perfectly attired butler. "Will you be staying, Sir John?"

"No, I most go make sure the cleaning up is being done to my satisfaction."

Simms went to organise coffee for his master.

"I understand another body was found on the road, trampled by the elephants."

Burleigh was putting on his grey dress gloves, despite the fact that the weather was still hot. His skin was very pale for a man who had lived for so long in the tropical sunshine. He reached for his hat and cane.

"You mean Brunt?" said Burleigh flatly. He knew the governor liked to feel in control. Nowadays he would seize upon any weakness he could find. Any chink in the armour which formed Burleigh's ice cold exterior. Burleigh was grateful that the governor, at least, had no comprehension as to how scared he had become in his own home.

"Wasn't he the one my wards' heroic tutor gave a whipping to?" pressed Raines with transparent relish.

"I think you exaggerate a little, Governor," answered Burleigh coldly. "Brunt was a fool and failed me," he went on. "People who fail me tend not to live long. Now, if you will forgive me, Governor, I must take my leave. Good day to you, sir." Burleigh walked to the door, paused and straightened the front of his slate grey frock coat.

"So you killed him then?"

"My dear, Governor, as you already said yourself, an elephant killed him," replied Burleigh in a tone of exasperation. He placed his hat on his head and left, colliding with Simms, who had returned with piping hot coffee for the governor.

"Everything all right, sir?" Simms asked as he watched Sir John Burleigh saunter across the grand entrance hall to the exit.

"No, Simms, it is dammed well not all right." His butler put the tray of coffee down on the large curved desk.

"If there is anything I can do to be of assistance, sir?" he said.

"What, oh yes, yes, you can, Simms."

The elderly butler realised that the governor's mind was already distracted.

"Major Baldock of course," Raines was talking to himself. "I need to speak to the good and proper major." He turned to the butler as if remembering that he was still there. "Simms, fetch me Major Baldock. He may think he's paid his debts to me, but he hasn't even started yet."

Mrs Moffat had made the children have a quiet day. When Sydney and I returned from the library, we were greeted by the delicious smell of homemade soup and a big ham roasting slowly in the big oven. We had argued all the way home about the wisdom of our planned trip out to the reef.

"Would you mind if I was to go out for the day tomorrow, Mrs Moffat?" I asked. "Sydney and I have had the offer of a boat trip out to the reef. It would be most invaluable research for my book on the islands."

Victoria and Rupert often liked to eavesdrop on the grown-ups. They had learnt lots of interesting things that way. So although they had been sent to wash before tea, they had, in fact, remained by the open door to learn what we had been doing with our day.

"I can watch the children for you, Mr Anders, but you should know that they spotted a pirate watching them again today. You will need to reassure the boy that the pirate woman isn't about to murder him in his sleep. I have tried, of course, but he doesn't appear to listen to me."

"I'll talk to him, Mrs Moffat, I promise."

"Why not tell the kid the truth?" demanded Sydney sulkily.

"Shut up, Sydney," I said threateningly.

"Now, now, gentlemen, there will be no falling out in my kitchen, if you don't mind," scolded the housekeeper. "I've said there would be no problem and there won't."

"No, I just don't get it anymore," persisted Sydney. "Why don't you tell the child that Prudence Fairweather has become a good friend of yours? Explain to him that this woman he is convinced is trying to kill him is in fact his tutor's lover."

Mrs Moffat gasped in shock. Rupert and Victoria were still standing unseen in the doorway. The look on Rupert's face said everything. He looked at me with more disdain than a child so young should be able to muster. The one person in the world in whom he had trusted had let him down. At that moment, Rupert was sure he would never trust anyone ever again. He turned and ran from the room.

"Rupert!" I shouted after him. I was going to give chase, but Mrs Moffat blocked my path.

"I am absolutely sure you have a good explanation for this, Mr Anders, but just at the moment, I doubt very much if the boy would be listening, would he now?"

"Sydney," I said under my breath.

"Look, I'm sorry, old chap. I didn't know he was standing there, did I?"

"I am going to kill you anyway."

"I'll go tell him I was joking."

"You weren't joking and he wouldn't believe you anyway. He is not stupid. I have devoted my waking hours, when I am not finding ways to kill demons, trying to make those children feel loved and wanted."

"I better be going, Mrs Moffat," said Sydney uncomfortably.

"I think you're right," agreed Mrs Moffat, firmly ushering Sydney to the door. "I don't want blood all over my kitchen floor, that's for sure," she added, pushing him out into the back corridor and shutting the door on him.

Nobody said anything for a few minutes. I stared intently at the swirling patterns in the grain of the ancient wooden table. Victoria stood motionless at the doorway as if frozen in time. Mrs Moffat stood by the back door through which she had just evicted Sydney. She was rubbing her hands down the front of her white apron, as she did when troubled by anything, only much more vigorously than usual.

"I need to go and explain to Rupert that Prudence means him no harm," I said, breaking the silence.

"You would be wasting your time, Mr Anders," Victoria said in a very matter-of-fact way. "I am afraid he just won't believe you."

"I'm afraid she's right," agreed Mrs Moffat unhelpfully. "I am not sure yet if I believe that myself, Mr Anders." She sat down at the table opposite me and folded her arms across her large bosom.

"Do you really know the pirate Prudence Fairweather?" Victoria was unable to hide her excitement any longer. She came over to the table and sat down next to Mrs Moffat, her eyes sparking with excitement.

"Well, Mr Anders?" Mrs Moffat spoke fiercely. "The child is waiting for an answer."

The *Serpent King* rounded the headland on her approach to Heffen Harbour. Admiral Samuel Gilding stood forward, the breeze blowing his long blue-grey hair from under his tri-cornered hat. He was a grotesquely fat man, entirely due to excessive eating and drinking and little real exercise.

His ship was almost as ugly as he was. A four-mast affair that was claimed to be not only unsinkable, but also capable of blowing any ship afloat out of the water. Like its master, the *Serpent King* had a corpulent look to it. The hull had been constructed to be both longer and much wider than the average vessel, to enable even more cannons to be carried. The hull had also been constructed to almost double the thickness normal for a vessel of similar size. Overall, this strange and ungainly craft imbued a sense of gloom and suffering. Part of the vast hold below had been converted into Gilding's playroom.

The admiral's idea of play was to cause as much pain as possible to others. Rarely did he torture people for something as mundane as information. Mostly it was just for the fun of it. A special chair had been constructed to lower the admiral by a system of ropes and pulleys from the deck to his chamber of horrors. It was the only way that he could get there nowadays, for his repulsively corpulent frame would no longer fit the generously wide stairway.

If he had no prisoners to put on the rack or tie to the wheel, he kept a small number of slaves especially to keep him entertained. Any member of his crew showing the slightest sign of insubordination could well find themselves facing a slow and agonising end. Gilding's proudest boast was that it had once taken him more than two weeks to kill a man.

"We will be birthed within the hour, Admiral," said a young officer.

"See that someone runs up to the palace to let Governor Raines know that we have arrived. A little more wind and we would have made the grand ball. Still, it can't be helped. Who was in charge of that watch?"

"I was, sir," said the young man.

"Really. I didn't realise." The fat-faced man smiled. He signalled to a toothless sailor with long lank greasy hair. "Fifty lashes for this young man," he ordered. "Please don't start the punishment until I get there." He turned to the speechless and terrified young officer. "Never rely on the wind to get you out of trouble on my ship, young man."

The *Serpent King* docked at Heffen Harbour at almost the same time the first dark rain clouds began to form over Niildia. The first bright orange flames had begun to lap around the top of the volcanic mass.

Hidden where nobody could hope to find him, red eyes glimmering in the half-light, Efulric the Apprentice feasted on the evil and pain around him. As he did so, the power of this malevolent spirit that had been so weak for so long continued to grow, stronger and stronger. Soon he knew that nobody would be able to stand against him. Not even that silly female creature. Efulric had long since ended any serious threats, killed the one who could have destroyed it.

The chilling cry that came from behind the blood red eyes was not as it sounded a cry of excruciating pain, but a cry of total pleasure.

Chapter 15

$\mathcal{M}$y conversation with Mrs Moffat had been most uncomfortable. Rupert would not even speak to me. Only Victoria seemed to be impressed and very excited at the idea of my friendship with her idol. I was glad for the early start that morning. I was up, dressed and hoping to leave before anybody else had risen. I crept down from my room, managing to avoid all the creaky floorboards. My hand was slowly turning the doorknob leading to Mrs Moffat's kitchen. I was holding my breath as I slowly pushed open the door.

"Mr Anders," Victoria called to me in a loud whisper from the top of the stairs, making me jump out of my skin.

"Please don't do that, Victoria," I complained. "My nerves are already wrecked."

"I was wondering, could you steal me something from Prudence Fairweather, Mr Anders? Stealing from pirates can't be wrong, can it? Just one of her head scarves perhaps, or maybe some of those big earrings she sometimes wears." Victoria looked as if she was becoming upset. "You will come back, Mr Anders, won't you? Only Rupert and I need you, even though Rupert doesn't think he does just now."

I went back up the stairs and gave her a hug. "Friends of mine are watching over you both. I will be back very soon, Victoria. Please do as Mrs Moffat tells you, won't you?" I ran back down the stairs and through the little kitchen to the back door.

"I have made you some food up," said Mrs Moffat. She was standing by the door, holding out a parcel at me. "I have no idea what you are getting yourself into, Mr Anders," she went on grimly. "Still, I know a good and God-fearing man when I see one. So I suppose I'll have to trust you. Please don't go getting yourself killed, young man, if you can help it that is. I am not sure the children could cope with that."

Mrs Moffat got a huge hug. "Look after my young charges for me," I said, pretending not to notice the tear in Mrs Moffat's eye.

I came down the road from the palace as dawn broke in the sky over the harbour. The greyness patched in random blotches of blue and bathed in pastel pinks and reds. Everywhere was quiet. It was as if the whole island had become suddenly deserted.

I was heading for the same place Sydney and I had started our short safari from. We had agreed that Prudence would send a boat there to collect us. As I scrambled down the cliff path, I wondered what Sydney was doing. I realised now that I had probably been a little unreasonable. This paradise was not quite what poor old Sydney had expected.

Sliding down the last steep stretch of the path, I landed with quite a thud on a pebbly stretch of the beach. A little winded from the unplanned speed of my final descent, I was not immediately aware I was no longer alone.

"Our cab has not arrived yet," said Sydney. "I thought I better still come along to keep an eye on you, old chap. Let's face it, that temper of yours could get you into all sorts of trouble. I am pretty sure you are going to need a chaperone as well."

I looked at my tall and aggravatingly good-looking friend. He, in turn, looked sheepishly back at me.

"Is that your wife-stealing look by any chance?" I asked.

"I don't steal them, Thomas," argued Sydney, the hint of a smile playing on his lips. "I only borrow them. I always put them back again later, exactly where I found them."

The governor's palace was very busy for a Sunday. The talk everywhere in the building centred on the governor's unpleasant visitors. Major Baldock had been in again early and breakfasted with Raines and his guests Lady Catherine and the British ambassador.

Simms and his staff were kept very busy commuting from the big kitchen to the small dining room with trays of sausage, bacon, beef and potatoes. Fresh bread and cheese with a variety of preserves were also provided. A keg of ale for the ambassador supplemented the obligatory pots of tea and coffee for the other guests.

Simms understood that he was getting no younger. All this running up and down stairs was becoming very tiring indeed. At the first opportunity for a break, he sank into one of the comfortable chairs by the fire in Mrs Moffat's back kitchen. She had told him all about the goings-on of the night before.

"Perhaps you would have a word with young Rupert when you're rested, Mr Simms. It would do no harm. The boy is convinced the pirate has done away with Odi." She was putting on a fresh apron. "She killed my husband, so for all I know the lad could be right."

"There are more evil goings-on in this palace today than you will ever find on the *Black Albatross*," Simms spoke with considerable conviction. "How that woman Catherine Ridley has the nerve," he went on through partially clenched teeth, "how she has the nerve to come back here, I really do not know. As for the so-called ambassador, I am frankly surprised he dares even to show his face." The old butler, who never seemed to get ruffled, put his face in his hands. "You know I am getting to old for all this, don't you, Mrs Moffat?"

Mrs Moffat smiled and patted his arm. "The governor would be lost without you, Mr Simms, and you know it."

"I know that it is wrong of me to hold any opinion of our guests. The ambassador, however, is a wretched man, Mrs Moffat, if you will forgive me being so frank." He let out a hollow laugh. "He is, however, nearly a saint compared to a certain Admiral Samuel Gilding, who I have heard arrives at the palace today. He is, they say, to rid our seas of pirates and brigands." He looked very tired. Mrs Moffat smiled gently and took hold of the old butler's hand.

"All these people have sold their souls to the devil, if you ask me. You can be sure no good will come of it for any of them, Mr Simms, you mark my words." Mrs Moffat was dismissive of these powerful men. Simms recognised that the words, however, were spoken more as a result of her strong faith rather than through any insight into the future. "I used to think that there was hope for our employer, but I reckon he's as bad as the rest," she added sadly.

She handed Simms a steaming mug of dark coffee, exactly as Mr Simms liked to drink it. Uncharacteristically, her hand was shaking a little, spilling the scalding liquid onto the head butler.

"It's not like you to get all of a do dah, Mrs Moffat," said Simms, jumping from his chair as the housekeeper busied around with wet towels. "Stop fussing, woman, it was only a drop got on me." He gestured for her to stop rubbing his hand.

"Can't you feel it, Mr Simms?" There were tears rolling down her handsome face. Simms knew well that the stern but caring housekeeper, who constantly scolded everybody, was the rock on which the palace staff relied so much. That she was a strong woman able to cope coolly and calmly with any crisis made this all the more disturbing for the butler.

Simms was not good in such situations at the best of times. "Pull yourself together, Mrs Moffat." He stood stiffly upright and wooden, but with genuine concern mixed in with his ill-disguised awkwardness. So funny did the poor man look that Mrs Moffat began to laugh and cry at the same time.

"Sister Marion at the convent was just like you," she told the bemused Butler whilst trying to regain control of her emotions.

"Sister Marion?" exclaimed Simms, obviously horrified to be compared to a nun.

"Please forgive me, Mr Simms." Mrs Moffat was wiping tears of laughter and pain from her eyes. "She used to tell me off exactly like you just did. Miss O'Brien, she would say, will you pull yourself together at once, child? Then she would go on and on about how much we upset God himself if he saw us weeping."

"Well, as long as you are all right now, Mrs Moffat." Simms shuffled from foot to foot. "My fault, I suppose, talking about all those awful people."

"So you don't think the pirate Prudence Fairweather is engaged in the devil's work then?"

Simms sat cautiously down again. "She is no angel, Mrs Moffat. I do not pretend she is, but her soul is her own, and if you want my opinion, the devil will never get his evil hands on it."

"Well, you cannot blame the way I feel," replied the housekeeper firmly. "Although I admit, I have always thought you a good judge of character, Mr Simms. Then it would seem that Victoria idolises this pirate woman too. And what about our hard-working tutor, Mr Anders? I confess to have grown quite fond of him, in a maternal kind of way, you understand. If Mr Greenburgh were to be believed, it would seem that young Mr Anders is head over heels in love with this pirate. Not that I would trust that Mr Greenburgh, not as far as I could throw him, which is not going to be very far, now is it?"

"I am not sure what you are trying to say, Mrs Moffat," confessed Simms. "I am inclined to share your opinion of young Mr Greenburgh, however."

"I am trying to say you can't all be wrong." She got up and went over to check her stove, although there was no reason to do so. "I am sorry I got upset, Mr Simms. It won't happen again and I would be most grateful if you didn't mention it to anyone."

"Of course I won't."

"It's just with so many unpleasant people around and Mr Anders going off doing dangerous things. I mean, let's face it, the young man is not cut out to be a hero, now I ask you, he's not, is he?" Victoria ran into the kitchen at some speed from the backstairs.

"How many times have I asked you not to run like that, young lady?" scolded Mrs Moffat sternly.

"Sorry," gasped Victoria. Simms smiled to himself. The fight had not been knocked out of the housekeeper yet. "Only I can't find Rupert anywhere," she added.

Upstairs more guests had arrived, the first of these in the shape of the unbelievably grotesque sailor, Admiral Samuel Gilding. In sharp contrast to this hideously fat and ugly man was the suave and debonair figure of Sir John Burleigh. The portrait of the governor's namesake and grandfather, Silas Brand, stared threateningly down on the two new arrivals.

Despite being clothed in a smart and very expensive uniform, the admiral looked all wrong. He was of average height but extremely wide. His head, which appeared to be constructed from rolls of fat, was nevertheless too small for the inflated body on which it sat. He had obvious difficulty moving, although once he got going, the admiral could move surprisingly quickly. His uniform had been cut well by highly skilled tailors. Despite their skills, they had noticeably failed to add any grace to the obese man's bloated body, probably because such an achievement would be impossible. Samuel Gilding clearly did not belong in a uniform, especially such a high-ranking one.

After a few minutes' wait, Simms came up the stairs from the servants' quarters to show them into the small conference room. This was an L-shaped extension to the governor's offices. It was not often used nowadays. The governor preferred to hold any meetings in his main office. Not surprisingly, this explained the very musty smell that hung in the room.

A large circular table almost filled the space available, leaving barely enough room for the chairs. The curtains were drawn across, blocking out the bright sunshine. Two oil lamps flickering pathetically on the table did little to lift the gloomy darkness of the room.

The ambassador was already in his seat. His clothing carried evidence of his more than adequate breakfast, and he smelt of stale beer and three-week-old sweat. Burleigh made a point of sitting as far from him as possible. Unfortunately, the size of the room and its claustrophobic and airless quality made avoiding the vile stench of the man impossible.

The admiral didn't seem to mind squeezing his bulk into the chair next to the ambassador. Nobody spoke for a full five minutes. The only sound was of a mosquito buzzing loudly around the two uniformed men. If it bites the admiral, it will surely die instantly, thought Burleigh to himself. He watched with ill-concealed disgust as a great bead of sweat ran down the admiral's podgy face.

The governor, the handsome Lady Catherine on his right arm, entered the room. Burleigh guessed that the countess, having breakfasted well, had most probably enjoyed the governor for dessert. Clearly Raines had not been in the mood for such activity, especially before such an important meeting. Silas Raines was a worried man.

Lady Catherine, in contrast, although unashamedly flushed from her recent exertion, was both serene and confident. Today she wore a simple ivory and red dress, cut low on her full bosom. She was both amused and flattered that Burleigh's eyes were drawn to her prominent and plentiful cleavage. She made a point of leaning forward more to tantalise the suave businessman.

The last to arrive was Henry Jessop. Although he tried hard to look as dapper as Sir John, it was difficult to conceal the threadbare nature of his once fashionable garments.

"Now we are all together, the floor is yours, Sir John," said Silas Raines glumly.

"Not all I fancy, Governor," pointed out Jessop as he took his seat. "We have apologies from, let me see, Maurice Jones, Richard Boscastle, oh and…."

"That will do, Jessop," snapped Raines, interrupting him. There was no need for introductions. Everybody around the table knew each other well. Not one of them would have chosen to socialise with any of the others if given a choice. They no longer had a choice.

"Thank you, Governor." Burleigh had risen to his feet and bowed courteously to his host. "Today we begin the first phase. It befalls our esteemed governor to return to the place where they were found. I refer, of course, to the four segments of the amulet."

"I hope you know what you are doing, John darling," said Lady Catherine. Her fingers were stroking a delicate gold chain that hung between her breasts.

"People have doubted me in the past, Catherine my dear, and they no longer care." His narrow mouth curved into a smile more chilling than usual. "Everything is in place for this demon to die, for us to take his power, and with it, unimaginable wealth and influence in our world. This is not a time for the faint hearted."

"I don't understand why I needed to be here, that's all," explained the woman, looking around at the others.

"Nor I," agreed the ambassador, "although it was a dammed good party, Governor. Got any more of them young girls for me to try before I leave, Burleigh?"

"My stocks are a little low after last night, Ambassador, but I am pleased you enjoyed yourself," replied Burleigh coldly. "In answer to the countess, I must be guided by Peckham. The demon killer knows his profession well. He suggested that it was essential all those who wished to share in Efulric's power should be present on Heffen."

"That's if he can be trusted. You said yourself he may well be a government agent," interrupted Raines.

"What's this?" wheezed the vile Admiral Gilding, gobules of sweat trickling down his sagging jowls. "I cannot have government agents interfering, you know that."

"He will be dealt with," Burleigh reassured him. "When he has killed our demon for us, naturally."

"So what is our next move then?" The admiral had a sugary almost effeminate voice which was in stark contrast to his grotesque body.

"As I said, the governor returns the four segments to the place they were taken from."

"Who is going to be with me?" asked Silas nervously.

"Only the boy, Governor." Burleigh sounded as if he was tired of repeating himself. "You are the only one here who was at that meeting, remember?"

Silas Raines shuddered. His mind returned to that day, the table in the wooden shack, that dreadful dead place. The oil lamp swinging back and forth. The creature in the dark shawl with those dreadful blood red eyes.

"I thought we didn't need the boy. Weren't you going to have him killed?" The odious admiral's menacing question was intended to be rhetorical. "I'm sure I even offered to do the honours myself," he added with a leering grin. "I shouldn't have charged much."

Silas Raines rose from his chair, his face purple with rage. For a moment he seemed unable to speak. "My sister's child," he was almost choking on the words. "Understand me well and mark my words, the boy will not be harmed in any way. I thought I had made that clear, Burleigh."

"Do you even remember the little brat's name, Silas dear?" enquired the countess.

"I thought you were happy having the lad, you know?" The ambassador pretended to cut his throat with a fat stubby hand. "Didn't you hire in a chap called Skeet to do the dastardly deed, Sir John?"

"Oh dear, you were being a bit of a cheapskate, Johnny," observed Lady Catherine, smiling from similar cold lips.

"I would have done it for free and enjoyed every minute," pointed out Admiral Gilding, his fleshy features breaking into a vile and toothless grin. "And the girl, now I would really enjoy that," he added, wiping his dribbling nose on the back of his sleeve.

"I swear I will kill him in a minute," roared the governor, who looked like he was about to burst a blood vessel.

"Don't do that, Governor. Our fat admiral here is the only person who can get you through the reef and safely across the Fault," pointed out Burleigh. "You will take one of the yachts in the harbour and just a small crew. Only you and the boy must go up the path back to that place."

"Then what happens?" asked Jessop, who was looking particularly bored.

"Things will take a week or so to come to a head," replied Burleigh. "If you want a share of the power, we all have to join Peckham before the final kill." He looked at Silas Raines, who had now calmed down. "Governor," he said coldly, "I apologise for the misunderstanding with Mr Skeet. The boy will be in your charge, so I am sure he will come to no harm." Nobody believed for one minute that Burleigh meant what he said.

As the meeting broke up, Lady Catherine caught hold of the admiral.

"We do not want this boy to return. You do understand. A little accident perhaps?"

"A gentleman is entitled to his bit of fun," complained Gilding, wiping a mixture of sweat and spittle from his flabby jowls. "Accidents are just not fun," he added sulkily.

Burleigh walked over to the governor, who still looked very flushed. He had no desire to return to the rock. Silas had been dreading the coming of this day. It wouldn't have been so bad if the others had been with him. To go up to that cabin alone, except for his nephew, sent a cold chill through him. He was not the bravest of men in normal circumstances.

"Are you sure the boy has to come along?" he demanded of Burleigh. They were alone in the room now. He already knew the answer and knew the question to be a pointless one.

"As long as the child lives, he owns his segment of the amulet, you know that." Burleigh was trying hard to be patient. "The owner must return their segment to the table. Those were the clear instructions. I confess, I am unhappy that you have chosen to become sentimental about the boy. I suppose, however, it is understandable and something I should have foreseen." He laughed a hollow humourless laugh. "My fault entirely. Should have had them killed before you set eyes on the little brats." Burleigh ushered the governor to the door. "The boy is in the reception room and the admiral waits your pleasure. Cheer up, Governor. You'll be back in time for tea."

"Trouble." Simms's face was as white as a sheet. "Terrible trouble." He was shaking like a leaf. Mrs Moffat found him a strong brandy and waited patiently for the head butler to calm down. Victoria had been telling her that she still hadn't found Rupert, and Mrs Moffat was starting to become concerned at that. When she thought Simms might be able to talk, she took the glass back from him. Victoria stood, watching the old butler with a serious and concerned look on her pretty young face.

"Right, Mr Simms," Mrs Moffat said. "What on earth has got you into such a state?"

"I just met the notorious Admiral Gilding," he said.

"I heard he was not a pretty sight," said the woman.

"Nor is he Samuel Gilding," replied Simms. "At least that is not what he is known as in these parts."

"Who is he then?"

"His name is Jessie Crooks," said Simms bitterly. "Most feared pirate we ever had in these parts and with good reason. It was Jessie Crooks who killed your husband."

"It was Prudence Fairweather who killed my Bernard," she insisted.

Simms's normally expressionless face creased into a frown. "Who told you that then?" he asked. "Let me hazard a guess. Our governor perhaps?"

"Well, yes, as a matter of fact, it was Silas Raines, if you must know. He was very kind to me," Mrs Moffat reminded him. "Everything we had was destroyed."

Simms laughed. "Because he was forced to turn a blind eye to the crime. Bernard was getting in Sir John Burleigh's way. Affecting profit margins he was. I knew something was going to happen so I went down to warn him."

"Why have you never told me this before?"

"I am not much for gossip, Mrs Moffat, as you well know. If I am honest, I also feared you would go straight to the governor. I do not come out of this looking well myself." Simms looked sadly at her. "Your husband would not listen to me. He would not heed my warning. We argued and it became violent. He accused me of helping the slavers."

"He was both a stubborn and violent man, Mr Simms," said the housekeeper softly. "Believe me, I know that better than anyone."

"He drew a pistol and began to brandish it about. We struggled and the pistol went off." Simms paused, taking out one of his well-starched handkerchiefs and mopping his forehead. "I think he was quite badly wounded. I said I would go for help. Seconds later, there were explosions everywhere. Crooks and his cutthroats had hit the boatyard."

"But others saw Prudence Fairweather there," insisted Mrs Moffat. "Cornelious Jakes told me she was responsible."

"That is for you and him to discuss. He helped me get away and your son."

"My son?"

"His old crate set sail from the harbour ablaze. He must have managed to get to the lad. I had seen him shouting to him and then was distracted. I saw your boy on board later, during the storm, only for a moment or two, but I swear I saw him. It blew us into the Fault. Somehow Jakes kept the ship from running aground, but it was a close run thing and not an experience I would ever wish to go through again. We lost a good few hands overboard."

"He never told me any of that. Why wouldn't he have told me that?"

"He said he had never seen him."

"But you don't believe that, do you, Mr Simms?" Mrs Moffat reached across the table and took hold of one of Simms's ancient but well-manicured hands. "You think Cornelious cannot face the truth, so he is blocking it out. My son was washed overboard in the storm."

Simms sat as stiffly as ever, displaying his usual poise and air of calm dignity. He needed to say nothing for the Irish woman to know she was right.

"That is the true reason you have never told me this," she said. "It is all right though, Mr Simms, I have known my baby was dead for a long time."

"It was one hell of a storm brewing, and there was something less than human screaming in the fire," explained Simms sadly. "Niridia was spewing out molten lava. Had it not been so frightening, it would have been breathtakingly beautiful. Nature taking control. The Fault, too, was at its most dangerous, thick in mist. Even the ship's chronometer was showing the wrong time. There was chaos everywhere." Simms paused for a moment. "Before we left shore, he was trying to get to Bernard, but he would never have made it. Prudence stopped him. Otherwise, he would also have died that night."

Mrs Moffat looked shocked now. "But Jessie Crooks, he was hung, surely he was. I remember the young Philip Baldock carried out the sentence."

"I thought that too," Simms agreed. "Perhaps the good major couldn't find a rope strong enough," he added sarcastically.

Mrs Moffat sat down at the old kitchen table. Her hands were shaking as she tried to wipe away her tears. She never liked to show emotion to others. She had always considered it a sign of weakness.

"I am so sorry," said Simms flatly. "I should have told you all this a long time ago. I just didn't know how to."

"It doesn't matter now, Mr Simms, now does it? What matters is that all of a sudden all these terrible people, I thought our little paradise well rid of, are coming back." She looked up at Simms, her homely features a mixture of fear and sadness. "First that blaggard Henry Jessop, then Lady Catherine and now Crooks," she added.

"You do realise what else this means, Mrs Moffat?"

"Frankly, no, I don't, Mr Simms," she confessed. "To be honest, this is all too much for my small brain to cope with."

"Jessie Crooks is a pirate, and therefore, he has the knowledge. He knows how to navigate the reef and in theory the Fault."

"But that is where Mr Anders and Mr Greenburgh have gone." The housekeeper was beginning to panic.

"And the pirate Prudence Fairweather, it was due to her intercession Crooks was caught. I doubt if the sadistic monster has forgotten that," added Simms.

"They must be warned," said the housekeeper. "We must warn them."

When Mrs Moffat was sure Simms was gone and certain she was alone, she broke down and sobbed for her baby. Neither of them noticed until a long time later that Victoria had disappeared.

We were once more on the *Albatross* which, with a good wind behind us, was bouncing along in the choppy waters far too fast for my liking. It was clear, even to me, that we were approaching the reef. It was also our first view of Niridia. Local people hereabouts called the volcano "The Rock." It was not difficult to see where it had got this name. There seemed to be nothing living on Niridia. It was a rock, not withstanding the fact that it was a very large one.

It was a foreboding and desolate place, rising high into the dark clouds. Thick grey smoke, spilling from the mouth of the volcano, mingled with the gathering gloom. The flickering orange glow was barely visible. It was as if the dark skies were happening on cue. The sun continued to shine everywhere except on Niridia. At least that was how it seemed.

"Good morning, gentleman." Prudence had come from her cabin to greet us. She was clothed only in a brief white vest and short pants. The beautiful girl was barefoot, but she did have her shiny auburn locks covered with a bandanna.

"Aren't we going a bit fast?" I enquired.

"Is that why you are going a bit green again, Mr Anders?" Prudence smiled sweetly.

"Don't you have to navigate the reef carefully?" I shouted over the noise of the wind on canvas, and the creaking and groaning of the great ship as it cut its way through the choppy waters.

"Why don't you go and lie down below, old boy, and let others worry about driving this thing," suggested Sydney. He was looking very uncomfortable himself and desperately trying to hide it. "We'll call you when we need your superior intellect."

"I am better here thank you," I shouted back through the wind. I was hanging on to a convenient rail, trying hard not to be sick, or indeed look like I was trying not to be sick!

As it was, Prudence was paying little attention to Sydney or me. As the *Albatross* rode through the waves, leaning heavily to port in the strong wind, Prudence was shouting orders to the helmsman. He, with the help of a couple of musclebound pirates, was constantly turning the big wheel one way then the other as it weaved its way through the reef.

Gabrielle's Reef circled the waters in which lay the small group of islands inhabited by the pirates and some native Heffians. Part of these formed a narrow strait between the north island coast and that of Niridia. The small islands were themselves hidden from the Rock by the high peaks of the north.

The *Albatross* was now moving into the wind. There was frantic activity amongst the crew as sails were adjusted for the new challenge. Before us, through the salty spray, we could now see the eerie mist that hung just off the rock.

"Try and get us into the sheltered bit, Mr Ashcroft, behind those rocks." Prudence soaked, as we all were by the spray, pointed at a small island of rocks. This looked to be less than half a league from the Niridia shoreline and very close to the mists indeed.

Orders were being shouted in all directions now. Most of the sails were down, and there were men dropping lines over the side to check the depth of the water. The *Albatross* was now moving very slowly into the position Prudence wanted. The rocks offered shelter from the wind, whilst the pirate ship was hidden from the view of the far shore. In the unlikely event that another ship came through the reef, the *Albatross* would not be visible either.

The water was a deep clear blue where we had dropped anchor, although it turned to a cold slate grey nearer to the Rock. Prudence, her wet clothing clinging to her tall frame, walked over to where I stood, still clinging to the rail.

"You can let go now," she said in her sweetly sarcastic way.

"What next?" I said, brushing wet strands of hair from my face.

"We will have a bit of a meeting in my cabin, then, Thomas Anders, you are going to put my swimming lesson to good use."

"I can't swim," moaned Sydney.

"Just as long as you can sink," Prudence smiled, "and learn to keep your eyes open under water, we will make sure you don't drown."

Prudence's cabin seemed dark and stuffy compared to the bright light and fresh breeze up top. Harry and Arthur were arguing as usual, and Joshua was watching with obvious amusement. Arthur smiled at us as Sydney and I ducked under the low doorway into the cabin.

"You must understand what you're dealing with here, gentlemen," began the rat-faced sailor. "I am as honest a thief and a con-man as you will find in these waters. Any attempt at dressing in the cloak of respectability has invariably been for a transparently dishonourable purpose. Harry here, on the other hand, is not, are you, my ugly friend?"

"If I am ugly, then, my brother, you are monstrous. Efulric I fully expect to be handsome by comparison."

"He was once a respectable man who had a wife and two fine children. Then one day he left home and set sail to far-off places. In fact, Harry has been captain of his own ship. I am, of course, talking many years ago, before the relentless advance of age and senility. I mean, how can you possibly trust such a man who was once so respectable?"

"I was once respectable too, Arthur," pointed out Prudence as she entered the cabin, clothed as before but without the bandanna. The hot sunshine had dried us all out quickly.

"At least I sired just two fine children, Arthur, and both to the same mother and not half the population of Heffen."

"You and Arthur sound like peas from the same pod," I said to Sydney. We were all stood or sat around the big table that took up half of the L-shaped cabin.

"Will you all shut up?" demanded Prudence irritably. "There are only so many hours of daylight left, and we have no idea how long we have altogether."

"So what exactly are we looking for?" enquired the gigantic black man.

"I'm not honestly sure, Joshua," admitted the girl. "We know from Gabrielle's notes that if we destroy the Fault, we destroy Efulric the Apprentice and his demon hordes to boot. Or, at the worst, we at least prevent it from releasing them. This sounds easy, except that his carefully documented and detailed description of how we go about destroying the Fault would appear to be just a handful of ashes. The idea is to take a look and see if there is anything obvious. A weakness we can exploit, that kind of thing."

"From my research into local myths and legends, the destruction of the Fault can be brought about by setting explosives at certain points," I explained. "I don't pretend to fully understand the concept myself, but in simple terms, the Fault is a long crack in the Earth's crust, probably caused by one of Niridia's previous eruptions. My guess is that a series of large explosions would at least temporarily seal up the crack, thus refusing our demon the chance to reunite with his body, or his demon army for that matter."

"We think that, at the worst, it will have to wait another hundred years," interrupted Prudence. "If we are very lucky, I might get the chance to kill it. One thing is for sure, it will be a very dangerous day's work."

"How can we be sure of any of this when the scholarly Mr Anders admits to it being taken from myths and legends?" demanded Harry. He lowered his tall, deeply bronzed frame into a chair. Harry was still in very good shape for a man of such advanced years.

"You should perhaps read a little more, old man," said Arthur smugly. "The legend is clearly related in many different books and old scrolls. Nor should you forget what you and I have seen with our own eyes."

"I doubt I ever will," said Harry softly.

"Nor me," admitted Arthur. "Nor me."

"I know it is happening," said Prudence quietly. "And I am part of the legend for some reason."

"What about the spy?" demanded Joshua. "If everything else is true, then the spy will ruin everything."

"From what I understand, we know that the spy is in fact a demon hunter," Prudence explained. "The little man Thomas saw in the library that day."

"The nasty little creep Peckham, Harry and I saw," put in Arthur.

"So who killed the old man Boscastle?" asked Sydney. "I mean, he was a cantankerous old sod, but definitely not a demon."

"I don't know yet," admitted Prudence. "I am guessing Burleigh and his demon killer, but I have absolutely no idea why. I did drop in on the old man the other day. He was still very frightened, as he has been for at least the last ten years, since he killed his wife. My father liked Richard Boscastle, which is odd really, because my father was usually a good judge of character."

345

"Speaking of dead bodies, any news on the body Monkey and Meg found on the beach?" asked Harry cheerfully. "To be perfectly honest, I am more at ease with a good old-fashioned murder than all this demon talk," he explained to Sydney and me.

"He had no clothes on, no means of identification. Nobody has a clue who he was," replied Joshua.

"Probably just some drunken deckhand," suggested Arthur with a big and wicked grin. "One minute scoffing more than his ration of rum, the next, feeding the fishes, easily happens," he added.

"Stark naked and with a look of sheer terror on his face," said Harry. "I think my grotesque friend here is missing the point, not that he ever gets it anyway."

"Look, children, you can bicker at each other later," snapped the girl, glaring at the two rogues. "Let's not waste the daylight, gentlemen." She turned and looked me up and down, mischief in her brown eyes again. "Mr Anders, you are a little overdressed to go swimming. Harry, have a couple of boats lowered. Let's go see if we can work out what Gabrielle saw a hundred years ago." She looked at Sydney, who was looking horrified at the prospect of swimming. "And somebody find Sydney some water wings," she added.

Less than half an hour later, a small rowing boat moved closer to the unnatural mist that hung above the dull grey water. The *Albatross* was now hidden from view. Our little craft felt very exposed in the shadow of the awesome visage of dead rock looming high above us. The wall of cold grey stone rose in gloomy magnificence from the water's edge. I felt so small and our little boat so insignificant in this place. What possible difference could we ever hope to make?

"Joshua, please ensure that Sydney doesn't drown. I will endeavour to keep Mr Anders floating." Prudence turned to look at me. Sydney, sat next to me in the back of the boat, was as white as a sheet, despite a good tan. "I suggest we have one more practice, Mr Anders, before we go swimming near the Fault. It might be better, Joshua, if you and Sydney worked from the boat."

Without warning, Prudence took off her top. Before anybody had time to admire her lovely breasts, she had slipped over the side into the warm water. I looked nervously at Sydney and Joshua, pulled off my shirt and trousers and dropped over the side to join her.

She was swimming away from Niridia, looming so ominously above us. The austere mountain was in its own stark and barren way quite beautiful. The water was quite calm close into the shore and warmer than I had expected. Prudence stopped swimming and waited for me to splash ungracefully towards her.

"You will never be mistaken for a fish, Thomas Anders," she shouted back. Only her head and broad shoulders were visible above the water line.

"The sea is deep here," I gasped. I had reached the girl at last and must have swallowed a few gallons of seawater in doing so. I was now having some difficulty treading water.

"Hold onto me," said Prudence. I was close up to her now. My arms were on her shoulders. I am ashamed to say I was in danger of panicking.

"Hold onto my waist and relax, Thomas," Prudence said firmly, sensing my fear. "You are not as bad a swimmer as you think you are. Just relax and worry less about getting your face wet."

The soft touch of her skin against mine, as our almost naked bodies pressed together, was both very sensual and very relaxing indeed. The panic melted away and the water seemed more able to support my weight.

I kissed the pirate girl and she kissed me back.

"You're not drowning anymore," she said softly, pushing wet hair away from my eyes. Her full lips were still almost touching mine.

"You made me forget myself for a minute," I confessed.

Prudence laughed. "I meant to," she confessed. "Now your body knows that even when you are out of your depth, the sea will support you, if you will only let it. Now come with me, Thomas, and I will show you a world more wonderful than anything you have ever seen before."

Prudence pushed me away and dived down. She had shown me how to swim down to the seabed before. After I had come up spluttering from a couple of failed attempts, Prudence resurfaced.

"Are you coming or not?" she demanded crossly.

On my third attempt, I managed to remember to keep my eyes open. Quickly becoming used to the gloom, I was confronted by one of the most magical sights I could ever hoped to have seen. I found I was swimming down towards a mountain of coral. Little fish, of many shapes and in a multitude of bright colours, were weaving their way around the intricate design of this enchanted, underwater paradise.

The pirate girl's voluptuous curves were silhouetted for a moment against the sun as she swam gracefully down towards me. I could have dwelt on this vision forever, had I not been forced to return to the surface for air.

"What do you think?" gasped Prudence Fairweather, coming up for air next to me.

"Beautiful," I said, trying to catch my breath.

"Come on, I'll show you some more. Then we can go take a look at the Fault." The girl disappeared again below the surface. I took a very deep breath and followed her down. We went deeper this time, being careful not to touch the coral, which was very brittle and easily damaged. I could see that there were also a lot of sharp rocks looming up to the surface. These would rip the bottom out of any passing boat with consummate ease.

Amongst the rocks and the coral, in the ghostly green light, I could make out the wrecks of at least two ships on the rocks. Like monstrous phantoms from a dream, they lay at awkward angles, their backs broken, shimmering in the unnatural light. I almost forgot that I needed to breath air, so enchanted was I with my strange and surreal surroundings.

There were creatures living in the coral, or amongst the rocks, stranger than anything I had ever found in books in Heffen's unique library. Prudence tapped me on the shoulder and pointed to the surface. I put both arms around her slim waist and we glided slowly and gracefully back to the surface. It took both of us a little time to catch our breath that time. We had stayed underwater too long.

"Will you swim closer to the Fault with me now?" Prudence asked.

"As long as you let me rest a few minutes more," I agreed. We swam back to the boat, where Joshua pulled us both on board without any effort.

"I had a little look round whilst you two were practising."

"That's what they call it nowadays," muttered Sydney, who was still sulking in the back of the boat.

"Sydney's jealous," said Prudence, who was still all most naked, with her long legs pulled up to her chest and her back to Sydney and me.

"If you would like a swimming lesson too, Sydney," Prudence fluttered her eyes at him. Sydney grimaced and did his best to ignore her.

After we had rested for a while, Joshua took the small boat to the very end of the mists. Here it was so very easy for your mind to start playing tricks. At first I thought I could hear the most wonderful music I had ever heard coming from somewhere in the fog. Something else, I am not sure what, seemed to be trying to suck us in. It was nothing tangible, nothing you could reach out and touch.

Now and again though, I was convinced that I saw the shapes of things moving in this peculiarly unreal fog. There were momentary glimpses of good people lost forever in the mists, and sometimes the vague and indistinguishable form drifting past was that of a demon spirit trapped in an alien world. A ghostly silhouette of a young man, then an old pirate, seemed to loom out of the fog towards me. Were these ghosts from the many shipwrecks down below, or just our imaginations playing tricks on us?

For some unaccountable reason I did not question any of this, although there was clearly no way of knowing what, if anything, I was truly seeing. Prudence and I explored everywhere that we could. Each time we came back to the surface for air, I could see our little boat moving amongst the rocks, whilst Joshua and Sydney explored the surface, as well as keeping an eye on us. I was beginning to become very tired and even a little cold.

"You all right for one last look?" The pirate girl's face betrayed her total disappointment and frustration. Close to the mists, the underwater landscape was little different, although much darker and gloomier. Here, the creatures I saw clambering over the rocks and coral reminded me even more of giant monsters. I had seen so many such beasts portrayed so colourfully in the pages of books. Stranger-looking animals than these misshapen creatures would be difficult to find. Some had countless legs and eyes on stalks emanating from the most unlikely part of that particular crustacean's shell.

I did not want to let Prudence down. In truth, our search was quickly proving to be hopeless. It was becoming harder all the time to understand what we had been hoping to find. I forced a smile and followed her once more into the murky depths. My limbs were aching now and I had to go up for air much more often. I was also experiencing cramps in my legs.

It was in this tired state that the creature attacked. All I saw in the dark green light was the shadow of something, or someone, approaching very fast. Blood red eyes shone so brightly from the blackness of the creature's face that a strange red light mingled with the watery green that my eyes had become so accustomed to. The speed of this apparition was impossibly quick. I felt something brush against my side as I flung myself sideways in a desperate attempt to get out of its path. I was swallowing water now. The cramp returning to my calves made me scream in silent and excruciating agony.

Prudence had also been attacked. The girl, however, could swim like a fish and fortunately for me remained calm. Her dark brown eyes searched the gloom for me until her lungs were bursting. She glided up and took a great lung full of air before plunging back into the darkness. When she found me, I was barely conscious. I had passed the moment of panic and had been overcome by a strange sense of calmness. My surroundings seemed less real than ever.

The girl kissed me, forcing air into my lungs. Then she pulled me free from the coral and seaweed. She put her arms firmly around my back and launched back to the surface. Joshua had seen that we were in trouble and had brought the small boat round to pick us up. He effortlessly pulled me in first and then helped Prudence back on board.

I must have passed out for a moment. As consciousness slowly returned, my eyes focused back onto the world I had so nearly left. I decided that I must have died after all and gone to heaven. Prudence Fairweather was straddling my body, pushing down on my chest. Her hair hung dark and straight on to her broad shoulders and bare breasts.

Her beautiful big eyes were filled with real concern. I was coughing up foul-tasting saltwater.

"You were not supposed to drink the sea, Thomas Anders," she said softly, as I focused fully on her.

"Is he going to be all right?" asked Sydney. He sounded touchingly concerned.

"He will be as good as new, Sydney," Prudence assured him. "I suppose I should be very grateful for that. God knows we need something to be thankful for." She looked at Joshua and Sydney moodily. The olive-skinned girl looked uncharacteristically depressed. It was clear that just for now she did not know what to do next.

"I don't know what I was expecting to find," she explained sadly. "I always knew it was going to be a long shot, so I suppose I shouldn't be surprised that we found nothing."

"That's not true," I spluttered. "That thing that attacked me, did you see it?"

"It would be an exaggeration to say I saw it. I got a glimpse of something," admitted Prudence.

"Sounds like you saw a shark to me," muttered Sydney. He would have normally dreaded coming across sharks, but oddly at this moment; it seemed to be the better option.

"No, I don't think so," I disagreed. "Not unless sharks round here have arms and legs and bright red eyes. According to the books, demons guard the gateway to hell. I am pretty sure that was one of those guardians. This must surely mean that there is some kind of a weakness just there. That creature was only defending that part of the reef. It didn't try to chase us back to the boat."

"We have something to be grateful for then," Sidney shuddered.

I had started to shiver. It was going much colder in the little boat and it felt much later than it was. With the power in Joshua's huge muscular arms rowing, we set off back in the twilight gloom towards the *Black Albatross* at a good fast pace.

"Where have you been all this time?" demanded Harry.

"The old fool has been frantic with worry," mocked Arthur in a camp way.

"We have only been a couple of hours," I said, still shivering.

"We thought we had lost you," explained Meg, hugging Prudence. Prudence must have been looking very perplexed by now.

"You've been gone for more than two days," said Monkey. He was looking back into the mist intensely as if trying to see something in particular.

"That's impossible," argued Prudence. "Thomas is right. We can't have been more than a couple of hours."

"Except that you entered that," said Monkey, pointing into the swirling mists. "That makes anything possible."

I don't think I had even begun to understand the powers that lay within Gabrielle's Fault until that moment. I imagine everybody else was feeling the same. We all stood on the deck, staring back out into the bleak and foreboding half light, as if hoping to find some answers.

"Do you know that it is said that this place is the gateway to more than a million other worlds, many running parallel to our own?" I said. "A million Prudence Fairweathers to fall in love with," I added without thinking. I felt myself going red again.

"Perhaps you should find one with a milder temper," suggested Arthur.

"There couldn't be a million more of him, surely." Harry pointed at the tall thin rat-faced thief.

"I wonder if there really are a million of this pair bickering somewhere," laughed Joshua.

"Imagine if they all found their way here," chipped in Meg. "Then our world would really be doomed."

Everybody was laughing now. A much needed release of nervous energy. The green mists continued to swirl about the Fault, and stood in the ghostly light, it was ever so easy for us to believe in myths and fairy tales. Prudence turned to my companion.

"Clean him up for me, Sydney," she said, gesturing at me. "If he feels up to it, he can join me for supper," she added. "Or perhaps it's breakfast, who knows?"

I remember thinking that the girl was working hard to put a brave face on things. There was paleness to her golden brown skin. Dark shadows had formed under her clear brown eyes, which themselves betrayed how unsure she was in her fight against this unseen enemy. My theory might have given us some hope, or perhaps we were just grasping at straws. Nobody had any notion on how to close up the crack and destroy the Fault.

We were confident that if this could be successfully accomplished, then Efulric the Apprentice and his demon hordes would be banished from our world. There were now even signs of disagreement on board the *Albatross*. Far deeper differences of opinion than the bickering between the two older men. Arthur was keen to get as much gunpowder as he could carry and seal up the Fault forever. Surprisingly, Harry, for once, was in agreement with his weasel-like companion.

Whilst Prudence and I were largely in favour of Arthur's plan, Joshua remained on the fence. Monkey was, however, set very strongly against the idea. The usually relaxed young pirate was quite passionate and most articulate in his arguments against such a course of action. Meg was also against it, although it seemed most likely that this was because Monkey was. This had to be the place where the Fault was vulnerable.

"A wise man would not attack the nature of things, Mr Anders, sir. Especially without the knowledge and understanding of what he does," Odi said to me a little while later. "He may triumph over one particular demon, but who knows how many others he would let escape into our world." He looked up at me through eyes filled with the captivating innocence of a child. "Odi may not be good at sums, Mr Anders, sir, but he knows this."

Chapter 16

Dear Thomas,

It was so lovely to hear from you at last. Your short note has served much to relieve a mother's natural inclination to worry herself into an early grave. Your father's gout also seems to have noticeably improved since reading your letter and as a result he is far less tetchy. He thought it sounded rather dull on Heffen even for you, dear Thomas. He wanted me to ask you if nothing exciting ever happens there. Poor Sydney must be having a terrible time with so little happening and so little to do. Father was also wondering if you had met any nice girls out there. We are both confident Sydney would have found a few, but do be careful the disgruntled husbands don't come after you. Your note does not mention much about the social life there. I do hope you are not working too hard, Thomas. The climate is not, as I understand, suited to hard labour. Oh and don't forget to drink a lot of clean water, so you don't dehydrate, dear.

We have had four more letters from your brother, now very deep in the Amazon somewhere. In contrast to your brief note, he writes rather long-winded accounts of his adventures I find. Odd when you think that you are the professional writer in the family. Anyway, he is having a wonderful time, although apparently, he gets homesick a lot. No hairy mammoths yet as far as we can tell. Everyone else is well including the new boy we've taken in. I don't think Father's too pleased, but they seem to get on very well. Try not to work too hard and do get out and enjoy yourself a bit. Don't be letting Sydney get you up to anything too dangerous though. Father wants to know if there is anything much worth shooting at out there. I think he means rabbits, the silly old thing.

We love you so very much, my darling. Please take care. I catch your father asking God to look after you at least once a day when he thinks I am not looking. Please write again soon.

Mama

Under dark and foreboding clouds, a different craft landed on the dusty pebbled shore of Niridia. Two large and unusually ugly pirates jumped out onto land, heaving the boat out of the water. The huge bulk of the Admiral Samuel Gilding, better known to many as Jessie Crooks, was helped onto the shore. The governor and his small and very frightened nephew followed.

Rupert was terrified. He was still sure deep down inside that the pirate Prudence Fairweather was to blame. Sensing his irrational fear, his uncle had chosen to encourage it, to the point of making up some elaborate and quite implausible story as to why they were now on the rock.

It was impossible now for Silas Raines to hide his own fear either. The path that led upwards from the shore into this dead mountain climbed ominously away before them.

"You will wait for us here, Jessie," demanded the governor, looking for some reassurance.

"Please don't call me that, Governor," replied the fat man in his inappropriately high-pitched tone. "May I remind you that the man you refer to died a very long time ago." The admiral smiled a mouthful of rotten teeth at Silas.

"I know," replied the governor bitterly. "I signed the death warrant if you remember. Forgive my confusion, Admiral. It's just that I thought poor Admiral Gilding was dead."

"He is." The fleshy man smiled. "Only took two days," he added sadly. "Still, he screamed for most of that," he added, cheering up. "We will be here with the boat, Governor, but don't be too long. There is a storm brewing and I do not want to be stuck on this place all night."

The governor took hold of his nephew's hand firmly and they began to walk slowly up the winding stone path. The sides of the mountain closed in upon them, desolate and lifeless, as the path cut its way through solid rock, winding slowly and steeply upwards.

Rupert saw the shadow of a tree ahead, which gave him an odd feeling of hope. When they got there, it was the petrified remains of what once had been organic matter. Rupert reached out and touched the ghostly white bark. The tree collapsed into a pile of dust.

"Don't touch anything," hissed his uncle, his voice smashing down the unbearable silence of this place as it echoed off the rocks.

From time to time, Rupert was sure he caught the shadow of something or someone out of the corner of his eyes. Whatever these things were, they could move about with impossible speed.

The climb was becoming steeper, and although the late afternoon air was much cooler, the man and the boy were very hot.

The lake was an extraordinary sight. They had climbed quite high to reach it. A vast stretch of coal black water loomed out of the gloom. It was sprawled out a little below the narrow ledge on which they were climbing, like a sheet of glass reflecting the cold grey surroundings around the narrow strip of shoreline. There was no sign of birds, or fish, or any form of vegetation.

There was a small forest of trees reflected back from the ebony depths. They looked as if they had been dead a very long time.

Rupert had never liked the dark. Although there was still a little light, this haunted place was terrifying.

"Why did you make me come to this horrid place?" he asked his uncle nervously, as they rested and drank some already stale water from their pouches. He had never spent time with his uncle since coming to Heffen. He and his sister Victoria had been convinced that the governor strongly disliked, if not disapproved of, his niece and nephew. They had, as a result, always found him to be very unapproachable.

The governor did not answer Rupert's question.

"Please tell me, Uncle Silas," begged the frightened child.

"It was much better than the alternative, child, believe me."

"What was that?" pushed Rupert.

"If you must know, lad, the alternative was death." He paused in deep thought for a moment. "I couldn't have let that happen. My sister would never have forgiven me," he added almost to himself.

"Is it the pirate Prudence Fairweather you are protecting me from, sir?"

"You or me, what difference does it make who is being protected?"

"Why does she want to kill me? I have never done anything to her. I told nobody about Mr Skeet." Rupert was becoming upset, which was the last thing the governor wanted right now.

"No more questions. I don't think it's much farther now. Let's get this over and get back to the boat, shall we?" He looked sadly at the frightened child and cursed his greed and his stupidity. "Be brave for your Uncle Silas, just a bit longer," he begged. "We will soon be safely away from this horrid place, I promise you. We just have to return something your father and I borrowed a long time ago, that's all."

The governor had enjoyed too much good living in recent years and was finding this journey tough going. At last they came to the old settlement nestling close into the rocks. There were a number of empty houses and one or two grander buildings. They looked somehow familiar to the child.

All the buildings gave the impression that they had only just become vacant. The abandonment of the town had been very sudden. Perhaps this was the reason for the strange feeling that the occupants might return at any moment to finish what they had been doing. It was also true, thought Rupert, that should he reach out and touch one of the buildings, it would collapse, just like the petrified tree had into a pile of dust.

Separated by some distance from the main buildings that had once formed a thriving community, there stood a solitary wooden hut. A pale yellow light flickered in the tiny window.

"Come on, child, that's where we are going."

Rupert could feel his uncle trembling with fear. "There's a light on, Uncle, is somebody in there?"

"I hope not," replied the governor grimly. He took the child's hand again, and the two of them walked slowly up to the door of the ancient wooden shack.

"Open it." Uncle Silas nodded at the door.

"Will it not turn to dust?"

The governor pushed Rupert impatiently aside and pushed open the door. Nothing had changed in ten years. The table stood as before, and just for a moment, it was as if his former companions were looking up at him as he entered the shack. There was even a younger and much thinner Silas Raines, soon-to-be governor of the Heffen isles. A position he had hankered for since it had become vacant some years earlier.

Rupert saw none of this, just the oil lamp swinging backwards and forwards from the low-beamed roof, sending a constantly moving cascade of shadows across the room. There was a strange hollow shape cut into the centre of the table, almost directly under the swinging oil lamp.

The governor took a small velvet pouch from his pocket and took out three small pendants. The first slotted easily into its place, as if it was pleased to be back where it belonged. The second fitted next to it and the two seemed to bond together before their eyes. Silas looked even more nervous as he took the third pendent. There were beads of sweat forming on his high forehead. He seemed, to the boy, to be saying a silent prayer. Silas Raines was not known to be a religious man.

He dropped his last pendent into its place. There was a moment of tension. The squeaking of the swinging oil lamp was the only noise to be heard. Rupert found himself wondering why the lantern was swinging so, as there was not even the slightest breeze. The air on Niridia was absolutely still. The third piece of the jigsaw blended in with the first two and the governor breathed a sigh of relief.

"Your turn," he said to the boy. His voice was weak and shaky and he sounded breathless.

Rupert reached inside his jacket and pulled out a package which he unwrapped awkwardly. From it he took the final pendant. This was the one that had belonged to his father. He had never known his father and he had so wanted to keep this pendant. It was the only thing he had that he knew belonged to his father. He quickly returned the paper in which it had been wrapped back inside his coat. He did not want Uncle Silas to see the picture of Prudence Fairweather.

Rupert stepped apprehensively forward to the table and dropped his treasured pendent into the remaining space. Almost at once there came the most hideous and blood-curdling scream. This transformed into something cold and dreadful that could best be described as insane cackling laughter. Only it wasn't laughter, because the creature didn't quite understand that emotion yet.

The oil lamp exploded with a terrible bang, showering tiny fragments of glass over the man and the boy. It also had the effect of plunging the small room into total darkness. The ground beneath the shed was beginning to shake. Rupert yelled out in fright. His uncle grabbed him and dragged him to the door.

"Pull yourself together, child," he hissed through gritted teeth. "We have to get off this island quickly now."

They could not go too fast because it had become so dark. Rupert kept seeing red eyes staring out of the darkness at him. High above them, they could see the very peak of the rock spewing out boiling red lava. Around them blinding orange flames would burst out of the earth without warning. The Rock was burning. The lake was on fire and everywhere was becoming very hot. The ground was beginning to shake even more.

"Uncle, what have we done?" Rupert picked himself up from the rocks, his legs cut and bleeding.

"Opened the gates of hell!" shouted Raines bitterly. "But Sir John Burleigh has everything under control, or so the fool thinks. How in God's name can any man control this?"

As he spoke, the moving earth flung him from the path and into the coal black water. It was quickly apparent that the governor could not swim. More fires were exploding around him. Rupert, forgetting for a moment how frightened he was, jumped down onto the black dusty sand and grabbed hold of his uncle, who was being sucked towards one of the great orange infernos burning on the surface of the lake.

Silas fought for his life, and with the child heaving him back towards dry land, he managed to pull himself out of the thick black mud which sat just below the surface of the water. With one last huge effort, the two fell backwards onto the shore.

"Thank you, child," he gasped. For a moment, he looked at his nephew, lost for words. "Let's get out of here," he suggested, after he had got his breath back.

The two ran down the twisting path towards the boat. It had started to rain now, and out beyond land in the orange glow of all the fires, the fog was moving in.

"We were about to go without you," said the admiral in his squeaky voice.

"I want off this island!" yelled Silas over the wind that had suddenly started blowing across the shore. In the confusion, the admiral turned to a pirate he had borrowed from Burleigh.

"The boy stays here," he hissed. "Feel free to enjoy, but remember I am looking forward to a play myself." He gave another grin showing off his mouthful of rotten teeth. "A boat will take you off this hellhole as soon as we are away." The big oaf with the drooping lip tried to smile and dribbled instead.

In the confusion of the wind and rain, the air on Niridia was no longer still. In the bewilderment brought on by the shaking earth and the fires now burning everywhere, Crooks managed to get Silas into the boat without him realising that Rupert was no longer with him. They were back on the yacht before Silas realised his nephew was missing.

"Admiral, have you seen the boy?"

The pirate-turned-admiral looked over at his crew. "The governor's nephew, lads, what have you done with him?"

"We thought he was with you, sir, and the governor," said one of them innocently.

"Take me back to the Rock!" screamed Silas Raines.

"I am very sorry, Governor," explained the grotesquely obese brigand. "You can see the weather for yourself. It would be impossible to get safely back there. The mists are moving too. It is unwise to sail too close to the mists, you know that yourself, Governor." He patted the governor on the arm. "It was always going to be a dangerous trip for such a pretty little boy, Governor. He must have fallen over the side in all that wind and rain. I don't suppose he suffered at all."

Silas Raines began to sob uncontrollably.

"No, he won't have suffered much." The disgusting man smiled. "Not yet anyway." Jessie Crooks left the governor of Heffen to his sorrows and went to find some beer, tobacco and perhaps a little entertainment.

Prudence looked refreshed when I joined her in her cabin. She had not moved the *Albatross* away from the reef yet. The girl was now clothed in a long silk dressing gown, embroided with colourful Oriental depictions of birds and fire-breathing dragons. After my usual exchange with the parrot, I went over and sat next to the girl.

"How are you feeling now?" she asked, not looking up from the map she was studying.

"I'm feeling ok, thanks to you," I said.

"It really was a pleasure, Mr Anders." She looked up and smiled at me.

She had tried to sleep earlier but with little success. Her mind kept drifting back to that night when her family had died.

Arthur had not come back to the tree, so the girl had explained to the man Douglas that she had to go and find him. Arthur was the only person who could lead them to the coast and the ship that was waiting for Douglas. The only place close to where they were was Boscastle's place. She decided that this must be where Arthur had gone. They managed to avoid any more of Boscastle's traps and were soon at the end of the forest, looking out onto the clearing where the famous architect George Mansfield had designed this grand and spacious wooden-framed ranch house.

In the dark it was hard to be sure, but Prudence was convinced she could see somebody hiding in the shadows. Something in her brain told her they must wait in the trees, silently watching the ranch. There was something very wrong here. She could almost smell death. Douglas nudged her and pointed to the arrival of the handsome young army captain.

"Stay here, Douglas," whispered the young Prudence. "If our rat-faced friend is in there, we need him back to guide us to your ship." She slipped unnoticed into the grand hallway of the ranch. She had always been good at getting into places without being seen.

Prudence did not want to see any more carnage. She had already seen much more than such young eyes should ever have had to look upon. This sadly would not change the fact that Boscastle's young bride lay dead on the stairs. Two red stains on her body indicated that she had probably been shot at close range.

The handsome young army officer, Philip Baldock, was there. She had looked forward to his visits to her father's ranch. As she grew older and became aware of her body and then of the interesting if slightly puzzling effect it had on men, she would flirt wickedly with the shy young captain when he called. Although his complexion sometimes matched his scarlet jacket, there was no doubt Captain Baldock enjoyed her attentions.

Indeed, his visits became noticeably more frequent. Prudence liked him. He was the kind of heroic figure she liked to fantasise over. Now he stood motionless, his pistol pointing at her rat-faced guide. Arthur was crouched by the girl's body.

"Stand where you are," ordered Baldock at the beak-nosed weasel in the striped shirt. The cornered man's eyes were darting about the great hall, looking for some way to escape. "One sudden move and I will shoot you dead where you stand," barked the soldier. The young girl looked down at the body of the manservant. He had, it seemed, also been shot, perhaps with the pistol now lying at the girl's side.

Why hadn't the handsome captain stopped all this killing? She was angry now. What use was a smart red tunic, what use were soldiers, when a massacre like that at her daddy's ranch was allowed to happen? She had even heard said that the army had been seen helping the pirates.

"Captain, please put down your gun." Prudence tried to sound as authoritative as she could for a girl still only in her middle teens. Still, her father and her brothers had often accused her of being too bossy. The captain dropped his pistol and turned to face her. The girl's face, although young and innocent, was that of a child who had been to hell and back. Her clothes were torn and covered in blood. Her eyes, deep brown and very beautiful, were filled with hatred and anger. She looked as if she had been crying for a long time.

"You," she snapped at the rat-faced man in the striped shirt. "Turn down your offer of free passage, did she?"

"I never got the chance to ask her," said the man sadly. "And before you ask, I have nothing to do with this and that is the honest truth. I swear on my mother's grave."

"So why are you here?" persisted the girl, one pistol trained on him still.

"It's a long story. I told you, she was a friend."

"I thought you had deserted us," the girl said quietly, lowering the pistol trained at Arthur. "This has been another bad night, Captain," she said, turning back to face the young Baldock.

"Yes, it has," agreed Baldock. She wasn't sure if he recognised her or not.

Prudence left her message with the young captain. It was obvious, she told herself, that somebody had tried to make it look as if the poor servant had killed Patricia Boscastle.

"Why would he do that?" Prudence was back in the present, looking into my eyes.

"Do what?" I asked. I was aware that the pirate's mind had been somewhere other than her cabin. I was about to make my excuses and leave.

"Richard Boscastle killed his wife in a moment of passion," she explained.

"I gathered that from the other night," I agreed. "It was one of the worst kept secrets on Heffen, and Philip Baldock is to this day racked with guilt for not hanging him for it."

"And they used a badly staged coverup involving a manservant, which nobody believed, to save the man's hide. Everybody on the islands, including Boscastle himself, knew he had done it."

"What's brought all this on?" I asked nervously. Prudence was a little volatile tonight. She looked at my concerned face and smiled.

"You really are a very sweet man, Thomas," she said. "I have been going over in my mind the things that happened the night my family was murdered. I am sure that Patricia Boscastle's murder is connected in someway. We are asked to believe that a drunken and very angry Boscastle returns to his house, shoots his wife in cold blood and then shoots a servant, who has always been totally loyal. All this in the hope somebody would believe the poor servant capable of murdering his mistress." I must have looked very confused.

Prudence laughed at my puzzled expression. Although she still looked tired, her captivating brown eyes sparkled as she tossed her head to flick her long curls from her face. The front of her gown had opened just a little

"I sometimes drive you wild, don't I, Thomas?"

Those, I thought, were the most true words spoken since I had set foot on these islands and for that matter for some considerable time before. She leaned forward seductively and was whispering something nonsensical in my ear. A longer slender finger ran down my face and rested on my lips. The front of her gown had now fallen completely away from one shoulder, and one long shapely leg had become bare from the top of the thigh. Prudence was breathing heavily. Her mouth touched mine.

"You always drive me wild," I said kissing her.

"Not now, Mr Anders, control yourself." Prudence pushed me away. I must have looked quite hurt. "Passion you see. A man's lust for a woman," said Prudence, her big eyes still teasing me, "can sometimes drive him to do terrible things." She did a graceful twirl, letting her gown drop slightly before pulling it back round her. Her eyes were sparkling even more. "Passion," she went on, stroking her fingers down the curve of her long golden brown leg. "Passion is being out of control, filled with wild and uncontrollable desires and emotions." She sat up and covered her leg and smoothed back her tangled mop of hair.

"So you find I am cheating on you, Thomas Anders, with a good dozen different pirates a day. So would you kill me in cold blood, in a cold, clinical and calculating way, two clean shots at point blank range? Or would you strangle the life from me in a moment of jealously, despair and terrible rage? Loving me as you tell me you do, Mr Anders, would you then make a pathetic attempt to pass the blame onto a loyal servant, or would you lie sobbing with grief and remorse for the terrible thing you had done?" Prudence clutched at her chest and fell dramatically onto her bed, where she lay still, pretending to be dead.

"I am not certain I would feel that much remorse," I said, smiling again.

"Now I don't believe you." The corpse opened one eye. "Anyway, the point is, and you know I am right, poor Richard Boscastle went to his grave believing he had killed his beloved bride. When, of course, he hadn't," she added sadly. There was an urgent knock on the cabin door.

"Come in!" shouted the girl. Harry entered. Although not a giant like Joshua, he still had to bend a lot to get in through the low doorway.

"Niridia has visitors," Harry announced. "Important visitors at that."

"Who would want to visit the dead rock at this time of day?" Prudence looked surprised.

"Would you believe the governor? He has a child with him. We think the boy is probably his nephew."

"Rupert!" I jumped up, banging my head on the low ceiling.

"Calm down." Prudence had risen from the dead and was pacing up and down by her big desk. "I must admit I wasn't expecting this and I probably should have been. I don't think the boy is under any immediate danger though." She looked at Harry and I. "We do need to get him off there though and soon."

"Wasn't someone supposed to be watching him?" I asked.

"We were protecting him against those who want him dead," explained Prudence. "The people who want him dead would not have let him come to Niridia. The danger now is that they will almost certainly not want him to leave the rock again."

"We have a couple of boats ready."

"I wonder who navigated through the reef, Harry? We know everyone who can do that. If you will excuse me, gentlemen, I will get dressed again. Mr Anders, it might be better if you stay on the boat this time."

"Not a chance," I replied stonily. "He's my charge and I will be in the rescue party. Don't forget, this child is scared of pirates and especially of you," I added.

It was very dark outside now, although the macabre mass of Niridia could still be made out even before we were close. We had not taken a direct route, so as to try and avoid a direct confrontation with the enemy. As we drew closer, Prudence slipped over the side and swam towards the shore. Joshua slipped into the water after her. After my experience of earlier, I did not feel much like a swim. I did not, however, want to be left behind so I followed.

Once onto the shore, we crept forward to where two men were standing by a small boat which had obviously brought the party to the island. Farther up the beach, on the black sand, stood three more men. One was a nondescript type; another looked to be constructed out of great rolls of fat. The last, also a big man, I recognised at once from the deformed lip. There was no sign of Rupert or the governor.

Prudence let out a stifled gasp of surprise.

"It's the thug who attacked me at the library," I whispered.

"I know the fat one." Prudence looked shocked. "He is even fatter than he used to be. That man used to be known as Jessie Crooks, and he is the most evil and despicable man you will ever meet, Thomas."

"You look surprised to see him here, like you have just seen a ghost?"

"Your friend Major Baldock was supposed to have hung him," explained Prudence, "so perhaps I have just seen a ghost." She looked around her, trying to see into the pitch black. "Do you get the feeling that there is something watching us?" she asked. We were flat on the ground, behind rocks, looking out across the gloom. The beach party, who was expecting no other visitors, had put up quite a few lamps and also had torches burning. I, too, could feel the presence of something else.

Now and again, a shadow darted across the rocks. It always stayed in the dark, moving so fast it was impossible to tell its shape or size. It could well just have been our imagination playing tricks. It had been decided that if they all got back in the boat and left, we would signal the *Albatross* and follow. Prudence, however, was sure that this was not what was going to happen.

"This place gives me the creeps," I said.

"I am afraid we are going to be here for a while," apologised Prudence. "They have gone up the track to the hut. The governor and Rupert I mean. We could follow, but we might just miss them, or more likely put them in even more danger." So we settled down into the ash and stone behind the rocks and waited for something to happen.

"After we left Boscastle's place," Prudence told me, "it seemed sensible to put as much distance as possible between that sad place and us.

"Arthur had us moving very fast over terrain, which was, to say the least, difficult. Poor Douglas found it hard going. In the end, I got mad with Arthur and told him we had to stop and rest. He was angry about Boscastle's wife. I think she must have been very special to him, although he has never talked about it.

"So Arthur went of scouting ahead, whilst Douglas and I rested." Prudence paused in her story. "He was a nice man Douglas," she went on, after a few moments' silence. I had learnt that it was best not to try to rush her. I also knew that nobody had ever been told this story. "Douglas was about the same age as my father, I suppose. I never did understand why he was there. It did, however, become more and more obvious that the people pursuing us were after him, not me.

"You have been very kind, child," he said. "I would have perished a long time ago had it not been for you and your grumpy friend."

"It is good to be of some help."

"You must leave me now, Prudence, because what is chasing us is more dreadful and more evil than anything you can ever imagine. It no longer matters if it gets me. I do not want to put your life at any more risk."

"We are not leaving you, Douglas. I don't care if you are being chased by a giant hairy mammoth, I am not leaving you."

"Did you say giant hairy mammoth for any particular reason?" I interrupted foolishly. "Only one of my brothers is hunting them in the Amazon."

"Shut up Thomas."

"Sorry."

"Whatever it was continued to follow us all the way to the coast. We dodged soldiers and pirates and highwaymen on the way. In fact, we had a few unimportant adventures I might consider telling you one day."

"When we are old and grey?"

Prudence looked at me, her beautiful eyes trying to read my mind. "You still see me going to your papa's church," she observed quietly. "And sitting as good as gold through one of those impossibly long sermons you talk about, don't you, Thomas?"

"He would know what to do about a few hell demons," I pointed out. "It would involve his biggest shotgun and the dogs of course. He does almost nothing without his dogs."

"You miss home, don't you?"

"Yes, sometimes."

"So do I."

The ground had begun to shake beneath us. Great geysers of fire plumed upwards out of the dead earth. From somewhere in the distance came a terrible inhuman scream. Above us, the rock Niridia showed her anger to the world. From out of the acrid smoke came Silas Raines, clutching his nephew. In the deepening gloom, now lit more by the random fires than the insipid light of the sailors' lanterns, they exchanged words with the men waiting.

It was exactly as Prudence had predicted. In the confusion on the grey beach, the hideous fat man had guided the governor to the boat. For such a big man, the pirate Crooks could put on a good turn of speed. My old friend with the fat lip had grabbed Rupert. Holding a hand over his mouth, he held him back. Rupert was struggling to free himself, but his efforts were futile against the pirate's strength.

A great ball of flame burst from the ground close to us. Although the source of the flames was more than fifty feet away, I felt the heat burning at my flesh.

"Shall we go?" said Prudence. The ground seemed to have almost stopped shaking. The tall girl pulled herself to her feet and strode down the rocky path towards Rupert and his captives. It was easy to see what Rupert was thinking as Prudence Fairweather came into his view.

The pirate girl walked forward towards the two men, her cloak swirling about her in the strong wind. She had one hand on the hilt of her sword.

"It is well known throughout these isles, gentlemen, that this boy is mine and absolutely no one else's. I'd like him back please."

"We have no desire to await the admiral's pleasure on this hell hole," slobbered the big pirate. "Believe me."

"We have no stomach for what he plans to do with this little boy either," added the nondescript one. "So as long as you can give us free passage off this island, you can do what you will with him."

"But if the boy must be killed, make it a quicker death than the admiral had in mind," finished the big man, wiping his drooping lip.

Prudence walked up to the boy. "First you try to drown me and now you drag me out to this foulest of places, child, and at such an ungodly hour." She looked at the two men. "Are you not Sir John Burleigh's cutthroats?"

"He lent the admiral some men, as his own are busy preparing the *Serpent* for the attack on the pirate stronghold," explained the one with the big lip.

A few of Prudence's men came up the shore to take the two men to the boat. As they came closer, the ground began to shake even more violently. A huge ball of flame burst out of the ground, engulfing the smaller of Burleigh's men. His screams of agony were dreadful to hear

The ground exploded in further places at random around them. Rocks were becoming dislodged from the places they had rested for years. It felt as if the devil himself was hurling them at us.

I was not far behind Prudence, steam rising from the barren earth around me.

"Go to Mr Anders," snapped Prudence at the child. "There is somewhere I need to go."

I looked at the big man who had tried to kill me.

"It was just another job, teacher man," he explained with the usual pronounced lisp. "My friends call me Chisel. There was no offence meant."

"None taken, Chisel," I shouted over the wind and the sound of crashing rocks.

"Course," he added glumly, "you fair ruined my reputation as a good assassin, Mr Anders. Couldn't even kill a teacher man they're all saying. That's why he wanted me to kill kids, said it would teach me a lesson, only I've always liked kids myself." Some rocks fell dangerously close and another fountain of orange flame shot from the ground close to where we stood.

"I won't be long," shouted Prudence. "Ask Joshua to come back for me." She turned and headed off up the path, carrying one of the torches.

"Chisel, when you get back to Heffen, it might be worth telling all your business contacts that it was not some inept school teacher who confused your plans, but the notorious and much feared pirate Prudence Fairweather. The lad here will confirm it." I looked at the frightened boy who nodded. The ugly man's face brightened almost at once. It was as if I had lifted a terrible burden from his shoulders. "Now, can I trust you to get the boy safely back to the *Albatross*, Chisel?" I asked. "If somebody could come back for us I would be grateful."

"Of course I will." Chisel gave a huge lopsided grin. "I owe you something for trying to kill you I suppose."

Something told me that Rupert would be as safe in this hell with Chisel as with anyone. I grabbed another torch and set off up the path to catch up with Prudence.

Prudence knew where she was going. I was not quite so sure. There was, however, only one track. I guessed by the width in places that this had once been a road for mules to drag carts up and down. In places it had now crumbled away to form little more than a narrow ledge. With the ground shaking so much, it was difficult to know how long some of this would hold.

The wind was becoming stronger and some of the rocks falling from above were white hot. I caught up with Prudence alongside the lake. Much of it seemed to be on fire. The shiny black surface was bathed in an orange glow.

"You just can't take a hint, Mr Anders," shouted Prudence. Her face was blackened with smoke and dirt.

"No, I can't," I agreed. "I had this dreadful feeling I might end up reading about this in a book and I wouldn't have liked that."

"What about the boy?"

"Chisel is going to get him back to Joshua."

"Chisel?"

"The man with the lip."

"Oh, that Chisel. You make friends quickly for such a shy man."

"I think the trying to kill me bit brought us closer." I put a hand on her arm. "What are we doing up here?"

"Trying to recover something that belonged to my father," explained the girl. "If we could, it might help stop all this."

We kept going up the path. It was raining now, although this seemed to have little effect on the fires burning around us. It took considerable effort to keep going, but Prudence would not let me rest.

"Please," I was trying to catch my breath, "can we not rest for just a moment?"

"You wanted to come, Thomas Anders. Nobody, as I recall, invited you," I was told coldly.

At last we reached the ancient settlement of Neeraheffen. This had once a long time ago been the financial centre for all of the islands. Merchants and bankers had quickly recognised the potential of this place. Placing the various banks and money lending houses here, in the truly inhospitable environs of Niridia, reduced considerably any risk of pirates, or for that matter anyone, helping themselves to the wealth of these islands.

Niridia was by no means a dead rock back in those days, but it had always been exposed to the elements. There was only one poorly maintained cart track leading to Neeraheffen. This wound its way through difficult and often unpleasant terrain which offered little in the way of shelter, even for those who had come here on legitimate business.

Taking in our surroundings as we struggled to catch our breath from the stiff climb, it was easy to understand how any attempt to attack this place would be nigh on impossible. It was equally clear that somebody, or more likely something, had. Prudence and I looked at each other. We both could feel a distinct uneasiness in this place. It looked as if the money lenders, bankers, insurers, actuaries and accountants had only left a few moments before we arrived, and yet there was something oddly unreal about the buildings. In places some were almost transparent in the gloomy twilight. Others bathed in the orange glow from burning lava seemed almost skeletal.

This whole place gave off an overpowering feeling of death. Something terrible had happened here, we were left in absolutely no doubt of that. Some of the buildings in the settlement were quite imposing. The most important building had a hint of Greek or perhaps Roman. What appeared to be massive stone columns held up the monolithic structure. A huge wooden ranch house nearby seemed uncannily familiar to Prudence. There was another similar structure set some distance behind.

The bizarre and gloomy ghost town was bathed in the eerie orange glow of the many fires. Great clouds of light grey powdery dust were blowing in our faces. Before either of us had chance to ask where this stuff had come from, the ranch house in front of us began to slowly disintegrate before our eyes. The timber walls seemed to slowly transform into particles of silvery dust that momentarily continued to hold the form of the building.

For a moment the great house became fluid as the thousands of tiny particles of the old wooden building were sucked up into a funnel of air. It seemed to be swirling around us higher and higher and then all of a sudden it froze for a single moment and then very slowly separated into another pile of dirt that blew across the empty street.

"Over there," shouted Prudence over the worsening storm, pointing at a small wooden shed. A bright orange glow at the window suggested that the building was already on fire. I followed the girl across the broken roadway to the shed. Swinging open the door, we could see that a fire was already burning inside. I saw an altogether different scene.

There was no wind; in fact, the air could not have been more still than this. In an uneasy and unnatural silence, four men sat around a table, an oil lamp swinging slowly to and fro just above their heads, suspended from a creaking rusty chain. One of the men looked rich, one was in rags. Another looked learned; the last one was clearly terrified. Only the persistent groaning of the slowly swinging lamp broke this unnatural silence. Why the lamp was swinging in this way was difficult to comprehend, as the air was so still. The movement of the light created strange moving shadows that seemingly at random plunged different parts of the room into total darkness.

In the centre of the table was an amulet in something that looked like dull gold. I have heard some call it the devil's gold. It was an ugly thing, on which was carved the shape of a dragon. At the head of the long table, in the shadows that were almost still, sat a tiny figure cloaked in black, a dark shadow blocking its features, from which shone bright blood red eyes. The tiny form was of an innocent, the presence within it I knew at once to be of pure malevolence. I felt such terrible fear welling up inside me.

Slowly and carefully each of the men rose from their place at the table. Each took a peace of the amulet from its resting place. Having done so, they returned trembling to their seats, each clutching their small piece of devil's gold. I recognised the governor of Heffen as one of the men, and Richard Boscastle as another.

The face of one remained obscured by the creaking oil lamp, although I was certain I already knew the identity of this man. The tall and awkward-looking young man was clearly even more frightened than the others. Although I had never seen him before, I was sure that I was looking at Rupert and Victoria's father.

Prudence did not see any of this. The amulet, however, was clearly visible to her in the centre of the ancient table, fire licking up around the legs.

"I have to get to the table," shouted Prudence.

There was nobody sat in the burning chairs now, but the shrouded figure still sat at the head of the table. It rose from the chair as if not impeded in anyway by gravity. The cloak fell away from its head to reveal a face from far beyond any sane man's nightmares. For the few seconds it was visible, huge green eyes burning blood red at the centre glared out at us. It had some kind of a mouth contorted into the most horrible scream. Then it was a child, an innocent, used and discarded as it always did.

The table exploded into a sheet of white flame. Prudence and I were flung backwards out of the door with tremendous force. That was all that saved us from melting in the flames. We were still too close to the shed, too close to the intense heat from the fire. Even now I could still see clearly inside the burning hut, although my eyes were stinging from the heat, smoke and dust. The table began to crumble and the ground beneath began to open.

We clung on desperately to each other in a futile struggle to stop ourselves from being sucked back into the cavernous hole that had opened in the ground. My eyes could not believe the things I was seeing beneath us. Flashes of other people's lives, in other faraway places, in countless distant worlds. The noise of an infinite number of living minds came close to destroying mine.

Then I saw the creature's army. Thousands upon thousands of the most unimaginably hideous things, stretching back as far as it was possible to see. Some were recognisably human or at least if not human, ape, most were not. Prudence grabbed hold of me and, with considerable effort, dragged me stumbling away from the heat. Where it had been so still before, the wind now struck us at hurricane force.

"So it is true that worlds collide," I yelled. "Nobody will ever believe what we have seen today. To be honest I am not sure I believe it myself."

A moment later the hut exploded, sending wood and splinters in every direction. Once again we were hurled across the clearing with considerable force. I was badly dazed. As my eyes came back into focus, I could taste blood in my mouth and one of my legs was in agony. Prudence had a nasty gash on her forehead, blood was streaming down her face.

I was lying on the floor. The girl had pulled herself up to look down on me. Her face had gone a terrible colour. I knew at once that she had been badly hurt by the second explosion.

"Have I failed my destiny, Thomas?" she asked weakly. Prudence looked confused and disorientated. I could see that she was fighting to stay conscious. "Is this the end?" The ground was shaking even more ferociously beneath us now.

"No," I answered grimly. "This can surely only be the beginning."

Prudence didn't answer. She stared blankly at the burning shack for at least a minute and her eyes rolled. Then she let out a soft cry and collapsed on top of me.

Chapter 17

Prudence the child had seen the rock Niridia before, but never so close as she had seen it now. Arthur had brought her and Douglas to the home of a lady friend, high up on a hillside overlooking the coast. The ship that was waiting for the gentle grey-haired man was sheltering in the shadow of the great volcano. A large ship, it looked tiny against its magnificent backdrop. Niridia, in its cold and austere, natural beauty, reminded the young girl of one of the great gothic cathedrals her father had shown her pictures of in books. These she had always thought must be places to worship an angry god.

Down below, on the road they must cross, Prudence could see a small group of people. They were dressed in black from their turban-style headgear to their shiny leather boots. Some carried crossbows, all of them were armed with knives.

"Are they waiting for you?" asked the girl.

Douglas nodded. "I am afraid so and there is no way round them." The kindly man looked sadly at Prudence. "I came here to do something and it is successfully done, although at far too greater cost. I think they will give up once they have me. I would be very grateful if you could get a message to the ship. The captain is likely to disobey his orders and try and save me, unless he knows not to do so. Now, I could do with some paper and a pen."

"Do you think for one minute, and after all we have been through, I am going to let you go off and get yourself killed?" Prudence sounded both angry and incredulous.

"You really don't know what you're up against, child," insisted Douglas. "I could never forgive myself if you were to be hurt on my account. My wife Carol is a wonderful woman. I will give you a short note for her. I promise you, child, she will love you as we do our own children."

Prudence had gone red in the face and looked as if she might stamp her foot at any moment. Arthur would become very used to these occasional tantrums.

"Will you stop calling me, child, old man!" she shouted. "Arthur, find us a way past these people. We have to get this very old and incredibly annoying man to his ship."

Douglas tried to say something.

"I am not discussing this, very old man, for I am just a child."

Arthur took the girl firmly to one side. "He's trying to tell you that these are trained killers. I am not exactly sure what they are, or where they come from. Mercenaries paid for by Sir John Burleigh, or perhaps loaned by my little darling." He took hold of the girl's arms. For once, the look in his eyes was not the usual cavalier one. "What I do know, Prudence, is that if we interfere in this, we shall probably be killed."

"Listen, my rat-faced friend, you would probably be dangling on the end of a rope if I had not rescued you." Prudence was aware she sounded very close to the spoilt child she was trying so hard not to be. "I don't know what evil has spilt into our lives, Arthur, but I intend to fight it. If that means dying, then, Arthur, we die." She smoothed her hand across his creased and rather lopsided face. "Now I have come to realise that you are a cunning and clever rogue, so I am confident you can find a way to get us to the ship."

It was on that day that Arthur first knew Prudence Fairweather was unlikely to ever lose an argument. The old man had given the *Albatross* to Harry. Arthur couldn't stay after that. He had been with the old man as long as Harry had. Harry wasn't even really a pirate. Deep down Arthur knew he probably wouldn't have made a good leader, he wasn't really a pirate either, although he had always been a crook. In truth, he hadn't even wanted the responsibility. Knowing that didn't make him feel any better. Twice he had had something important stolen from him by the same man. Arthur looked at the pretty young girl, stood hands on hips, glaring haughtily back at him.

"It simply can't be done, Prudence," he said.

Later that day, a mule and cart headed down towards the coast. A pretty young girl was sandwiched between two old ladies. These were two of the ugliest old hags a man could ever set eyes on. The one driving was the worst. She had the look of a rodent about her and an enormous beak of a nose. The ruse appeared to work and the cart pulled up on the shoreline just before dark. Douglas's ship was signalled with a lamp and then they sat back and waited for a boat to be sent.

Arthur, still wearing traces of the old lady's makeup, was chewing on a clay pipe. His eyes darted to and fro, one dark shadow to another. He was listening intently, and now and again, Prudence thought she saw his large nose twitch, as if smelling for something. Seeing her looking at him, the rat-faced man scowled.

"Too easy, Mistress Prudence," he said. "All much too easy."

It was at almost exactly that moment they attacked. There was about four of them. Arthur had rigged up various traps before they had settled to wait for the boat. Only two of the attackers lived to enter the camp. There were horrible screams that indicated strongly that the other two had befallen Arthur's well-planned welcome.

Of the two who had made it, one was fighting Arthur. The other, ignoring Prudence, who was screaming and shouting, had sent Douglas to the ground and raised his curved sword to finish him. The girl picked up the sword she had carried these last few days. Years ago, a friend of her father's had taught her to use it. She had never needed to employ such a weapon in a real fight.

Prudence managed to delay the assassin, but he was too good for her. At last he skillfully flicked the sword from her hand. He was about to thrust his weapon into her chest when Douglas flung himself onto the black-clad warrior's back.

The assassin was able to throw the brave Englishman to the ground and, turning on his heels, raised his sword high to plunge downwards into the fallen man. Prudence flung herself at his legs, unbalancing him, so that they both fell forward into the sandy ground.

The professional killer had pulled out a long knife. He and Prudence rolled over in the dirt until he had her pinned down. Douglas tried to pull him off her and was flung against some rocks. The long knife was pointing downwards into the girl's chest and she was weakening.

Suddenly, the killer froze. His eyes widened and blood spilt from his mouth onto the struggling girl. Then his eyes rolled around in their sockets and he plunged forward across the girl, staring lifelessly out at the empty coastline. Arthur pulled his dagger from the dead man's back.

"I can't believe you could be so stupid as to risk your life for a silly old buffer like me, child," said Douglas, gently wiping a wound on her forehead. "You did not need to do that."

"I've told you I am not a child," replied the girl haughtily.

"No, you are no longer a child, are you?" he agreed sadly. "In just a few days, you have been forced to grow up. That is very unfair. You will like my wife Carol and my children. We will make you feel at home and maybe, given time, you can salvage something of what is left of your childhood."

"I am not coming with you, Douglas," said Prudence softly. "I met somebody on the road who told me I was important here."

"The lady in the tree, you mean?" said Douglas.

The girl was lost for words. "So you did see her?"

"I was very ill and very weak as I recall. I think I was probably dying, wasn't I?" he said. "I thought I might have imagined her, but when I woke up in the morning feeling so much better, I knew I had not." Douglas put a rough hand on the young girl's face. "I always knew you would choose to stay here," he confessed sadly. "I have already seen at first hand that there is absolutely no point arguing with you." He gave her a rueful smile.

"I wish you could stay and look after me," said the girl, tears welling up in her eyes. "All I am is my daddy's very spoilt little princess. You are right, my body may be changing, but I am still only a child."

379

"Those are not the words of a child," Douglas pointed out gently. "As for me staying here to look after you, my family would have lost their daddy too, had it not been for your stubbornness and bravery. I was fortunate indeed that you found me when you did."

Prudence was crying again now. She was angry with herself for letting her emotions show, annoyed that she was making such a spectacle of herself. The boat had arrived. Arthur, who had kept his distance, his senses still alert for further attacks, walked over. He did not know yet that Prudence was not leaving with the man from England. He felt oddly depressed at the thought of her departure. In truth, the old man had been right. Arthur needed direction and leadership, someone to give him back some belief in this wicked world.

He could not, however, go crawling back to Harry under any circumstances. He was surprised when the Englishman thanked Arthur warmly for risking his life for him. Arthur was not used to people thanking him for anything; it felt good. He was taken even more off guard when he was told to look after the girl.

"I thought you were going with him?" he said, looking at Prudence.

"Sorry, Arthur." The filthy girl smiled through the thick layer of dirt on her pretty face. "I am afraid you are not going to get rid of me as easily as you thought."

"Now there's a surprise," muttered the rodent-like man.

Douglas put his arms on the girl's strong shoulders. "Your father was an exceptional man and your mother was a very special person, too. Like all of us, they made mistakes in life. They have, through their bravery and enormous sacrifice, bought us time. You are much stronger than you realise, Prudence Fairweather," he said, looking into her tearful brown eyes. "I will never forget you, or what you have done, you know that. One day, I give you my word, I will repay your kindest to me. You will not fight this evil alone, I promise you." He embraced the girl to his own bulky frame.

"And besides, I will always have somewhere to come and stay in England," she said, wiping the tears from her face, whilst trying to smile and sound brave at the same time.

"Always," he said, a big finger affectionately touching the end of her pretty nose. "You would have to wash that dirty face though," he added. He turned and ran down to the water. Clambering into the boat, he turned and waved.

Prudence watched the rowing boat until it was just a small dot alongside the waiting ship. Her head was throbbing with pain from banging it against the rocks in the fight earlier.

"You all right?" asked Arthur.

"I think I need to sit down for a minute," said the girl. Arthur caught her as she collapsed.

About ten years later, I struggled to drag the unconscious girl away from the remains of the burning hut and the searing heat. The fire was still burning fiercely. Any attempts to wake her had proved unsuccessful, and although I kept telling myself that everything would be all right, I knew deep down that Prudence was very badly hurt.

I had no real way of telling how bad she was, but the signs were not good. I could feel little or no pulse. The deep wound on her forehead looked very nasty. The rock Niridia, on which we now seemed to be trapped, was threatening to shake itself apart, that is if it didn't explode into one giant ball of orange fire first.

I knew I didn't possess enough strength to carry the girl all the way back down the steep and twisting track to the shore. However, it did seem the only course of action left open to me. With some difficulty and much cursing, I managed to lift her across my back. Prudence was heavier than I had expected and I had sustained some injury myself in the explosion.

I struggled, stumbled and staggered along the narrow path away from the nightmare of Neeraheffen. More of the once grand and opulent buildings so reminiscent of the architect Mansfield had collapsed slowly into fragments of dirt and dust before my eyes. Much of the clearing was on fire. Any attempt to gain access to the hut would have been futile. I was not even completely sure what Prudence had been trying to recover.

The air was full of thick acrid smoke, which had a pungent smell that choked the lungs. At least further down the path, the air was clearer. I slipped and slid down the dead mountain, the pirate girl thrown across my back. Progress was slow. I needed to take plenty of rests. Prudence was becoming heavier with every step I took. The conditions were anything but favourable.

There were times when every joint in my body screamed in pain. I was close to exhaustion and when I rested it became increasingly harder and harder to make myself carry on. It began to feel that I just could not manage another step. More than once, something inside my head told me that this was a good place for two lovers to curl up and die in each other's arms.

Maybe this was what my dreams had been about, perhaps this was our destiny, to die together on the dead earth of Mount Niridia. I could see ghosts again, shadowy spectres of dead people, floating in and out of my line of vision. I would catch no more than a glimpse of a stark white face or lifeless, staring eyes.

There was what appeared to be a family floating on the track directly in front of us. They were dressed as you might expect a merchant and his family to dress, a man, woman and two children. The young ones I guessed to have been much the same age as Rupert and Victoria when they died. I could see right through their translucent forms down the track towards the beach and a chance to get away from this place. Large lifeless eyes stared back at me. All four of these apparitions were beckoning me towards them and calling my name, as if they had something exciting they wanted me to see.

"Thomas, Thomas Anders."

For a moment I stood rooted to the spot in frozen terror. Then, just as suddenly, the fear was gone and I didn't feel quite so exhausted. For the first time since we had begun our long descent, I began to believe that we could make it. These poor people wished me no harm; far from it, they were urging me on.

I stumbled and staggered down the rocky track, the ground continuing to explode and fall away around us. Many times the earth beneath me gave way, plunging down into the blackness below. I must have fallen a hundred times. I was becoming delirious with pain and exhaustion, but I still swear that more than once something or someone helped me back to my feet.

By the time I reached the shore, I was beyond exhaustion. My legs, no longer able to carry us, folded beneath me. I was vaguely aware that the path we had just come down was now a raging inferno. Had I taken just one more rest, we would most certainly have perished in the flames. Now, barely conscious, I felt myself fighting against the odds to stay awake. I did not know if Prudence was breathing or not. I remember that she looked so very still. Then I saw the face of the ugly pirate with the twisted lip leering down at me. A moment later, everything went black.

Silas Raines had never been so angry as his carriage bounced along the road towards the great Burleigh folly. If the architect George Mansfield had been inspired by some Arabian fairy tale in his design for the governor's palace, then Burleigh's home was in the spirit of a gothic nightmare. It was hard to believe that the same man whose genius was behind such wonders of our world as the governor's palace and Heffen Library could have conjured up this monstrosity.

"Go faster!" yelled the governor to his driver. The sight of the governor's glistening golden coach and four white horses hurtling through the rain-swept night at great speed, lamps blazing, had an unreal quality. The sight of Sir John Burleigh's monstrous home, silhouetted against the orange glow of the burning rock Niridia, was both awesome and grotesque.

Burleigh was still getting unwelcome visitors. The children were playing in front of the big fireplace. The flames from the fire were clearly visible through their transparent bodies. Although just ghostly apparitions, the children looked up as he strode into the room. They were smiling at first, but quickly became sulky and belligerent.

By the time Burleigh had settled into his much loved armchair, the children could no longer be seen. Trying to make himself comfortable in front of the blazing fire, he felt the cold iciness in the air around him, where a few moments earlier the unwelcome spectres had been. Lady Catherine entered the room looking a little flushed.

"You are very much better in bed than that fool of a governor John." She smiled and deliberately stood so that her large breasts, barely covered by a pretty sky blue chiffon gown, were at eye level with the seated businessman. "I look forward to doing that again very soon," she added.

Burleigh did not answer. He was coldly studying the fading outline of a hound that lay chewing on a bone by the fire. Burleigh had never liked dogs much. Silas Raines stormed past the butler, who was trying to announce him to Sir John, pushing him out of his way. He glared vacantly at the countess, not registering the significance of her presence in Burleigh's house.

He turned to Sir John, anger blazing in his eyes. Burleigh thought the governor's sagging jowls were vibrating, so mad was he. His face was purple with rage and he could hardly speak.

"This is your doing, Burleigh." He was still tripping over his words. "First you let my sister die and now my nephew. How low can you sink?"

Burleigh laughed. There was, as always, no genuine humour in it. "Governor Silas Raines," he spoke scornfully. "Would you believe, Lady Catherine, that our appointed leader has suddenly got himself a conscience."

"I would go further, Sir John," suggested Lady Catherine smoothly. "He seems to have almost developed a sense of right and wrong."

"A little late in life for that, Governor, don't you think?" Burleigh's thin grey lips were shaped into something as close as he would ever get to a smile again.

"Did he not murder his brother-in-law, Sir John?"

"And turned a blind eye to the activities of Jessie Crooks, who he arranged with the complicity of the good Major Baldock to walk free of the gallows."

"He has never asked to give up the power or the position," said Lady Catherine, walking over to Silas Raines.

Burleigh handed the governor a brandy. "We could not have risked the boy at the main event, Governor, you must realise that. There is no telling how he would have reacted. Everything could have been put at risk."

"Sir John tells me that Peckham, the demon hunter, also urged us to dispose of the boy."

"Once again, Governor, all I am guilty of is to relieve you of the problems of making hard and difficult decisions," pointed out Burleigh calmly. "The countess is right of course. You have brought on much of this pain because of your own failings. I did warn you all from the beginning that which we all seek came at a very high price indeed."

Raines flung his drink into the fireplace. "I do not understand how you can be so clinical, Burleigh. Catherine would sell her own mother into slavery for a few sovereigns. You let a child die today. No, correction, you had him killed."

Burleigh grabbed hold of Silas Raines by the coat. "We have a demon to beat, Governor, and I would have thought that you, of all people, would want Efulric destroyed. If he is not, we all burn in the fires of hell for an eternity."

"I forgot, but didn't you also just have another of your best friends murdered?" interrupted the countess. She was admiring herself in a mirror she had taken from her handbag.

"Be quiet, Catherine," said Burleigh sharply in his ice-cold way. "The governor understands now."

Silas carefully and deliberately removed Burleigh's hands from his coat, never taking his eyes off the icy grey eyes of the other man. Straightening his coat, he picked up his tall hat, which he had dropped earlier. He wiped the side of the topper with his coat sleeve. Glaring for a moment at Burleigh and the countess, there was an unbearable silence.

"I will bid you good night then," he said. Turning on his heels, he charged from the room.

"That man is becoming a liability," observed the countess.

"He will be fine for another week or so," said Sir John, almost to himself. "After that, we don't really need him anymore."

Shortly after the governor stormed out, the Countess Lady

Catherine Ridley excused herself and retired for the evening, leaving Sir John Burleigh alone with his ghosts.

My surroundings slowly came into focus. Sydney's worried face was the first thing to converge into something recognisable. The good-looking man was looking at me with what appeared to be a mixture of sadness and concern. It took me a little longer to realise that I was in our small and austere cabin on board the *Black Albatross*.

"Thomas, how are you feeling?" He poured me a glass of water from a jug by the side of my bunk. "You've been out for the count for nearly a day."

"Prudence?" I sat up and grabbed hold of my friend. "How's Prudence, Sydney?" My mind was beginning to collect together all the confused thoughts and fragments of memory from before I had passed out. Prudence had been so still. I had carried her lifeless body all that way down the rock without feeling any movement. A sudden sense of great loss began to overwhelm me.

"She'll be fine." Sydney had never sounded less convincing.

"You don't sound too sure."

"The physician is a little worried about her, Thomas," replied Sydney sadly. "We are nearly back at their little island. They will be able to make her more comfortable. She took a nasty bang on the head."

"I need to see her." I tried to get up and my head began to swim.

"As soon as you feel a little better, Thomas, of course," promised Sydney.

The *Albatross* dropped anchor as close to the shore as it could get. A boat took us the short distance to the golden sands and palm trees of a truly paradise island. The man with the big lip, Chisel, scooped me up and carried me to shore as if I weighed nothing. He carried me up the small hill to a strange but beautiful place called Sunshine. Now he had decided not to kill me, the big man could not do too much for me.

Prudence was already lying quite still on her bed, still with the wound to her head, which did not look so angry now. She looked very pale but otherwise as radiant as ever. Harry was sat sombrely by the bed, holding her hand.

"What happened?" he demanded of me. There were tears in his eyes.

"Is she dead?" It had taken all my inner strength to ask. My heart felt as if it would explode at any moment. I dreaded the answer.

"The physicians say they can do no more for her. They think she will fade away. She may, however, just sleep like this for years."

"I love her, Harry. I mean I really love her. She liked me a little too I think, although I am not a fool. I don't think she saw herself settling down with some lunatic like me." There were tears streaming down my face.

Harry looked sadly at me. "We all need her," he said. "I taught her to use a sword you know. Her father, Old Man Fairweather, was a good friend once, until I let him down that is."

"Let him down?" I asked.

"Passion is a wonderful thing, Thomas, when it is aimed in the direction of something good. You proved that beyond any doubt today. What you did in getting Prudence from halfway up Niridia back down to the shore was physically impossible. Monkey might have been able to do it, Joshua has the strength, but with respect, Thomas old lad, you don't."

"I took too long."

"You did it in remarkably quick time according to the others. You shouldn't even have made it, man. Somehow, passion drove you to achieve the impossible. Unfortunately, my passion was for a lady who is as evil as any woman alive in the world. My passion led me to do things I would not normally be capable of doing. With my help, she almost destroyed a good man, her own husband." Harry reached shakily for a bottle of rum, nearly sending it flying from the low table onto the stone floor. "I had a family too," he continued, his mind drifting back to the sound of children's laughter. "I paid a big price for my indiscretions, Thomas. I have never seen my own children since."

"Here, let me help you," I said, grabbing the bottle before it fell.

"Old Man Fairweather could not understand why I had stooped

387

quite so low." Harry laughed. "The woman I loved had, of course, already turned on me. That is how I came to be less than respectable, Mr Anders. I wasn't always a rogue like Arthur you know." He smiled sadly and put a hand on my arm as if to offer comfort. "Perhaps that is part of the reason why this annoying woman is so special to me," he whispered hoarsely. "I know you love Prudence. It is, frankly, the worst kept secret in these parts. I cannot tell you how she feels naturally, except that I know she likes you."

Harry stood up. For the first time since I had known this man, he looked his age. Old and tired, he offered me the chair in which he had been sat.

"Her father and I made up in the end, and I promised him that I would look after her," he said softly. He walked to the cabin door. I noticed the parrot was missing.

"I haven't done a great job of looking after her, have I?" Harry looked at me, his eyes filled with despair. "I need to go and cause Jessie Crooks some confusion. Prudence would never forgive me if I let him onto our little paradise, and I don't think I could stand that." Harry picked up his hat. "Look after her for me, Mr Anders," he said quietly. He came back over and kissed her forehead. "I will not let Jessie Crooks into our sanctuary, Prudence, I promise." He kissed her again and left.

Still very weak myself, I almost fell into the chair Harry had been occupying. I had forgotten poor Rupert until I saw the frightened child in the doorway of Prudence's room.

"She's going to die as well, isn't she?" he said sadly. He still looked frightened of the pirate, despite it being clear she could cause him no harm. He approached the bed very cautiously.

"She is beautiful like Mother," he said. "Why is it always beautiful people who die?"

"It isn't always, Rupert," I said, wiping a hand across my tear-stained face.

"Do you love her, Mr Anders?" He looked at me strangely.

"Yes, Rupert, I do."

"Did she love you?"

"I think she liked me."

"Like's not the same as love."

"I don't know then, Rupert. Probably not."

"If she hadn't needed to kill me like pirates do," the boy said carefully after some thought, "I think she could have loved me, Mr Anders, don't you?"

"I know she would have loved you, Rupert, and anyway she didn't want to kill you."

"When she dies, is it going to be my fault again?"

I must have looked very confused by this question. "How can it be your fault, Rupert?" I asked incredulously.

"The woman at the workhouse said that Victoria and I were to blame for our mother dying," Rupert answered in an almost clinical tone.

"Why!" I, on the other hand, had become quite irate. It was not just my body that was exhausted. My nerves were shattered by all the different emotions that were choking me. To hear how some terrible and unfeeling woman could have been so cruel to two small, frightened and heartbroken children beggared belief. "Why could your poor mother's death be your fault, Rupert?"

"She said if Victoria and I had not been there, she would have found better work. She said Mother should have sent us out to work. We were idle and useless." Rupert was crying now. "It's my fault people die!" he screamed and ran from the room.

Sydney was in the corridor. "It's all right, old boy, I'll go find him. You look after your pirate."

I went back into the room and sat down by the bed, and took hold of the girl's hand. It felt cold to touch. Some attempt had been made to clean her face, but it was still quite dirty. Surely I could not have lost her so soon. I began to feel anger. Kicking back the chair, I began to walk about the room. Closing the door and locking it, I walked to the fireplace and back to the large bed.

"Prudence told me about you!" I shouted. "You told her what her destiny was. You can't just let her die now. If I am to believe in this dreadful evil, this pure malevolence that is threatening to throttle our world, if I am to except something so wicked exists, then there must conversely surely be some powerful good out there somewhere. My guess is Prudence met that power of good in a tree ten years ago. She is the only one who can save us all from Efulric the Apprentice and his demons from hell. How about you get the hell down here and save her like you saved her companion ten years ago. Or am I being unreasonable?"

I heard the music first, gentle, soothing music, which I was convinced was coming from inside me.

"The old man was accurate when he spoke of your passion, Master Thomas Anders."

I was looking at the woman that Prudence had described so well to me. Except she perhaps wasn't as tall as I might have expected. She had, however, an ageless beauty, reminiscent of a fine statue or a great work of art.

"I am not used to being ordered about either, young man."

"Please forgive me, my lady. I would never presume to order you about."

"You just did and rightly so. Even angels need a kick up the backside once in awhile." She smiled at me. "Your trip from home has been very educational to you so far," she observed.

"Please save Prudence, my lady," I begged her.

"For you, Thomas Anders, or so she might save the world?"

"Both," I said.

"I have no control over what this child feels for you."

"I understand that and I wouldn't want it any other way."

The beautiful creature looked sadly at me. Her simple flowing gown came from the earth and fitted well to her slim and shapely frame. She seemed so delicately built and yet there was great strength in her vibrant green eyes.

"As a learned man, a man of books," she spoke softly, "you will no doubt have read of the prophesies of failure by a demon hunter. I think you know of whom I speak, Thomas Anders. Whether the ancient ones could see the future is quite another matter. Perhaps they simply understood, even in the old days, how weak those entrusted with this pretty little world of yours really are. It was always written that unless the people of the world stopped their petty squabbling and learned to be more kindly disposed to one another, then this terrible demon Efulric could well be victorious. You see, it feeds not just on pure evil, but on the weaknesses in our minds." She sighed.

"Then there is no hope," I said, wiping a hand across my pale and tear-stained face.

"It struggles hard to understand us, as you, Thomas Anders, struggle even now to accept its terrible existence. It is already beginning to understand that the only one who had the strength and purpose to destroy it is dead. Efulric the Apprentice also still has its protector. Prudence has at least rescued the child Rupert from the demon, and that has been a serious setback to the creature. The child Rupert is as important to it as the child it fears. Sadly though, Prudence failed to stop it before it recovered and reassembled the key. Now it is able to reunite with its own flesh, no matter how rotten and decomposed that might be. It is then a simple matter for Efulric the Apprentice to release hell's terrible army into our world to slowly devour every last piece of it."

"Is there no one but Prudence Fairweather who can stop this thing?" I asked, looking down upon the lifeless girl on the bed.

She sighed again. "She is the only one who can kill this evil thing, Thomas. It is her legacy."

"Then we are finished," I said sadly.

The woman smiled, a gentle smile that seemed momentarily to take away the pain and hurt. "You have been very busy with your research in Heffen Library. You know a demon hunter's importance in all of this," she continued in the same gently soothing tone. "If he or she can use the great powers they have inherited wisely, then that person could do much to help the slayer kill this foul thing."

"But the prophecies say that the demon hunter is a fool and a coward, and as a result of this weakness our world will perish!" I shouted in a mixture of confusion and dismay. "As for the slayer, she lies here cold and still." Tears began to stream down my face again.

"All is not lost yet, Thomas," she said, "although you understand that I cannot in any way guarantee the outcome of the terrible battle that lies ahead. It is never too late for a demon hunter to make amends for his mistakes you know. Indeed, with the help of a brother, such action could make all the difference. I can help Prudence because there is still the slightest spark of life and that is thanks to you, Thomas Anders. I know not if she deserves your love. I do know that without it the tiny spark would surely have been snuffed out. I would then have not been able to do anything except to rescue her soul." She smiled again and I marvelled in her gentle and heavenly beauty. "It has always been true that where there is life, there is also always hope."

She walked over to me and put her hands on my head. At once I felt a comforting warmth flow through my veins.

"Now lie down next to her and hold her tight. You are exhausted, Thomas Anders. Do not fear sleep, my young hero. You must rest if you wish to go on helping her defeat this evil, however ungrateful she might seem to be." She took me over to the bed. I did as I was told and lay down next to Prudence.

"I can offer little further help for now," she said. I tried to say something. "Shush now, Thomas." She put her hands on me once more. The gentle music in my head grew louder. It seemed to soothe my aching limbs and rest my troubled mind. "Sleep now," she whispered. "Dream good dreams and tomorrow be refreshed."

I drifted slowly into a deep and rejuvenating sleep. I knew even in my dreams that I could find a ship out of Heffen if I so wished, heading in the direction of home. The comforting smell of Mama's cooking beckoned, as did my incorrigible father's interminably long sermons and my foolish collie dog with his oversized ears. Even the familiarity of the cold, damp climate back home, I missed, although I probably complained about the northern English weather as feverishly as anyone did before discovering the hot and humid climate of Heffen.

I wouldn't miss bumping into the likes of Sir John Burleigh, Jessie Crooks or the lovely countess, nor would I miss the suggestion that this terrible demon Efulric was close by. I suddenly realised that I had a very good idea what Efulric the Apprentice looked like. Not from all the books I had studied in Heffen's magnificent library. Nor from all the colour plates I had found depicting various devils and demons. Not even from the briefest glimpse I might have had of this terrible thing seconds before the hut exploded and the ground opened beneath us.

It was when I slept that I had seen the image of this creature, just as I had seen the image of Prudence Fairweather long before we had ever actually met. A fact I still found strangely odd. I was dreaming now and once again I was on the beach. One again I could see the hideous face, hewed out of solid rock. It was not the face of anything human, more beast than man, and even in the calm of deep sleep, I could feel terrible panic begin to well up inside me. For this was an effigy of such terrible mind-possessing evil, I found it difficult to even look upon it. How could anyone hope to defeat this terrible thing?

But then, as before, I could no longer see the awful face of Efulric.

Instead, draped gracefully over the rocky outcrop, her long and shapely legs dangling down over the twisted face and into the clear water, was Prudence Fairweather. It was at that moment I was certain that this girl alone could save us all and kill this evil and the evil on which it feeds. It wouldn't be easy, of course, and the cost would most likely be a high one. I do not consider myself to be a brave man, but if the pirate Prudence must die to save our world, then I would be happy to die with her.

"Mr Anders!"

I awoke with a start to see Prudence sat up on the bed, looking indignantly at me. Her long wild hair was more tousled than ever. Her beautiful eyes were on fire.

"Whoever said you could sleep in my bed?" she demanded curtly.

There was no mark visible on her forehead. Her skin was back to its usual smooth golden brown colour. Her large brown eyes sparkled. She looked rested, refreshed and very angry.

I fell out of the bed.

To Be Continued

Printed in the United Kingdom
by Lightning Source UK Ltd.
106074UKS00003B/40-51